THE MISSION, IF SUCCESSFUL, WOULD TURN THE TIDE OF THE WAR

Under the Espionage Act (U.S.C. 50:31:32) this publication shall not be carried in any aircraft on combat mission or when there is a reasonable chance of its falling into the hands of the enemy.

Krug smiled. No problem.

Reaching into his cap for pencil and paper, he copied out the critical performance data from the flight operating charts, tables, curves, and diagrams, including the Engine Calibration curve. Since the specifications and measurement numbers were non-metric, he copied them as they read, though his notes were in German.

The return swim was uneventful until he was nearly at the fence—

"HALT! Halt right there!" the young male voice commanded again. "Come up out of the water!"

Krug did so, saying lamely, "I was just hunting for clams and oysters, sir." Above all else, he must prevent this guard from summoning others. He undid the button of his right shirt cuff.

For a moment it appeared to Krug that the guard did not know quite what to do next; then Krug saw him reach for his whistle lanyard.

At the same instant, Krug lunged at him.

BY MICHAEL GANNON

Operation Drumbeat
The Dramatic True Story of
Germany's First U-Boat Attacks
Along the American Coast
in World War II

Secret Missions

ATTENTION: ORGANIZATIONS AND CORPORATIONS

Most HarperPaperbacks are available at special quantity discounts for bulk purchases for sales promotions, premiums, or fund-raising. For information, please call or write:
Special Markets Department, HarperCollins*Publishers*,
10 East 53rd Street, New York, N.Y. 10022.
Telephone: (212) 207-7528. Fax: (212) 207-7222.

SECRET MISSIONS

MICHAEL GANNON

HarperPaperbacks
A Division of HarperCollinsPublishers

This is a work of fiction. The characters, incidents, and dialogues are products of the author's imagination and are not to be construed as real. Any resemblance to actual events or persons, living or dead, is entirely coincidental.

HarperPaperbacks *A Division of* HarperCollins*Publishers*
10 East 53rd Street, New York, N.Y. 10022

A hardcover edition of this book was published in 1994 by HarperCollins*Publishers.*

Cover illustration by Bill Dodge

First HarperPaperbacks printing: August 1995

Printed in the United States of America

HarperPaperbacks and colophon are trademarks of HarperCollins*Publishers*

❖ 10 9 8 7 6 5 4 3 2 1

To Vince, who would have enjoyed this

*In war it is not so much the men
as the man that counts.*

—NAPOLEON

CHAPTER 1

THURSDAY, JANUARY 15, 1942

To Peter Krug it seemed that his handlers could not have picked a less fitting site at which to test him for a mission to sand, sun, and aquamarine waters. The Pas-de-Calais coastline presented a scene of cold compact ground under sullen clouds, the kind that came off the English Channel and hung forever in the winter. But, as Krug recognized, the atmosphere was irrelevant. The essentials were here: a military airfield, warplanes, and guards. On that basic stage his performance during the next twelve hours was all that mattered.

Worried that he might be challenged by forward sentries or by farmers who owned the land beneath his feet, though he saw no one in the dusk's last light, he hurried north over the brown fields, still furrowed where leeks and sugar beets had been extracted, and waded across the canals and irrigation ditches that, twenty months before, had barely slowed elements of the 10th Panzer Division that passed this way on their advance to Calais. Ahead he could smell the salt air of the Channel beaches where, in the years before the war, the Parisian petite bourgeoisie took its pleasure in the summertime.

One last time he considered which sequence of the test requirements he would follow; then, as twilight deepened, he began walking the final few kilometers through the woods that bordered the south perimeter of the old French airdrome at Le Touquet–Paris–Plage, now a key base of the famed Luftwaffe fighter wing *Jagdgeschwader* 26.

Nearing the edge of the woods he expected to hear the guttural warm-up of engines as the first night fighter arm *Staffeln* prepared to lift off against radar-detected British Wellingtons, Stirlings, and Hampdens on the first legs of their generally useless bombing flights across the Lowlands into western Germany, or, to the south, against the capital ships at Brest and the U-boat bunkers at Lorient.

But Krug heard nothing. Through the trunks and branches he did see, just turning on, the bright rotating airfield beacon and then, other lights, operational, maintenance, and air strip, of the airdrome. A number of thoughts went through his head. Coastal radar must not be painting incoming enemy aircraft near this sector or the lights would not have been lit. And that.would account for the absence of night fighter scrambles. Except for a small glow in the mist above the airfield lights, the descending night sky, just one day shy of new moon, was lampblack dark. Perhaps the moonless conditions persuaded the RAF to stay on the ground tonight: they were not hitting much of anything with a moon, how could they expect to find their targets without one?

Before exiting the woods he triangulated his position bare-eyed using the beacon, a cluster of radio antennas, and a water tower. From his shoulder bag he withdrew a pair of dry heavy socks, which he donned to replace his wet ones, a pen-sized flashlight, a notepad and pencil, a towel, a pair of clean cotton gloves, and a can of aviation engine oil, which he emptied over his face and head, hands, arms, and lower legs, as a precaution against dogs. Then, under the abundant leaves, he buried the bag which also contained tightly wrapped bread, sausage, cheese, and water rations for the morrow.

It was a good thing he stopped where he did, since only meters ahead, as he now saw dimly, he would have stumbled upon three Luftwaffe ground crewmen walking at 90 degrees to his course toward a squared-off clearing in the wood line. Sighting heater units, starter motors, and wheel chocks in the clearing, Krug deduced that this was a parking site under tree branch canopies that provided concealment for aircraft that could taxi from it straight onto the airstrips for takeoff.

As he knelt to listen in on the crewmen's chatter, hoping

to pick up information that might be useful, the night air was shattered by the loudest loudspeakers Krug had ever heard. The speakers were everywhere, some above him in the trees: "ATTENTION! ATTENTION! GROUND CREWS PREPARE TO RECOVER AIRCRAFT!"

Now many crewmen could be seen scurrying out of wood huts and maintenance hangars to Krug's left and taking up positions at other chock-down sites imbedded in the wood line. At the same time, the first engines could be heard overhead as two-plane formations of aircraft entered the downwind leg of the airfield pattern and then, turning base and final, began throttling down to meter-per-minute approaches.

Krug, whose background was in bombers, could not identify the fighters from their engine noise alone, but as the first aircraft to land taxied straight toward him he saw from their twin engine configuration that these were Messerschmitt Bf-110s. One after another, the 110s touched down and taxied to their concealed chock positions, where the pilots would shut down one engine and use the other, in combination with brakes, to swing the aircraft 180 degrees around to face the airstrips.

The various series of the Bf-110 had not performed well as escort fighters in the battle over Britain during the summer and autumn of 1940; in fact, as Krug knew, in one three-week period the elite *Zerstörergruppen,* which flew this type aircraft, lost 40 percent of them to Hurricanes and Spitfires. As all-black-finish night fighters against British bombers, however, the 110s had redeemed themselves, and no doubt that was their use here.

But why, Krug wondered, were they landing now, just as night started? This was the hour, 1930, when night fighters usually were taking off! No question about it, though, the ground crews were chocking the wheels and settling them in for the night. Fuel trucks went down the line to top off the tanks, but, curiously, no armorers came forward to replace empty ammunition boxes, feed the belts through, swab the barrels, and cock the guns. Had no ammo been spent? Krug's mind returned to the basic question, which was, why were these night fighters in the air at twilight but on the ground at night? Was it only because British bombers were not flying, if indeed they were not?

As the crews completed their tasks they withdrew and reentered the warm huts and tents from which they had emerged. And all the lights, including the beacon, went out. It was not only the 110s that had gone to bed, the entire airdrome was packing it in, its missions apparently completed.

When Krug's eyes adjusted to the total darkness he could see slightly to his right and at the opposite end of the field a long series of sandbagged blast pens. Day fighters. It had to be. He walked slowly and noiselessly, he hoped, out of the woods and onto the airfield grass, turning his head smartly from side to side, like a bird. He froze when he saw a guard, to his left, at some distance away though, helmeted, rifle slung over his shoulder, pacing slowly, no dog, smoking a cigarette: a pinpoint of red light glowed on and off.

Krug was sure that he was too far away to be seen, but this was the first moment when he sensed fully—and with a short but healthy twinge of fear—the vulnerability that his civilian clothes imposed on him. Obviously he did not belong here. There was no masquerade, no impersonation, no cover that he could hide behind. In his black leather jacket and watch cap he was naked to the Wehrmacht sentries who secured Le Touquet. At any moment, perhaps without even challenge or warning, one of them could shoot him dead. And what would his handlers say about *that*?

Well, if this was to be his line of work he had best get at it. In a crouch he ran toward the black pens. Better to go boldly than hesitantly, he thought, though he was on wide open ground for much longer than he liked. Finally, he reached the nearest sandbag revetment and threw himself inside it. He was right, he told himself, panting heavily:

before him, in chocks, sat two of the older Messerschmitt Bf-109 day fighters with bright yellow paint from the spinner over the engine cowling as far back as the aft end of the supercharger air intake fairing.

After catching his breath he climbed onto the port wing of the 109 nearest him, opened the starboard-hinged cockpit canopy, and with the aid of his penlight located the map pouch from which he withdrew the pilot's handbook and logs. Next he reached for his notepad and pencil and began writing down the asked-for specifications for this type, which turned out to be Bf-109E-4.

Turning the handbook pages, he found the engine mark, Daimler-Benz DB601A, and the numbers for horsepower; gross weight; maximum level speed at various altitudes; cruising speed at various altitudes; rate of climb and time to altitude; service ceiling; turning radius; range; and armament. He quickly examined the airframe and engine logs for modifications, placed the documents back in the pouch, closed the canopy, stepped down, and then examined the adjoining aircraft in the blast pen, which proved to be of the same airframe type and engine series.

Emboldened by this success, and hearing no jackboots nearby, he proceeded to the next pen, and then to the next, and, during the following three hours, to the remainder of the day fighter pens until he was satisfied that he had obtained all the information his handlers required in this category. There were three types of day fighter on the base: a few 109Es, mostly 109F-4s, and Focke-Wulf 190A-2s. There were no examples of a new type he was asked to look for, 109G with the DB605A powerplant. The data asked for on each type were now in his notebook. The pages were oily but legible. He sat behind a 109F tail assembly in the last pen on the line, leaned back against the sandbags, and rested.

Bootsteps. Guards. At least two men. Very talkative. They came from the right and crossed the entrance of the pen. A dog on a leash preceded them. Krug placed a hand over his mouth and nose and closed his eyes, lest breath or tear give off a scent. The threesome passed by. Aviation oil had saved him. He breathed again and listened intently as the jabbering, for which Luftwaffe units and their guards were famous, faded. He checked his watch: 2350. Then he crept slowly along the 109 fuselage to the pen entrance and looked warily to his left and right. He saw the receding figures to his left, but no one else.

It was time to take the second test. Across the grass airstrips, barely visible as gray upon black, stood the two-story white wood-frame fighter control center with its railed, open observation deck on top. Three ground-level windows facing him showed thin streaks of yellow light around the edges of their blackout curtains. No doubt these were the lights of the operations room, which would be occupied by the duty officer and the dispatcher. Radar equipment, if that was where it was set up, would also be manned, but Krug did not think that the technicians worked in the light, or in that much light. He began his run in the same low crouch he had used before, knees thrusting up close to his face. Halfway across the grass strips he fell to his elbows and surveilled 360 degrees around the airdrome. No one. No movement. He concentrated on the control center. At this distance he could see rows of huts to the right of it that probably were officer-pilot quarters. Their lights were either shielded or out. No guards were visible. Security around here was certainly irregular and casual, he thought, which, in his case, could be either good or bad.

Up on his feet again, and running fast this time, he soon found himself close enough to hear music from a radio, then, quickly afterward, he was standing upright at a corner of the control center. When his chest stopped heaving he walked to the front of the structure and peered inside through a gap in the curtains. An officer sat at a long map table facing the left wall; he was reading a book under a desk lamp and blowing thick clouds of Gauloise smoke. Krug could see the blue pack and, through chinks in the window framing, smell its acrid product. To the right a flight sergeant, no doubt a dispatcher, slept soundly, despite the radio music, in a camp chair. Behind him an open door led into a darkened room, perhaps a communications center. To the far right was the office Krug had set his sights for. A painted wood sign identified the door: GESCHWADERKOMMANDEUR.

He crept around to the darkened window corresponding to the wing commander's office and slowly pulled on its frame. Latched. He moved to the next window on the right and tried its frame. Open! At age thirty-two he had the muscle strength but not the agility of his younger years; still, struggling, he managed to hoist himself up the wall and through the window. He worried about the noise of his shoes scraping against the outside wood siding, but as he fell inside he heard no reaction from the adjacent operations room.

He might have alerted both its occupants if the cry that left his lips had been in the audible range, but a bruise would certainly rise where in the darkness he barked his shin against a toilet bowl. No wonder the window to this room was left open. He took out his penlight and surveilled the lavatory. Then, careful not to knock anything over, he ran his left hand along the wall that faced the wing commander's space. There he found a door handle and pushed it down—of course, the CO would have his own private access—opened the door and quickly entered the office where, this time, he shone his light about before making the first move. Then he donned the clean cotton gloves.

Dead ahead, where its drawers faced the window, was the CO's desk, its front top heavy with bric-a-brac and battle souvenirs. Krug stepped in front of the wood swivel chair and swept his narrow lightbeam over the papers on the desktop. They were combat reports and correspondence—interesting, but noncritical. One by one he opened the drawers and examined their contents, which were mainly routine operational, maintenance, and personnel orders and forms, nothing worth stealing or copying. The third drawer at bottom right was locked. Krug drew a steel pin from his pocket and had the drawer open inside ten seconds. He pulled from it twenty or so folders containing typed forms and pages and one oversized envelope stamped *Geheime Kommandosache*! The papers in the folders dealt with disciplinary matters: pilots and crewmen who had knocked up respectable French girls or smashed mirrors in cafés or been derelict in their duties—the administrative detritus that one would expect to find in a CO's confidential drawer. The envelope marked *Command Secret* had to be of a different order.

It turned out to contain a lengthy land-line cipher transmission by Siemens Geheimschreiber T-52 teleprinter and, attached, an Enigma machine German-language decryption of the message. Krug recognized its importance at once. The sender was General der Jagdflieger Adolf Galland. After reading it through, he began copying the entire cover sheet, which was the heart of the transmission. When finished, he reread the following pages, which contained flight schedules and procedures. Then he placed the envelope back in the drawer and turned the lock shut with his pin.

Hearing nothing but music in the adjoining operations room, Krug considered it safe to spend a short time more examining the CO's office. There were no file cabinets. They must be in a clerk's office, he guessed. On one wall he found an operations chalkboard with flight schedules that corresponded to the documents he had just examined. The reason why the night fighters were in the air at dusk but not at night was now apparent. On another wall he found a set of RAF aircraft silhouettes, including one of the twin-engined Avro Manchester on which someone had drawn stretched wings and two additional engines. Curious.

It was time to go. He was pressing his luck. From his jacket he withdrew his small towel and used it to wipe clean the front of the CO's desk chair of any aviation oil that might have come from his clothes. In the lavatory he wiped clean the door latch and, as he exited the window, he did the same with the sill and siding. Putting the towel back in his jacket, he walked to the rear of the control center and scouted the routes back to the wood line. He decided on a course that would take him south then east around the hangars and crew quarters. He began walking, maintaining, as usual, a close watch for guards. Before long he would have to meet up with a guard, but it would be when he was prepared, at his own time, and on his own terms.

Without incident he made the trees and, treading softly over the leaf-strewn ground, he found the spot where he had buried his bag and, before anything else, slaked his thirst from the water canteen. The time was 0210. With his still-gloved right hand he removed tropical-weight tan overalls from the bag and donned them to cover the engine oil on his clothes and body. Then he used his towel to wipe his gloves clean.

More than two hours passed before Krug found his moment. He had begun to worry that the night would drag on and that sunrise would spoil his chances to pass the third test requirement. But now, to his relief, a lone guard, without a dog, came into view on his left, ambling in a lazy, nonmilitary gait, a Mauser strapped over his right shoulder. He held a lit cigarette in his right hand. So he was right-handed. He could hardly be the same guard Krug had seen eight hours before when he first stepped out of the woods, since that sentry detail would certainly have been relieved by this time. All that remained was to check the man's collar patches. His eyes strained in the darkness to make out the rank. When he was satisfied, Krug made his move.

From a kneeling position where, still as a statue, he summoned up every vital power and mental edge, he crept out of concealment onto the airfield grass behind his target. Then with a rush he went after him. The corporal turned to his right when he heard Krug coming, lowered his rifle strap and gripped the stock, which immobilized his right arm, at which instant Krug's own right arm slammed against the sentry's right side, turning him around. Krug knocked the gun away and pinned the sentry's right arm behind his back at a painfully acute angle while, using the crook of his left arm, he pulled his victim's head back in a chokehold that he gradually increased in pressure. As the guard gagged and fought back with his heels and a flailing left arm, Krug whispered the only words of the encounter: "I'm sorry you didn't make sergeant. . . . If you're a believing man say your prayers. . . . Be proud that you died for the Fatherland."

As the body sagged, Krug sagged with it to a kneeling position, exerting just enough pressure to cause asphyxia without leaving a bruise. Against his chest Krug felt the body's last warm tremors. He maintained the hold until, with his right hand, he felt no more pulse in the superficial temporal artery.

He then picked up the body by pulling it over his shoulders and carried it to the edge of the woods where he placed it in a seated position against a tree trunk. He straightened up the tunic and brushed the hair. Then he went back to the site of the engagement and picked up the Mauser and the corporal's helmet, both of which had fallen to the ground. He also knelt and examined the grass for broken soil or other signs of struggle with his hands: there seemed to be none. Next he placed the helmet on the corpse's head and strapped the Mauser back in place. Standing over his handiwork, he whispered, "I think this poor fellow—can't be more than twenty—had heart pains, sat down to rest, and simply died. It happens more and more these days."

Krug had killed before, many times, but from 10 to 20,000 feet, never at ground level, never head to head. He was gratified that the kill had gone just as he had practiced it in training. At the same time, he was surprised how naturally, as though he was born to it, cold blood passed through his veins.

Recalling the maxim, *Der Mensch fängt mit Leutnant*

an—Humanity begins with the rank of lieutenant—he supposed that, for this test, his handlers had lowered the threshold to sergeant.

Well! Damn! He was hungry. Back at his bag, he made a sandwich from the bread, sausage, and cheese. Newly fortified, and with all his test requirements met, he began retracing his path out of the woods, across the fields, through the water courses, and toward the gully between highway 143 and the River Canche where he had hidden the Peugeot 346cc motorcycle.

Before he broke out of the woods, while pausing to take a leak, he heard the loudspeakers and then the starter motors and the cough and growl of ignitions as the 110s in their nests revved up for predawn takeoffs. It was all according to schedule. A couple of hours later the 110s would come home and stay on the ground until late afternoon when, refueled but not re-armed, they would go aloft again. In the meantime, sixteen-plane waves of 109s and 190s would struggle over the grass on their retractable undercarriages and then, rotating quickly off the airstrips proper, snarl into the air, form up under the estimated 400 meter ceiling, and fly west over the slate-gray seas and whitecaps of the Channel Front, where most would never once climb into that low cloud cover. It was all in the plan.

He found his moto, raised it from its concealment in the gulley, kicked the starter, and accelerated east along the Canche, then south through flat, open countryside to Conchil-le-Temple, then on D940 east to Nempont–St. Firmin, where he turned onto No.1 south, which skirted the western edge of the Forêt Dom de Crécy and took him to Hautvillers-Ouville, where he left it for tertiary roads that led to the airdrome at Drucat, above Abbeville.

There he found his copilot and crew standing by the JU-88A-4 *Schnellbomber* that would take them back to Hamburg. After he returned the borrowed moto to its airdrome owner and tossed his bag through the aircraft's bomb-bay aft fuselage access, Krug took the left cockpit seat and directed the copilot to light the twin Junkers Jumo 211 engines.

It was good to be starting home, he considered, but then he had never been more alive than when he was running around the airfield at Le Touquet. He felt even more alive than he had a year and a half back when he was flying bombing runs over Britain, or when, earlier in the same year, he penetrated the office of the United States naval attaché in Berlin. Already he missed the danger and the challenge. There was one more exhilaration to come, though—when he presented his handlers back in Hamburg one very much alive made-in-Deutschland bombshell.

CHAPTER 2

KRUG HAD SLEPT DURING much of the return flight, leaving the flying chores to the right seat. And now, at 0900 on Saturday, after a relatively good afternoon and night at the Klopstock boardinghouse, where he and the other Abwehr I trainees were put up, and after several hearty meals matched by an equal number of large steins of Holsten Pilsener on the Reeperbahn, followed by one particularly fine orgasm, he sat at a conference table in IT/Lw, the Tecknik/Luftwaffe offices of the Abwehr I post in Hamburg, Army District X, which occupied a dreary three-story concrete building on Sophienterrasse in the residential subdivision of Harvestehude.

When his two handlers and a third man, who was unknown to him, entered the room, Krug stood, but not at military attention, for all signs of military bearing and manners had been drilled out of him during the last four weeks. His two handlers motioned him to be seated while they took chairs opposite. The third individual, a tall dark man in his forties, balding, with jug ears, settled into a chair near the door of the bare off-white room.

Facing him on the left was Hans-Joachim Groskopf, director of the air intelligence technical section, a man of medium height, with a ruddy, intense face, and thick black hair. To the right sat Wolfgang Kettner, of the SD, *Sicherheitsdienst,* the SS intelligence and security service headed by Reinhard Heydrich. Kettner was tall and dark-blondish with deep eyes placed close together and a mouth so thin and slanted it appeared to be a slash scar across his face. Both men held Krug's own rank, that of major.

From local Abwehr gossip Krug had learned that Heydrich and Admiral Wilhelm Canaris, head of Abwehr, though publicly good friends, were in fact rivals for control of Germany's intelligence services. Heydrich had insisted that one of his own men, Kettner, be involved in Krug's training, since so much counted on this mission's success. Four weeks were hardly enough to prepare an agent with the thoroughness that both Groskopf and Kettner preferred, but the surprise Japanese action at Pearl Harbor and the opening of full-scale German-U.S. hostilities had placed everyone on an accelerated schedule. Krug was the emergency point man.

"We're glad to see you back, Krug," Groskopf said. "No scratches?"

"No scratches," Krug answered.

Groskopf smiled, something that Kettner never did.

"Let's get down to business. We gave you three test requirements. Which did you choose first?"

"The day fighters," Krug said. He handed Groskopf the pertinent oil-stained pages from his notepad. "You'll find all the performance figures there."

Groskopf opened a folder containing typewritten data sheets and began comparing Krug's data against his own for each day fighter type stationed at Le Touquet. It was not a cursory examination. Groskopf labored at it, while Kettner looked over his shoulder. Groskopf's motto was "Victory Through Numbers."

Under Groskopf's exacting tutelage, with help from Hauptmann Hermann Sandel, deputy chief of air intelligence, Krug had learned, if not mastered, use of the usual tools of espionage, including radio operation, the standard Abwehr agent cipher, Morse code, invisible inks and their reagents, false papers, microdot photography, and passwords, most of which would be of no use in the mission at hand. Even radio telegraphy would be no use, since he would be so far away from base, over 3,000 miles, that the small 10-watt Telefunken-made *Agentenfunk,* or Afu, shortwave transmitter-receiver normally issued to agents could not carry the distance, and since both Abwehr high-power stationary transmitters in the United States, at

Centerport, Long Island, and on Cauldwell Avenue in the Bronx, had been seized by the FBI in a massive agent round-up seven months before. A third clandestine station in Mexico City, with which an Afu might work in relay if atmospheric conditions permitted, was not itself capable of reaching the Abwehr receivers at Wohldorf, a small country town outside North Hamburg. And, so far, except for making contact with one agent-radio operator in Florida, no radio relay agreement had been worked out with the independent-minded signals people of the Ubootwaffe or with its commander-in-chief, U-boats, Admiral Karl Dönitz, in part because of a longstanding enmity between Dönitz and Canaris, under whom the former had served, disagreeably, in the early 1930s.

The FBI raids in June and July, netting in all forty-five individuals, including a dozen producing agents, had destroyed the principal prewar Abwehr ring in America. At fault was an agent become double-agent, William G. Sebold, codenamed "Tramp," who betrayed the entire apparatus. Hauptmann Sandler had been his case officer. Only six senior agents, or V-men, remained in the country, although there were still scores of subagents and informants including, Krug knew, the radio operator, who was also a skilled forger, in Florida. No one left had the knowledge or background required to provide reliable high-grade military intelligence. Now that war had been declared, the Hamburg post, which handled Great Britain and the United States, was desperate for hard data on U.S. aircraft performance. That was what Groskopf emphasized: *performance*.

As Krug well knew from the Luftwaffe's miscalculation of the British Spitfire in 1939–40, design was one thing, performance was another. Just to have known that the Spitfire's Rolls-Royce Merlin II engine was being fed American-shipped 100 octane gasoline would have alerted Germany's pilots to the enemy's surprising rate of climb, and to have known the Spitfire's turning circle would have led to different fighting tactics. Now that the Americans had entered the war with both feet, the air over Europe would be filling soon with numerous fighter and bomber types of American design and manufacture. The Luftwaffe simply had to know at the earliest possible date their flying and fighting characteristics. What was needed now, Groskopf and Kettner had told him, was a *grossagent* of superior familiarity with military aircraft, a man of single-minded intensity, unquestioned reliability, unbounded energy, daring, and proven devotion to the Fatherland. They had decided that he was that man.

"Very well done, Krug," Groskopf said, lifting his eyes from the spread of papers. "You obviously got to the cockpit handbooks and logs."

"Obviously," Krug answered.

"And you copied the data exactly, which is important," Groskopf emphasized. "We need to know the performance envelope in minute detail. Blue sky figures do not help us."

"Neither do exact figures, Groskopf," Krug corrected him, "if an aircraft's handling characteristics have been altered by modifications. For example, I know from listening to fighter pilot gossip that the one-oh-nine F-fours with the R-one modification—that's the MG one-five-one cannon installation—tend to fishtail and porpoise. That's not something you'd learn from cockpit documents. Also you have to factor in the skill and agility of the pilot if you want to know full performance capability."

"Yes, of course," Groskopf said, recovering. "Do you suppose a Tommy or Yankee agent could have gotten these same numbers at Le Touquet?"

"Absolutely," Krug said. "The security there is porous. I had no trouble at all. Neither would an enemy. A saboteur could easily torch the planes and blow up the fuel depot. I don't know how we're winning the war—if we are."

"That's enough of that," Groskopf cautioned. "The next requirement—"

"I'd like to jump to the third in the order I chose and get it out of the way," Krug said, looking at Kettner's hard face. "I killed a guard, as instructed, and I made sure he was not a sergeant. You can check."

Kettner spoke for the first time. "I already have, Krug. The base flight surgeon reported a sentry dead from apparent heart failure, nothing missing from his person— or from the base. He noted the faint odor of engine oil on the body and uniform, but explained it in terms of the environment. So you did well. But let me warn you, not every physician is going to be as matter-of-fact and accepting as a flight surgeon. A trained pathologist would have discerned the true cause of death, through autopsy, and the discovery of soft tissue hemorrhages in the strap muscles of the neck. So don't think you're going to get away with the kind of death certificate you want every time."

Kettner leaned back in his chair and nodded for Groskopf to continue.

"The, uh, last requirement," Groskopf said, "was to penetrate the base commander's office. What have you got for us there?"

Krug tore three pages from his notepad and handed them to Groskopf.

"What you have there," he explained, "is a command secret message from general of the fighter arm, Adolf Galland, at Goldap, dated thirteen January, and addressed to the Jags twenty-six and two air wing and group commanders at Le Touquet, Caen, and Schiphold.

"It describes a new fighter training program for an operation called *Thunderbolt.* Bf one-oh-nine and FW one-ninety squadrons will conduct training missions during daylight hours. Bf one-ten squadrons will train at twilight and at daybreak. Trial runs of the operation will be conducted beginning twenty-two January. Twelve additional Bf one-oh-nines to participate in this training will be dispatched to Le Havre from the operational training unit in Paris—"

Groskopf interrupted him to read from the notepaper: "'Be certain to keep an exact record of all flight data, including times, distances, winds, ceilings, visibility, and fuel remaining. This applies to radar decoys as well as to operational aircraft—'"

"Yes," Krug went on. "More detailed instructions will be sent later to the commanders in sealed envelopes marked Thunderbolt and are not to be opened except upon direct order from Galland or upon receipt of the codeword *Thunderbolt.* And notice that, on order from the Führer, absolute secrecy about the training schedule is to be observed by all personnel and that includes any speculating among themselves or with others about the exact nature of the mission for which they're training."

"But—" Groskopf objected, "but Galland states here: 'Fighter pilots may be told only that a new bomber offensive will be mounted against England.'"

He looked up, beaming. "Krug, you really got something there. I never thought you'd come out of Le Touquet with a document like that. I knew something was up when I heard that the one-oh-nines at Paris were being posted to Le Havre. And you found the reason—a new bombing offensive against England!"

He smiled proudly in the direction of Kettner.

There was a pause. Then Krug spoke: "Do you accept everything on its face, Groskopf? You ask for exactness, but how about a little imagination here? Why don't you ask me what the training altitudes are?"

Groskopf recoiled in his chair, as much from the impertinence as from the challenge.

"Look," Krug continued, savoring the patronizing tone he gave the word, "the training schedule I examined has most of the one-oh-nines out over the Channel at continuous low altitudes, never above cloud bases, and the one-tens flying only during the half-light periods of dawn and dusk, most of them also at low altitudes.

"Now what does that mean?" he lectured his mentors. "It means that on a given date, probably the next new moon, Jags twenty-six and two will fly protective cover for the break-out of capital ships from Brest and their—"

"Break-out?" Groskopf exclaimed.

"At Brest," Krug continued, his voice rising, "we have, what?, the battle cruisers *Scharnhorst* and *Gneisenau* and the heavy cruiser *Prinz Eugen*. Since the loss of the *Bismarck* they've been frozen in port, where their only utility is as a fleet-in-being that ties down the British Home Fleet and prevents its detachment to the Mediterranean. Fine, but being only a short distance from Britain the three ships or their dock areas are taking a hammering from RAF bombers. So why not move them to less-exposed ports in the Elbe or at Wilhelmshaven or in Norway even? And the only safe and economical way to do that is to take them out of Brest at night and under heavy fighter protection dash them in daylight through the Channel. The air side of the operation is what Thunderbolt is all about."

"Why that's preposterous!" Groskopf protested.

"Preposterous? How else do you explain over-water training flights on which most fighters never climb above cloud ceilings, unless their pilots are training for a mission of exactly that kind? Do you think by these means they are training for bomber-escort sorties over England? Have you ever heard of bomber escorts that never exceeded eight hundred meters in altitude? Can you imagine bombers themselves flying at those suicidal altitudes? Let me spell it out for you: The one-tens will fly air cover for the ships at dawn and dusk. The one-oh-nine air umbrella will try to control the dash lanes in daylight. At night, the ships will be on their own. The Navy probably has its own codeword for the operation.

"What is really preposterous, Groskopf, is the thought that Reichsmarschall Göring would divert bombers from Russia to the Channel Front just at this particular time when our panzer groups are mired in the snows before Moscow, and every Heinkel, Dornier, and JU eighty-eight in the inventory is desperately needed to support them. I was surprised you had an eighty-eight that I could use to get to Drucat.

"And don't you know that fighter escort strength in the

west has been drawn down, and I include the training reserves, in order to meet the emergency in the east? Except for the Paris fighters detailed for Le Havre? You should know that."

Kettner, who never smiled, now smiled, obviously taking pleasure in the discomfiture of his Abwehr colleague. A little Schadenfreude, Krug noted.

"Equally preposterous," Krug continued, "is the thought that we would undertake a bombing offensive against England during the worst flying months of the year in that country when God himself can't see through the cloud layers. I will be amazed, Groskopf, if the Jag pilots don't figure this out for themselves. Anyway, in an order that demands absolute secrecy about Thunderbolt we may be sure that what the pilots are to be told is not what they will end up doing."

Krug had finished. He sat back and drank in the faces of the two men across from his. It seemed that both had been totally captured by his logic and now were afraid to comment lest they be charged with collusion in the exposure of a state secret. The man by the door stood up and left the room.

"Who was that?" Krug asked when the door closed again.

"That was Oberst Hans Piekenbrock," Groskopf managed to answer, "head of Abwehr I, from headquarters in Berlin. He came over to hear your debriefing. You will be flying with him to Berlin this afternoon. His driver will pick you up at the Klopstock at thirteen-hundred hours. Tonight you will be driven to the home of Admiral Canaris, the head of Abwehr. SS Obergruppenführer Heydrich will be a dinner guest. Tomorrow, the eighteenth, you will be a passenger on the headquarters aircraft to Lorient, France, where you will report to Korvettenkapitän Viktor Schütze, commanding officer of the Second U-boat Flotilla. After that you're in the navy's hands. Your orders are cut—pick them up at the desk as you leave."

"Outstanding."

"Henceforth," Groskopf went on, "you will be known by a number and a cover-name. Your number is R-thirty-five eighty-eight. Commit it to memory. Your cover-name is 'Homer.'"

"Why 'Homer'?" Krug asked.

"Because you're going on a long odyssey."

"I think I'll accept it because of Winslow Homer, my favorite American watercolorist."

"Whatever," Groskopf said, irritably.

"One thing more, Krug," said Kettner, standing up to his full height and assuming what Krug thought was a posture of military attention. "Tonight you will be with the two most important men in our profession. Wear a dress blue suit. And be on your best behavior—if you have a best behavior."

"In other words," Krug said, standing now himself, "you don't want me to kill them."

Kettner bristled. "Insolence like that will do you in some day."

"Certainly something will," Krug said, smiling. "Why not insolence? I can't think of a more satisfying way to go."

CHAPTER 3

IT WAS WHAT PASSED for winter in St. Augustine. Temperatures in the high thirties after the passage of a dark cold front. The Florida sky a bright transparent blue again, with a dusting of cirrus. Minorcan men in jackets and mufflers played checkers in the antebellum slave market at the east end of the heavily treed Plaza de la Constitución, which was the center of town, now as it had been for most of three and three-quarter centuries.

Dirtied marsh hens scrambled from San Sebastian River at the city's western edge and squadrons of the gray-white gulls that waited for shrimp boats wheeled once more over Matanzas River, which separated the town from a narrow barrier island, Anastasia, and from the ocean beyond, while, three thousand feet above, droning flights of aircraft from Naval Air Station Jacksonville practiced after-early-chapel formation flying in what pilots called CAVU—clear and visibility unlimited.

Adjoining the old Spanish cathedral and fronting the plaza at its northwest corner was the parish rectory, a Second Empire style residence from the 1880s. Two sabal palms presented arms on either side of its paired front doors. Around the building and its narrow yard stood a three-foot-high molded-concrete wall.

Only the chilly temperatures made Father Anthony D'Angelo feel anything like at home in this rectory, 900 miles removed from his native Manhattan. From the window of his second-story room on the rectory's east side, he could look out on a slice of the plaza, the street in front, and, up close, the flanks of the cathedral and its campanile. He opened the double-hung window to take in the air, which both braced him and, because of the freight of memories it carried, deepened his melancholy.

This was the kind of northern cold air in which he had spent all his previous Februaries. Pictures of those winter times rose before him, particularly those from his boyhood years on Forty-first Street when he and his pals played potsy, Johnny-on-the-Pony, and roller-skate hockey with pucks from the candy store, shot water rats along the East River with BBs, ducked into the museums—the Met and Natural History—when it got too cold, traveled to the Bronx Zoo for a nickel and across to Staten Island for the same, hitched rides on the Third and Sixth Avenue els, built bonfires on election nights, watched the globe turn in the Daily News' lobby, bought two cents worth of nigger babies, rode their Flexible Flyers down the new snow in Central Park, played funny racket at Albert's Delicatessen, and taunted the police: "Brass buttons, blue coat, couldn't catch a nanny goat!"

Odd that he could not summon many images from the period after he entered Cathedral College downtown, and then major seminary at Dunwoodie. Piety, he guessed, was less memorable than mischief. After that—well, life became more regimented and respectable, but no less interesting since in New York just looking about when on vacation or on days off was something to do. He could hardly wait for spring training to see the Yankees in St. Petersburg.

It was not New York alone that he missed on this Sunday morning, however. It was having something to do, something other than Mass, baptisms, confessions, convert instructions, filling out marriage forms, saying the breviary—and golf. He was surprised how little he liked golf, which, it appeared, was every other cleric's avocation. Too slow, he thought. It took up too much of his free time. And there was no real exercise to it. Why wasn't there a handball court in town? Not that he was any good at it. But it was exercise.

St. Augustine just did not have that much to offer once you had seen the historic sites, which he had, or if you did not like golf, fishing, or the beach, which he did not.

There was a small art colony and a literary circle and an amateur theater company that was quite good. And some of the resident tourists he had met at the winter hotels, the Ponce de Leon, the Monson, and the Buckingham, in particular, were accomplished and sophisticated people.

Overall, the venerable Spanish town presented an aspect of drowsiness, as though it was wearied by the travails of long life and hard survival. The individual townspeople he had come to know, whites and Negroes alike, were faithful, generous, and good-humored. It was a joy to talk with some of them. But the town itself was pretty damn boring—except, you could say, on weekends when it filled with soldiers and sailors from nearby bases. Then it sometimes became the disorderly garrison town it had been in colonial times. But Tony saw little of that. Weekends were his busy time. Besides, rectory life and the collar insulated him from a multitude of sins, both civilian and military, that he heard about only in the confessional.

When Bishop Francis A. Garvey had entreated the bishops of the priest-rich Northern dioceses to lend him clergy to assist military chaplains in caring for the exploding numbers of Catholic soldiers, sailors, and airmen at Florida camps and bases, Archbishop Francis Spellman of New York, alone among them, had responded, and sent him Tony. It was not what Tony himself had wished for. He had begged Spellman's auxiliaries and chancellor—a priest just recently ordained like himself would have had little direct access to Spelly—for permission to enter one of the military services as a chaplain. From his soul he detested the fascism that had ruined his father's Italy and had assumed huge and wanton power in Germany, and he zealously willed its final destruction. Serving as a uniformed chaplain would give him something to do in the practical order that would have direct, positive bearing on the war.

Instead, Spelly sent him on loan to Garvey so that he might replace a Florida priest who *did* go into the chaplaincy. That hurt. Badly. Though, in charity, he tried not to, in justice he harbored a deep resentment toward Spelly for that inconsideration and put-down. He prayed for help in overcoming those feelings, but the God of Battles was slow to respond. Perhaps He felt the same way about Spelly. Anyway, here he was in St. Augustine, filling a space.

Yes, he could see that he was needed, as, in fact, many more Northern clerics were needed here in priest-poor Florida; especially now that war had been declared and the diocese, which covered the entire state east of the Apalachicola River in the Panhandle, was filling up with tens of thousands of service men and civilian base workers, most of them from the North, a large percentage of them Catholic, whose spiritual needs exceeded what the base chaplains could supply. Pastors and assistant pastors who had parishes within driving distances of the bases were having to work many hours overtime providing Mass and the sacraments to make up the shortfall. The diocesan chancery, which previously serviced 70,000 Florida Catholics, was now doing as much dispensation and casework as a diocese with 200,000 souls.

The army's Camp Blanding, an hour's drive into the interior, had 12,000 tents and was expanding to hold over 90,000 men. Soon it would be Florida's fourth-largest city. Its neighbor, Starke, once a sleepy strawberry hamlet, had filled with civilian workmen to become a neon-lit boomtown. The Naval Air Station at Jacksonville, thirty miles north of St. Augustine, was growing rapidly, as were similar stations at Sanford, Banana River, Fort Lauderdale, and Miami. Engineers were laying out auxiliary stations elsewhere. Tens of thousands of Army Air Corps personnel were training at MacDill Field in Tampa, at Miami Beach, where four or five of the largest hotels had just been taken over, at Sebring, Fort Myers, and dozens of small fields from the Panhandle to the Keys. A huge new Air Corps test facility, Eglin Field, near Fort Walton, was filling with airmen. Even Royal Air Force cadets were learning to fly at Arcadia, Lakeland, and Avon Park.

Elsewhere there were plans to establish programs for service women—WACs, WAAFs, and WAVES. Florida was becoming a garrison state.

Garvey had explained it all one night over Black Label in his sitting room on the rectory's second floor. "We're surrounded by fools, Tony," he had said.

"Which ones, Eccellenza?" Tony had asked, using the Italian form of address, which the bishop enjoyed since it recalled for him fondly remembered years in Rome when he was attaché to the papal secretary of state.

"These Northern bishops who don't understand that if the Church fails to provide spiritual service to our young soldiers and sailors, we're apt to lose a generation of young men to the Church," Garvey answered. "I've appealed time and again to the North for help. I would be recreant to a sacred trust if I did not do so. Facing us is nothing less than a spiritual emergency. 'Feed my lambs, feed my sheep.' But hardly a bishop has stepped forward to say, Here's a good man, take him, put him to work. Spellman of New York lent me you, of course, perhaps out of some obligation he sensed to me as the man who succeeded him at Rome as American *Addetto alla Segreteria di Stato*. But, as one of the *Romani*, shouldn't he be counted on for more than just one priest *in hora necessitatis*? Good grief, here is a prelate who has been named military vicar of the armed forces! And since nineteen thirty-nine he has presided over a seminary, St. Joseph's at Dunwoodie-Yonkers, that from nineteen thirty-seven to nineteen forty brutally purged its candidates for ordination from fifty-four in number to eighteen—to get rid of the surplus. The surplus!"

"I was one who survived the purge, Eccellenza," Tony interjected.

Garvey snorted and leaned forward in his chair, his eyes flashing. "The rest of the episcopal pack are a craven, selfish lot, a disgrace to the purple," he went on. "O'Connell of Boston promised two priests, but then backed off. Stritch of Chicago suggested that I should recruit more young Florida youths to the priesthood, not alluding to the fact that it takes eight years after high school to make a priest. The emergency is now. Pittsburgh patronized, as is his wont, saying that his priests joined that diocese because they wanted to be near to home. How nice! Brooklyn responded with generalities about Communists, Jews, and the Roosevelt administration. Baltimore and Fort Wayne are also slackers in this whole sorry business. What the Church needs most, Tony, is about five or six first-class funerals."

Tony closed the window and looked at his watch: 11:05. Getting close to Mass time. He curled and uncurled his hands. They were good hands. Angela Fanelli had told him so in the eighth grade. "You have such beautiful hands," she had said, turning them over and under, giving Tony his first rush of sexual arousal in the presence of another person, and making him think of uses for those hands that, he was sure, his mother would not approve. Nor would the Marist Brothers, at St. Agnes on Forty-fourth near the Chrysler Building, where Tony had more than his share of schoolyard imbroglios and Brother Matthias made him hold his palms at arm's length while he whacked them with a length of inner tube.

Eleven-oh-five. Better get into his shirt and cassock. Bishop Garvey required that every priest in the house— there were three—wear a dress white shirt under his cassock. Garvey looked for shooting French cuffs, and, Tony mused, if everyone in the house should get saintly all of a sudden, Garvey would probably be looking for *hairshirts* with French cuffs.

God only knew how much saintliness, if any, was in this house, and that was something you could say literally. The bishop probably had a dose of it, ex officio. The legend on his episcopal coat-of-arms read, *Virtus in Arduis*—virtue in hard work—and the man worked all the time, so he must have built up a lot of *virtus*. Tom Murphy, the interim pastor, worked less hard, but if kindness and humor were virtues, Tom was making good grades, too. He liked Tom's way with his dog. "A Jack Russell terrier," Tom would say proudly. "*He'll* take a varmint to ground!" His only fault, so far as Tony could tell, was an excessive taste for the wee drop. Tony enjoyed Tom's irreverent observation, meant as wit not as fact, that the three owls rampant on Garvey's heraldry meant that the bishop didn't give three hoots.

The one man in the house who was a clean shot to be another St. John Vianney or Don Bosco was Larry Byrne, the other assistant and Tony's lookalike. So closely did he and Larry resemble each other in build, facial features, and hair color that the bishop, who liked to use nicknames, sometimes called them Cosmas and Damian, after two Christian blood brothers who were martyred in Arabia during the reign of Emperor Diocletian.

With Larry's pious, obliging, joyful nature this latter-day Damian was heaven-bound, no question about it. As for himself, Tony was looking at a long stretch in purgatory—unless: he had a scheme he would like to twit Larry's nose about.

He stepped into his Rogers Peet black worsted cassock and buttoned it up close to the military collar. From the top drawer of his dresser he took a fresh white linen collar that Mattie Mae, one of two Negro housekeepers, had primly pressed, wrapped it around his neck, and fastened it in back with a brass stud. After joining the last remaining buttons and holes on his cassock, he checked the results in the dresser mirror, combed his black hair, wet his right index finger and ran it across both bushy eyebrows which, when he raised them up and down rapidly, caused the girls at St. Joseph Academy to squeal. That was one feature that Damian didn't have, the eyebrows. But Damian wasn't a teaser, so he didn't need them. And the lips. Damian didn't have the full lips.

Eleven-ten, got to go. He opened the door to his room and walked down the second-floor hallway toward the stairway. Passing Larry's door, he rapped and asked, "Larry, you helping with communion?"

"Yes, Tony, I'll be down," Larry answered through the door.

Making his way to the bottom of the stairs, Tony paused by the hatrack table to read the headline and lead story in that morning's *Sunday Times-Union* from Jacksonville:

SURVIVORS TELL OF TORPEDOING.
EIGHTEEN IN TANKER CREW ARE REPORTED MISSING IN ACTION.

In one of the most dramatic sinkings reported in the war to date, the 8200-ton U.S. tanker *Pan Massachusetts*, with storage tanks holding 55,000 barrels of gasoline, was sunk in Florida territorial waters by a German submarine, U.S. Navy sources reported. Eighteen men were reported missing, eighteen others, suffering from burns, shock, and exposure, were brought to Jacksonville by a rescue vessel. Survivors stated that the ship was hit at night on the starboard side by two torpedoes simultaneously, causing the gasoline to erupt in a blazing inferno, and that the U-boat then surfaced to shell the blazing hulk . . .

Tony lay the paper down and walked toward the sacristy.

"Holy shit!" he thought. "The damned Nazis have come to Florida!"

CHAPTER 4

AT JUPITER, FLORIDA, a U.S. Navy radio technician, operating a directional antenna, intercepted an encrypted Morse code transmission in five-letter groups from a German U-boat somewhere off the Florida coast. He guessed that it might have originated from the U-boat that sank *Pan Massachusetts* and, according to a report just in, a second tanker in the same general region, but because it was in cipher there was no way for him to know. Word quickly arrived by land-line teletype that other high-frequency direction-finding ("Huff-Duff") stations at Amagansett, Long Island, Cheltenham, Maryland, Poyners Hill, North Carolina, and Charleston, South Carolina, had made the same interception.

At Net Control in Washington, D.C., a navy Huff-Duff analyst, with all the reports in hand, stretched strings across a chart of the Atlantic seaboard waters. Each string started at a Huff-Duff station as shown on the chart. Based on the compass bearings reported by each of the stations, the analyst drew the individual strings across his chart and pinned their ends into the chart paper. The second string, from Cheltenham, intercepted the first from Jupiter at a point off the north Florida coast. The third, fourth, and fifth strings, representing the other intercepts, or cuts, crossed the first and second strings at the same general position.

"We have a fix," the analyst reported to his superior, "between a hundred and two hundred miles due east of north Florida."

The rough weather front through which U-*Böhm* just passed was only the latest misery among the many that Peter Krug had suffered as a passenger aboard this bucking, twisting submarine, which its commander, Kapitänleutnant Günther Böhm, never let *be* a submarine, but obstinately rode across the ocean surface, scorning the tall and angry waves, as though he pined to be a rodeo rider in the decadent country toward which they were headed.

A lookout just down from bridge watch told Krug there was a sky above as chaste as German crystal, visibility severe clear. They should be seeing Florida palm trees anytime now, he jested. Krug donned a leather jacket over his sweater and climbed the aluminum ladder from *Zentrale,* the control room, into the conning tower from which he could see clearly through the open bridge hatch above him a circle of cerulean blue brushed with horsetails. He used the helmsman's voice pipe to inquire of the first watch officer on top, "Permission to go topside?" To which his ear, pressed to the pipe, heard back a laconic "Nein."

Damned arrogant Saxon, thought Krug of Oberleutnant zur See Wolf-Harald Franz, *1. Wachoffizier*, or Number One, who unlike Böhm, never explained his orders and denials. Thinks he's so goddamn professional when in fact he's only an automaton, like a Siemens machine, totally lacking in imagination, not to mention proper respect and courtesy toward those who are far more important to the Reich than he is by any scale. What Franz needs is a good long weekend at Prinz-Albrecht-Strasse 8 where some of Krug's instructors can suggest how very fragile and painful are his various body parts.

The helmsman, sensing Krug's anger, spoke up. "Herr Krug, we've entered the Gulf Stream and they say there's lots of American air bases ahead, and we might have to make an alarm dive, so the Old Man has ordered no personnel on top but lookouts. That's what I heard, Herr Krug."

Krug nodded. Don't tell *me* about the American air bases, he said to himself. Grabbing hold of the ladder he went below again into the dank, reeking dungeon that had been his home for five punishing weeks. Breathing the fresh dry air on top would have been a delicious respite from the U-boat's foul enclosure, but, unlike the rest of these poor bastards, he should be off this fucking boat by tomorrow night, so he took comfort from that fact as well as from the calmer seas, which meant that for the first time in weeks he did not have to spend every waking minute bracing himself against the railing of his bunk or against some stanchion protruding elsewhere from the interior of this narrow steel cylinder, while Böhm and his merry sadists drove it westward through every winter storm they could find in a plunging, yawing corkscrew that had him puking into buckets or into the one available head when it was not occupied, as it usually was when he needed it most. God! how he was wearied by the ceaseless hammering of the diesels aft, by close, slithering physical contact with so many other men in this sewer pipe, by the darkness made light by continuously burning, harsh, wire-guarded bulbs, and by the clammy feel of every surface that he touched, including his own body.

Least of all, when he made land, he would miss this putrescent atmosphere he breathed, to which, with no fresh water on board for washing, he and the fifty-one officers and crew had made their own gamy contributions. He gasped as he inhaled the accumulated vapors of stale, humid air, diesel oil, battery gas, bilges, oven fumes, soiled trousers, unbrushed teeth, urine, vomit, semen, and the foul odor that emanated from thick, cheeselike smegma collected beneath the foreskin.

From the edge of a bunk he watched idly as Second Watch Officer Klaus Baumann laid the heavy *Marine-Funkschlüssel-Machine M* on the wardroom drop-leaf and began deciphering a transmission handed him by the radio room. Laboriously, Baumann punched the letters into the device, which resembled a typewriter except that its top had four turning rotors instead of a carriage and its front presented a tangle of wires and plugs. He read the results from glow holes above the keyboard and wrote the

German text letter by letter onto a pad. After completing the decryption and reading the message through, Baumann looked over at Krug.

"You might want to come with me while I hand this F.T. to the Old Man," he said. "It's a transmission intercept from U-one twenty-eight to BdU, Admiral Dönitz's U-boat headquarters at Kernével near Lorient where we left port. It's got some stuff you would find interesting, if the Old Man wants to share it."

By this time Krug was familiar with the abbreviation F.T., which stood loosely for radio message, and he knew from the chief radio operator, whom every one on board called *Puster*—"Blower"—that messages to and from the home base and from boat to boat were being transmitted since February 1 in a new U-boat cipher key called Triton that used four machine rotors instead of three. He followed into the control room where Böhm was bent over the navigator's table examining the dead reckoning line drawn on an overlay placed above the meter-square Atlantic chart *Nord-Atlantischer Ozean Wegenkarte*.

Krug had spent a lot of time examining that chart on his own. Drafted in 1940 to a 1:6,250,000 scale, it could hardly be expected to show much detail of coastal Florida, but to Krug's amusement, neither Jacksonville, that state's largest city, nor Miami, its most famous, was shown at all, while little "Eden" was prominently displayed between "C. Canaveral" and "Jupiter." Emil Lorenz at Eden will get a laugh out of that when Krug tells him. A pineapple town of only fifty to sixty people and it makes the *Wegenkarte!* But V-man Lorenz had earned it.

The Old Man acknowledged them as they came aside. "We got a good sun sight today, Number Two, after these last several days of weather and cloud cover. Our DR line was not that far off."

"Yes, Herr Kaleu," Baumann repled, using the accepted diminutive form of Böhm's rank. "The radio room tells me that we also have a good fix on—let's see," he said as he looked at his notes, "WSAV Savannah and

WIOD Miami. And here's an F.T. I've just decrypted. I thought you might want Krug to know about it, too."

Böhm took the decrypt from Baumann's hand and studied it: "*Ausgang F.T. Nr. 222 Grönland . . .*" He read it to the end, then looked back down to the DR overlay and said, "It looks like our refueling boat has had some successes."

"Refueling, Böhm?" Krug asked.

"Yes, U-one twenty-eight, that's Ulrich Heyse. Part of his mission is to top off our diesel fuel. His is a type nine C boat, which has larger fuel bunkers than our nine B, two hundred and eight tons of oil to our hundred and sixty-six. Originally, it was hoped we would have the first 'milk cow' at sea by this time, U-four fifty-nine, which is a large, defanged boat containing nothing but oil and provisions— no torpedoes. But when it became apparent in January that four fifty-nine wouldn't be able to leave Kiel until March or April, BdU Op had to make other arrangements.

"At first it was thought you should go to Florida on one twenty-eight, which was supposed to have left for New York and Cape Hatteras with the *Paukenschlag* force last December, but could not because of mechanical problems. Then when she was ready you were not. The one thing Admiral Dönitz cannot abide is a U-boat sitting idle. So one twenty-eight was sent on ahead with orders to reconnoiter south along the Florida coast to determine how much traffic is coming up the Straits of Florida from the Gulf of Mexico and the Windward Passage. Before she gets too far south on that coast, however, she's to rendezvous with us and discharge all the fuel she can spare."

"You said she's had some successes," Krug said. "Is she also sinking ships?"

"Oh yes, she was given license to sink anything that came her way but not, I'm told, to maneuver any great distance after targets, so as to save fuel. According to this F.T. she reached Florida in forty-two days. That's a week longer than it's taking us. She probably economized by running alternately on one engine then the other, at seven knots, as I've done a number of times."

On a boat where after five weeks everybody looked about the same—pallid, haggard, bearded—Böhm stood out, not because of his uniform, since no one on board wore a uniform as such but all ranks dressed in either standard issue winter gray-green leathers or in nondescript shirt-sweater-pants combinations of their own choosing; not even because of his *Schirmmütze*, or peaked officer's cap, with the tropical white cover that only a commander wore to make him easily recognizable on the bridge at night. He stood out because of his bright, round, pleasant Bavarian face that was nearly always crinkled in a smile under curled dark hair—unlike the stark, featureless faces Krug saw on most of the men, and certainly unlike the face of that bastard Franz, whose face and anus had been switched at birth.

"The time one twenty-eight spends rendezvousing with us tonight," Böhm continued, "will not be shown on her KTB—that's the war diary a U-boat keeps—instead, BdU will cover that space with a gloss of some kind, fictional data, probably navigational, in order to guard the secrecy of your mission, whatever it is, from the eyes of navy bureaucrats in Berlin and elsewhere to whom copies of the KTBs go as a matter of course, but who don't have 'need to know' clearance. For the same reason they'll fake my KTB for the whole period."

"Is that often done?" Krug asked.

"Not often, but Admiral Dönitz has required it a couple of times that I know about. Anyway, I want to repeat, *whatever* your mission is, since I haven't the slightest idea why we're bringing you here or why we're picking you up. But we're trying to be good soldiers about it. And we do get our turn at the Great American Turkey Shoot after we let you off."

"Turkey shoot," Krug repeated, relishing the allusion.

"Our orders are to proceed at slow cruise to Hatteras, where the *Paukenschlag* boats of Hardegen, Zapp, and Kals found such good shooting last month, sit on the bottom during the daytime to save fuel, and surface at night

36 **MICHAEL GANNON**

to torpedo anything that passes by. Then, on the appointed day, we'll return to pick you up off Eden and go home."

"You better be there, Böhm," Krug said.

"*You* better be there," Böhm replied, smiling. He handed Krug the F.T.:

> OUTGOING RADIO MESSAGE NO. 222
> GREENLAND CIRCUIT.
> ARRIVED OFF FLORIDA FORTY-SECOND DAY. ON 19
> FEB. SANK TANKER 3000 GRT IN DB 9546. NOT
> ZIGZAGGING IN VISIBILITY 1-2 MILES. ON 22 FEB.
> SANK TANKER 12000 GRT IN DB 9439. NOT
> ZIGZAGGING BUT BLACKED OUT IN CLEAR FIRST-
> QUARTER MOON. PROCEEDING TO R/V AT 2230
> TODAY IN DB 6848 WITH U-BÖHM FOR
> REFUELING. QU 6793. 134 CBM. U-HEYSE.

Krug handed the decrypt back. "Two ships in three days," he said. "Is that considered good?"

"Oh yes, for someone who's pretty much standing still to save fuel," Böhm said. "There's supposed to be another boat operating nearby, Poske's five-oh-four." He turned to Baumann. "Any intercepts from Poske?"

"None yet, Herr Kaleu," Baumann answered.

"Very well, let's stick to our own business."

Krug pointed to the decrypt in Böhm's hand. "It states there," he said, "that one twenty-eight will meet us today at twenty-two thirty hours."

"Yes," Böhm said, "which is seven hours ahead of local war time, so it will still barely be daylight. We stay on German time, as you know. BdU established the rendezvous point, day, and time before our two departures. The only problem we have now is finding each other. DB 6848 is—" he pulled off the *Wegenkarte* to reveal beneath it *Karte* 47/3480, a large, detailed grid chart of the Florida peninsula and adjacent waters—"here," he said, pointing to a position about 120 nautical miles due east of Matanzas

Inlet. "We are now—here—in DB 6839, very close by, with plenty of time to reach the established position.

"The grid chart takes us down to a mesh six nautical miles on a side, and you would think that we could find each other fairly easily with that kind of definition, but that's not always the case."

Böhm went on to explain the difficulties that faced him and Heyse three hours hence. Although the clear skies in wake of the cold front had given the two boats good sun sights, and the broadcast station intersects provided additional reference, and the two boats could even take fixes on each other's transmissions, it was as much a matter of luck as it was of skill that the two boats would be able to see each other at or near the appointed hour. Some boats, only a few miles apart, had been known to spend a full day searching for each other. One problem was the U-boat's low nap-of-the-water silhouette. It was always hard to sight from the surface, particularly in a mist, because of the camouflage-haze gray paint scheme. That was why the rendezvous with 128 was set at the time it was, an hour and a half before sunset, with an extra seventy minutes of twilight. After dark it would be impossible to see her.

A daylight rendezvous would not be attempted at any position where the RAF flew, such as the Western Approaches or the Bay of Biscay on the eastern side of the Atlantic, since the Tommies were particularly adept at sighting U-boats from the air, but here, off the American coast, enemy aircraft apparently did not fly that often or else did not know a U-boat when they saw one, if Böhm could judge from the impunity with which the Ubootwaffe had operated for over a month now off New York Harbor, the Jersey shore, the Delaware and Virginia Capes, and, of course, Hatteras. Still, the lookouts would keep their eyes peeled. There were a lot of airfields nearby. You never knew.

With luck, he said, the fuel hose connection between the two boats could be made while it was still light or twilight. The hoses were heavy canvas over inner tubes of rubber. To prevent them from sinking below the surface the crews would tie life jackets at various points along their lengths. Maneuvering the nozzles across the water and preventing the hoses from getting frayed by scrapes along the decks required the highest levels of concentration and proficiency from the two crews. Bleichrodt and Kals in *109* and *130,* respectively, had carried off such a IXB-IXC fuel exchange seventeen days before in grid square CB to the north without any problems.

Heyse would probably want to connect in echelon rather than in tandem, since it was a small sea and winds were only two knots from the northwest. Once joined, the two boats would pray for darkness to come on rapidly since, in their yoked condition, unable to dive, refueling U-boats were extremely vulnerable to enemy attack. Like beasts in copulation, they made a fat, inviting target.

"We should start receiving transmissions from one twenty-eight any time now," Böhm concluded. "In the meantime, Krug, enjoy the last hours of your cruise. I don't suppose you have any complaints?" He smiled.

"Yes, I have two, Böhm. First, I don't like that bastard Franz. You have a real asshole for second-in-command."

Böhm was quick to answer. "An officer's value to a U-boat bears no relation to his likability. On a U-boat all that matters is that each man do his job. On the performance of each man depends the survival of all. Franz is a performer. Yes, he's remote. He packs a tight seabag. But so long as he does his job that's all that concerns me, and I'll say no more about it."

He looked hard at Krug. "No, I take that back. Since you brought up likes and dislikes, I may as well say you haven't exactly made yourself very likable either. Everyone here is professional navy. The crew see you as an alien—not because you are civilian, but because your words and actions on this voyage convey to them a certain nature and intent not in keeping with navy spirit and traditions.

"It's something about the chill in your eyes, the acid in

your voice, the unnecessary salute you give each morning to the Führer's photograph on the ladder well, your unwillingness to engage in casual conversation.

"The only time anyone's seen you smile during the whole voyage was when the radiotelephone receiver told us about the successful Channel dash.

"You're a dark mystery, Krug. The crew don't understand you and they don't like you. If knowing that will help you conduct your mission, then I'm glad I said it."

Krug looked steadily ahead, expressionless. "You have something against the Führer?"

Böhm raised his eyes to the overhead. "Oh, don't be a fool. The photo is standard issue. We take it for granted. We don't feel that we have to light candles before it every day. We don't need to prove our loyalty and we don't need a Party guidance officer in order to do our jobs. You said you had another complaint?"

"Yes," Krug said, "I wish the navy would hurry up and develop a U-boat that is really a U-boat, an *Unterseeboot* in the true sense of the term—a boat that always travels smoothly underwater, as this one does for the brief intervals when you make trim dives. In all my years as a bomber pilot I have never experienced such turbulence as you create by careening about on the surface over every damn storm-tossed wave you can find. I know these boats weren't made for my convenience, but, yes, that's a complaint, and I wish you'd pass it on."

"It's a pretty damn silly complaint," Böhm said. "This is your only means of getting to Florida, not to mention getting back, unless you would have preferred to take a blockade runner to Argentina and then swim across the Rio Grande. As a matter of fact, there are boats on the drawing board that will do just as you say, steam fast and smoothly underwater for an extended radius of action. Professor Hellmuth Walter has designed such a boat powered by a mix of diesel fuel and hydrogen peroxide."

In his irritation with Krug, Böhm could not suppress a smile. "Do you remember your Shakespeare? *Twelfth*

Night? The sea captain? 'Like Arion on the dolphin's back, I saw him hold acquaintance with the waves.'"

"I think I remember," said Krug.

"Well, I'm Arion on the U-boat's back and I'm acquainted with the waves. I have to be. It's the only way we can travel. I thought the chief engineer explained all that to you when you came aboard."

"Did you read Shakespeare in the original?" Krug asked.

"No, I don't know English, though I should. My languages were Latin and Greek."

"In university?"

"At Heidelberg, before entering the naval academy at Flensburg-Murwik."

"A lot of good Latin and Greek did you there."

"Well, remember what Seneca said: 'It is better to have useless knowledge than to know nothing.'"

He was interrupted by the radio operator.

"F.T. from U-*Heyse*, Herr Kaleu."

"Very well, Puster." Böhm read the message that had been decrypted on the Schlüssel M by the puster himself, after which he abruptly ducked through the forward bulkhead hatch to draft a reply:

> AUSGANG F.T. AN HEYSE.
> YOUR TRANSMISSION ACKNOWLEDGED. PLEASE SEND
> CONTINUOUS SIGNAL AT 2000 HOURS SO WE CAN TAKE
> BEARING. BÖHM.

CHAPTER 5

LEFT AGAIN TO HIS BOREDOM, Krug climbed onto the soiled and still-warm blue-and-white check gingham sheets of the bunk he shared with one of the officers, lay back, and let his mind roam where it willed.

Böhm was right. Krug had been told on the first day at sea, by the chief engineering officer, and his head had accepted the information, though his stomach had not, that the boat was going to run about 98 percent of the distance on the surface. U-boats spent most of their time on the surface, the engineer had explained, because there the twin MAN diesel engines gave them high speed, as much as 18 knots in this type boat, and extensive cruising range. Submerged, the boat could only do 7-plus knots on batteries, and even at a slow 4 knots, electric power would give out after fewer than 65 nautical miles.

So, Krug really did understand why U-*Böhm* operated more like a motor torpedo boat than a true submersible, why when she was "on the march," as now, she traversed oceans on the surface, and why she launched her torpedoes on the surface—but at night when her low-riding hull and tower were hard for a target ship or a warship escort to detect. He had been unreasonable in his complaint to Böhm. But what the hell, he was just worn down by the hard seas. He was venting his aggravation. Didn't he have a right?

Two or three times a week, to Krug's unutterable relief, the boat had dived so that the control room could check the trim. Those blissful intervals, which persuaded Krug how great it would be to stand on level, steady ground again, enabled the engineering officer and his trim team to balance the boat and ensure that if it had to dive in an emergency, such as to avoid enemy aircraft or warships, it could do so safely without either broaching the surface or plunging out of control. Krug had watched the control room crew acquiring that balance underwater by pumping kilograms of sea water fore or aft into trim tanks in the bow and stern. It was an art, like walking while carrying an ice tray full of water. And Krug had admired the achievement.

Böhm was right about another thing. Krug had exhibited too much of his brittle military-political side and not enough of the persona he had adopted for his mission. He should have used these weeks for practicing a smile, for projecting a certain warmth and friendliness, however feigned, for perfecting his conversational skills, and for establishing the look and eye of an artist, for those were the attributes he would have to display after landing.

A man could be hard in the conduct of his military and political responsibilities, yet soft in matters of art and the heart. On his other side, Krug persuaded himself, was the draftsman and painter of nature, the man of gentle habits, refined manners, and cultural high taste. That side of him he had kept hidden behind the sterner exterior that statecraft and war required. Now the artist in him could serve the State for a special while, and the representational painter that he once had been years ago, in Chicago, before the family moved back to Hannover, before the Party caught his fancy, and then the gliders, and then the Heinkels and Dorniers—that artist would emerge again.

Watercolorist was to be his cover. He had proved to Abwehr and SD officials that, like riding a bicycle, using a color wheel was a skill one never forgot. His demonstration paintings had not been substantially less creditable than what he used to turn out, exhibit, and, in a few cases, sell in Chicago. In fact, though his freehand was a little shaky and his brush technique required work, his sense and use of color had matured. He looked forward to transferring the landscapes of Florida onto cold-pressed 140-pound paper.

Reinhard Tristan Eugen Heydrich, in fact, having seen the sample watercolors, had encouraged him to take up the brush again regularly and to make pictorial art his leisure avocation during wartime.

"An eye like yours should not be wasted," Heydrich had said to him during dinner that night at Betazeile 17, Admiral Canaris's home in a garden suburb near the Grosser Wannsee in southwest Berlin. "Just as," he had added, "I try not to waste my ear."

The SS Obergruppenführer's meaning became clear when, following coffee, he opened a violin case on Canaris's piano bench and, after tuning its strings and allowing for the noise made by the other dinner guests turning their chairs on the oak floor to subside, he performed a Beethoven *Spring Sonata* of manifest virtuosity and surpassing beauty.

Krug found himself rendered breathless at the sight of this tall, big-hipped, hawk-nosed, blond, blue-eyed god of a man in field-gray SS service uniform tunic and breeches with black boots and brown shirt—fencer, fighter pilot, chief of the SD, the Gestapo, the Security Police, and Deputy Reich Protector in Bohemia and Moravia, who was also capable of tender grace and delicate emotion! Heydrich was the ideal mix, Krug exulted, of brutality and sentimentality—the perfect Nordic type, Siegfried incarnate—the model National Socialist. God, he would love to be such a man!

Krug watched the flowing bow arm and the exquisite fingerwork. He took pleasure in the lyric tone quality and the crisp staccato. The sound that filled the room aroused in him a strong, contemplative delight. When Heydrich finished and lowered his bow, it took all of Krug's reserve and discipline to prevent his applauding louder than the other guests.

Frau Canaris then produced a viola and the duo, Reinhard and Erika, played a moving Mozart *Concertante* with wonderful legato and deep mellow tone. It was obvious that they had performed together before.

When, finally, the mini-concert was over, and the guests snaked their chairs around to their proper places for more coffee or schnapps, Heydrich stowed his violin and came around to where Krug sat.

"Now we must talk, you and I," he said, and walked briskly toward an adjoining salon where he picked up a thin leather briefcase and quickly checked its contents. Krug followed *con brio*. When he stood alone before Heydrich, he said, sincerely, "Excellency, I enjoyed your performance."

Heydrich dismissed the compliment with the wave of a hand. "Thank you. And, as I said, I liked your watercolors. Actually, Erika and I have played together for some time. The admiral there"—he nodded toward the small, stooped figure of civilian-dressed Canaris, whose fingers drummed nervously on the dining room table and whose face, canted below snow-white hair, bore a weary, melancholic expression—"was first officer of the training cruiser *Berlin* when I first met him. In fact I served under him."

"You were in the navy, Excellency?" Krug asked, surprised.

"For a short time—nineteen twenty-two, twenty-three. The navy and I had a falling out. Anyway, we renewed our acquaintanceship, Canaris and I, here in Berlin in the early thirties. We had homes near each other in Döllestrasse in Berlin-Südende, then later, about thirty-seven, our two families moved here to Schlachtensee. My house is just around the corner."

"But you live in Prague now, do you not?" Krug asked.

"Oh yes, but I still keep the house here. And I use it when I come to Berlin on business, as today."

"Important business, I am sure." Krug checked himself. "I shouldn't have said that."

"That's all right. My office has a villa overlooking the Wannsee, which is nearby, and we have a conference there in a few days. I'll fly back to Prague tonight and then return for the conference."

Krug was relieved when Heydrich turned the conversation back to Canaris.

"He and his wife and I and mine used to play croquet

on Sunday afternoons in my garden. Of course, croquet is only a diversion. Fencing is really my sport. I practice an hour every morning before work. Then, on Sunday evenings, Canaris would cook dinner, like the saddle of boar he did for us this evening, and afterwards Erika and I would play together or invite other artists in for chamber music."

Heydrich took Krug by the arm and walked him toward a far corner of the salon. "In the war of fourteen-eighteen Canaris was a military and intelligence dynamo. He served on the cruiser *Dresden* in a number of notable battles, made a couple of overland escapes, crossed several borders dressed as a monk, and in the last years sank ships as a U-boat commander. Did you know he once shot and killed a priest?"

"A priest?"

"Yes. On one of his adventures he was arrested by the Italians at Domodossla, near the Swiss border. He escaped by coaxing the prison chaplain into his cell, killing him, and walking out of the prison in the priest's cassock.

"The story has always amused me, since, like Reichsführer Himmler, I was raised a Catholic."

"I, too," said Krug.

"And that's the kind of thing you have to do in this business. We need active, aggressive men. We need totally ruthless men. That's why I insisted on our SD people having a major role in your training.

"Canaris and I have an agreement we call the 'Ten Commandments' that gave my SD people the right to be involved. As a bomber pilot you've killed indiscriminately. Now you know from us how to kill selectively."

Heydrich reached for a folder in his briefcase and opened it up. "Let's see: Peter Krug, born in Hannover, twenty-three April nineteen oh nine—son of Walter Krug and Barbara Dohler, pure Aryan bloodline, baptized Catholic, taken by family to Chicago in America at nine years of age, attended Lake View High School, took painting courses at the Art Institute, exhibited watercolors at

Thurber Galleries, returned with parents to Hannover in twenty-nine, attended university at Freiburg in Breisgau, joined the Party in nineteen thirty-three—what was it exactly that led you to join the Party, Krug?"

"It was the Führer primarily, Excellency. He expressed all my hatred for the Jews."

"You, an American school graduate, what would you have known about the Jews?"

"Like my parents, I remained a German citizen, Excellency. And in Chicago my father had many disagreeable experiences with the Jews, both German and Russian. He owned a dry goods store in the Lawndale district and the Jews came in from Maxwell Street on the Near South Side and drove him out of business by undercutting his prices and selling on Sundays. The same thing happened to other Aryan German store-owners in other neighborhoods. I learned early on to be an anti-Semite, and when my father decided to return to Germany to live again in a pure Aryan environment, I was glad to go with him. My father helped to enforce the Führer's boycott of Jewish businesses in Hannover in nineteen thirty-three, and I joined the Party in the same year."

"Very well," Heydrich acknowledged, and returned to his brief. "You entered the glider program on the Borkenberge, received a commission in the Luftwaffe six August nineteen thirty-five, served as military aide to Foreign Minister von Ribbentrop—God, what a fraud he is—in thirty-eight and again in forty, flying bomber missions in-between, in Poland and France.

"In fact, what brought you to my attention, Krug," he continued, looking up, "was the pinch you made in the naval attaché's office at the American Embassy in nineteen forty. Did you act on your own or at Ribbentrop's instance?"

"On my own, Excellency," Krug said. "I was not a trained agent. I did it as a lark. A deputy minister asked me to accompany him to a formal function at the embassy. Ribbentrop didn't go since the American ambassador had been called home as a protest over something or other. During the reception I noticed that the Marine guards were dipping into the whiskey back of the kitchen, and I went up the stairs unnoticed.

"I tried the handles on several doors. The naval attaché's door was unlocked. I saw a sealed file cabinet, which I couldn't get into, but the desk drawers were open, and in the right top drawer I found a photostat that I folded and placed in my jacket pocket."

From his briefcase Heydrich held out a photostat for Krug to see.

"This one," he said. "It was a bold damn thing to do."

Krug took it from Heydrich's hand and read it. Yes, this was the document. He had not seen it since he handed it over to Ribbentrop:

```
              Navy Department
   Office of the Chief of Naval Operations
                Washington
                                    22 May 1940

   SECRET
   FROM:     The Director, War Plans Division
   TO:       The Chief of Naval Operations
   SUBJECT:  Disposition of the U.S. Fleet in
             the event of the surrender of the
             British Fleet to Germany
```

1. In the event of the surrender of the British Fleet to Germany, it is believed that at least one year would expire before the Germans could operate the vessels of the British <u>as a fleet</u>. Individual surface vessels and submarines might be ready to operate in a period of a few months but their operations would be restricted to commerce destruction or raids.

2. In the event of these circumstances, the disposition of the U.S. Fleet is recommended as follows:

(a) A force of 1 division of battleships, 1 division of heavy cruisers, 1 aircraft carrier, and 3 squadrons of new destroyers, be maintained in the Pacific to guard the line of communication from the United States to Hawaii.

(b) Base the remaining strength of the U.S. Fleet in the Atlantic, with a strategical concentration in the Caribbean area, employing the Canal Zone and Guantanamo as bases, with a carrier group, consisting of a carrier and a division of heavy cruisers, based on Narragansett Bay.

R. S. Crenshaw

"Too bad we couldn't have used that knowledge," Heydrich said, sotto voce, as though taking responsibility for the Messerschmitts.

"Yes, too bad," agreed Krug, with equal chagrin, taking responsibility for the bombers.

"Göring is to blame for what happened over England, Krug. We had the RAF on the run so long as we were attacking their airfields. But then the fat man switched us to the cities.

"We could have had England! And her fleet! Stupid! And now he's going to lose some more air battles for us by refusing to acknowledge the quality and production figures of American four-engined bombers. We're going to be seeing a blizzard of those planes later this year."

"B-seventeens and B-twenty-fours," agreed Krug.

"Göring has been telling the Luftwaffe that the Americans are good at making fast cars, razor blades, and refrigerators, but that they don't know a damn thing about making war planes. And he ridicules the American aircraft production figures as mere bluff."

"The new B-seventeen E may be a better bomber than anything in our own inventory, including the four-engine Heinkel HE-one seventy-seven, which is still in the testing stage," Krug said. "The early model of the B-seventeen that the RAF used briefly did not perform well, I think in part because the British didn't know how to use it. Also, it may not yet have been a combat-ready offensive machine."

"That's what you have to do, Krug, find out the performance characteristics of the American bombers, how the Americans intend to use them, what their weak spots are, and so forth. And you're going to establish your *schwerpunkt* in Florida?"

"Yes, Excellency. The bases there are full of bombers, I'm told. Fighters, too."

"Have you been there before?"

"Once, with my parents. It's a beautiful place, much of it still wilderness when I saw it."

"How's your English? Is it accent-free American English?"

"Better than that, Excellency. It's Chicago English."

"And that means?"

"When commercial network radio began in the States sometime in the late twenties or early thirties, the Chicago, or Midwest, voice became the standard for announcers. Americans associate big-time radio with the Midwest pronunciation. Like what the Southern English and the BBC call the 'received pronunciation' in that country.

"The larger radio stations in the South, where people speak with a pronounced drawl, all have Midwest announcing staffs. The Southern people can't stand to hear their own accent on the air. So what I mean,

Excellency, is that I have a very acceptable pronunciation that would give me entree anywhere in America."

"Good. Now listen. A few things I want you to bear in mind. First, you must be absolutely cold-blooded. In total war there are no noncombatants. Where you can be soft, be soft, but where you must be hard, be hard as a diamond.

"Second, never leave a trail. Be a bloodhound yourself, but never leave a trail.

"Third, always be alert to data you're not expecting. Abwehr's mistake has been to send agents on narrow searches. I say you never know what you might stumble onto, such as your 'Thunderbolt' document that Kettner told me about, such as your naval attaché's document.

"Finally, be alert to anything that might help the Japanese. Remember we're in this thing together now, for better or for worse, and I'm not confident which it's going to be. One thing, though: our Asiatic friends can keep a lot of Americans occupied in the Pacific and off our backs here. Anything you find that can help them, by all means bring that home, too.

"And, in that connection, when you *do* return, Krug, see *me* first before you see Canaris. . . ."

Krug was jarred out of the sleep into which he had drifted by the puster's hand against his shoulder.

"U-one twenty-eight is in sight, Herr Krug," the puster said. "The Old Man says you can go topside to watch the refueling."

"I thought no one but lookouts were allowed on the bridge," Krug said, acidly.

The puster laughed. "It doesn't make any difference now. We have so many men up there for refueling we'd never be able to get them all back in the can in order to make an alarm dive, if we had to. And when one twenty-eight gets its penis into us, forget it!"

"Thanks, Puster." Krug grabbed for his jacket and mounted the control-room ladder. Climbing through the tower hatch onto the narrow steel bridge above, he took a position alongside Böhm, who, like the rest of the bridge detail, was wearing double-breasted, gray-green leather coat and pants. God, the air smelled good!

He let his eyes follow the Old Man's binoculars to port across the late afternoon sea. There! It *was* a U-boat. He could see it with his bare eyes—gray against a lapis lazuli sea—headed almost directly toward them, hull down, its conning tower leaning left and right with the waves. It was a startling sight, and yet reassuring after these many weeks of having seen nothing else of human manufacture, much less other human beings, and fellow nationals, at that, whom he expected to come into view momentarily.

He looked at his watch. The rendezvous was running a little later than planned.

"How do you know that's Heyse and not Poske—or an American submarine?" Krug asked Böhm.

"We exchanged blinker signals," Böhm answered, not lifting his pupils from his Carl Zeiss 7 x 50 glasses.

To either side of Böhm, and aft, four lookouts surveyed the surrounding sea and sky, sweeping the sectors assigned to them with 7 x 50s held tightly against their sockets, searching for dots and anomalies that might mean danger to their boat and to themselves.

Meanwhile, on the casing abaft, a ten-man deck force snaked a fuel hose out of its container and secured the nozzle at one end into the starboard fuel bunker. Krug watched their movements.

Böhm let his Zeiss barrels fall slack against his chest. "Heyse will supply a hose for the port bunker," he explained. "The new fuel will displace saltwater on which the oil sits as it's expended."

Now U-*128* was pulling close and turning to face the northwest, in echelon with Böhm.

Krug could see Heyse's deck force similarly engaged in laying out a hose and tying life jackets at various points along its length. Heyse's crew also had a rubber dinghy on the fore casing, which several men were inflating with compressed air from a line that ran out of the tower.

When *128* was close aboard and the two boats lay to, bouncing from trough to wave at steerageway, three to four knots on electric motors, Böhm used a megaphone to call across to Heyse: "Heil one twenty-eight! Congratulations on your ships! We're ready to suck!"

"Thank you!" Heyse shouted back. "It's nice to have company! Welcome to Florida! If you're ready I'll send the dinghy with our line and bring back yours!"

"Agreed!" Böhm yelled.

While the two deck forces proceeded to their urgent and delicate business, passing lines, pumping oil, guarding against chafing of the hoses, Krug had leisure to lean against the periscope housing and take in the sunset. A vivid and perfectly formed tangerine sun hung just above the horizon. Suffusing the atmosphere around it was a glow that Krug could not decide was peach or rose. Looking up, he saw the color change in luminous grada- tions to cerulean blue, broken on top by dark blue-gray formations of altostratus. It was a mackerel sky.

Ordinarily, following Homer Winslow's technique, Krug painted wet-on-dry in order to obtain crisp forms and sharp edges. But this marine scene would tempt him, if he had brushes and pigments in hand, to try wet-on-wet, laying down a wash of various hues that soaked into each other for a misty, soft impression. Upon that liquid tone he would tip in a sun of yellow and red-orange, and then streak the sky above it with a subtle mix of cobalt violet and ochre.

He was turning his attention to the pan colors that best responded to the sea below, when from the starboard quarter he heard the dread scream—

ALARMMM!

FLUGBOOT!

At once Böhm turned to see the lookout's hand chop- ping excitedly five points starboard off the stern. He raised his glasses and confirmed the sighting—"Bearing right at us, about a hundred meters off the deck!"—then took his megaphone to warn Heyse—*"Heyse! Flying boat!"*—chopping like the lookout in the plane's direction.

Diving was out of the question. And the connecting hoses meant that the boats could not even maneuver. There was only one defense: "Gun crew to anti-aircraft!" Böhm shouted. Directly behind the bridge was a semicircular flak platform with three sweeping rails called the *Wintergarten*. On it stood twin 2-centimeter C/30 antiaircraft machine guns. These the AA crew hurriedly manned, two men feeding ammo belts from their watertight container, another two cocking and clearing the barrels.

"Fire on my command!" Böhm ordered, taking precedence over his Number Two, Baumann, who ordinarily would command guns. "Lookouts maintain observation of all quadrants!"

With the fear that filled men who knew that death approached them in a form from which there was likely no escape—Böhm remembered his Shakespeare: "And more inexorable far/Than empty tigers or the roaring sea"—the bridge details and the deck forces on both boats braced to await the inevitable bombs.

Krug turned to Böhm: "If you lend me your glasses, I should be able to tell you something about that aircraft." Böhm nodded and removed the strap from around his neck. Krug swung the 7 x 50s around toward the aircraft, focusing with his fingers for a sharp image.

"It's a Consolidated, Böhm," he said. "Two engines. It's a PBY-five Catalina. American Navy Patrol Bomber flying boat. The type that located and tracked the *Bismarck*. Carries four depth bombs on exterior racks attached on either side to hard points on the wings. . . ."

Krug paused, lowered the glasses, squinted, raised the lenses to his eyes again, focused for maximum acuity, and gave the glasses back to Böhm with one of his rare smiles.

"I don't know what lucky star you were born under, Böhm," he said, "but that plane's got no bombs."

"No bombs?"

"The racks are empty, and there's no interior bomb

bay. The most he can do is spray your crew with machine gun fire. But you can give back as good as you get."

"What's he got?" Böhm asked.

"A flexible gun in the bow turret, I'm guessing thirty caliber, and a couple of fifty calibers in waist blisters, maybe another gun below or behind. The point is, he's slow, a big target, more vulnerable to small gun fire than you are. I think the combined anti-aircraft of both boats can easily fight it out with him."

"Good!" Böhm raised his megaphone to port, "*Heyse! Enemy Bee has no bombs! Repeat no bombs! Guns only!*"

The Old Man looked around to make sure his three other lookouts were sweeping the horizon for possible other aircraft, then returned his attention to the "Bee." It was slow, like the British Sunderlands that the U-boats called "Tired Bees." And its wingspan was enormous. The damn thing was still coming straight on—and dropping altitude.

With his megaphone again he yelled fore and aft: "Deck force take cover forward of the tower!" Then he pushed past Krug and a lookout to direct the guns.

"Look alive now," he encouraged the crew. "Target is descending to about thirty meters. Aft gun neutralize the bow turret gun. Forward go for the wing tanks"—he turned to shout—"Krug, where are the wing tanks?"

"Probably close aboard the fuselage!" Krug did not know exactly, but he thought it a good guess. He watched, fascinated, as the PBY swooped down on them like a giant condor.

"Close to the fuselage," Böhm directed. "Here he comes—steady—take your aim—he's *in range*—*commence firing!*"

The guns shook angrily, *Dacca-dacca-dacca-dacca. . . .*

CHAPTER 6

PATROL PLANE COMMANDER Lieutenant j.g. Beauregard Burke pushed the carbon mike close to his lips and called for a new heading from the second pilot, who was taking his turn at the navigator's table below and aft in the PBY Catalina designated 2-P-10 out of NAS Jax.

"Navigator—course home!"

Burke's much-abused ears barely heard the navigator's reply over the thunderous din of two 14-cylinder, 1200 horsepower Pratt & Whitney R-1830-82 engines above his head.

"Two-nine-zero, Bo."

"Two-nine-zero," he acknowledged, as he reached for the throttle quadrant overhead and fine-tuned the power to 2,000 rpm, 30 inches manifold pressure. To First Pilot Ensign Raymond A. Hope, seated at the yoked controls on his right, who was scanning the ocean ahead with Bausch & Lomb 7 x 50s, Burke gave the first good news Hope or any of the six other men on board had heard after ten straight hours of flying: "We're headin' for the barn, old son."

Burke disconnected the auto pilot, then muscled in the ailerons and rudder.

After what seemed like five full seconds the inertia-devoted flying-boat responded. A slow turn to 290 completed, and the high, long, flexing wing level again, Burke handed over the controls to his PP1P.

"You have it," he said to Hope, jiggling the control wheel.

"I have it, Bo," Hope acknowledged, setting his binoculars on the cowl of the instrument panel, and jiggling back.

Burke eased his stiff frame out of the left seat.

"I've overdosed on this noise and vibration, Ray. Going

to hit Boys Town and then stretch out a few minutes. Crank two-nine-zero into the autopilot and maintain altitude. Call me when you see the river."

"Aye, aye, Bo."

Burke removed his headset and ducked aft through the watertight bulkhead into the anodized yellow-green interior of the hull, passing through the navigator's and radioman's compartment, then the bunk compartment and the waist gunner's compartment, and, finally, entered the tunnel, where he lowered his pants, edged his bare bottom onto the cold head, and deposited the remains of his breakfast and lunch into a wax paper poopie bag.

That accomplished, he returned forward and selected the lower port bunk, where he flopped down heavily. Even though the engine noise was less intrusive here, the so-called living quarters were hardly a home away from home. Occasionally, an off-duty crewman, lying flat in one of the four canvas bunks, got airsick from the turbulence, since the aircraft flew most of the time at 1500 feet or lower, particularly when there was a weather front, such as the one the aircraft penetrated two days before. As a result, the compartment had a certain lived-in aroma. Burke thought that the color of the zinc chromate paint contributed to the nauseating environment.

Just as there was no engine noise buffer in the airframe, so, too, there was no weather insulation—and no heating system. In the still chilly wake of the front, Burke, like the other officers, wore his NAS-issue winter flight gear. The white hats, or ratings, wore their dungarees, foul-weather jackets, and watchcaps.

Burke zipped open his jacket and withdrew a letter from his shirt's left front pocket. The blue stationery was frayed along the fold lines from many openings, readings, and refoldings. Despite the pain it inflicted, he read the letter again:

Dear Bo,
    You know that I'm a pretty direct person, so let me

say right away that, as fond of you as I am, I've decided that the best thing, certainly for you, is to break off our relationship.

You have been the kindest, warmest, most considerate man a woman could desire. It has been an honor to be courted by a man like you. We had such good times together, at Surfside and the Officers' Club.

But, Bo, I am just not in a position to tie myself down right now—the way so many girls and women have done in this city, committing themselves to soldiers or sailors, whom they rarely see, and may never see again. And they spend their days and evenings sitting around, unable to "go out" with anyone else, which means being totally immobilized—maybe for years.

Fortunately, I'm not the sort to need a man's company to go where I want to go and to do what I want to do. Still, engagement, which is what I think you were getting around to suggesting—am I presumptuous?—would tie me down psychologically at just this moment in my life when I'm thinking of breaking new ground.

I'd like to go into military aviation myself and ferry airplanes. After the war, I'd like to go off somewhere for a graduate degree in aeronautical engineering. There are lots of things I would like to do, and the kind of commitment that engagement and marriage represent, while they are something that I do want at some later point in my life, would frustrate me at just this time when I feel very different yearnings and ambitions.

In other words, why should we tie ourselves down with promises that we know I can't keep?

It hurts you to read these words, of course, but I feel that you will understand. There will be many more people in your life. Who can resist your blue eyes, your dark brown hair—I never saw you without a crew cut, more's the pity—your sun-bronzed handsome face, your strong build? Your Louisiana accent? Who will not admire your fine mind and wit? You have so much going for you, Bo!

I know that you will have a wonderful life. Thanks with all my heart for being a short part of mine.

And most important—be careful! Protect yourself. Don't let any Germans or Japanese hurt you. Keep your wings level and maintain airspeed!

All the best,
Belle

Bo felt all alone. He missed his family in Plaquemines Parish. He missed his dog. He missed his former football teammates at LSU. He missed his fellow aviation cadets at Cuddihy Field, and doing barrel rolls and Immelmanns in N2Ss, and eating steaks as long as his forearm at the Driscoll in Corpus. He missed what he could have been, but was denied the chance to be, a fighter jock on a carrier. Most of the guys who filled out Navy Preference Sheets at Cuddihy opted for the safer craft—land-based bombers or cruiser-based float planes or PBY and PBM P-boats. He was in the minority who wanted the dangerous birds. So what did the perverse godddam Navy do? Sent 70 percent of his class to carriers, 15 percent, including himself, to P-boats, 8 percent to land-based bombers, and four guys to floats.

Bo daydreamed a lot about what could have been. He saw himself strapping on a F4F Wildcat, thundering off a CV deck in the Pacific, and drawing beads on various Mitsubishis, Nakajimas, and Aichis. But when his mind reawakened, as it did now, he was just a Catalina truck driver, and the biggest thrill allowed him in *this* craft was a 30-degree bank.

God, he felt down. And Belle's letter was the knife-twister.

He remembered his first sight of her, at the tiny municipal airport north of St. Augustine: a tall slim figure in leather jacket and jodhpurs, long blonde hair going on brown, a wet puckish mouth, rose cheeks that looked like port and starboard insignias. And what a vocabulary! She actually said what she thought. She was challenging—and irresistible.

He had always liked high-spirited girls back in Louisiana. And he had lucked into the prototype here in Florida. She even flew and loved to talk airplanes. The only problem was, she preferred talking airplanes to kissing. He could tell over the last few weeks, though he denied it at the time, that she was pulling back rather than drawing closer.

His misery was mercifully relieved by the first radioman who leaned low to report in a flat but respectful voice: "Lieutenant, a ciphered CW from base. Marked priority, five Ps."

Burke looked up at the ARM2c. "Okay, Sparks. Decrypt it. And please don't tell me it says the galley at base has run out of hot food."

"Aye, aye, sir."

"And make a note for me to write up a yellow sheet on our broken hotplate."

"Aye, aye, sir."

Burke refolded Belle's letter, stood up to stretch, then worked his long legs through the hatch forward into the radio-nav compartment. He stood patiently behind Sparks's aluminum swivel chair that faced the communications equipment on the starboard hull waiting for the decrypt. Finally, the radioman swung around and handed Burke the readable message:

PPPPP X 2P10 X COMINT RDF NET REPORTS U/B
APPROX POSITION 29N 79W X INVESTIGATE AND
REPORT X VP2JAX/23242/1705

Burke turned around and lay the message before Second Pilot Ensign Samuel O. Singer at the nav table.

"How does this position square with our new course, Sam?" he asked.

It took Singer only a moment to check the coordinates. "With just degrees, no minutes, shown, that's a pretty big area, Bo. But, to answer your question, our course home is taking us right through what you've got there."

"Thanks," Burke acknowledged, and sprang for the pilot's compartment. In the port seat, he donned the headset across his overseas cap and took the controls from Hope: "I have it, Ray. Message received that a U-boat transmitted from somewhere ahead or around us. Let's sweep the glasses."

With the 7 x 50s Burke and Hope surveyed the ocean port, ahead and starboard. The calm water was deep gray, except for the long, narrow hemorrhage of orangish-red color that poured from the dying sun; visibility unlimited, the horizon knife-sharp.

"Bo!" Hope pointed. "Two objects three points off the port bow!"

Burke focused his lenses. "Two? Oh yeah, I have 'em. Must be shrimpers. About eight miles off."

P-10 flew on at 110 knots indicated, making fewer than two nautical miles every 60 seconds. Burke had been so sure that what he saw were fishing vessels—the report was that one U-boat stood somewhere near this position—he was reluctant to admit to himself the contrary evidence that gradually took shape within his glasses.

"Jesus, Ray, if those are shrimpers, they're the first two I've seen with conning towers!"

"I know, Bo. I was about to say, look at how long they are. And they're pretty far out to be shrimpers. Those are subs! Maybe they're ours. How can we tell?"

"Only way is to dive on them," Burke said. "Tell tower to set mixture at auto rich. Give me forty-three inches and twenty-four hundred. Going off autopilot. I'll trim."

"You say dive on them, Bo, what will that do?"

"Well, if they're ours, they'll wave, and if they're not, they'll shoot."

"Wonderful," Hope said. He looked over at Burke anxiously. "It's just that I was thinking, Bo. We have no depth bombs, no guns, no ammo boxes."

"Tell me about it," Burke said. "The rest of the world has gone to war, but we're still training. Get used to it, Ray. The Florida coast navy is going to train until we get it right. The Krauts may sink five hundred ships right under our noses in the meantime, maybe win the whole friggin' war, but we're not going to make a move until we're parade-ground perfect."

"Those subs are coming up fast, Bo. I don't see any flags or markings."

As P-10 on glide attack mode descended to 100 feet at 140 knots indicated, keeping the two submarines slightly to port ahead, Burke used the mike and interphone to alert the rest of the crew: "Pilot to crew, we're descending on two suspected Kraut subs. Hope they're ours instead. If they're not, prepare to receive ack-ack. So battle stations, everybody. Fasten your belts and guard your balls. Navigator, record exact coordinates, then break out your camera."

Now the two submarines were in full eyeball view, sufficiently detailed in line and contrast for Ray to see easily, as though it was happening in a silent film, puffs of light gray smoke lift from the towers of both boats and curl gently toward their sterns.

"They're *shooting* at us!" he exclaimed.

Burke looked up to the port wing just in time to see it perforated from the main spar diagonally across to the fabric-covered trailing edge and aileron, where tattered shreds of Grade A cotton and cellulose nitrate dope hung, flapping in the wind.

"Shit!" he said to himself.

"Turn away!" Ray yelled.

"Hell, no!" Burke answered. "Give him our whole broad underside? I'm going to bank against him—show him as little as possible."

As he stood on the rudder hard-a-port, Burke heard the metallic crack of rounds entering the fuselage. He hoped that none of his crew was in their paths. Damn this lumbering, slow bitch of a wagon! Fly! Fly! Fly! Move it! Christ!

During the bank, as Burke's port window passed directly across the U-boats below, his retinas received images at machine-gun speed, of which later he would remember two in particular: black hoses, two in number, connecting the boats, and, on each conning tower bridge, a man—an officer?—wearing a white cover.

When P-10 was past the guns and out of their effective range, Burke went to the mike again: "Crew muster! Normal sequence!"

He carefully checked off the replies: "Hope, starboard pilot, unhurt, okay; Singer, nav, okay; Bernard, plane captain, okay; Pratt, first radio, okay; McClusky, second radio, okay; Martin, first mech, okay; Simmons, tunnel, okay."

Thank God, no injuries.

"Bernard! Damage report on wings and engines! Martin on hull!"

The plane captain, as the flight engineer was called, who operated the engines and other systems from the tower, a windowed compartment in the cabane strut that connected the hull to the wings and engines above, counted thirty-plus holes in the two wings, none in the engine nacelles. The port aileron was shredded but still serviceable. Below, the first mech reported eighteen perforations of the hull, no damage to cables, lines, or communications gear.

The navigator handed up a slip of paper with the chart coordinates.

"Sparks," Burke called on the RL-24-A interphone, "send the following message to VP-2 Jax: 'Sighted and engaged two U/Bs at position twenty-nine point four two North, seventy-nine point forty-one West. Apparently exchanging fuel. Aircraft took incoming AA. Minor damage. No—repeat—no personnel casualties. Recommend dispatch warships and armed—repeat—armed aircraft to position.' Sign it P-ten and send."

Hope looked over and asked, through his mike, "What do you think they'll do back at Jax, Bo?"

"They'll do nothing," Burke said. "Absolutely nothing. There're no warships around that I know about, except the little seventy-five foot Yippies at Mayport—if you can call them warships. And our squadron has no depth bombs. They won't give us any. Hell, we're not scheduled to be operational until one April. I wouldn't be surprised if the war ended and we still had no bombs. NAS Jax will sit on its hands as many months as it can."

All the while Burke was jawing at the navy, Hope noticed that he had increased power to 2400, 42 MP, staying below 2450, where vibration began in the Hamilton-Standard propellers, and was making a slow turning climb back across the U-boats' position.

"You going back, Bo?"

"Yeah, but high enough to be out of their range."

"In your message you said we *engaged* the U-boats."

"That's because I'm about to do exactly that, Ray. Somebody in this friggin' navy has got to go to war."

"With what?" Hope asked.

"I'm going to hit the enemy with everything we've got," Burke said. He pressed the mike to his lips. "Pilot to Simmons. You still in the tunnel?"

"Aye, aye, sir."

"I want you to count the filled poopie bags in the head and report back."

After a moment, Simmons responded, "There's two in there, Lieutenant."

"All right, now I want you to open the tunnel hatch. On my order I want you to drop the poopie bags at two second intervals. Just count one-two between them. You got that?"

"I think so, sir."

Hope knew Burke well enough from ten weeks of joint training to know that he was not quite mad in one sense, but was plenty goddam mad in another. He decided to say nothing—especially since he had the wit to realize that in later years he could brag on being an eyewitness to one of the great moments in military history.

When Burke had established what he thought was the optimum point of obliquity above the target, he slowed to near-stalling speed and gave the order.

"Pilot to Simmons. Standby to drop—*now!*"

Seconds later, Simmons reported: "Tunnel to pilot— bags away!"

"Very well, secure the hatch," Burke said quietly.

It was the last word spoken in the pilots' compartment for the next five minutes while Burke resumed normal navigation and cruise numbers. Then he nudged Hope's left arm and said over the interphone, "Better go aft, Ray, and check on morale."

"Aye, aye, Bo."

Hope returned ten minutes later to report. "Everybody's okay, most of them in good humor except for Singer and McClusky, who are both shaking uncontrollably with chills."

"The danger they went through got to them after the event," Burke said. "Someone just tried to kill them. I wish I had some bourbon to give out. I could use some myself."

"I wrapped 'em in blankets and put 'em in bunks and told 'em to stay there until we're on final."

"Good idea. I'll send 'em over to sick bay when we get down."

Fifty minutes later, Burke raised NAS tower on 8210 kilocycles, in the clear: "NAS JAX tower, P-ten, east southeast of you, crossing coast below Ponte Vedra, inbound landing, seadrome."

The acknowledgment crackled in the earphones: "NAS tower, P-ten, wind three-three-zero at two, straight-in approach approved, report five miles south of buoys."

"Roger."

The air station was situated eleven miles southwest of downtown Jacksonville on a point of land that jutted out into a particularly wide expanse of the St. John's River, sheltered water that was now enveloped in darkness. The landing path would have been swept by an inshore patrol boat to make sure there were no floating obstructions. Five miles out, Burke sighted the twin lines of lighted buoys that marked the landing path.

"NAS Jax, P-ten, five miles."

"P-ten, cleared to land."

Burke began letting down at 75 knots, 200 feet per minute, careful to watch instruments since there was no visual horizon. The propeller governor was set at low pitch, the mixture control at auto rich, and the cowl flaps at open. Not forgetting Singer and McClusky, he ordered them helped to their seats and strapped in. In sequence, he eased back on the throttle to bleed off airspeed, signaled the plane captain to lower the retractable wing tip floats, and trimmed for a touchdown halfway down the lights so as to minimize taxiing distance to the ramp. Soon, the two lines of lights began to level off and rush by them as the long flexing wing responded to the cushioning of ground effect off the black water, slowing the rate of descent without any further change in throttle setting. Burke pulled back slightly on the yoke. The V-shaped bottom of the aluminum hull touched home, tick—tick—*tishhh.* . . .

As the aircraft slowed and settled in, Burke adjusted throttle and prop settings and ordered out sea anchors—cone-shaped canvas bags streamed aft in the water from the waist gun blisters to slow taxiing speed and improve maneuverability.

"Sea anchors over and holding," first mech Martin confirmed.

Closer to the ramp than he thought he would be, Burke blipped the ignition switches to slow the engines below idle speed. Then he approached the anchored buoy 100 feet from the ramp and maneuvered so that a crewman on the bow could hook the buoy line and lay the loop end over the bow stanchion. When that was done, Bo looked up to see an unusual number of lights and a considerable crowd at the top of ramp three.

"Looks like we've attracted quite an audience, Ray," he said to Hope. "Everyone wants to see what a shot-up Cat looks like."

With the buoy hooked, he idled the engines at 800 rpm and signalled the plane captain to secure engines. With the engines shut down, he pulled the master switches to off and sat back to fill in log numbers, while a beaching crew in rubber waders up to their armpits floated out beaching gear, which they attached to the forward sides of the hull and to the tail. When that was done, the same crew hooked a heavy towline to the tail tow fitting. With the buoy line lifted off the bow stanchion, a ramp tractor at the other end of the towline swung the Catalina around and pulled it, tail first, out of the water and up the ramp on its newly installed wheels. When the aircraft became level on the tarmac apron, the waiting crowd of pilots and mechanics pressed forward to study the holed aluminum and the shredded wing and aileron fabric.

Squadron Operations and Training Duty Officer Lieutenant Frank Hudson walked up to Burke's port window.

"Good to have you safely back, Burke. We'll talk in my office as soon as you hand your Cat over to the line chief. Sure you had no injuries?"

"Thank you, Lieutenant. Yes, I'm sure, but I've got two men with chills, Ensign Singer and Radioman McClusky. They ought to be looked at in sick bay, and, if I may say so, sir, given a stiff drink."

"I'll see to it," Hudson said. "Debriefing in forty-five minutes?"

"Aye, aye, sir."

Lieutenant Hudson motioned Burke to a chair in front of his desk at squadron headquarters and handed him a paper.

"This is a form MIKE that Fifth Naval District Norfolk has been using for operational reports. Yours is the first boat to have an operational experience locally, so you get to be the first Cat driver here to fill one out. It looks easy enough. Be sure to give me as much detail as you can on the two subs—what they looked like, course and speed, armament, camouflage, that sort of thing."

"Actually, they weren't moving at all so far as I could

tell," Burke answered, "and I couldn't see any camouflage—they looked dirty gray and rusty."

"Whatever," Hudson said, "just put it down on the form. And, when they're developed, include your photos. I'm anxious to see them. Now what was it you meant in your message when you said that you 'engaged' the two subs?"

The tall, half-balding, sandy-haired duty officer leaned back in his chair, allowing a slight but indulgent smile to crinkle his face, since he was well aware that Burke's PBY was toothless.

Burke began by explaining why he had dived on the boats, since, he asserted, that was the only way he could determine if the subs were friends or foes. He had been given no silhouettes or recognition books.

"And you sure as hell found out, didn't you?" Hudson noted, his smile going full-beam. "It's a good thing they didn't take out one of your engines. The Cat's single-engine performance is marginal. And at your altitude, and no time to jettison radios and anything else loose, and high time on those engines—"

"I could be riding to Germany in a submarine," Burke agreed.

"You got it."

Encouraged by Hudson's friendly manner and seeming approval, Burke decided to tell him straight out about Operation Poopie Bag. "Set for a spacing of forty-five feet at seventy knots," he concluded. "Released manually."

Hudson clapped his hands to the top of his head. "I love it," he said in a high-pitched voice. "I love it. Jesus, I love it."

The O and T officer then sat upright and placed his forearms on the desk. "That doesn't mean," he said, suddenly serious, "that the squadron skipper or the base commander will find it funny—one damn bit. Not when one of their bureau aircraft is shot up to hell. And let me clue you in on something, Mister."

He paused to put on an official face.

"You're not the first fly guy in Florida to drop something on the Germans. Yesterday evening about seven or so we lost a ten thousand ton tanker, loaded, the *W. D. Anderson*, off Jupiter. And very early this morning"—he reached for a teletype page from which he read—"at oh-one-fifteen, a navy type SOC-three scout from NAS Miami, Lieutenant Ostromm piloting, sighted by moonlight and attacked a sub on the surface fifteen miles bearing zero-five-zero degrees true from Jupiter Light, scoring what the pilot judged to be a hit—results unknown."

"Well, how come Miami has depth bombs and we don't?" Burke protested.

"I don't know," Hudson said, in a tone that revealed his own exasperation. "Fleet Air at Key West and Banana River also have DBs, and they're both training units. Maybe it's because Key West is on operational training and Banana River's on transitional, while we're still intermediate, I dunno. We're not scheduled to go operational here, as you know, until one April."

"That's what ticks me off, Sir. When they finally get around to it, what's 'operational' going to mean here?"

"According to the plan I've seen," Hudson said, "we're gonna fly Cats out of here four times daily, seventy-five miles north, seventy-five south and twenty-five to sea."

"Twenty-five!" Burke exclaimed. "Why that's nothing. Sir, I would never have sighted the subs I did if I'd been limited to twenty-five. In a boat that can fly fifteen-plus hours if you press it, I could patrol what? Five hundred out? I'm doing more now in training flights than they're planning to do in operations. Hell, I hear even the Civil Air Patrol is going to send patrols *sixty* miles out—in Cessnas and Luscombes, for godsake. What are the other navy units doing?"

"PBMs at Banana River are scheduled to go out fifty miles. I don't know if they're doing it yet."

"Sir," Burke broke in, "except for the instructors, I'm the senior active Cat pilot here. My crew has the top marks in the squadron. Can't you give us some bombs and ammo? Thinking about those subs sitting out there pretty as you please makes me madder'n hell. Getting shot at by them doesn't help, either. Meanwhile, sending me and my crew out on training flights with no weapons or protection or even recognition books, in the middle of a war front, and asking us to 'investigate and report' is like sending a Boy Scout troop out on a camping trip into Bataan peninsula. Don't you agree?"

"Yes," Hudson said. "Point taken. I do agree. And I'll talk with the squadron skipper about it. If we can't get you on a war footing here, maybe we can detach you for a time to VP eighty-three at Norfolk, where you can load up with all the bombs you want and go to war every day. We'll see. It would be good for one of our boats to have that kind of operational experience. We'll talk about it."

"Thank you, sir."

"Meantime, with your skin shot up you're off the flight schedule until it's fixed." Hudson rose and walked over to the schedule board and wiped Burke's plane number from the Duco finish.

"While your skin's in A and R, I'll assign you and the officers to lectures," he went on, "so you can bone up on navigation and cloud forms—all those good things. And I'll put your ratings into semaphore, blinker, and signal flag drill."

"They'll love that," Burke said, dryly.

"Being off stick time means you can have hard liquor at the O Club," Hudson added. "I'd suggest you hit the galley, shower and shave, and then high-tail it down Mustin Road for a double blackjack."

"Aye, aye, sir."

"But finish the form MIKE first."

"Of course."

"And don't gun deck it. If you don't know the data asked for in a space, leave it blank."

"Got it."

"And leave out the poopie bag attack."

"Right."

• • •

His legs rubbery, and his mind elastic, Bo Burke departed the O Club at closing time and walked loosely south on Mustin Road, the winding drive he thought to be as beautiful as any drive he had seen through any college campus, and doubly so tonight under a first quarter moon. Indeed, the whole base, he had been told by senior officers, was one of the most beautiful naval reservations in the country. Speaking of senior officers, the senior BOQ, also regarded as one of the most beautiful BOQs anywhere, was looming into view. In fact, everything was one of the most beautiful tonight, he decided, with the light-headedness of one who had just successfully flirted with death and also gotten mildly drunk.

His call to Belle from the club had gone about as well as could be expected. For security reasons, he could not tell her what had happened to him and his plane earlier that day, though he was dying to, and he almost did.

"Don't you want to have a family someday?" he had asked her.

"Someday. Right now, like you, I want to fly. Jacqueline Cochran's organizing twenty-five women pilots to ferry warplanes for the British Air Transport Authority. I'm trying find out how I can join up."

"You're talking about some pretty hot airplanes," Bo protested. "The Brits are not fighting in J-three Cubs."

"Now you're condescending," Belle corrected him. "Of course, I'd have to be trained. Of course, I'd have to get checked out. In the meantime, I'm building hours. I have six hundred plus. I'm quitting my job next week so I can fly with the Civil Air Patrol, hunting submarines."

"What?"

"A CAP unit is starting up at Flagler Beach. Frank Upchurch and Roy Barnes have already painted a CAP insignia on their Aeronca Chief here at St. Augustine. Frank says when we fly as CAP we can get avgas instead of the car gas we've been using. Also, the CAP is going to give us one hundred pound bombs—"

"What?"

"Bo, I've got to go. I won't change my mind about what's best for both of us. However, if you need a friend to write to, I'll be glad to receive your letters, but on two conditions. One, just news, no romance. If you break that rule, I'll have to have your mail returned to sender."

"Okay and?"

"Two, buy some Ovaltine and send in the top for Little Orphan Annie's secret decoder pin. Then send your messages in Annie's secret code. I'll respond in kind. That'll keep our letters short."

"What?"

"Goodbye, Bo."

Probably it was not his best idea, it occurred to him now, with a lucidity that belied his condition, to be rambling about in the vicinity of so many senior officers. Making a stiff, formal about-face, as he had first learned to do in the Boy Scouts and had learned to do again in naval reserve basic training, he reversed course toward Yorktown. He thought he would talk with the guys around the pool at the student officers' area. But that was a stupid thought; it was too cold for anyone to be around a pool. Then, he decided, no, he would go down to the river and just sit for awhile on the bank, which is what he did, except that he did not sit upright for long, and once he let his back rest gently on the grass and his head on his cover, and after he pulled the collar of his topcoat around his neck, he fell hard into a warrior's sleep.

It was not only the morning sun that finally woke him, it was machinist's mates, cadets, and pilots warming up scores of aircraft for primary and intermediate training flights. Harsh combustions filled the air from N3Ns and Stearmans, SNJs, SNCs, and OS2Us. Soon, he knew, the loud but underpowered PBYs would join the chorus. What a night! And here he was lying on the grass in one of his best uniforms. Good that no duty officer or shore patrol type had sighted him zonked out this way on the beach.

He knuckled his eyes, stood up, and tried to look alert and businesslike. It was hard to do, given his head. But he brushed himself down, patted his hair, found his shave still halfway presentable, and adopted a stance that, if anyone was watching, might suggest that he was studying the water for take-off conditions. He prepared a speech to that effect in case a superior officer asked: "Just observing the surface here, sir—it's mirror-finish calm—too calm for the hull, even with a step, to break the suction—need to send out an inshore patrol vessel to rough up the water—only way to get airborne today, sir." That was what he would say. But, looking around, he gratefully saw there was no one he had to say it to.

His watch showed him he had ample time to clean up and report. So he stayed a short while longer to watch the sun paint soft Necco Wafer blues and yellows in the mist that hung over the flat river, framed on both sides by moss-covered water oaks. In the early light, Burke noticed, he could see into the water itself, which was tea-colored with the tannic acid that drained from leaves and twigs and organic ooze in the forests where the river had its origins. Later in the day, he knew, when the sun was blazing, about the time he would be seated in class, transfixed by some rapturous lecture on celestial navigation, only the impenetrable glassy film of the surface could be seen, sparkling like a northern lake.

He reached into his left breast pocket and retrieved the letter from Belle. Without reading it one last time, he tore it into small pieces and, kneeling, tossed the pieces gently into the water.

CHAPTER 7

BELLE HART BARELY AVERTED the sight of the sprawling pile of seashells looming to her right in the late afternoon light as she ran after two boys across the fort green at St. Augustine. The seashells, each smaller than a fingernail, came from Anastasia Island across the river, where, two million years before, they and their surprised mollusk inhabitants were thrown up on the ocean shore by violent storms. Over time, the shells, whole and broken, fused together to become soft yellow rock.

In the last quarter of the seventeenth century, Spanish engineers learned how to quarry the rock in the large slab form that gave it load-bearing strength, to leave it in the sun until it hardened, to lighter it across the river on barges, and to place it, slab on slab, to form the walls and bastions of a castle—Castillo de San Marcos.

The castle was out of Belle's line of sight now as her Keds pounded the angular path across the flattened remains of the old Spanish glacis. Those kids, twelve or fourteen years old, were fast, but she bet they didn't have her conditioning. They could beat her in the short distance, but not in the long. Besides, they were weighted down with the decorative brass pipes they had stolen from Orange Street Elementary.

By chance, Belle had seen them on her walk home from her WPA job as assistant recreational director at the playgrounds of Davenport Park in North City. The boys were hauling brass pipes out of a maintenance door, obviously to sell for scrap, probably so they could buy candy or go to the movies.

Darn those kids! They were turning down Water Street, the last place in town where they should be. Those families were going to be shocked by this foot race past their front porches. Belle picked up the pace. Her lanky athletic frame bent to her will, and her dark blonde hair flounced on her shoulders. As she made the turn onto Water Street along the river she saw the two boys halfway down the street, flagging, drop the brass pipes with a series of loud clangs, then attempt to run farther without them, finally go limp, double over with their hands on their knees, and gulp for air.

Belle caught up with them just as the quiet, sequestered Water Street community threw open its windows and responded to the now rolling, ringing pipes.

"What in the *world!*" exclaimed one resident.

"Heavens to *Betsy!*" added another.

"We've *never* had a noise like that!" confirmed a third.

Belle grabbed both boys by their collars and stood them up. "See what you've done?" she scolded them. "Disturbed these kind people in the privacy and peace of their homes? Now pick up those pipes, and don't you bang them together!"

When the boys had the pipes under arm again, she said, "You two come with me and get off this street—right away! Tommy Williams and Bubba Davis, I am surprised. Your parents will be ashamed of you."

"My folks don't care," said Tommy. "We just wanted to see the movie and have a freeze at the Mat Shop. We didn't hurt no one."

That was just the problem, Belle reflected. So many parents in this city didn't care. Time and again the police had taken juvenile offenders home to confront their parents only to have the parents take the kids' side against the police. Well, there was a second step in place now.

"Where're you taking us?" Tommy asked.

"To Mr. Corbett's home, the school superintendent," Belle told him sternly, "so you can return his pipes and apologize for what you've done."

"All we wanted to do was see *Captains of the Clouds*, with warplanes and James Cagney," Bubba said.

"And Mr. Corbett will ream you out pretty well, and

tell you that if you ever do anything like this again, he will see that you go before Judge Mathis, and Judge Mathis, despite anything that your parents say, will send you straight to State Reform School at Marianna. And you won't like it there at all, believe me. No freedom, no friends, no shrimp, no mullet, no oysters—think about that!"

As they exited Water Street and entered the fort green, Belle asked, "Both you boys go to St. Joseph's Academy?"

"Yes'm."

"Yeah."

"Don't the sisters there teach you the Ten Commandments?"

"Yes'm."

"'Thou shalt not steal?'"

"Yes'm."

"Maybe you need some goals in life. Don't the sisters point out things you can do when you grow up—provided you stay out of trouble?"

"What's there to do, Miss Hart?" Tommy said. "Shrimp boats, railroad, Miller Shops, hotels, tourist stuff, that's the only goals in this town. Unless being a recreational director like you."

"You don't need to stay in this town if you don't want to. The one thing you do need is an education. Do well in school and you can do anything, go anywhere."

"Well, how come you're here, Miss Hart?" Bubba asked.

"Because I happen to like it here," Belle said. "Besides, you can add interest and excitement to your life wherever you live."

"Like what?" Tommy asked.

"Like flying."

"Flying?"

"Yes. When I was in college, I set myself a goal of learning how to fly and I now have a private pilot's license from the Civil Aeronautics Administration. You can do something yourselves that's equally interesting."

"Whatta-ya fly—*bombers?*" Bubba said, and both boys banged their pipes laughing.

"I'm going to whack you both over the head!" Belle said, mock threatening them with her arm. After a moment, she resumed, with a certain pride in her voice: "Piper Cubs, Aeroncas, Taylorcrafts, Stinson Reliants— planes like that. Private flying's been restricted since the fifteenth, but there's talk of starting a Civil Air Patrol here, and I'm going to join."

"Doesn't it cost a lot of money to fly?" asked Tommy.

"Not that much once you've soloed. If you belong to a club, as I do, it's only two dollars an hour, otherwise four."

"I'd love to go up in a plane sometime," Bubba said.

"Tell you what I'll do, if wartime regulations permit," Belle offered. "Stay out of trouble the rest of the school year, get grades of B and above in all your subjects— including deportment—and come June, if your parents give permission, I'll give each of you a ride."

"Wow, that's neat!" Bubba said. "Can we go out over the ocean?"

"A short distance, maybe," she promised.

Suddenly, Bubba shot an arm in the air. "Look!" he shouted. "There's a plane!"

Belle looked up to see a small blue balsa wood and paper model airplane, its rubber band engine spent, gliding in to a landing on the green, where two figures were running after it.

"Neat!" Bubba said. "That's Paul Ohlenburg from school. And Father D'Angelo's with him."

Belle asked, "Paul's at St. Joseph's, too?"

"Yeah, Saint Joe's. He's a senior. We're just first year."

"And Father D'Angelo's from the cathedral?" Belle asked.

"Yeah," they said together. "Everybody likes Father D'Angelo," Tommy added.

"A right guy," Bubba agreed, "not like some of 'em."

"Well, maybe I'd better talk with him about you two."

"Oh, no!" they both protested.

As Belle led them over to the priest, Bubba asked, "Do you go to the cathedral, Miss Hart?"

"No, I attend First Methodist."

Tony D'Angelo and Paul were examining a damaged landing gear when Belle approached with her two young miscreants.

"Hello," Tony acknowledged them.

"Father, I'm Belle Hart, a recreation director at Davenport Park. These students of yours stole brass pipes from the Orange Street School and were going to sell them for cash so they could go to the movies. Do you know them?"

"Yes, I do." He addressed them, "Is that right, boys?"

"Yes, Father," they answered softly in unison.

Belle explained that she was taking them to the home of the school superintendent, and that he could handle the situation from there.

"Well, if you don't mind, Miss Hart," Tony responded, "I'd like to go with you and see what I can do for the boys." He turned toward them. "I really am disappointed in both of you."

The boys' heads hung in appropriate shame.

Then he said to Paul Ohlenburg, who was holding his wounded plane, "It's about time for your ride to come, anyway, isn't it, Paul?"

"Yes, Father."

Tony explained to Belle as they began walking toward San Marco Avenue, "Paul's father usually picks him up after school and drives him home. They live at the beach. But his father called the school to say that he was sick, and Joe Capona, the night watchman at Marine Studios, is going to give him a lift home on his way to work."

"That's nice of him," Belle said.

"Yes, it is. Tell me, Miss Hart, do you often spend your afternoons chasing down thieves?" He smiled.

"If you'll tell me, Father D'Angelo," she shot back, "if you often spend yours playing with model airplanes."

"Touché!" he laughed. "I deserved that. The answer is, no. Paul just finished building his plane and I asked if I could watch his test flights. It was fun. I didn't build model planes when I was a kid. We didn't have much space for flying them where I lived in New York."

As Paul peeled off to await his ride, the remainder of the procession crossed San Marco and headed toward Valencia Street. Tony repeated his intention to work with the two boys.

Belle responded, "You know that, if you don't succeed, the next step will have to be Judge Mathis and Marianna."

"Marianna maybe," Tony agreed, "but Judge Mathis has been called into the service. Judge Eisenbach has taken his place."

"All right," Belle said, "Eisenbach. I didn't know that. What I do know is that the city is fed up with these youthful offenders and is dealing with them tough. The earlier policy was to drive them home and scold them in front of their parents. But the parents sided with the boys. So, on a second or third charge, Judge Mathis started sending them to Marianna, and the delinquency rate fell right away."

"It would be terrible if anything like that happened to Tommy or Bubba," Tony said, looking down at them. "Wouldn't it, boys?"

The two nodded their heads energetically.

"I have to tell you, Father," Belle continued, "I don't think you give much moral guidance to your Catholic people. Look at these boys. And look, by the way, at your Negro members. A third or more of the Negroes in this town call themselves Roman Catholic, but their behavior scandalizes the rest of the Negroes, particularly the Baptists, the Methodists, and the AMEs, and I'm sure the unchurched besides."

"Just a minute," Tony interjected. "We have two mission churches that work directly with the Negroes, St. Benedict the Moor on Central Avenue in Lincolnville, and St. Joseph's in West St. Augustine. And two full-time Josephite priests conduct that ministry."

"Well," Belle answered straightaway, "from all I've heard from the Negro ministers, the Catholic Negroes lower the moral tone of the whole community. Go to Mass and then do as you please, seems to be their motto. They sell Cuba and Bolita tickets. One of them sells Palm Valley shine at a blind tiger on Saint Francis and Oneida streets, including Sundays. And it's the Catholics who form the majority of the crowd at the Sunday midnight dances."

"Midnight dances?" Tony asked.

"You don't know about the midnight dances? Beginning fifteen minutes after twelve o'clock every Sunday night at the Odd Fellows Hall on Saint Francis and Washington? They last sometimes until daylight, so that people are hardly able to go to work on Monday mornings. The Catholic church could do something about that if it cared to."

"Well, what is your church, Miss, and what have you done?"

"First Methodist," Belle answered, "and I think we have a pretty good record of showing our concern for these people. Our charities are very generous—"

"No more so, I venture, than the St. Vincent de Paul Society," Tony interrupted.

"Perhaps. But at First Methodist we also have a program in which our young people's division, as we call it, visits the schools and churches of the Negroes in order to get to know them better as fellow human beings, fellow Christians, and fellow citizens. Do you do that?"

"No," Tony confessed, "we don't. We should. It sounds like a fine idea."

"But you won't do it," Belle said, "because you're too committed to segregation. You have separate churches and separate ministers."

"But you do, too," protested Tony.

"Yes, but our young people are trying to cross that bridge. If you, the dominant religion in town, ever told me that your young people were doing the same thing, I'd feel a lot better."

During the pause that followed Tony reflected on how odd it was to get dressed down by a young woman. It had never happened to him before. He had never met anyone like Miss Hart. It was an unsettling experience.

"The other thing I wanted to say to a Catholic priest one day," Belle continued, "is that, as I see it, real Christianity is not a matter of doctrines and prohibitions and cere-monies—or uniforms, either, like that black suit you've got on, if you'll excuse my bad manners—but personally taking care of people who are poor and without hope. And I think that if you did more of that rather than parading about in fancy vestments we'd all be a lot better off."

"And again," Tony said, "I suppose you think the Methodists have a better record?"

"No, I don't," Belle allowed. "It's just that with your one true church pretensions, the failure of Roman Catholics to practice real Christianity is just more glaring and damaging. You're always making brave public state-ments about Jesus and the poor, but maybe the best Christians in town are neither Romans nor Methodists."

"For example?" Tony asked.

"Did you ever walk down Granada, south of Craig's Funeral Home?" Belle asked back.

"Sure," Tony said, "to get an ice cream cone at the Iceberg. It's the best I've had outside the Italian shops on Forty-first Street in New York."

Belle laughed and her green eyes blinked. "I love it, too," she said. "Satin finish coffee is the flavor I get. You know that that Negro place and a drug store in Palm Beach have the highest ratings for sanitary cleanliness in the whole state?"

"No, I didn't know that," Tony acknowledged. He was beginning to relax a little now. There might be a sense of humor or pleasure behind this Savonarola facade after all.

"Well," she went on, "just before you get to Bridge, at number forty-six, you see Saul Snyder's wholesale grocery. That man is a saint. All during the Depression he's kept I don't know how many Saint Augustine families alive, both Negro and white. 'Just pay me when things get better,' he's told them. He's made no speeches, taken no public positions, totally unpretentious. No man is more loved or respected by the poor. There's no better Christian in church on Sundays, your church or mine. And Saul Snyder is a Jew."

Tony stared at the sidewalk and let Belle's story sit in his mind for a moment. He shrugged his shoulders in discomfiture. What could he say? Probably humility was the best position to adopt.

"I've learned a lot from you," he said to Belle.

She smiled. "I apologize if I've been too bold. Sometimes I'm a little direct. I like to go from point A to point B."

"Point A?" Tony asked. "I'm unfamiliar—"

"Oh, that's piloting talk. I fly. A lot of pilots enjoy just going upstairs and flying around the pea patch. I don't. I like cross-country—going from point A to point B—direct."

"I see."

"If you'd ever like to go flying, give me a call at Davenport Park. I can get you closer to heaven than you've probably been before—at least physically."

The invitation was a stunner. Not since he entered the seminary had any girl or woman suggested that she and he be alone together in an airplane or a car, or in any other confined space. Nor had he forgotten the clerical rule: *Numquam solus cum sola*—Never be alone with a woman.

"I'd like that," he said, totally surprised at himself. He wondered if the double-entendre of "heaven at least physically" had occurred to Miss Hart. He hoped not. But, then, another side of him hoped it had. Unnerving.

"Private flying's been curtailed for a couple of weeks while the CAA gets its rule book organized for wartime," she added. "We're supposed to start up again on March eighth. Call me anytime after that. I think you'd enjoy it. I'll show you how to handle the stick," she smiled, mouth and eyes in unison.

Tony, totally undone, reached for his handkerchief and blew into it as hard as he could, grateful that they had reached the superintendent's house, where Belle pressed the doorbell.

There had already been one national FBI round-up of German aliens, in December, and twice since aliens had been ordered to re-register. Paul wondered how much longer he and his father Hans would be able to escape detection. They had re-registered, as ordered. Their last name, Ohlenburg, was too obviously German for them to do otherwise, especially since they were not on the rolls as native-born or naturalized citizens. But his father, as an Abwehr contact and facilitator, was skating on the edge of active espionage.

If the FBI caught on to his father, and he was arrested, Paul would likely go to prison with him, and the thought was thoroughly depressing, not just because he feared what the Americans might do to his father, and perhaps to him, but because the wonderful, familiar world Paul had grown up to love during these high school years would disappear from his reach, perhaps forever.

That world was the ocean, the beaches, and the intracoastal waterway. Living on St. Augustine Beach, where his father operated the White Surf Cottages, Paul was confessedly addicted to his surroundings, which were a never-ceasing source of sensory pleasure. Morning and night, his nostrils savored the briny air. Daily, his eyes feasted on the changing colors of the sea's expanse, from the moment the eastern sun rose upon it in an orange explosion, to the hour of soft light that fell upon the surf at evening tide, when his afterschool chores were done—that magical quiet time when the dun of the beach shaded into gray and the blue sea melted into ash.

Paul's heart lifted to the pelicans that glided past in tranquil V-formations, and swam with the gams of porpoises that surfaced in the distance to open their blowholes. His hearing resonated to the high-pitched tone of sea gulls that dived off shore for mullet, to the mid-range, everlasting roll of swells becoming breakers, and, especially in the summer, to the deep baritones and basses of thunder from the western sky.

Underall, the sand, both loose and packed, produced its special tactile pleasures to the bare foot, even one as calloused as Paul's. He recalled the lines from Gerard Manley Hopkins, taught him by Sister Seven Dolors at St. Joe's: *Generations have trod, have trod, have trod . . .* What was the rest of it? *Nor can foot feel, being shod.* Something like that. Paul valued the barefoot life.

And taste? Forget your cattle, your farm-grown meats, and your game. No fare compared in taste to what he brought in daily from the ocean pier and the waterway: sea trout on an artificial shrimp lure—he caught more trout on that lure than old-timers caught using live shrimp; pompano and Spanish mackerel on a red head clothespin plug; stone crabs in wood lattice traps; flounder that he gigged at night on the shallow banks of the waterway with the aid of a Coleman lantern.

Paul knew why so many people who lived in St. Augustine or on the beaches would live nowhere else, why they did not mind if the tourists came and went and left their money here, so long as they went; did not mind even that the tourists tasted these ocean delicacies at Rector's or at the Neptune Grill or at the Blue Heron—fried shrimp, all you can eat, fifty cents. But the locals did not want outsiders to know how much this good life was free for the taking, did not want them to come in large numbers to settle on the beach and spoil it for those who were already here. "Build a wall around it," was what most locals said.

Paul had once been taken back into the oak woods behind the beaches by old-timers who showed him the bare remains of subdivision streets that developers had carved out during the 1920s land boom. As though being shown the darkest, most foreboding tracts of hell by Dante himself, he had heard from the old-timers how those pre-development schemes, if successful, would have jammed the beaches with people and cars, ruined the swimming and the belly surfing, raised tall sun and breeze blocking hotels, and killed the fishing, killed it dead—"like Miami Beach," they said, conjuring the most frightful possible image.

When the weather turned warm there would be belly surfing on the big wood board. No matter how hard it was to work the board across the breakers, no matter how dangerous it was risking a hit on the head from a sudden movement of the board's edge or an unexpected run-out that had carried more than one swimmer out to sea, it was worth the peril to gain the indescribable spiritual experience that came from catching exactly the right swell and riding it as a breaker into shore.

That was his world, and the closer the hour came when he and his father were to pick up an agent named Homer, from the same purple-blue surf, the more apprehensive Paul became.

This afternoon, thanks to the ride from Mr. Capona, he was able to get a little work in before dark. From the office cottage roof he cleared sand and debris that the recent weather front had deposited in the 33-foot east section of the sheet-metal storm gutter that his father had separated from the downspouts in order to use it as an antenna, connected to his National HRO receiver, for picking up continuous wave Morse code transmissions on the 20-meter band, which his father guarded nightly at 2100, 2300, and 0100 hours.

Such a transmission, in one-time pad cipher, had come in two nights before from subagent Emil Lorenz in Eden, near Stuart. Lorenz relayed confirmation from the U-boat carrying Homer that the agent's landing was still on for just north of Marine Studios at 2300 tonight. That was just four and a half hours off, and with his father bedridden with intestinal flu, Paul anticipated that he would have a role in the landing somewhat larger than his father had planned.

Paul's stomach was not doing so well either, but it was not from flu: the sharp pain that ran down his gut came from stress and fear. He had not felt at all like flying his model plane today. But Father D'Angelo had asked him to bring it in, so he went through the motions. When the landing gear broke it was like his own legs collapsing. God, what would Father D'Angelo think about him if he knew what he and his father were doing? What would his senior year classmates at St. Joe's think?

At school he was a member of the volunteer civil defense team. He had helped crosshatch all the school windows with surgical tape to prevent their shattering from the concussion of German bombs. He was head, in fact, of the student chemical decontamination squad, and in that capacity, with the Mother Superior's approval, he had placed buckets of sand throughout the ground floors of the school and convent that could be used to counteract poison gas canisters dropped from Nazi planes.

No one at school ever mentioned the fact that he had a German name. Maybe the sisters knew he was originally German. None of the kids seemed to know, or care. He spoke cracker English as well as they did. Every morning, standing at his desk, he pledged allegiance to the flag of the United States, and to the nation for which it stood, and he gladly sang "America," which Sister Seven Dolors had changed in part to read, "land of the Spaniards' pride," instead of "Pilgrims' pride," since the Spaniards had founded St. Augustine fifty-five years before the Pilgrims came to Plymouth Rock.

Paul honestly liked America. He liked the people, the casual life, the total freedom, the swing music, the movies, the chocolate shakes, "Fibber McGee and Molly," the American hymns at Mass, the cigarettes, except that the good ones were now off the market and the All-Americans and Fatimas that replaced them were not as good; the cars, he loved the cars, especially the convertibles, but cars were going to be around less and less, what with the halt in auto manufacturing and the onset of tire and gas rationing. In fact, there was hardly anything about America he didn't like. So why was he trying, secretly, to destroy it?

"Because of the higher principle," his father kept telling him, though Paul was never sure he understood what the higher principle was. Because of loyalty to his father, that was really why.

"In total war everyone is a combatant," Hans had told him. "We are all in the trenches. No one is exempt from the great struggle."

Paul prayed that something would happen to the U-boat, or to Homer, so that he would not have to be in the great struggle. He prayed that he might somehow be carried away from all this reality, the way he was transported to other spheres when he rode his board in the summertime.

But, later that evening, Paul's father, white and drained from his fever and retching, told him, "Son, I think you're going to have to drive the pickup yourself tonight."

CHAPTER 8

TONY LIFTED THE WINDOW to drink in the twilight air, and then opened his breviary, with its gilt-edged leaves and multicolored ribbons. He had every intention of getting in Vespers before supper. *Deus in adjutorium meum intende. . . .* But his mind was not on his prayers. The words dribbled off his lips but his concentration wandered. It had happened to him a lot recently. He reproached himself with the words from Matthew: "This people honors me with their lips but their hearts are far from me."

He lay his head back on the off-white linen antimacassar and listened idly to the hooves of the last horsedrawn tourist carriage to make its rounds of the plaza before dark.

He couldn't believe that he had said yes to that invitation. Was it only a primal reflex action to show that he was not intimidated by her aggressiveness? God! Bishop Garvey would kill him if he heard that he went up in a plane with a young woman—a blonde at that! In his imagination Tony could see the stern-faced chancellor of the diocese handing him a return train ticket to New York.

But Belle—should he think of her by her first name?—Belle was more than a person of the opposite sex. She was an *event*—completely unlike any woman he had met before. Physically attractive, yes. But an independent mind. Apart from her sexuality, *that* was what had gotten to him. She thought her own thoughts, not others'. She probably made her own rules. Was that why he was so taken with her? Deep down, did he wish he had the same independence? And assertiveness! She did have moxie! That was another thing he liked about her.

Better face up to it, pal, he told himself. Without

intending to, he could now say he was sure, she had made ripples in his pool. And there was a moment, in front of the superintendent's door, when he had had to think hard about the Yankees.

Was he missing out on something here, something very crucially connected to being human? His older, married brother Giulio would say, no.

"You're gonna solve people's marital problems?" Giulio asked incredulously one day when Tony was still in major sem. "You won't know anything to say about marriage unless you get married yourself."

"A doctor doesn't need to have TB to treat TB," Tony had answered.

"Tony, you poor son-of-a-bitch," his brother replied, condescendingly, "you're so naive. Marriage isn't like TB. It's worse. Being criticized to death is a far more tortuous way to go. You'll never understand it unless you go through it, which, if you continue on present course, you won't, you lucky shit. Just don't tell anyone later on you know all about it, 'cause you won't know doo-doo."

Giulio was right: Tony didn't know. What he was taught at major sem was a semen-centered moral theology and a canon law fixated on marriage as a contract. Of marriage as a relationship he learned nothing. Of marriage as a problem-riddled experience he knew only what he encountered in the confessional or in the office, or overheard in parish conversations. The many times he heard it said, for example, "The woman is a saint," he knew that the canonization cause was being promoted by a domineering, probably abusive husband. To which pain the only remedy the Church provided a priest, should the woman seek it, was the formula, "Offer it up."

Giulio had to be wrong about marriage. Tony had been in too many happy family homes to be as cynical as his brother. Sure, there were problems in marriage sometimes, maybe often. If Giulio wanted to emphasize the problems, then that was Giulio's perspective. It didn't have to be his. Living with someone like Belle, Tony thought, should, overall, be a warm, happy, and exhilarating experience—if he could trade wits fast enough. He decided not to think about the sexual part of it right now. He might have an impure thought.

He laid his breviary aside and stood up to climb into his cassock. It was nearly time for Mattie Mae, the Negro housekeeper, to ring the supper bell at the base of the stairs. He looked himself over in the dresser mirror. Better slow down, he told his image. Your head is racing out of control, not to mention your loins. After supper better whip out a spiritual master, maybe Jacques Millet's *Jesus Living in the Priest*, so you can reinforce the theory that celibacy is a higher good.

Better shape up, Tony.

Sneakers off, feet propped on a wicker ottoman, Belle Hart let go slack the leg muscles that had competed with Tommy's and Bubba's, as well as the cortex that had competed with Father D'Angelo's. With a puff of breath through puckered lips, she reached for that afternoon's *St. Augustine Record*.

The front page was all war:

STATE OF FLORIDA IS GOING ON WAR FOOTING
CITY TO HAVE AIR RAID ALARM DRILL THURSDAY
LOCAL FLYER COMPLETES BASIC TRAINING AT RANDOLPH FIELD, TEXAS
TRIBUTE TO COLIN KELLY PENNED BY LOCAL POET

"Colin Kelly, Colin Kelly,
Knight of the Eastern Sky . . ."

And all of page three contained instructions, with pictures, on what to do in an air raid.

An air raid?

There was a knock on the half-open door. "Come in, Mother," she said.

A trim, slightly graying woman, in a suppertime apron,

came in with a cup of hot tea. "I thought you'd want this, dear. It's getting chilly out. Did everything go well today?"

"Oh, yes, I survived the little rascals again."

"I also wanted to ask you about those warnings in the paper about air raids. You're an airplane pilot. Do you really think we'll be bombed?"

"Oh no, Mother! From where? Vichy-controlled Martinique is the closest place. But how would the Germans get their short-range bombers, and that's all they have, to Martinique? They could occupy the Azores, but that's too far for them to send bombers here and expect to get them back. No, this is all ignorant hysteria. The Germans may send a battleship or something, but no planes."

"Oh, I'm so relieved. I'd just hate to have to go through what the people did in London."

"No need to worry. Saint Augustine is the last place they'd be interested in, anyway."

"I'll get back to my beans," her mother said, closing the door behind her. "Don't get a chill."

Who would have predicted air raids in her college group at Florida State College for Women—in the chapter of the Student Peace Service that they had founded in their senior year? The six of them had discussed the Sino-Japanese "conflict," as the 1938 yearbook called it, and they had taken turns reporting to the group on such things as the Ludlow War Referendum and the Hill-Shephard Industrial Mobilization Bill. But those events and concepts were remote—almost abstract. What of air raid drills here in Florida?

Who would have predicted it—their chairman? What was her name? How could she forget? Just four years ago.

She reached for the yearbook, *Flastacowo,* on the lower shelf of her wicker side table and turned the pages to "Organizations" in the back. Virginia Allen, of course, and the program chairman, Sara Lewis. Maybe they foresaw air raid drills in Florida. If so, they never said it.

A flip through the front pages raised many already distant memories—processing in cheesecloth tunics, pledging to the Torches Three, loitering over Goody Specials in the Sweet Shop, singing "Pals" at twilight . . . , Mortar Board, Phi Beta Kappa, the Junior Minstrels, Senior Hall, dancing in evening dress to the swing of the Auburn Knights.

She reread the caption to the two-page photographic spread on herself: "Gray-green eyes, long bobbed wavy blonde hair. 'F' sweater and skirt, cuff socks and saddle Oxfords. Straightforward, adventuresome, disarming, irresistible. Flying lessons at the Tallahassee airport. Perfectly coordinated athlete. An original, the new American Girl."

She wondered how the passage might be brought up to date—"Living now on a Works Progress Administraton salary and a trust fund from her late father"? "Killed by Nazi bombers in Florida during the war . . ."?

She put the yearbook back and walked to the dresser mirror. Not especially liking what she saw, she fussed over her now shoulder-length hair with the matching comb and brush set, and let her eyes fall on the 5 x 7 framed photo of her navy pilot in Jacksonville: "Thinking of you, Bo." She should have filed it away in her memories box days ago. Which she now did.

Then, turning on the bathtub faucets, she mumbled the words and notes of *Alma Mater:*

> GARNET AND GOLD
> AND MAY WE EVER LOYAL BE;
> AS IN DAYS OF OLD
> THY DAUGHTERS BORE THE TORCHES THREE.
> FEMINA PERFECTA . . .

Femina perfecta?

To Tony the dining room looked no different from a hundred other clerical refectories, chosen at random. The table, chairs, and sideboard were what he called Heavy Dark Rectory, relieved only by the pressed white linen table cloth and a centerpiece of blue and white bachelor's buttons. Above Bishop Garvey's chair, that is, to the left of

Tony's chair, hung a gold-leaf framed oil copy of Raphael's *Alba Madonna*. Between windows behind Larry's place, opposite Tony's, were a Celtic cross and a somewhat mildewed engraving of Rheims Cathedral. Over acting pastor Tom Murphy's chair, which stood at the end opposite Garvey's, hung a bad religious goods store painting of Saint Teresa of Lisieux, which Murphy favored, but which Garvey disliked having to look at during meals, because it was manifestly bad art and because the Little Flower, as the nineteenth-century French Carmelite nun was called, represented a contemplative lifestyle that ran against Garvey's own activist form of Christianity, and especially because it was the Shrine of the Little Flower in Royal Oak, Michigan, that harbored the pro-Nazi, Jew-baiting radio priest Charles E. Coughlin, whom Garvey detested.

A long walnut-framed mirror stretched over the sideboard behind Tony.

While the three priests stood at their chairs waiting for Garvey, Tony decided to twit Larry on a point of theology.

"Larry," he said to his cassocked lookalike opposite, with only the slightest trace in his voice, he hoped, of mischief, "I've found a sure way of getting to heaven without your having to worry any longer about good works or personal behavior."

"A sure way, Tony?" Larry asked, genuinely surprised. "Isn't that a sin of presumption?"

"I don't see why," answered Tony, "if the Church gives it warrant. Here's how it works. I found two prayers, one of which, when you recite it, carries a plenary indulgence at the hour of death. That remits all the temporal punishment due to sin, right? Now—"

Larry interrupted hesitatingly: "You forgot something, I think. Don't you have to—?"

Tony finished the question: "Be in the state of grace at the time to receive a plenary indulgence?"

"Yes."

"That's where the second prayer comes in. Recite it and you're guaranteed to be in the state of grace at the hour of death. The two coincide"—Tony joined his fingers—"and zing! When you die you go rocketing straight up to heaven. So, you can recite those two prayers and then relax. Sin all you want. Have some fun! Just as Luther said, *Pecca fortiter sed crede fortius.*"

Larry looked confused. "There has to be something wrong with that," he said.

"I'm only telling you what's in the *Raccolta*," Tony concluded, just as Bishop Garvey, in black cassock with purple buttons, sash, and piping, entered the dining room. A native of Des Moines, forty-eight years old, slight of build with a square granite face, thin lips, and balding pate, Garvey walked in a slightly hunched-over position, the result of chronic hypertrophic arthritis of the spine from the upper dorsal to the lower lumbar and sacral regions. Standing behind his chair, he made the sign of the cross and gave the blessing:

"*Benedic, Domine, nos et haec tua dona quae de tua largitate sumus sumpturi. Per Christum Dominum nostrum.*"

To which all at table, and Mattie Mae, standing in the kitchen doorway with a steaming bowl of Minorcan chowder, responded, "Amen."

"Good evening, Your Excellency," Tom said.

Garvey nodded with a pleasant smile.

Tuesdays and Fridays were seafood nights at the rectory. As Mattie Mae ladled soup into Garvey's bowl, Tony asked her what the fish was.

"Red snapper, Father."

"Good, my favorite. Thank you."

When Garvey's bowl was filled, he laid his wire-rimmed spectacles on the table. Tony knew it as an unmistakable sign that the bishop was about to pontificate. During six years at the Vatican he had learned well how to do it. What was it to be tonight? Garvey's favorite supper table themes were the Nazis, Charlemagne and the Unification of Europe, the Failure of the German and Irish Bishops in America, and Religious Orders of Women—what Tony called his Sisters *Genitori Genitoque* speech. Tonight, it turned out, the subject matter was a mix of one and three.

Garvey began with a recital of what the Nazis had done in Europe, as he had followed them from his post at Rome: the crushing of the Catholic peace movement in Germany; the pogrom against the Jews; the *Anschluss* in Austria; the seizure of Czechoslovakia; the invasions of Poland, Denmark, Norway, the Lowlands, France; the air bombardments of civilians in Warsaw, Rotterdam, and London—"and now" he said, bringing the recital home and up to date, "just in the last number of days, the sinking of *four* American ships right off our Florida coast—in the territorial waters of my diocese!"

He named them: *Pan Massachusetts, Republic, Cities Service Empire,* and *W. D. Anderson.*

"Think of the loss of life," he said. "*Requiescant in pace.* The dragon is here, Fathers. It has arrived just as I said it would, but very few in the American church were listening."

Garvey explained that even before he left Rome for St. Augustine he had been dismayed by the number of articles and editorials he had seen in the American Catholic diocesan and national press suggesting either accommodation with the Nazis' program of European domination, or, at the least, silence in the face of it. He named the *Brooklyn Tablet, Pilot, Evangelist, Tidings,* and Coughlin's "scurrilous sheet," *Social Justice.*

"And then you had the radio broadcasts, texts of which I received in Rome. On the one hand you had Monsignor Fulton J. Sheen, who insisted that the Communists, not the Nazis, were our number-one threat, and on the other, you had a pro-Nazi anti-Semite orator like Father Coughlin, who blatantly displayed his sympathies for the Führer over his own national radio network. Coughlin was particularly dangerous. At one point that demagogue had a national audience of many millions."

"I heard him lots of times," Tony said. "But not recently."

"His ordinary, Archbishop Mooney, of Detroit, was finally able to shut him up," explained Garvey, "with help from the National Association of Broadcasters. In the meantime, you had a situation where, with most of the bishops and their priests practicing, if not an overt sympathy for the Nazis, an isolationist silence about them and their global menace to what our president has called the Four Freedoms—you had a situation where there was a likelihood that among our more thoughtful lay citizenry we would see taking shape the kind of continental anticlericalism from which our country to date had been spared."

"Why the pro-German bias, Your Excellency?" Tom asked.

"Why the pro-German bias? Why the conspiracy of silence? Well, look at what kind of leaders we have up there in the Biretta Belt. A German-Irish axis. The Germans for ethnic reasons, the Irish because they hated the English so blindly they could not see past their Guinness noses that if the Sceptre'd Isle fell, the Emerald Isle would not be far behind. I looked at them good and hard when I got here to Florida fifteen months ago. . . ."

Back in his room after supper, Tony reflected on what Garvey had said about the bishops. Although he had no direct knowledge of politics at the episcopal level, as Garvey did, he had no reason to doubt Garvey's description of the two American cardinals as nonentities—O'Connell of Boston with his senile criticisms of women's fashions, Dougherty of Philadelphia with his iron regime and his piratical exactions; and many of the archbishops and bishops as no better—Dubuque making cheap bids for publicity, Cincinnati playing the scholarly shrew, Albany and Buffalo both votaries of the Roman Coughlin Church, Los Angeles twisting the lion's tail with all the vigor of an 1848 Irishman; even New York strangely silent; Cicognani, the Italian apostolic delegate, hushing everyone.

No doubt it was true, as Garvey argued, that there had been too much soft speaking, too much anodyne, too much ambiguity, too much avoidance of the issue by the brighter heads in the hierarchy, while the dim bulbs among them had been allowing editors of diocesan press to establish the Catholic Line. And the line was that Communism was America's number-one enemy; whereas, in fact, Garvey had insisted, the first enemy of humanity, the killer of priests, the despoiler of temples, was the Nazi. In combatting one army, the editors were caught broadside by another. *Incidit in Scyllam qui vult vitare Charybdim.* In seeking to avoid the whirlpool of Communism, they steered their barks straight into the rock of National Socialism. Those editors had to be shocked, when Germany invaded Russia and the Ukraine.

Then there was Garvey's radio speech that Tony had heard on the CBS network last July. Maurice Sheehy, the chief chaplain at NAS Jacksonville, had arranged it with his friend Bill Paley of CBS. Garvey had had to go up to WJSV in Washington to make the broadcast. In his memory, Tony recapitulated part of what Garvey said about the radio speech at supper that evening:

"Then I tried to describe the magnitude of the German menace, pointing out that our country, and Central and South America, too, were honeycombed with Nazi agents—enemies of Christ by definition, which gave me the right, I thought, to speak on the subject. The agents' cross, I said, was the hooked cross of National Socialism, their god the recluse of Berchtesgaden. It was only a matter of time before these operatives, advance guards of the Nazi lust for world domination, would welcome the enemy onto our own Atlantic shores.

"I said that churchmen simply cannot allow the interests of religion the world over to be placed in jeopardy by a ruthless persecutor of the Church of Christ. Goodness knows, we quote scripture to government often enough. I said that there are times, and that this was one of them, when government had a right to quote scripture to the Church: 'Render unto Caesar the things that are Caesar's.'"

Heady stuff, Tony thought. You could not hear its like in too many rectories, and he included cathedral rectories.

One thing you could say about Garvey: the man was a fighter. Tony wondered what pablum passed for discourse at Spelly's table in New York.

Paul Ohlenburg had the red Ford pickup gassed and packed with everything his father had said to take along: flashlight, binoculars, socks, blankets, and a thermos of hot coffee.

"Don't leave here until one hour before the scheduled time," his father had told him. "You don't want to be hanging around down there any more than you have to. Remember, there's a watchman at Marine Studios. Keep well to the north, where you're supposed to be, a half-mile north of the Studios. Cut your lights after you cross the toll bridge. Park on the shoulder where I showed you."

Paul's father, Hans, was sicker tonight than he had been that afternoon and still he was refusing to call a doctor to come out for fear of being ordered to a hospital. Hans simply could not miss this contact. He had too many things that had to be said, adult to adult, even if they had to be said from a bed. Paul was savvy and dependable, but the agent, Homer, would not have any confidence being briefed by a boy.

So Hans took aspirin to lower his temperature and drank a little turpentine for his stomach, while he guarded the 20-meter band on his National receiver, as he usually did at this hour, and watched the clock.

Paul was an emotional mess. He fidgeted, moved about his room, stared out the window. A half-hour to go, just the half-hour for "Fibber McGee and Molly" on Tuesday evenings. He tuned his Zenith portable to WJAX and half-listened, unable to smile, much less laugh, as his mind kept switching to a world that was crashing all around him.

Finally, at ten o'clock, he grabbed his jacket, told his father that he was off, climbed into the Ford, and drove out the crushed coquina driveway onto the beach road south.

CHAPTER 9

KAPITÄNLEUTNANT BÖHM came down from the bridge wearing red goggles, so as not to lose night vision acuity, and leaned against the opening to his cubicle where he watched Peter Krug shave at the small wash basin underneath the hinged, lift-up writing table.

"I appreciate your lending me your cabin, Böhm," Krug said, catching Böhm's face in the small mirror and making short strokes with a straight razor.

"It's hardly a cabin," Böhm answered. "More like a friar's cell. Just a hole in the wall with a curtain. But you're welcome to it. That pitcher of fresh water is just for you, so you'll look presentable on shore."

"I'll save some of it so you can shave, too," Krug said, pouring a dash over the lathered blade.

"Not a chance," Böhm said. "No commander is going to arrive back in Lorient without a full beard. He'd be disgraced."

In the mirror Böhm watched Krug's long bony face emerge as the black whiskers fell away, like marble chips from a sculptor's chisel. It was a taut face, suggesting tenacity of will, with a wide mouth and piercing blue eyes.

"Ever decide what those objects were that the navy patrol bomber dropped around us?" Krug asked.

"No. The chief engineer thinks they may have been dye markers. They were not metallic. They floated for a while, as you saw. In retrospect, I probably should have put out the dinghy to pick one up. We just don't know much yet about the American defenses."

"I've been practicing my English with the puster's help. He let me tune in the Miami and Charlotte stations on the broadcast band. It all sounds very familiar."

"What about clothes?" Böhm wondered. "Is what you've got on there authentic American?"

"Yeah, the labels are all American, but they told me in Hamburg that the styles are probably a little out of date, particularly this belted jacket and the shoes. Nothing will give you away faster than shoes. My first task in the morning will be to stock up on clothes and shoes from a variety of stores. I've certainly got enough dollars."

"I hope their serial numbers are still in circulation."

Böhm reached down to his bunk blanket for the *Handbuch der Ostküste der Vereinigten Staaten, 2. Teil,* and opened it to pages 210–211. Flotilla headquarters had told him that his drop-off marker was Marine Studios, a saltwater aquarium of some kind. "Sits all alone on the beach two or three kilometers south of Matanzas Inlet, is quite large, squat, cream-colored, easy to see in a quarter moon." That's what they said—information they had gotten through a U-boat relay from Eden. But the bridge had not sighted it yet, even though they were running awful close at three miles off the beach. What worried Böhm was that the place was not listed in the 1941 coastal pilot handbook. It listed the St. Augustine lighthouse, which he had homed in on and could still see, and Matanzas Inlet, which he could not see in the darkness, and then a wrecked four-masted schooner, which he could not see, either, and after that, Flagler Beach, which was well below the latitude where Marine Studios was supposed to stand. So it was a mystery. Anyway, they were ahead of time.

"I'd better get back on top," he told Krug. "I'll let you know when we're ready."

On the conning tower bridge Böhm lowered his goggles and raised 7 x 50s toward the shoreline. His lenses joined those of First Watch Officer Franz and the two starboard lookouts in sweeping the shore in search of a structure that Lorenz told Lorient no one could miss. Meanwhile, the two port lookouts scanned the seaward sky and horizon for possible enemy planes or ships.

An attack on him now would be particularly dangerous, Böhm worried, since he had very little shoal water in which to dive, should that become necessary. Mindful that the tide tables showed him just fifteen minutes past the low tide mark, he leaned forward to the voice pipe and yelled below: "Navigator!"

In the control room the petty officer *Obersteuermann* answered, "Navigator here!"

"What's your fathometer reading?"

Checking the *Lotapparat* gauge on the gray wall to starboard, the navigator reported: "Fifteen meters under the keel, Herr Kaleu!"

"Very well. Report any lower numbers as they occur."

"*Jawohl,* Herr Kaleu."

Staying at the pipe, Böhm ordered the helmsman: "Come to course two-five-zero." He would close the beach as far as he safely could for a better view. "Both ahead slow. Make four knots."

The voice of the helmsman in the tower acknowledged, and the shrill drag of his telegraphs came up the open hatch. Böhm kept both diesels on line in case he had to order the boat back emergency full. He leaned against the periscope housing, raised his glasses, and strained again to find their target. Fast-moving clouds obscured the moon.

"Ten meters, Herr Kaleu!" the navigator cautioned from below, as U-*Böhm* crept closer to the beach, and Böhm thought he saw the white crests of breaking combers. Just then, the forward starboard lookout stiffened.

"Herr Kaleu!" he shouted.

Böhm lowered his glasses and aligned the barrels with those of the lookout. Then, raising the rubber-cushioned eyepieces to his brow bones again, he stared along the same visual pathway. Yes!

"I see it." A narrow band of gray broke the black horizon. "That has to be it, a little to the south. We just hadn't gone far enough."

He returned to the voice pipe. "Both engines stop! Deck force to the fore casing!"

"Number One," he said to Franz, "have the deck force break out the dinghy."

"*Jawohl*, Herr Kaleu."

Within a minute's time the deck force was inflating a black rubber dinghy with air from a line that led through the tower to the Junkers compressor in the maneuvering and electric motor room below. An expandable aluminum frame provided the six-meter craft additional rigidity. Two oarsmen stood by for launch.

"Number Two," Böhm called down the pipe, "bring Herr Krug to the bridge."

"*Jawohl*, Herr Kaleu."

When Krug came up the hatch onto the tightly packed bridge, Böhm led him down the exterior ladder to the fore casing, where the oarsmen were lowering their *Gummboot* overside.

"My instructions are to make certain you haven't left anything on the boat," he said to the freshly shaved Krug, more than usually alien in his American clothes. "Will you check one last time for the record?"

Krug shrugged and obliged him. From inside his jacket he withdrew a waterproof bag and checked off its contents: one birth certificate, two lock picks, two penlights, six batteries, three bottles of pyramidon headache tablets, and $5,000, including $1,000 in $100 bills. Then he pulled up his right sleeve and showed Böhm a narrow steel dirk in a leather wrist sheath.

"It's all here, Böhm."

"Then we'll see you off Eden on thirteen March," Böhm said seriously, and shook his hand. "Good luck."

"Thanks. Same to you."

Krug looked up to the Number Two, Baumann, on the *Wintergarten* and waved briskly. Franz, standing nearby, he pointedly ignored: they had been two scorpions in a bottle; no desire now to change his relationship with that bastard.

"The oarsmen will take you slightly north of the Studios building," Böhm advised, as Krug, stepping into a rope ladder, made his way down the side of the gently rocking hull onto the starboard saddle tank, then into the pitching rubber dinghy. The oarsmen pushed off and began rowing smartly toward the shoreline, as excited, it appeared to Krug, to be off the U-boat as he. Krug did look back, though, fascinated to see, for the first time since Lorient, the full broadside of the sea monster in which he had been riding. Truly, a thing sinister. *Auf Wiedersehen.*

Then, peering ahead, he tried to discern signs of a shoreline. The sea was inkwell black, with a moiré sheen from the reappearing moon. Semi-solid in appearance, it looked as though it could be walked on. In the wake of the oars, he saw its surface broken by flashing schools of small fish. Soon, in the distance, he heard the rumble of the rolling surf, and, not long afterward, he could see with his bare eyes, off to the left, a long gray structure which must be the Marine Studios that Böhm had mentioned.

Now the dinghy began to move with its own momentum, carried forward on the incoming tide, lifting with the swells and racing with the breakers. The crewmen used their oars to steer, and the rubber bottom bounced on the American beach.

One of the crewmen made a gesture for Krug to disembark, while the other, reaching down, filled his pockets with enemy sand. No sooner had Krug stood up in the swirling surf than the oarsmen, switching positions, rowed vigorously back against the breakers. He knew that they would be using a flashlight beamed seaward, so that if they could not find the U-boat, it would find them. He watched the dinghy for a short while, until it merged with the black velvet air.

Well. Here he was back in America.

He turned to face the beach.

After leaving his truck on the road shoulder and marching through the quartz sand, saw palmetto, cordgrass, and sea oats, Paul took a position in the dunes where he could sweep the surf with his binoculars. At once he was stunned to see a lone fisherman heaving his line into the surf. There *never* were fishermen at this place at night. Darn! He took a closer look.

It was Mr. Capona! What was he doing *here,* fishing? He was supposed to be watching the Studios! Is this what he did at night instead? Paul watched him walk back from the surf with a spool and a long cane pole. He set the pole as deep as he could in a sand dune and sat down no more than twenty yards from where Paul was sitting. After about five minutes the pole flexed steeply—he must be using cut mullet to get channel bass—and Mr. Capona ran down into the surf, wrapped a yard or two of line around his open left hand and elbow, and ran back toward the dunes as hard as he could, hauling his bass behind him. Good size, Paul thought, must be about twenty pounds.

Then the fisherman set his hook another time, heaved his sinker and hook, and walked back to the dunes. For ten or more minutes, while his heart pounded, Paul moved his glasses from pole to surf, from surf to pole. Then, again, the pole bent sharply, and Mr. Capona ran down to the surf—at exactly the moment when, some fifty yards to his left, Paul saw a black bulbous form emerge from the surf and a man step out of it into the water up to his shins.

The boat from the submarine! The man had to be Homer! He could see him plainly. So, too, it appeared, could the fisherman, who let his line drop and ran heavily toward the boat, which was already receding from view by the time he reached its passenger. The two men stood facing each other on the beach, the fisherman gesticulating out to sea. Paul could not make out anything they said. He only knew that this was the worst possible foul-up.

Then, in the blink of an eye, the man from the surf grabbed the fisherman by a wrist, spun him around, and yanked his head back in a chokehold. For over a minute the two shadowy figures locked in a violent embrace. The struggle ended, finally, when the fisherman, like a bass caught on cut mullet, stopped thrashing and fell limp on the wet sand. Homer was on top of him in an instant, turning the fisherman's head to a side. From his right wrist, he drew a thin bright object that he placed in the fisherman's ear and drove home with the ball of his right hand.

In the dunes Paul lurched to his left and vomited.

Disposing of a human body was not something that Paul thought he would ever be doing at any time in his entire life. But here he was, with Mr. Capona's feet in his quaking hands, while Homer held the head and shoulders, hauling dead weight to the soft sand of the fore dunes, where Homer said they should bury him.

"Better to have a man disappear than to have him die of suspicious causes," Homer said. "We could have faked a drowning, but an autopsy would prove otherwise. So let's just shovel out as much sand as we can with our hands and deposit this fellow where he won't be found until the next—what?"

"Nor'easter," Paul said, shakily.

"Nor'easter, huh?"

Was this really happening? Paul anguished, as he dug furiously in the sand. He had done everything that he had prepared to do—flash his light, acknowledge the name Ohlenburg, and explain why his father was not there. But watching a man he knew being killed and helping to bury his corpse—a murder victim?—was not anything he had even speculated doing. Wasn't this just a bad dream?

When they finally had the hole dug large enough, they lifted the body into it. Homer pushed the cane pole as deep in as he could alongside, and threw the spool, line, and three bass on top of the body. Then, he and Paul filled the hole, Paul finding that he could not bring himself to throw sand on Mr. Capona's face or hands. He knew that the questions that chilled his mind at this moment would never leave it as long as he lived: Was he really dead? Would he perhaps "wake up" in this sandy tomb and claw desperately in the wrong direction until oxygen deprivation killed him for sure? Did he really have to be killed in the first place?

It began to rain.

"That's good," Homer said. "It'll mottle and pack the sand so that this dune will look like every other dune. Let's get to your vehicle."

Paul led the way to the truck. When they reached it, he gave Homer the dry socks, thermos of coffee, and blankets.

"My father said you should ride in the back of the truck under these blankets," he said, "until we pass the toll bridge."

Homer jumped in the back. "Okay, let's go."

Paul started up the engine and made a U-turn on the narrow coastal road. It was only a couple of miles until they reached the creaking wooden toll bridge across Matanzas Inlet where Paul handed the tender a dime. A quarter mile past the bridge he stopped so that Homer could move into the cab, and so that he himself could dash around to puke in the rain-filled grass.

When he took his place behind the wheel again and resumed driving, Krug, smelling the fresh vomit on the boy's breath, sought to change the subject.

"Where are we now?" he asked.

"We just passed Summer Haven."

"Who lives there?"

"The Mellons."

"And they are?"

"Rich people from Pittsburgh."

"No one else?"

"A man named Passos or something who writes books."

"What kind of books?"

"I dunno. Did you really have to kill him? He was a *friend* of mine." Paul broke down bawling.

Homer looked over at him with a mixture of understanding and cold logic. "Let me tell you something, young fellow—is it Paul?—you have to realize, Paul, that in total war everyone is involved. On the other side there are no civilians, there are no innocents, there are no friends. I told that man I was a fisherman—that my fellow workers on a fishing boat were just dropping me off. If he had accepted that, he would still be alive tonight.

"But no. He said no fisherman he knew was ever dressed the way I was dressed, and he was probably right. And he said no fishing boat carried a dinghy like the one I rode in on, and he was right again. And he said any bunch of fishermen who had to come ashore would have sat around the beach for awhile instead of taking right off, and I think he was probably right there, too. Then he asked me flat out, are you a saboteur or something?

"And that's when I knew he had to die." After a pause he asked, "Are you feeling better?"

"No."

They rode in silence for awhile. Homer tried again to lighten the mood. "What's this road called?"

"Ocean Shore Boulevard."

"Boulevard," Homer repeated with a condescending laugh. "I wonder what they'd call a four-lane road."

In the main White Surf cottage Homer sat by Hans's sickbed and, after commiserating, described the events of the landing.

"Your son said he knew the man."

"He gave Paul a ride home after school today," Hans said. "It's too bad the boy had to experience that. If I weren't so weak I could have handled the business myself."

"Can we depend on the boy's secrecy?" Homer asked warily. It was an important question. Any sign of doubt in Hans's answer and—

"The boy is absolutely obedient and reliable," Hans answered. "He will say nothing. I'll stake my life on it."

Maybe you just did, Homer said to himself, then added aloud: "Well, it's over now, and we can also forget the code-name. I'll be going by my real name, Krug. Peter Krug."

"Yes, I know your real name, since Lorenz sent me the documents you'll be needing."

He reached for the general delivery envelope and opened it. "Here's your Illinois driver's license, an auto insurance policy, and the title to a car. It's parked outside in back, a forty Pontiac with Illinois plates, what I thought a Chicago man might be driving. Here's a Selective Service System Notice of Classification, four-F—you have a heart murmur. Be certain you carry that card on your person at all times. A Social Security card, three Army Air Corps ID's, a private pilot certificate for conventional aircraft, and the medical certificate that goes with it."

Krug examined the documents closely. "They certainly look authentic."

"Lorenz does good work," Hans said. "Now there're some hitches with the pilot's certificate and the Air Corps cards. First, private flying's been suspended for a few weeks. You'll have to watch the papers to see when it resumes. Second, before the eighth of last month, every pilot in the country had to obtain a second validating ID, because of security concerns, obviously. The new card, like the license, is issued by a regional Civil Aeronautics Administration office. It contains a photograph, fingerprint, and signature of the pilot along with a CAA signature— Lorenz sent me a blank card with forged Chicago CAA signature, a sample completed card, and some fingerprint ink.

"Tomorrow morning, before school, Paul, who's very good at cameras, will take some photos of you, and print out a small square glossy that we'll gum to the card. Then we'll have you sign it and affix your right thumbprint. Now the Air Corps cards need the same kind of work: photo, fingerprint, and signature. We'll do them at the same time. We've got three cards: one in the grade of captain, one, major, one, full colonel, all with the same serial number. Lorenz sent up an Army olive drab shirt with propeller and wings insignias on the collar. We'll use that. He typed in color of hair and eyes—and type O blood; I hope that's correct."

"It doesn't matter."

"And religion, Catholic."

"It doesn't matter."

"Any questions?"

"Yes," Krug said, "my watercolors."

"Oh yes, thanks for reminding me. In the trunk of your

car you'll find a complete set, with the kind of paper Lorenz told me you requested, and a folding easel and stool. I picked up everything in Jacksonville—used, as Lorenz instructed."

"Good. My whole purpose in coming to this particular city first is to establish myself as an artist. That's my cover. I want my name and work to become known to a few other artists in case I need them to vouch for me. St. Augustine is supposed to have a winter art colony of some repute—"

"I don't know about the repute. I know there's an Art Association here headed by a man named Benoni Lockwood."

"I'll make myself known."

"Now, about your quarters. I've got you a room at the Alhambra Hotel, in the middle of town, starting tomorrow."

"All right, that's fine."

"The night clerk there is a man named Miles Zeigler. Everybody calls him Zig or Ziggy. He's seen everything, done everything. He's a fund of information about the city and Florida. But don't press him—he's a real American patriot type."

"Okay," Krug agreed. "In that connection, is there a chance that you and Lorenz might get picked up by the FBI simply for being aliens?"

"Oh yes. There've been a number of aliens seized already. And Lorenz has heard a rumor that there's a plan to round-up and intern every German and Italian alien on the Atlantic Seaboard—the way they're planning to intern all the Japanese on the West Coast."

"Well, I hope they leave Lorenz for last. I'll be needing him."

Hans leaned up on one elbow and pointed down the hall. "We've got a room for you here tonight, second door on the left. Tomorrow, after we fix up your cards and licenses, Paul will take the truck to school. He'll have to be a little late for classes, but I'll write an excuse. Can Paul get you something to eat or drink? I'm not being a very good host."

"No thanks," Krug answered. "I appreciated the coffee in the thermos. It warmed me up. The ocean was a bit chilly on my legs and feet. I don't want to catch a cold."

"The temperature's going down to the forties tonight," Hans advised.

"But I have to tell you, Ohlenburg, that that was the worst tasting coffee I ever had."

"Oh, I have to apologize for that, Krug. The water out here is from artesian wells and it's sulphurous. When I first moved here I thought it smelled like rotten eggs. But I guess I've gotten used to it. Maybe somebody will invent a pill that will remove the sulphur."

"Maybe," Krug said, getting tired and bored now, and wanting a good night's sleep to prepare himself for all he had to do tomorrow. He let Ohlenburg talk on a few minutes more.

"Like they did down at Marine Studios," Hans continued. "When they opened that place in thirty-eight they found that the sea water they were pumping in by the millions of gallons to keep those specimens alive clouded up with so much algae no one could see anything through the portholes. It looked for awhile as though the whole multi-million dollar project was a bust. Then, the curator there, a fellow named McBride from the American Museum of Natural History in New York, found that if you added minute traces of a copper compound to the water, the water cleared up completely."

"In other words," Krug said, "little things mean a lot."

"I guess so."

"One little thing you need to do tomorrow is see a doctor," Krug said, standing up.

"*Ja,* I guess so."

"*Gute Nacht.*"

"*Gute Nacht.*"

As Krug walked down the short hall, he caught a glimpse of Paul in his room. The light was out, the room silent. The youth was seated at the window, staring out to sea.

CHAPTER 10

THE DAY BEFORE, after checking into the Alhambra Hotel, Krug had walked the short distance to clothing stores on St. Augustine's King Street and Cathedral Place. At one, he purchased a $40 navy blue Worsted-Tex gabardine suit with vest, a less expensive Glen Plaid double-breasted suit, a brown houndstooth sport coat, a tan sweater, several pairs of trousers, and an assortment of shirts. At a second, he bought a topcoat-raincoat, a mackinaw jacket, two pairs of shoes, one military style, the other double wing-tip brogues, a gray snap brim hat, ties, and underwear. At a third, he found a money belt and a large suitcase. Back at the hotel, he changed into one of his newer sets of clothes, then walked several blocks to the street where he had left his car and placed his U-boat clothes in its trunk until such time as he could dump them. Then he wandered about the small city center.

Although he had not visited St. Augustine on the tour of Florida he had taken long ago with his parents, he recognized many of the same north Florida oaks and sabal palms, the same ghostly gray Spanish moss and thick-leafed grass, the same Prussian blue-ultramarine-touch of ocher sky, though the clouds here were of a completely different tone and density from what he remembered seeing in the more balmy southern counties; the same briny air, and the same slow pace of life; except that, where the local residents ambled, the winter visitors, identified, a merchant told him, by their darker clothing, fairly quick-marched down the streets. Most of the pedestrians, locals and visitors alike, wore semiformal attire, the men in suits and hats, the women in dresses and hats. Some wore topcoats.

Certain of the downtown streets, like European-narrow Aviles, Charlotte, and Marine near the river, were evocative of the city's Spanish origins. There one saw numerous houses of native coquina, ground floors stuccoed over in age-mellowed gray and ocher, and, on the second floors, weathered wood plank balconies that did arabesques over the brick pavement. Patio walls in antique patina sheltered gardens bright with annuals and red bougainvillea, green with hibiscus, oleander, and coral vines. What peach-colored afternoon sunlight did not fall directly on these scenes sifted as gentle shade beneath fig, pomegranate, and sweet orange trees. No wonder, Krug thought, the quarter attracted artists. Every splash of the palette on paper would re-create some real color here before his eyes.

The next morning, in his room, he broke out the water-color box and foldable tripod easel and stool that Ohlenburg had obtained for him. The varnished hardwood box had the look of long use, as did its contents, which was good. Ohlenburg had purchased wisely, and better than he knew. The box had probably belonged to a professional, to judge from the quality and variety of sable and ox hair brushes, the selection of moist watercolors in tablets, with a few colors in tubes, particularly Payne's gray and some blues that were not ordinarily found on an amateur's palette, and the assortment of ancillary materials such as sponge, white wax stick, cotton swabs, masking fluid, watercolor varnish, and rubber cement.

He made a short list of materials he would want to add, starting with the first necessity—paper. The paper that Ohlenburg purchased was the wrong weight, in single sheets, and too small. What he needed were blocks of twenty or twenty-five sheets lightly glued at the corners, larger in size, cold-pressed, 140 pound weight.

After unfolding and refolding the easel and stool several times until his movements in doing so were easy and natural, he carried his equipment to Aviles Street where he found the city's only advertised art supply store. The proprietor regretted that he had left in stock only three single sheets of the weight and size Krug required. He would be glad to sell him those, and a shipment of large pads such as Krug wanted was due in Saturday afternoon. Could he wait until then?

Well, did he have a choice? He concluded he did not. Placing an order for three blocks of paper, he paid for the three available sheets and for a few additional articles from the store's otherwise good inventory, including a cardboard case for finished paintings.

There was much to admire in the oils and watercolors that hung outside on the bohemian street's coquina garden walls. But he could not linger long today to study other people's work. Instead, he walked south a short distance and set up his easel on the corner of Aviles and Cadiz, where, by moving about slightly, he could paint four different perspectives of the conjoining streetscapes on a single large sheet. He resolved to use just three pans of moist colors from his palette box: Cadmium yellow medium, Prussian blue, and Alizarin crimson carmine, plus the white of his paper. The paintings were only exercises, but more rewarding than he could have anticipated, since his near-final fourth effort caught the approving attention of a passerby artist, Tod Lindenmuth by name, who introduced himself, stated that oils were his medium, and that his wife worked in pastels, but he knew good watercolor work when he saw it.

Krug explained that he was just in from Chicago.

"I'm on my way to the Monson for coffee with Benoni Lockwood," Lindenmuth said. "Have you met him yet? No? Well, you should. If you're finishing soon, why don't you join us?"

"I've heard of him," Krug said. "Head of the local art club or association?"

"Yes," Lindenmuth said. "The Monson's just down behind you on Bay Street."

"Thank you," Krug said. "I'll pack up here in a few minutes and join you there."

At the Monson, over what was very good coffee, better, he had to acknowledge, than what was then available in Germany or France, Krug took advantage of the chance to imprint his name and face on Lockwood, who seemed a pleasant enough man, and certainly knowledgeable about every person who had raised a brush in St. Augustine. He named the artists who were active in the city that winter, which Krug made an effort to remember. It was all very interesting at first, and the conversation enabled Krug to establish his bona fides, but it came to be boring after awhile, and Krug was anxious to get back to his paints. Excusing himself, with thanks for the company and the coffee, he carried his equipment to the central Plaza de la Constitución, where he set up in front of the Spanish-Moorish cathedral.

St. Augustine, he found, was an incongruous amalgam of the old and the new, the miniature and the gigantesque, the tasteful and the shabby. Antique stuccoed remnants of the colonial past stood alongside flashy cocktail bars, and what might have been an Old World skyline was marred by gas and water tanks, neon signs, and, most obtrusive, an eight-story Exchange Bank Building that overwhelmed the palm-fringed plaza and the narrow streets around it. Indeed, though Krug was no friend of religion, he had to wince at the sight of the cathedral with its well-proportioned campanile diminished by the bank edifice rising only yards away—a juxtaposition not helped by the architect's attempt to "Hispanicize" the structure with Moorish domes, cast terra cotta ornamentation, and a watchtower.

He was particularly appalled by north St. George Street, called in the hotel travel folders the "oldest street in the country," in a town where everything was the oldest something or other, which was a joke because everything here was spanking new compared with what one found in the old cities of Germany. And in Germany one would never see such a junky collection of buildings as existed on St. George, made all the more ugly by power and telephone poles and webs of overhead wires. The spectacle made him appreciate anew the neatness, charm, and beauty of his native German cities.

Still, there were certain individual features of St.

Augustine architecture that were attractive to the eye, accounting for the number of artists here, and Krug decided to concentrate on those. Which he did for the next two hours, until he got hungry and headed back to the Alhambra.

In his bedroom he studied the weight and texture of the cold-pressed paper and decided that it was just what he had hoped for. He took the sheet on which he had painted the streetscapes and turned it to its reverse side. Then, on the dresser top, he arranged several items that he had purchased at Touchton's Rexall Drug Store that morning: two eye cups, a box of toothpicks, and three bottles of St. Joseph's aspirin. He opened the three aspirin bottles and dumped their contents into the toilet, after which he filled the bottles with the pyramidon tablets he had brought with him on the U-boat. Then he filled one of the eye cups with water and dropped in a single pyramidon tablet, stirring it with a toothpick until it was dissolved. With the toothpick and eye cupful of solution, he returned to the watercolor paper and, dipping the pick in the solution, wrote carefully on the paper. The moist lines vanished as they dried.

Krug let the paper set for an hour while he perused the morning paper. The headlines were not reassuring: RED ARMIES LAUNCH NEW ATTACKS ALONG BOTH ENDS OF FRONT . . . ALLIED PLANES RAIN NEW BLOWS ON JAPS' BADLY MAULED FLEET. He wondered how much of that was just propaganda. He would sooner trust the version in Berlin's *Völkischer Beobachter*. Far more worrisome was an AP story on the front page, datelined Palm Beach:

WEALTHY BARON IS ARRESTED AT PALM BEACH

(AP) Baron Fritz von Opel, wealthy Palm Beach and Nantucket, Mass. yachtsman and shooting enthusiast was arrested by Federal Bureau of Investigation agents tonight as a "potentially dangerous alien."

A quantity of guns and ammunition were seized at one of the residences involved in tonight's raid.

God! Krug thought, no one was more potentially dangerous than Lorenz at Eden! If Lorenz was picked up, Krug would have no way to get his information out—and no way to get home to Germany. Damn the FBI! Well, no good would be done by worrying over things that might never happen. Better to proceed as though everything would fall into place, as planned.

After an hour had passed, he plugged in an iron that he had borrowed from the front desk and slipped a dry towel under the section of watercolor paper on which he had written. When the iron was hot, he ran it over that section. As he did so, brown-colored letters clearly appeared: TODAY I HAVE FOUND PAPER THAT WILL SERVE JUST FINE.

He stood up straight to admire the result, and, after disconnecting the iron, took a pyramidon tablet in his hand, chuckled, and said to himself: Hans Ohlenburg was right—a little something in the water makes all the difference. Then he tore up the painting into small pieces, which he placed in his pockets for disposal later.

He wondered now what there was to do around this town while he waited for his paper pads to arrive on Saturday. He really needed to get to work! But there were no army airfields near by. All he could do was practice his paints, eat seafood, and go to the movies. He wondered if there was any gambling in town. That was the one side of decadent America that he had enjoyed in Chicago during his late teens, he had to admit it: blackjack, dice, and the horses at Arlington. It was his one vice. Wasn't he allowed *one?* He enjoyed it because he was good at it—or lucky. And now he had more money in his belt than he ever dared dream about back then. Of course, it was money belonging to the Third Reich. But he had not been placed under any restrictions as to its use, so long as he employed it in the fulfillment of his mission. And certainly that mission would be all the better served, he concluded, if he caused the money to grow. . . .

He decided to go downstairs to the desk and ask Zig, or Ziggy, or whatever his name was, if there was any action.

The referee used his shoes to tamp down battle scars on the tanbark pit. Then he raised his right arm for silence.

"Tenth fight!" he called out over the continued murmuring of bookies and bettors. He consulted his card. "Between Spanish Red—weight four-thirteen—and Single Malt—weight four-eleven and a half!"

Loud cheers from the crowd echoed off the ceiling of the open-sided pavilion while a fresh February breeze momentarily cleared the stands of tobacco smoke. Two men entered the pavilion with fighting cocks in their arms, stepped down into the pit, and presented the birds for inspection to the referee.

"Excuse me," Krug said to a man seated on his left in the stands, "can you tell me what's going on there now?"

"Referee's checkin' the gaffs," the man answered.

"The gaffs?"

"Yeah. You don't know nothin' about this?"

"No."

"The cocks got natural spurs on the back o' the legs and the handlers strap steel gaffs over 'em. They're about two-and-a-half inches long, curved, with sharpened points. The birds cut at each other with those things. And they have to be strapped on just so. That's what the referee's checkin'."

"Thank you," Krug said. "And do they fight rounds like in boxing?"

"No, usually they go at each other for twenty or thirty minutes until one of 'em is killed or declared a loser. Sometimes the referee will continue a fight in a pit outside."

At the referee's direction, the two handlers took positions on opposite sides of a line that divided the round pit that Krug estimated was five meters across, where they flaunted their birds at close quarters, leading the feathered contenders to bristle and peck wickedly at each other.

"Better get your bet down now, if you wanna make one," the man said.

"I don't know how to choose between them," Krug answered.

"I never give a tip," the man said. "Best way to make people mad at ya."

Krug nodded and the artist in him decided that he liked the bird with the gold, rust, and iridescent black-green feathers. He yelled at a bookie passing two rows in front: "One hundred on Single Malt!"

"Tall man a C-note on Malt!" the bookie confirmed.

The handlers stepped back from the center line, dropped to their knees, and placed their birds on the bark floor. When the referee yelled "Fight!" they released them.

The birds advanced toward each other warily, crouching and feinting, Spanish Red thrusting his long neck, Single Malt ruffling his feathers, each glaring at the other, waiting for an opening. Suddenly they exploded in a midair collision, their fearsome gaffs raking repeatedly at flesh. The crowd roared admiringly.

No sooner had the birds dropped to earth than they were aloft again in another blurry tangle of beaks, wings, wattles, combs, and polished gaffs that flashed in the afternoon light.

And so it continued, up and down, up and down, as shrieks from the crowd shook the cypress rafters. Krug found himself yelling, "Come on Malt, kill him! Kill him!"

Then the two birds came down together in a thud, and lay there, locked in an awkward embrace, wings beating slowly. The referee called, "Handle!"

"What's happened?" Krug asked the man alongside.

"Red's gotta gaff stuck in Malt's breast."

"Is that bad?"

"Bad fer yer money, not fer mine."

The handlers had rushed to their birds, separated

them, and rubbed their legs and thighs until the referee called again, "Fight!"

"Ten seconds is all they get to do that," the man said as fighting resumed. Red immediately sprang onto his wounded foe, leaping on top and striking again and again with his fierce weapons. At first, Malt appeared unsteady and defenseless. Then, remarkably, he lunged at Red and bowled him over, biting at his wattle with an angry beak, and attempting a cut with his right gaff. The recovery brought cheers from his worried backers.

But Red escaped the charge apparently unhurt and returned to the fray with dominating force, savagely holing the weaker bird, whose blood now stained the pit floor. When at last Malt lay motionless under the sharpened steel assault, the referee, confirming the obvious, declared loudly: "Fight won—by Spanish Red!"

The winner's fans whooped joyously while Malt's handler carried his vanquished, lifeless form out of the pit, and the bookies moved efficiently through the seats to settle wagers.

"I think dice is my game instead," Krug said to his seatmate.

The man laughed. "It takes a while to get to know the good birds," he said. "So you like craps? The cockers run a good game after the fights at the Alhambra Hotel about eight o'clock on. I've played a number of times."

"That's where I'm staying," Krug said. "In fact, it was the desk clerk there who told me about these fights going on here north of the city."

"That would be Zig?"

Krug nodded.

"Zig's a good man. When the cockers wanted to extend their crap table Zig had carpenters there in thirty minutes to take out the wall between rooms twenty-six and twenty-eight. Relocated the couple that was in twenty-eight. That's real service."

"Yes, it is," agreed Krug. "Thanks for the information."

As he waited for the next fight, Krug's eyes surveyed

the crowd, noticing for the first time how many of those in attendance were women, perhaps a third. It started him thinking about the advisability of linking up with a woman for cover purposes. He had not wanted to, and had said as much to Groskopf at Hamburg. He much preferred to travel alone. But Groskopf had insisted. "Always travel with a woman" was Abwehr doctrine, since, as Groskopf asserted, a woman companion deflected notice from a man's activities and rendered the couple, in the eyes of otherwise watchful guards, innocent, feckless tourists. Isn't that how Kurt Frederick Ludwig had the success he did in April and May 1941? Groskopf argued. Accompanied by eighteen-year-old Lucy Boehmler, a Stuttgart-born beauty who could pose as either a daughter, a sister, or a springtime-winter wife, Ludwig gained entrance to military bases and camps from New York to Key West, and was able to send Hamburg a constant stream of data, including photographs, most with Lucy in the foreground. The problem with Ludwig was that, not being an aviator, he did not know what to look for, so there was nothing in his dispatches about aircraft performance. It was no great loss to air intelligence, therefore, when he and Lucy were caught up in the FBI's grand slam last summer.

There was another operative who came to Florida with a woman, Krug remembered. Groskopf had mentioned a Yugoslav businessman-agent named Dusko Popov, codenamed Ivan, who was sent out by Pan American Clipper from Lisbon last August expressly to report on airfields in Florida. He and the woman got to Florida all right but not a single item of intelligence came back from them. Groskopf figured that they spent all their Abwehr funds having a good time in Miami. Krug wondered if Popov turned double-agent.

Well, traveling with a woman no doubt had its advantages. But Krug wondered if those advantages were decisive. He had no doubt that he could pick up a woman. From a decade of bedding frauleins he knew that, when he chose to, he could project an irresistible force field. Even without trying, like Fighter Arm General Adolf Galland, with his crash-smashed face, he emitted an unconscious and automatic charisma.

The other sex would come to him.

He could afford to wait and see what happened.

Sally Parkins stepped down from her coach car on the Seaboard Air Line train from Miami and quickly entered the straw-colored Flagler System station.

"God, it's cold here," she said to no one in particular. "Isn't St. Augustine supposed to be in Florida?" Three people on the station benches looked up but said nothing.

A Negro porter put his head in after her. "You lookin' for a porter, ma'am?" he asked.

"Yes, I am," she said, smartly. "I have two suitcases"— she handed him the check stubs—"and be sure a trunk in my name, Miss Parkins, comes off the train and goes into Railway Express storage. And then get me a cab with a driver who knows the better hotels."

"Yes'm."

While the porter went about his business, Sally studied her pale reflection in a station window. Removing her hat, she patted her ginger hair into place, reflecting as she did so on what an unjust world this was, what with her skills as a hoofer, and being one of the nicer looking Jills around with a first-class shape in every respect, but the Miami clubs were hiring nobody but blonde tap dancers. No gingers, no brick-tops, no black heads. Didn't matter if a broad was square as first base with most of her weight in the knees, if she had blonde hair she was star-quality, $30 a week.

Well, Sally was damned if she was going to dye her hair for thirty per, and damned if she was going to do any heavy lifting, either—she hadn't left Manhattan to do that—besides, there was bigger money than thirty clams to be had hustling Daddy Warbucks at Hialeah and Tropical and at the dog tracks, and getting staked to a few Cs at the gaming tables at night and laying six-to-five that Daddy makes his eight. And the do-re-mi had mounted up, and she was living in higher style than any tap dancer, except that she had to bed down in a fleabag on Seventh Street in order to put money into high fashion clothes, which she needed to be escorted to various mansions by various daddies, but, hell, you were unconscious in bed, so who cared where you slept when you were alone.

And when a daddy likes a doll he will show it in diamonds, and she had collected her share, one as big as a manhole cover, which she kept, but the others she had sold to get cash because once the daddies started getting romantic with rocks they tended to neglect the bank-roll, as though cash was beneath the dignity of their new relationship, and that was when she had had to start rifling the daddies' wallets while they slept.

Which had caused all kinds of problems, what with one guy, a self-important Warbucks from Cleveland, planting a John Roscoe in her ribs to get his C-notes back, and another, a full colonel doll chaser, waving a six-piece and threatening to call the police, which she doubted that he would ever do as long as his little woman was still at home taking care of the kids and would not want to learn about this particular part of his military experience; and, in his case as she climbed out of bed and put on her bra, panties, dress, and shoes she recited several times as loudly as she could a war poem of her own composition:

> *The titties grow*
> *Row on row*
> *In Philanderers Fields*

and walked out, slamming the door behind her. She thought it was a major cultural statement the way she did it. But two rods in a row, *plus* mention of the police, plus the fact that word about her was bound to spread among the daddies, and she figured that her contribution to the Miami scene this season was over.

And so here she was in this pony burg St. Augustine, which people said was also a winter resort but without the tap dancers and the horses. There were plenty of daddies about, but most of them were upright prigs with their wives in tow. Still, there had to be pigeons somewhere here, and she didn't mean weekend soldiers or sailors with their frigging $21 a month.

"Got jer bag, ma'am," the porter announced through the doorway. "Trunk's in Railway Express, ma'am, jes as you say, an' the taxi's waitin' at the curb."

Sally handed him fifty cents, which she thought may have been excessive, but even these Negroes had a way of getting word around on who was important and classy, so she thought it was money well spent.

Getting into her cab, she directed the driver to head toward the center of town. "And fill me in on the best hotels," she added.

"That would be the Ponce, ma'am," the driver answered, "followed by the Monson, the Buckingham, and the new Castle Warden."

"What's the tab at the Ponce?" she asked.

"Ten dollars a day, American Plan."

Christ! she thought. That's as expensive as Miami. "How about European?"

"Ain't no European there, ma'am."

"Well, I only go European," she said, escaping that embarrassment. "Let's try one of the others you mentioned."

"They're all filled, ma'am."

"*Filled?*"

"Yes, ma'am. The cockfighters are in town."

Cockfighters? What the shit were they? Some kind of pervert boxers? But she didn't let on, of course, because it was important never to let on.

"Cockfighters," she repeated. "I should have remembered."

"They always come to the pit show here right after the Deer Island mains near Orlando, you know?"

"Yes. Well, is there another hotel you'd recommend where there might be a vacancy?"

"I hear tell there's a room or two at the Alhambra, ma'am, across the street from the Ponce. A bellhop told me earlier t'day some people checked out."

"Is it a decent place? I'm a respectable lady, as you can see."

"Oh, yes, ma'am. Just stay away from the bar on weekends when the servicemen are in town, and you'll get along just fine, ma'am."

The driver pulled up to the Alhambra entrance. As Sally got out, she looked resentfully at the huge Spanish-style, twin-towered goddam American Plan Ponce opposite, and pledged that somehow she would dance in its ballroom, if it had one, before the week was out. Her cabbie fetched a gray-jacketed bellhop and, after paying the fare, straightening her hat, and pulling on her wrinkles, she glided into the Alhambra lobby with as stately a step as she could manage and with a bearing of head and eyes that signalled to the desk clerk and to anyone else who might be present that she was gracing this establishment only because there was no place else in town for a lady to go.

"Good evening, ma'am," the clerk greeted her. "May I help you?"

"Yes, I'm told that in a very crowded city you may have a vacant room."

"One left, ma'am, I'm pleased to say." The clerk, a short, wiry, balding man, reached for a registration form. "On the second floor without a private bath. Two-fifty a night. Very clean. I'm sure you'll like it."

As she filled out the form, Sally heard a group of men approach the stairs behind her talking loudly about "shufflers," "gaffs," "drag pits," and sums of money, the last category, of course, catching Sally's immediate full attention:

"Two Gs I won on that roundhead," said one.

"All I had was dunghills," said a second. "Lost five hundred on the day."

"See you guys in twenty-six after food?" asked a third.

As they mounted the stairs, Sally ventured a guess to the clerk: "Cockfighters?"

"Yes, ma'am."

"And what is twenty-six, may I ask?"

"Oh, that's a room on your floor, ma'am, but far enough away that you won't be disturbed."

"I gave you my name, sir. What is yours, may I ask?"

"Zeigler, ma'am. Miles Zeigler. People call me Zig or Ziggy."

Sally leaned forward. "I'm very interested in people, Zig. What happens in room twenty-six?"

"Well, the cockfighters have a high-stakes dice game in there, ma'am. Not anything a lady like you would be interested in, I'm sure, ma'am."

"As I said, Zig," Sally confided, "I'm very interested in people. I'd like to observe that game."

"Well," Zig hesitated, "you have to show two C-notes— that is, two hundred dollars—just to be admitted—"

"Thank you, Zig," she interrupted with a knowing smile. "If the bellhop will take my luggage, I'll go on up to my room."

It was not hard to find room twenty-six after supper, as Sally simply followed the sound of brassy voices and the mixed fragrance of whiskey and tobacco. She was in her tightest, if not her best, dress. A confident knock and the door opened to a very smoky space crowded with bodies.

"Yeah?" said a guy packing a Betsy in a shoulder holster.

"Hi, big boy," Sally said, spreading two C-notes for his inspection.

The door guard smiled, said, "Come on in, doll, and fix yourself a drink," and followed her movements with a low whistle of approval, which did not surprise Sally at all since she knew she was a curvaceous scene.

Quickly, with a practiced eye, she checked the table: real money in front of the players, high denominations, no chips. And serious rolling, nobody rubbing the dice in his palms or blowing on them or saying, as they do in the streets, "Come on, baby!" These shooters were pros.

In shirtsleeves, some with suspenders, the men ranged in age, she figured, from low thirty to high sixty, each holding a fistful of bank notes in one hand and a drink, cigarette, cigar, or a broad in the other.

Sally checked the competition: one peroxide looker, maybe high twenties, in need of a bustle; one flat-chested tomato definitely faded around the edges; one wide doll, brunette, forty-odd; and a gray thing with alcohol eyes in an over-painted pan. The line definitely did not favor the house in this division.

She made her first move alongside a thick-set old crutch who held the biggest wad at the table and seemed to enjoy the hip contact more than he should, at his age.

"Oh, you're such a pretty sugar puss," he said to her, and slipped his right hand around her waist. "Bring me some luck, cutie. I've got plenty on the table that says Blinker George won't make his six."

And when Blinker George went belly-up on a seven, the old crutch celebrated by rubbing his hand several times across her panty line, which, of course, gave her the right to say, "If I had a daddy who'd stake me to a couple of Cs, I could have fun, too."

Which the old crutch did right away, knowing it was a small price to pay where someone this gorgeous was concerned.

And Sally immediately made good on a two-C side bet that one very handsome thirty-odd stick-out the rest were calling Lucky Krug would bang a ten stone cold.

She asked the crutch, "How long will you all be here, daddy?"

"Leavin' day after tomorrow's hack," he answered. "Goin' to the mains on an upper floor of an office buildin' in Jacksonville, then to pits in Fort Lauderdale an' Tampa. Keepin' the cocks movin'."

"How about these beautiful ladies?" Sally asked. "Do they travel with you?"

"Oh, yes. Some of them are wives, some aren't. Are you for rent, pancake?"

"No, I'm not, daddy. Only for long-term lease. Thanks for the stake." She moved quickly away to take a position in back of the man named Krug, whose gentleman's face was like java to her cream. Now, from behind, she admired his tall muscular frame. And, of course, she studied the green and gray contents of his left hand. Without question, Lucky Krug had it all—a wad, a pan, and a bod, in that order, which, as all the smart dolls knew, was a trifecta.

She eased up alongside his right side and clapped her eyes on his right peeper. After a moment, he turned to acknowledge her with a thin smile.

"Good evening, Miss."

"The name's Sally. How come they call you Lucky?"

He laughed. "Oh, I just joined the game an hour or so ago and hit nine straight. I got lucky and they started calling me that. Real name's Peter."

"I like Peter better," she cooed. "Are you a cocker, too?"

"No," he drew out the word, "I'm just a guest in the hotel. I'd never seen a cockfight until today."

"I think they're fun," she said. "What's your dodge?"

"Dodge?"

"Yeah, whadaya do for a livin'?"

"I'm an artist."

"You paint *pictures?*"

"Yes."

"Well, slap the mooch! You're the first artist I ever met. I didn't know artists gambled."

"Most don't, I suppose."

"Do you dance? You know, ballroom dance?"

"So so. It's been awhile."

"There's nothing I want more in all this world than to go dancing on Saturday night at the Ponce de Leon Hotel across the street. I asked the desk clerk when I went down for dinner if there was a band there and he said, yes, in something called the Venido Room, and they're called somebody and his Rainbow Room Sextet. I would just *love* to go dancin' to that New York sound. It's where I'm from."

"Well, why don't you?" Krug asked.

"I need an escort," she said, plaintively, and added, "You must think me forward for saying that," lowering her eyes in mock shame.

Krug paused for a moment, then said, "I have to stay here through Saturday anyway, so, sure, I'll take you."

Sally seized his right forearm. "Oh, Peter, you *are* a solid sender! We'll have a lotta fun! I'll go get us some drinks."

On her way, she swore that her hand had felt a shiv.

CHAPTER 11

AT NAS, NOB NORFOLK SEADROME, Bo Burke nursed his newly assigned PBY-5, Bureau Number 2359, into position for takeoff, taking care not to taxi so slowly that he fouled the engine plugs. This was his crew's first operational scouting and search mission in the two and a half days they had been here on detached duty from Jax, learning first how to load and fire guns and then how to arm and drop real depth bombs, not the 100- and 300-pound water bombs they had practiced with at Jax. Thank God their squadron skipper there had been able to get them out of lectures and signal drills and into operations here at Fifth Naval District (5ND), where everyone seemed to know there was a war on.

Bo looked out with satisfaction to port and starboard at the four Mark 17 325-pound depth bombs that hung in racks from hard points on the wing, hydrostatic fuses set at 25 feet. The crew had .50 cal guns in waist blisters, a .30 cal in the bow, and another in the tunnel, each with 450 rounds of belted ammo. Fifteen hundred gallons of 100 octane sloshed aboard the wing tanks, enough for twelve to thirteen hours of flight time. Everything worked out for weight and balance on the Librascope. Bo's Bombers were ready for bear.

Simmons in the waist-hatch compartment reported: "After station to pilot. Ladder is in, sea anchors are in, waist hatches secured for takeoff."

"Very well, Waist," Bo acknowledged.

After completing his checklist with Plane Captain Bernard in the cabane strut, Bo advised the seadrome controllers: "Norfolk tower eighty-three P-six in position and ready for takeoff."

"P-six you are cleared for takeoff," the tower replied. "Right turn out of pattern approved."

Bo turned to First Pilot Ray Hope in the right seat and said, "Ray, let's uncoil this spring."

Reaching overhead, he slowly pushed the throttles to the wall, marveling as he always did at the noise, vibration, and momentum that the throttles unleashed—although the rational side of him knew that, despite its initial displays of engine thrust, the PBY was basically underpowered and that it was always a challenge for the boat to break the suction and drag of the water's surface.

The longitudinal "V" of the hull's bottom provided initial directional stability as P-6 got underway between the buoys. The nose came up as power was applied and Bo held the elevator control back in his belly in order to prevent heavy spray from getting into the engines and reducing power. This was all the more critical today, since, with a freshening 8-knot wind, there was wave action in the sheltered water of the seadrome. The roughened surface had its advantages, though, since it would reduce suction. At 65 knots the boat was "on the step," riding on the notch, the discontinuity on the planing V-bottomed float, the last buoyant bit of the hull to stick to the water.

Abruptly, P-6 broke away and became airborne. The time: 1725, eastern war time.

Bo signaled Bernard to raise the wingtip floats, increased airspeed to 85 knots, in order to have control in case of an engine failure, and then began his climb out at 2450 rpm, 36 inches, or 800 feet per minute. In the interphone Ray sang, "Oh you'll never get to heaven in a PBY 'cause the goddam thing won't fly that high."

"I learned some lyrics to a song down at Breezy Point," Bo said.

"The PBM hangars?" Ray asked.

"Yeah. Those guys were established as VP fifty-five, you remember, and then redesignated seventy-four about eight months ago. Great guys. They can really party. Anyway, they've got an ensign there named Durant. 'Bull' Durant they call him. He started a squadron song. Part of it goes:

We fly in the daytime, we fly in the night,
Through weather that gives us a fright,
We cover the ocean
With tender devotion
But never a sub do we sight.
Now Norfolk, Virginia, the home of us all,
A helluva hole I recall,
Yet yearning and burning
We live for returning
While under the tables we sprawl.

"Hey, that's great stuff!" Ray said. "A regular Irving Berlin."

"Yeah, there's more. Who's playing navigator? Singer?"

"Affirmative."

Bo pulled the carbon mike closer to his lips. "Sam, you on the charts?"

"Aye, aye, Bo. I liked your song."

"Thanks. Better give me a heading. I'm leveling off at two thousand. The big bad Atlantic is dead ahead. I'm reading one-zero-zero."

"All right, Bo. Fly one-five-zero. That'll put us on the northwest edge of the search grid. I estimate we'll be on the corner off Oregon Inlet in about one hour fifteen."

"Roger that. One-five-zero."

Bo nosed over into cruise altitude, trimmed, and reduced power to 2000 rpm, pulling 30 inches, 110 knots indicated. Then he stood on the right rudder pedal and turned the aileron control slightly to starboard. The lumbering Catalina agreed, finally, to bank onto course 150 degrees.

As it did, Bo imagined that he was on the outside in another aircraft, watching his Cat make that move. In his mind he watched the 104-foot long wing flex up and down, admired the way its topside No. 71 nonspecular blue-gray paint scheme blended in with the Atlantic coming up below, and sensually approved the thin waist with the big tail—like a number of girls he had known. He even resonated patriotically to the flaglike red and white stripes on the vertical stabilizer. He would never forget how crushed he had been when he was first assigned to P-boats, but now that he had bombs under the wings, he and PBYs had come to terms.

In fact, Bo was one of the few navy pilots who thought that the PBY design was aesthetically pleasing, even graceful. Most pilots disdained the ungainly profile of the "yoke boat," as they called it. There was a saying in military aviation: "If it looks right, it is right." To many the Catalina just never looked right; unlike the new, larger Martin PBM Mariner—now *there* was a patrol bomber! But the Catalina looked perfectly right to Bo, and he had no desire to transition in PBMs. Hell, the PBM was even more underpowered than the PBY. At Breezy Point the day before, he had watched a Mariner try three times to take off from smooth water, without success.

As a matter of fact, he felt in his gut that the PBY would end up the war just as successful as the PBM, despite the latter's greater bomb load, longer range, and faster speed. Call it blind loyalty to make such a claim for a float boat that was technologically obsolescent, by even Bo's concession, but there you were. The Cat might just fool everybody—in everything but speed, of course. Certainly not even Bo could assert that the Cat was a good performer on the airspeed indicator. "She climbs at ninety, cruises at ninety, and glides at ninety." That's what PBY pilots said, but they said it affectionately. And it was an exaggeration to start with, since Cats regularly cruised at 110–115. Sure, even that was painfully slow, but let's just see, Bo would argue, what the Cat could do in the war. Kick a U-boat's ass, he bet.

To date, no U.S. Navy aircraft had clearly sighted and positively identified, much less attacked, a U-boat off the Carolina capes. Not a PBY from Norfolk or Elizabeth City. Not a PBM from Breezy Point or from Darrell's Island in Bermuda, BWI. Not an OS2U Kingfisher from Inshore Patrol, or any other aircraft of the Navy or the

Army Air Corps. Nor had any surface warship made the confirmed acquaintance of a U-boat commander, though the lone ASW vessel of any size to operate off capes Lookout, Fear, and Hatteras, the 165-foot *Argo*-class U.S. Coast Guard Cutter *Dione*, had been dropping depth charges on presumed underwater contacts since January. Meanwhile, the U-boats—no one knew how many were grazing in the Carolina pastures—had sunk sixteen freighters and tankers in this immediate vicinity alone since January 18, and sent two other ships, damaged, into port. And dozens more ships were going down elsewhere on the seaboard, from Canada to Florida. Not only ships, but hundreds of merchant seamen were dying, many of them in the rectangular search area where Bo and his crew were headed. Some were being blown apart, others drowned, some were being maimed by sharks, others dehydrated or starved. A great human disaster was taking shape on America's doorstep. Add to that the loss of desperately needed war cargoes that were funneled through these sea lanes from Florida, the Gulf of Mexico, and the Windward Passage: iron ore for steel, bauxite for aluminum, tin, rubber, phosphate, and cotton—"beans, bullets, and black oil."

Bo knew from his briefing at Norfolk by Section B8, 5ND, Operational Intelligence, that some ships and seamen could be saved by the simple act of keeping the U-boats submerged. It was known from British ASW experience that U-boats dived at the first appearance, however distant, of an aircraft, even at night. And that was important since, while submerged, under battery power, the U-boats' speed and maneuverability were greatly retarded: it was not possible for them to keep up with merchant traffic, much less to maneuver into optimum torpedo-launching position. So, if Bo and his crew failed tonight to sight and attack a U-boat directly, they might still perform a ship, cargo, and life-saving service by keeping some German commander's head down and out of the hunt. Or they might locate an open boat of survivors and vector a rescue vessel to its coordinates.

But, of course, Bo wanted more. He wanted a German commander's cap, with or without the head inside it. He remembered with searing anger and humiliation the greeting he received from the refueling boats off Florida. Apart from Belle's love there was nothing he wanted more in life than a U-boat kill, or two, or three—make it more. There was nothing like getting shot at to focus your hostilities.

"Navigator to pilot. You're at the corner," Singer reported from the nav station. "Take new course heading zero-nine-zero."

"Zero-nine-zero," Bo acknowledged as he wrestled the Cat to port and established the first leg seaward of their assigned search sector.

"Cranking in the autopilot," he told Ray. "Let's go to glasses." In the interphone he called: "Pilot to blister lookouts. Mark One eyeballs and seven-fifties. Continuous sweep. Stay alert. Report any disturbance of the surface, I mean the smallest speck. Any crease in the sea may have a periscope sticking out of it. Look for a feather wake. May be only two feet in length, last only for seconds. Out."

Ahead, the Atlantic was darkling gray as sunset approached and choppy from the passage of a mild, fast-moving occluded front and the backing of surface wind to northwest, force five. Estimated surface temperature 35 degrees. Light showers from cumuli that had preceded the frontal passage had cleared, and where P-6 flew at 2,000 feet below a four-tenth's cover of strato-cumulus at 2,500, there was relatively good visibility at dusk in all quadrants.

Sunset was fifteen minutes away. That was the time when U-boats, if there were any present, would start to appear on the surface. During the daytime hours they bottomed out on the continental shelf, both to conceal their hulls and to conserve their fuel. Then, with nightfall, they surfaced to ventilate the boats, charge batteries, and hunt for targets.

Contrary to popular belief, as Bo and his other pilot officers had learned at the Intelligence briefing, U-boats did most of their traveling and fighting on the surface, at night, when their low silhouettes were hard to sight and their high speed under diesel power, estimated at 18 knots, enabled them to maneuver around and past ship targets in order to make textbook bow position attacks. Underwater, their speed was too slow, and their battery power too limited, to make periscope attacks practical, except in rare cases.

There had been something of a lull in U-boat activity in these particular waters since the middle of the month. Most of the sinkings since the 14th had taken place off New Jersey, Delaware, and Florida. But the lull was bound to be broken, Intelligence said, by the sheer attractiveness to U-boats of the large number of ships, northbound and south, that nightly plied the dangerous passage around the Outer Banks and their extended underwater sand dunes, or shoals: Wimble, Lookout, and Diamond. "Vessels in mortal peril," the Intelligence officer had said grandiloquently. "A stately, doomed procession. Their U-boat killers will be back—and soon."

The briefer's rhetoric aside, he was proved right: the U-boats were back. The preceding midnight, off Wimble Shoals, a U-boat sank the American bulk iron ore carrier *Marore*, bound, loaded, from Chile to Baltimore. All thirty-nine of the crew got away in three life boats. The survivors aboard two boats were picked up by a passing tanker, *John D. Gill*, and the others were rescued by a Coast Guard motor surfboat and taken in to Big Kinnakeet Lifeboat Station at Avon, six miles north of Hatteras Light. Survivors reported that, following the torpedoing of their ship, the attacking U-boat used its forward deck gun to fire over 100 artillery rounds at the abandoned hulk. So intense was the shelling, some thought that there were three U-boats at work instead of one.

A copy of the Coast Guard official dispatch on *Marore* was posted at the VP-83 operations building for the attention of all pilots.

One or three U-boats, whatever the number, Bo wondered if he could *see* one, now that twilight had come on. He at least knew what a U-boat looked like. What two of them looked like, in fact. He even had pictures. That was why 5ND was eager to have him when Jax inquired if they were interested in an extra crew on detachment.

"You'll have a waxing moon, close to full," Intelligence had said. "And look for phosphorescence—the wake of greenish light caused by a sub's disturbance of surface organic material."

Bo had forgotten that. He called on the interphone: "Pilot to blisters. Watch now for phosphorescence—any band of green light."

Aye, ayes from the blisters.

It was probably too light yet to see something like phosphorescence. Twilight would last for an hour more. Bo darkened the instrument lights as far as it was safe to do so. Then he twiddled with the throttle quadrant, fine-tuning power and pitch, and looked over at Ray, who was sweeping with the 7 x 50s. Bo grabbed for his own glasses and joined him. They were coming up on some low-flying scud, wispy clouds left in the wake of the front, so that the ocean surface could only be seen in patches. He thought of going below the scud but decided to wait.

The Cat droned on—until: "Port blister to pilot!"

"Pilot. Go ahead."

"Sir, I have a long black object appearing on the port quarter! It may be a sub surfacing. I think it is, sir!"

"Good work! Keep it in sight. Plane is banking your side."

Automatic pilot off. Rudder and aileron hard-a-port.

"Pilot to crew! Battle stations! Weapons cocked and ready!"

Ray reached around behind the seats to throw the red cover toggle switch that activated the bomb release key on Bo's control wheel. "Firing key activated," he reported.

"Roger."

Bo kept a close watch on the turn and bank indicator to avoid a stall. At the same time, he pushed the yoke forward to begin a power glide, setting for 2,500 feet per minute.

"Port blister to pilot. I still have him, sir! Heading southwest. Not fully surfaced, I don't think. Decks awash. Scud makes it hard to get a constant sighting."

"Pilot. Roger. Ray, break out the Recognition Book. None of our subs are reported in this area."

With the turn nearly completed, Ray joined the chorus.

"Two points more to port and you'll be right on him, Bo. Three miles or less ahead, crossing our course obliquely from our port to starboard. Looks like a seven hundred forty tonner, according to the book."

"Okay. I don't see him yet," Bo responded. "Descending to two hundred. Speed one fifty. *Okay, now I see him!* I bet he hasn't seen us because of the scud! There're men on the tower. Now they're scrambling, going under, diving! I can't delay to get a better approach. Got to go for him now! Half a mile—quarter—"

"Bow gunner open fire!"

The forward hull of the aircraft shook from the recoil of the .30 caliber fire in the nose, which was Singer's station, while acrid smoke from burned gun powder filled the pilots' compartment.

Bo ordered, "Tunnel gunner! After bomb drop, sweep the deck with your fire!

"Aye, aye, sir!"

"Clear your gun now!"

"Aye, aye, sir!"

With the Intervalometer set for a stick of bombs at forty foot spacings, the DBs would drop in train rather than in salvo. Altitude now 200, descending to 100. Speed 150. Bo would have liked to go to 50 feet, the preferred bomb release altitude, but dared not with the sorry depth perception that twilight provided. He also would have liked to have a clean bow or stern-on approach and make a perfect straddle with his bombs, hoping that one or more would fall within the so-called lethal range of 24 feet. But he had to take what he could get, and at least this was better than a straight beam attack.

Now he saw the U-boat's tower in sharp detail, a narrow

black form passing through a gray mass of bubbles and foam generated by the sub's submerging forward hull. Wordlessly, in deep concentration, oblivious to the MG fire, and to Ray, intent instead on the dimensions and course of the sub, watching the foam, forward, the tower, now disappearing, center, and the rough, confused swirl of water forming at the sub's stern, he selected the exact moment to press the firing key, and watched eagerly as the DBs port and starboard severed from their arming wires in perfect sequence: one-two-three-four. No hang-ups.

"Four dropped!" the plane captain confirmed when the stick was completed.

Bo kicked left rudder, pulled into a climbing turn, and looked aft. He saw the water spurts sent up by Simmons's venom in the tail. Then, after sinking to their preset 25 feet, the DBs detonated in train, sending white water skyward in four violent geysers. Bo continued his climbing turn to 500 feet and began circling the attack position slowly, looking for results on top the tangled water.

In the narrow aft torpedo room, made all the more confined by the presence of three reserve torpedoes, each seven meters long, 1,608 kilograms in weight, Kapitänleutnant Günther Böhm began his stern-to-bow inspection of the U-boat interior before surfacing into the western Atlantic twilight. Wearing red filter goggles to adapt his eyes to the darkness outside, he watched the torpedomen, with hoist rings and chains suspended from an overhead I-beam, guide a grease-coated G7e electric torpedo back into number 5 tube after its every-three-day inspection and adjustment. The men, called "mixers," had examined every critical component of the "eel's" propulsion system, its gyropots and guidance controls, and its depth-keeping mechanism. On the eel's business end, or warhead, they had checked the Pi-G7H impact pistol, with its corrosion-inviting zinc guard flap, to make sure that upon impact with a ship's hull it would faithfully detonate the warhead's 280 kilograms of high explosive charge. Finally, they had ventilated the light lead storage batteries that provided power to the underwater missile and prepared them for recharge by the diesels when the boat surfaced.

"Number five eel inspected and ready for launch, Herr Kaleu," reported Petty Officer Karl Matz, on behalf of his smiling, oily, sweat-gleaming mixers.

"Very well," Böhm acknowledged. "We'll be surfacing shortly. I'll try to find you targets and free up some of this space."

He ducked forward through the circular watertight bulkhead hatch into the one clean compartment, apart from the galley, on U-*Böhm*. Here, in the maneuvering and electric motor room, were the twin Siemens-made dynamotors, or E-motors, that propelled the boat underwater, and the storage battery switching panels that dispensed power to the lights, radio, hydrophone, and other electrically operated equipment.

To the two E-mates, Axel Kremser and Hans-Gert Strack, Böhm said, "Prepare E-motors for surfacing."

"*Jawohl*, Herr Kaleu."

The next forward hatch led Böhm into the starkly contrasting engine room where he stood upright amidst the twin Buchi-supercharged, gray-painted MAN diesels, blackened hull walls, slippery floor plates, and thick sweet fumes of diesel oil. At the far end of the now-cold engine blocks, he sighted Chief Machinist Josef Schwendler oiling his nine-cylinder rocker-arm hinges on the starboard side. Schwendler respectfully stepped down and back when he saw the Old Man approaching, in order to let him pass. Böhm quickly moved through the shoulder-width gangway between the diesels and stopped before exiting forward.

"Schwendler," he said to the chief machinist, who held an oil can and a wad of cotton waste in his black-smudged hands, "I'm not going to order you to light the diesels until I'm sure we're alone topside. I'll keep us on E-motors for a few minutes in case we see something and have to dive. So if you feel the boat start to dance on the surface and hear nothing from us right away, don't be concerned."

"*Jawohl*, Herr Kaleu." Schwendler was always grateful when the Old Man told him personally what he was planning. It was not anything he had to do. On other boats, as Schwendler knew, commanders were content to communicate with the diesel machinists solely through the established means of engine telegraph, flashing lights, alarm bells, and loudspeaker. Böhm was considerate enough to take the petty officers and ratings directly into his confidence, which helped greatly to relieve the sense of isolation felt by crews in the after part of the boat. Even though the engine room was directly abaft the control room and tower, Schwendler and his machinist mates felt far removed from the boat's essential actions. Rarely did they have a sense of where the boat was, what it was doing, apart from diving or surfacing. Still more rarely—sometimes several weeks intervening—did they have a chance to see the sky.

In the control room, Böhm stepped around the periscope housing and checked the German war time clock on the port wall. According to local sun time in the almanac, advanced by one hour to U.S. eastern war time, surfacing should be safe about now.

"Chief," he said to Engineering Officer Heinz Brünner, "prepare to surface in ten minutes. I'll give the order after I inspect the forward torpedo room."

"*Jawohl*, Herr Kaleu."

Böhm stepped through the hatch that led to his private, curtained bunk space on the port side of the single-level gangway, and, on the starboard opposite, the radio and sound rooms. These were the domain of the puster Peter Krug had liked, Chief Radioman Kurt Schneewind, who alternated radio and hydrophone duties on six and four hour watches with another radioman, Hans-Jürgen Bauer, and two others of lower rank.

Beyond were the bunks of First Watch Officer (I WO) Franz and Second Watch Officer (II WO) Baumann, and the engineer. Here, too, was the wardroom drop-leaf where Böhm and the officers ate, conferred, chatted, read, wrote, or played the board game, *Mensch ärgere Dich nicht*.

Overhead ran thick bundles of cables and pipes, while underneath the floorplates from this point forward to the torpedo room bulkhead lay battery arrays numbers 1 and 2. The sixty-two-cell pasted-plate type storage batteries, which supplied power to the motors and panels in the maneuvering room, weighed close to 60 tons and were placed in the center to near-forward part of the boat to offset the weight of the diesels. Böhm checked the battery logs to make sure that the lead-plated energy cases had been properly inspected for acid levels and possible contamination by saltwater.

The petty officers' aluminum-frame bunks came next. Their heavy blue-and-white-check gingham sheets and pillowcases showed the grime and body stains of six weeks' continuous use as "hot bunks" by rotating sleepers. The stinking sides of the gingham, like those on all other bunks on board, including Böhm's, would not be reversed until the voyage home.

Next came the galley, to starboard, with its Vosswerke stove, two ovens, three hot plates, short standing refrigerator, sink, and busy cook, Rudi Hohmann. To port stood the lone working head with its elaborate step-by-step procedures for discharging fecal and urinal content.

Once through the next bulkhead hatch and into the forward torpedo compartment, which had four torpedo tubes to the after compartment's two, Böhm was relieved to find the "Lords," as naval ratings were called, alert, excited, even buoyant. They seemed to sense that something special would happen tonight, if only the launch of one or two eels, since that would allow them to place a reserve torpedo or two in the tubes and free up room to bring down the folding bunks that were now pressed flat against the hull. Because of the unexpended torpedoes, and the space they took up in an already cramped compartment, the torpedomen, technicians, and lookouts who were assigned to bunks here had been taking turns sleeping on the floor plates—"hard lying"—which was normally a form of at-sea punishment. Just finding a place to sit amidst the torpedoes and Rudi Hohmann's columns of tin cans filled with meat, potatoes, vegetables, lemon juice, and ready-cooked meals was a challenge, although standing upright and walking about in the compartment were less impeded now that the perishable breads and fruits that once hung from the overhead in nets and hammocks had been consumed. Of the fifty-one men on board U-*Böhm*, these bow-dwellers were the most inconvenienced by the boat's failure so far to find targets.

In various forms of warm clothing, mostly standard blue-gray fatigues with pullovers or jackets, the crewmen seemed to be warm enough, despite the fact that all else they had for comfort were a few space heaters. Humidity was high: fog formed in halos around the wire-guarded lamps. The air one breathed, now more than ordinarily fusty from twelve hours' submergence, was part oxygen, part noisome vapors, and no one could say which was the greater. Yet, these young men, eighteen to twenty-three years old, did not appear to mind their hardship and privations, their gray faces and weak voices. They were flinty, tenacious, unswerving, devoted, happy adventurers, and damn the inconvenience!

Böhm looked into the eyes of each petty officer and rating: Krauss, Sturm, Seidel, Erben, Wagoner, Borchert, and the rest.

"Men, I know that this has been a sour-pickle time. Six weeks delivering a passenger to Florida and then standing off Hatteras for a full day and night, and we can't claim a single ship in the locker. I have a feeling, though, that our luck will turn tonight. So look alive. Do your duty. I'll try my best to bring down a bunk or two for you hard-lyers."

The men smiled broadly at their commander and at each other as Böhm ducked out and made his way back through the fore-and-aft passageway to the control room, which, when he reached it, was poised for action.

II WO Baumann and four lookouts stood by in leathers

and blue wool forage caps, gloves, scarves, and night-adapting goggles, with long-cylindered 7 x 50 binoculars hung by straps around their necks.

Baumann knew that Böhm would want to be the first man up the ladder when the tower broached the surface, but after the Old Man's first quick reconnaissance around the compass rose, it was Baumann's turn to stand the watch.

He looked while the Old Man climbed into his own leathers, which he kept hanging from a stanchion near the navigator's table, donned his peaked cap with the white cover and verdigris-encrusted insignia, and reached for his 7 x 50s.

In the center of the control room, which measured ten paces fore and aft and five across the beam, the engineer Brünner awaited Böhm's order, as the planesmen and technicians in the control room awaited his own. Two planesmen sat facing the hull on the starboard side, in front of depth and trim gauges, with the palms of their hands resting on hand grips alongside the "up" and "down" buttons. Large black steering wheels served as backups to the electrically operated buttons. The planesmen's function was to operate protruding bow and stern hydroplanes, which, like an aircraft's horizontal stabilizers, caused a submerged, trimmed, and moving submarine to pitch up or down in the water.

On both sides of the control room, technicians stood by a warren of pipes, valves, levers, and red and black hand-wheels. Their task was to close vents on top of the exterior ballast tanks for the expulsion of seawater that the boat had taken on board when it dived; to release the compressed air that expelled the water; and, when finally surfaced, upon explicit order, to open the diesel air intake and exhaust valves that would permit the diesels to be engaged for surface propulsion and for flushing any remaining water from the diving tanks.

All the while, Kremser and Strack, at their controls in the maneuvering room, would provide E-motor power to help drive the boat dynamically forward to the water's surface.

"All right, Chief," Böhm said to Brünner, "keep the

boat heavy just in case. Be prepared for hard-a-dive. *Periscope depth!*"

The chief yelled: "Blow negative!"

At once, the always startling sound of compressed air filled the control room, while experienced hands, here as in the maneuvering room, whirred rapidly in unison among the wheels and levers, left, right, and overhead.

As ballast water vented, Böhm and his crew received the first sensible indications that the boat was rising: the plates beneath their feet moved, the welded high-tensile steel hull tilted upward, and Rudi's sausages, hanging from the overhead, began to sway like pendulums. The boat bounced once and then, as the depth manometer showed the engineer, began a steady ascent from its relatively shallow bed on the continental shelf.

"Boat rising slowly," Brünner observed. "E-motors ahead one-third!" he ordered the maneuvering room. "Bow up fifteen, stern up ten!" he ordered the planesmen, who with their brass buttons began "flying" the submarine skyward.

Böhm pounded up the ladder into the conning tower, followed by the bridge watch.

The bow planesman reported the depth in meters from the manometer until reaching 17 meters, when he reverted to the more accurate column of mercury in the periscope elevation indicator.

"Periscope depth!" he sang out at 13.5. Böhm took a quick look around with the sky periscope. "All clear," he said. "Surface!"

"Ten . . . eight . . . six-five," Brünner reported. "Tower hatch is free. Boat's on the surface."

While these reports were being given, Böhm and the watch clambered up the final ladder to the tower hatch wheel where Böhm disengaged the spindle and pushed the hatch cover open. Built-up pressure in the boat nearly propelled him up and out as he came up easily onto the dripping bridge platform, Baumann and the lookouts behind him.

Quickly, Böhm swept the horizon with his binoculars.

Nothing. No destroyers. No patrol craft. No trawlers. No merchant ships, either. Thin, low, scattered clouds overhead obscured much of the early evening sky. The lookouts took up their stations and began their rhythmic bridge vigil, scanning their lenses back and forth slowly, inch by inch, across their assigned sectors, holding the binocular barrels lightly on their fingertips and the rubber-cushioned eyepieces tightly against their browbones.

Böhm looked fore and aft with his bare eyes. It was nice to feel the sea again, he reflected, as the hull, still three-quarters submerged, pitched and rolled in the Atlantic swells. It was safe to light the diesels and come fully to the surface. As he moved toward the bridge voice pipe to give that order, it was not one of his lens-equipped lookouts who gave the warning, but Böhm himself, whose unaided eyes, quite by accident, caught the stark, dark, terrifying form of a twin-engine aircraft diving out of the clouds, four points off the starboard bow, three kilometers distant, and making for the deck!

"Flying boat!" he screamed. What he called down the voice pipe was: *"ALAAARM!"* As Böhm and the bridge party poured through the hatch in a blur, Böhm wheeling the cover spindle home in its bed, heads, mouths, hands, and feet below began a series of near-simultaneous, automatic actions.

Brünner ordered the ballast tank vents reopened to the sea, and banged the ball of right hand against the diving bell: *Brring! Brring! Brring!*

The bow planesman hit the down button and sang out: "Forward down twenty!" The stern planesman did the same: "Aft down ten!"

The chief bos'n, Böhm's Number One among the noncommissioned crew, shouted over the loudspeaker: "Every man to the bow!" Immediately, the stern torpedomen and the diesel machinists, though not the electricians, control room crew, or pusters, began stampeding the length of the boat, hunched and running down the narrow passageway, up and through the circular hatches, grunting and cursing, into the bow compartment, to join those who had been forward of the control room in a standing squash of flesh, whose weight forward would sharpen still further the angle of dive.

Böhm, his boots hitting the floor plates with a loud pop, ordered Brünner: "Rig for depth charge! Go to seventy meters!"

The chief noted the time on the dive: "Twenty-five seconds, Herr Kaleu," he whispered, following a speech habit formed by alarm dives to avoid the sound detection gear of warships, but unnecessary now. The bridge was below the surface again and there was ten meters of water above the hull. It would have taken ten seconds longer to reach that depth had the decks not been kept awash.

While the chief watched his depth manometer and inclinometer bubble, Böhm took a position by the navigator's table, and, like everyone else, held on.

"Fifteen meters," Brünner barely got out of his lips when—

Click-CLANG!

The boat shuddered and teeth shook. Off the starboard bow.

Click-CLANG!

The deck plates rattled and the hull ribs moaned. Again, off the starboard bow.

Click-CLAANG!

Instrument glass cracked, sparks sprayed, and knees buckled. Off the port beam.

Click-CLAAANG!

The pressure hull lurched, steel shrieked, glass flew from wall to wall, lights flickered. The boat listed at an angle of 60 degrees and began falling out of control. Off the port quarter.

Round-eyed men struggled to keep their footing.

The lights flickered twice more—and went out.

CHAPTER 12

BO'S WATCH READ: 0140. He could see the ranging 14-mile beam of Diamond Shoals Lightship coming up on the port bow, as 83-P-6 neared the finish of its last westward leg of the night.

Both Ray and Sam Singer had spelled him in the port pilot's seat, enabling him to stretch out for a while, though not to sleep, for who could sleep after the excitement, and the frustration, that he had been through earlier that night?

What he had expected to see on the ocean's twilight surface—cauldrons of water and bubbles formed by escaping air mixed with oil, floating debris, perhaps a body or a commander's cap—he did not see. Despite the fact that he had cruised over the position for forty-five minutes, he did not sight the least damn evidence of a sub's destruction. Nor did anyone else on board, even when he released the port and starboard flares.

It was a textbook Class C attack—the sub just under water, the swirl plainly visible, the DBs an imperfect straddle maybe, but a straddle. He had every right to claim a kill. But the German Navy had not cooperated—goddamn them, anyway.

He looked at his watch again. They should be back at base in an hour forty. He double-checked fuel remaining with Bernard in the tower and made a decision.

"The lightship is where we're supposed to break off and head home off the banks," he said to Singer, who was on the controls as first pilot in the starboard seat. "I say let's continue on over Hatteras and go up the land side instead."

"Sounds good to me, Bo," Singer agreed. "A few spits of land, a few lights, would look good right about now."

"Just wish I knew what happened to that sonofabitch sub," Bo said, irritably, at the exact instant when McClusky at the radio bench, who was on split phone watch, monitoring two CW circuits, Norfolk on one ear, ships' distress frequency on the other, began writing quickly on his message pad. When finished, he switched his left ear to interphone, "Radio to pilot."

"Go ahead, Sparks."

"I have a distress signal on five hundred KCs: 'Triple-S, Triple-S, Norwegian motorship *Leif* torpedoed at lat thirty-four, forty-five North, long sixty-nine, twenty West. Sinking rapidly. Need immediate assistance.' End of message."

"Okay, Sparks, rebroadcast that in its entirety to base, in case they didn't get it. The brass pounders at Norfolk can vector a merchant ship to pick those people up."

"Aye, aye, sir."

"Ray, you on the phone?"

"Aye, aye, Bo."

"Well, the lull in sinkings is definitely over. Where is that position Sparks gave relative to us?"

After a pause, Ray reported, "Way the hell behind us, Bo, and to the south, off Cape Lookout. We could never make it there and get home, on our fuel."

"Not much we could do there, anyway," agreed Bo. "Whadya think? Is that the work of the U-boat we attacked?"

"I'm inclined to doubt it. Our U/B was east of Oregon Inlet, latitude thirty-five, forty-seven. I don't think a U/B could grind away that many degrees south and east in the time we're talking about. I could be wrong, but I doubt it."

"So we have more than one commander out there tonight," Bo suggested.

"Looks like it. Unless the guy we went after is dead."

"Well, we can't prove that even to ourselves," Bo conceded. "Anyway, we sighted one of the bastards and bombed him balls-on. That's more than anyone else at Norfolk can say. It might gain us a few illicit drinks at the BOQ when we get in."

"For breakfast?" Ray asked, laughing.

"They can slip it in our bug juice."

As the Catalina came on top of the lightship, Bo asked Singer, "How'd you like to serve on a lightship like that, Sam?"

"Be good for readin' and for fishin'," Sam answered.

"That fellow who gave us the briefing at section B-eight told me some things afterward about Hatteras and the lightship," Bo said. "The guys who serve on that ship— there're sixteen of 'em—stay on station there for a year at a time. Locally, they're called 'wave wallowers.' The Hatteras people are supposed to be descendants of shipwrecked English sailors. They have a Devon accent, the guy said, and use words like 'heerd' instead of 'heard,' and 'couthy' for 'capable,' and 'fleech' for 'flatter,' and, lemme see—'scunnered' for 'disgusted.' I'd like to hear people using those kinds of words sometime."

"We could drive down on a day off," Sam suggested.

"I know the rest of you guys are ready for a day off, and we get one tomorrow. Remember, we're scheduled to go out again later today, at fourteen hundred, maybe a different sector. For myself, I'd just as soon go out every day, I'm so pissed. But I can't ask that of the rest of you."

"Hey, Bo," Ray came on the interphone to say, "speaking of words like you were a moment ago, how about another verse of your song?"

"Okay. The only other words I know are:

Elizabeth City in North Carolina
Is a place where we spent too much time.
In the Starlight Club hazy
We thought we'd go crazy;
It drove us from women to wine.

First, there was the slender stalk of the sky periscope and the short, foaming V-wake that followed it, as the U-boat commander, seated at the saddle of the periscope sight in the conning tower, just below the hatch and above the control room, trained the lens around the sky with his left foot pedal, while, with his right hand, he focused the eyepiece in its rubber housing. Then, that periscope down, he elevated the attack periscope and surveyed the ocean surface. In the darkness, neither scope was likely to disclose an enemy's presence, especially the attack scope with its inferior light transmission, but the commander thought his actions prudent and appropriate.

Finally, the entire wide frame of the U-boat broke the surface bow-high, in a froth of bubbles, like a shark's head, ugly with menace, fanged. It rose to its full buoyancy, as heads quickly appeared on its narrow bridge, and glass lenses bristled in all quadrants, reflecting glints of moonlight from the now scudless sky.

In the belly of the steel tube oil-black hands fired the diesels, starboard ahead one-third on its shaft and propeller, port on line to the dynamos for charging batteries. The diesel air intake valve on deck was kept closed momentarily so that the engines could take a suction through the hatch and ventilate the sour air inside the boat, as far as that was possible, which was never very far.

With the valve opened, finally, and the diesel exhaust fumes fouling the night air aft, the U-boat sliced slowly through the dark surface, seas pouring out the limber holes where the forward deck met the diving tanks, and gray suds scalloping from the bow wake. The exhaust roar of explosions from eighteen diesel pistons filled the air. Astern, the starboard bronze propeller left a greenish trail of phosphorescence, which was barely visible in the competing moonlight.

The night was clear, with good visibility, wind northwest four, seas running three. The breaking tops of whitecaps came across the foredeck in sheets of spray, as the boat rose and fell, and, what the Type IX was wont to do, circled slightly at the top of a roll, to do an elephant dance.

On the bridge, the white-capped commander took one last look around and ducked below.

"Maintain two-two-zero, one-third ahead," he instructed the watch officer, who, with the lookouts, continued the painstaking bridge watch, straining through long lens barrels to sight any sign of merchant traffic: a curling trail of smoke, a pair of mast tops, a white bridge screen. Expecting that any ship in these lanes would be blacked out, they focused not where it might be on the horizon but slightly above it, for those were the experience-learned quirks of optics. At the end of each sweep, they allowed the 7 x 50s to hang on their chests while they unwound their triceps and monitored the sea and sky with bare eyes, each man harnessed to the bridge brackets as a precaution against being washed overboard by a freakish wave, as had happened numerous times, most recently on 31 December when Second Watch Officer Weinitschke was lost overboard off U-701 en route to Newfoundland in force four seas and medium swell. Then, with glasses in hand again, they swept the bloomed Zeiss lenses back across their sectors, looking, seeking, hoping.

At exactly 0930 German war time (0230 EWT), the port forward lookout, scanning from his right to left, stopped still like a seized engine. After five seconds, he shouted to the second watch officer, "Herr Leutnant!"

The officer positioned his binoculars in parallel with the lookout's. Then, he leaned forward to the voice pipe, "Commander to the bridge!"

Instantly, Kapitänleutnant Böhm was on the ladder to the top, where II WO Baumann directed him to two points off the port bow.

"Running with her damn lights on!" Böhm observed. "Red and green position lanterns and lights amidships. Doesn't she know there's a war on? Coming out of a mist. I estimate four miles distant, crossing south to north."

"Can't be British or Norwegian," Baumann offered.

"No. They'd know better. Probably American. A good bit out from shore, wary of the shoals. We don't have much habitation, it seems, on the Outer Banks, so there's little chance to silhouette her against shore lights. But the lighted Wimble Shoals buoy will help. And we have the moonlight, and her own damn lights, which is the best help of all."

"Both ahead half!" he ordered the helmsman in the tower. "Come to two six-zero-five."

The drag and trill of the engine telegraph came up the hatch from the red-lit helmsman's station. The boat leaned slightly to port as she answered the rudder.

Böhm and Baumann watched the target come to them on her heading around the shoals.

"Must be feeding time," Böhm said. "Just before I came up, the puster handed me an intercept from Feiler in U-six fifty-three, who's operating in our same naval square. He sank a Norwegian motorship in square CA ninety-nine. About thirty-five minutes ago."

"Do you know Feiler, Herr Kaleu?" Baumann asked.

"Never met him. He's not in our flotilla."

"Are you certain about the number—six fifty-three?"

Böhm asked down the voice pipe, "Puster, say again the number of Feiler's boat."

"Six fifty-three, Herr Kaleu," came the reply.

"That's curious," Baumann continued. "The construction series five fifty-one through six eighty-six are all Type Seven C. I know, because I served on six fifty-two, you remember."

"Damn curious, then," Böhm agreed. "A little boat like that has no business being this far from base. How does she ever expect to get back? What's she got for fuel?"

"A hundred and thirteen tons starting out."

"She'll never make it."

"I've heard of Seven-C commanders who increased their radius of action by filling their torpedo compensating tanks and even their drinking water tanks with fuel."

Böhm shrugged and grimaced. "Well, I'll worry about Feiler later. We have our own worries, although I must say our bomb damage was not as bad as I feared when we went plunging toward the bottom the way we did. The chief did a first-class job in righting the boat. We lost nothing serious, mostly glass. A few bent valves and busted pipes. We shipped some water. That's all. We should thank A. G. Weser, Bremen, for building us a stout hull.

"We—I—simply have to do better in anticipating those flying boats. This was the same kind of aircraft, Consolidated something—isn't that what Peter Krug told us?—that caught us off Florida. And this one had Wasserbomben. And the Wabos stung. A Seaman's Friday, I bet the crew are saying."

"Estimating three miles now, Herr Kaleu."

"All right. You and Franz get into position."

Böhm put his mouth to the pipe, "Battle Stations!"

Franz brought up the UZO, the target-aiming binoculars, and attached them to the UZO post forward of the periscope housing. By turning its fourteen-inch barrels on the post he connected its line of sight, or relative bearing to target, mechanically to the Siemens-made electric deflection calculator in the tower, which Baumann now manned and switched on. Following the directions of Böhm's glasses, Franz placed his eyes in the tubular spray shades and foam-rubber eye cups.

"I have her in sight, Herr Kaleu," he reported.

With the dimmer lever near the right eyepiece, he adjusted the movement of the luminous graticule, or aiming line, to the optimum brightness between light and dark.

"UZO is set, Herr Kaleu," he reported from his half-stooped position.

"Very well," Böhm acknowledged. "She's not zigzagging." Lowering his glasses, blinking hard, and raising them again, he observed, "Very little superstructure. She's a tanker, and riding low. Not large but loaded. And she has no gun."

Minutes later, Franz reported, "Target speed eight point five knots, judging from the second bow wake and time of her lights across the graticule."

"Launch one eel," Böhm ordered. "Set the depth at

three meters. Aim one point abaft the green lantern. That should get you inside the engine room. Permission to launch when ready."

Franz shouted down the hole to Baumann, "Open bow cap two! Set for three meters! Target speed eight-point-five, course three-five-zero! Range one-five-zero-zero! Angle on the bow Green fifteen! *Following!*"

At the calculator lamp board Baumann cranked in the numbers, including U-*Böhm*'s own course and speed. When the trigonometric solution came up in the gauges, he called back, *"Following!"* Seconds later, another *"Following!"* came by loudspeaker from petty officer Fritz Sturm in the forward torpedo room whose announcement confirmed that Baumann's solution, complete with an aim-off heading, was being transmitted through the torpedo launch receiver into the guidance system of the eel that occupied the now-flooded number 2 tube. Point four seconds after launch, on-board gyros would steer the eel's rudder vanes onto the exact aim-off heading.

"Range nine hundred!" Franz called, and, almost immediately after, hit the electromagnetic launch button, "Tube two—*launch!*" From the torpedo room Sturm confirmed, *"Launched!"*

The blast of compressed air that sent number 2 eel onto its independent, self-propelled, self-guided course toward self-immolation could be felt as a small jolt on the bridge. Below, one of Sturm's mates vented the excess compressed air inboard, a normal precaution against exterior bubbling, while Brünner in the *Zentrale* took 1,608 kilograms of seawater into the overhead regulator cells to compensate for the lost weight.

Baumann called up, "Running time fifty-eight seconds!"

Böhm leaned over the bridge coaming to watch the phosphorescent track left by the eel as it sped toward its long, low target. "Running hot, straight, and normal," the puster reported from the sound room. Franz had a perfect bow ahead attack angle of 90 degrees. If he did his numbers right, this one was a lock.

At one second past the time predicted—
WHACK!

A fierce white, eye-narrowing detonation just abaft the tanker's funnel sent a column of yellow-red flame, smoke, oil, water, and ship's parts two hundred meters into the air, obscuring the Western stars. White clouds billowed from the wooden deckhouse, and tongues of fire licked their way forward to ruptured deck plates and oil nozzles where, soon, deep red torches spat a more ugly smoke in dense, wind-blown plumes. "Crude oil," Böhm said to himself. "Bunker C."

The stricken hull immediately lost way and listed to starboard as falling shards and splinters fell hissing and steaming around it. Through his glasses Böhm watched grimly as knots of crewmen gathered at the starboard davits to lower a lifeboat, but had difficulty doing so because of the list. Finally, their boat came crazily down, hanging vertically for a moment in the forward falls, the men inside it toppling out like toys, and other men still on deck jumped one after another into the water to join the boat as it righted itself. A second boat appeared to be lowering with more success on the side opposite.

The crew had to abandon ship, of course. A tanker with a flooded engine room was doomed, even if its fires could be contained.

But now the men in their two boats had to contend with a flame-wrapped sea. Burst compartments forward of the bridge spilled flaming oil down the hull sides and into the water, where it spread rapidly in the swell action of sea state three. At times, the boats were lost completely to Böhm's view behind curtains of fire and thick black smoke, where he feared their occupants might either be fried or suffocated. Finally, both little crafts emerged seaward of the tanker, which was settling by the stern, and the survivors rowed hard toward the U-boat, which was the safest direction out.

Böhm would wait until the crew were safely away from the burning hulk before taking any additional action, if it was needed. Because of their compartmentation, tankers did not always sink after being holed by one torpedo. But he did not want to waste a second torpedo on a ship that, upon closer examination in this funereal light, was smaller even than he had thought—maybe 5,500 gross registered tons.

He would use his forward deck gun.

He turned to see Franz staring bare-eyed ahead, his features bright red from the fire, and his eyes focused in what looked to Böhm like raw fury. So fixated was that stare, the I WO did not train his eyeballs the few millimeters right it would have taken to return Böhm's glance, but, instead, like a dog on point, remained rigidly immobile in visage, position, and posture. Even when Böhm said, "Good work, Number One, perfectly placed," Franz showed no normal visible response.

The puster reported from below, "No radio message transmitted, Herr Kaleu. No SOS or SSS."

Good, Böhm thought. The radio shack must have taken a hit. A quick military response was unlikely, therefore, from Norfolk, the nearest base. And there were no warships or aircraft in sight.

Böhm looked down the hatch at Baumann in the tower and told him, "Number Two, alert your forward gun crew. I'm going to pass through the lifeboats, get an identification if I can, and see if we need to ventilate that tanker's waterline."

"*Jawohl*, Herr Kaleu."

Böhm returned his attention to the tanker. "Both ahead dead slow," he ordered, "starboard two."

It did not take him long to meet up with the lifeboats. He called Baumann, who spoke English, to come up with the megaphone and interrogate the survivors:

"What ship are you?"

A voice replied, "*Hennapoil.*"

"What registry?"

"USA."

"Is the master among you?"

"No. We're missing nine or ten."

"What is your tonnage?"

"Five thousand something, GRT."

"Take a heading of two-seven-zero and you will make land safely."

Böhm instructed Baumann, "Tell them I'm going to finish off their ship with artillery fire."

After Baumann did so, and then leaped down the outside ladder to command the 10.5-centimeter gun on the fore casing, Böhm ordered the gun crew to action stations.

Within less than a half-minute, the 10.5-cm aimer, layer, and loaders were in position. Ammunition ratings passed the heavy shells from magazines below teak planking on the lateral sides of the steel casing.

Böhm shouted, "Permission to fire!"

Baumann gave the order:

CRACK!

The first bright orange ignition cleared the barrel, startling Böhm with both the muzzle flash and the loud report. It had been awhile since he had used the gun. A specter of white smoke drifted aft. The second shot clearly struck the tanker forward, where a dark red wound appeared. A slight correction of the elevation enabled the gunners to hit the waterline seams, which they now proceeded to perforate from stem to stern. The pungent smell of cordite hovered over the U-boat bridge and stung the nostrils. Heat from the tanker inferno burned the face. The singing of shrapnel where the shells landed alternated with the sound of the gun.

In the noise and excitement of the artillery action, Böhm had not noticed that Franz had gone below and returned with one of the two handheld machine guns on board. Taking a position on the *Wintergarten*, the I WO opened fire on the lifeboats!

At first, Böhm's ears incorporated the MG fire into the general noise of exploding powder. Then, with a start, he made the distinction and wheeled around.

"Halt!" he yelled when he saw what Franz was doing, and ran through the lookouts to the *Wintergarten*. "Halt!"

he yelled again, and reached for the bucking hot barrel. "Halt!" he yelled into Franz's eyes as he wrenched the gun away from him.

"How dare you fire without an order. How dare you shoot survivors in the boats."

Franz turned a cold face toward Böhm. "They are our enemies, Herr Kaleu."

"They are *not* our enemies!" Böhm said sternly. "Not until they reach shore! Get below to your bunk." When Franz did not move, Böhm shouted, "At once!" Böhm took him roughly by the arm, and pushed him toward the hatch. The lookouts stood open-mouthed, their glasses at their chests. Böhm had to order them, "Carry on!"

With the mortally wounded frame of SS *Hennapoil* going down fast and hard by the stern, her funnel making water in a shower of sparks and her blunt bows heaving like a wounded hippo, Baumann had ceased fire on his own. He looked up to the bridge for further orders, where Böhm nodded and said, "Cease firing! Well done, Number Two. Stand down. Secure your gun." Böhm was now less interested in the tanker than he was in her crew.

"Both stop. Both back one-third," he ordered the helmsman at the telegraph.

"Bring up the searchlight," he ordered a lookout.

As the boat reversed course, and the bright yellow sword of the searchlight trained on the two lifeboats lifting on the swells, Böhm anxiously peered through his glasses for signs of damage or injury. When he came within megaphone range, he had Baumann shout over the grunting exhaust, "Has anyone been hurt?"

"Two in this boat," answered a soft voice.

"No one in this boat, you fucking bastard!" answered the other. "But thanks for the holes!"

Through Baumann Böhm addressed the first boat, "How bad are your injuries?"

"One man is dead," answered the same voice. "The other has an arm wound."

When Baumann translated this for Böhm, the latter

instructed Baumann to offer them iodine and dressings if they came close aboard. Böhm then ordered both engines stopped.

There was no answer for a full minute; then, the men in that boat bent to their oars and came alongside. A young seaman who could not have been eighteen or nineteen, Böhm thought, stood erect in the boat and said, "We'll take the medicine and bandage, sir. Our first-aid supplies went overside when the boat fell down the falls."

After this was translated for Böhm, he turned to the nearest lookout, "Go down and bring up iodine, dressings, food, water, and a compass."

"*Jawohl*, Herr Kaleu."

"Are there officers in your two boats?" Böhm had Baumann ask the seaman.

"No, sir. They was all in the bridge and poop."

"Dead or missing?" Baumann asked in Böhm's name.

"Yes, sir, and we're missing six others."

"Was your dead man there killed by the machine gun fire?"

"That's a fact. Tore half his head off, as you can see. An old fireman."

When he heard the translation of the man's reply, Böhm told Baumann to say, "I sincerely apologize for shooting at you. I'm the commander, and I am responsible. The shooting was not done on my order. And the man who did it will be punished. Please report that to your authorities."

"That I will, sir."

"Will you take the body ashore for burial?"

"We just talked about it, sir, but, Harry, he been a seaman all his life, and it seems proper-like to leave him here."

When this was translated, Böhm asked Baumann, "Don't we have some canvas shrouds in the forward compartment?"

"Yes, Herr Kaleu."

"Have somebody bring one up. And also weights of some kind."

After Baumann gave that order, Böhm thought for a

moment and added, "Number Two, assemble the entire boat's company on deck except the on-duty pusters and diesel machinists—and Franz. Go down and tell Franz personally that I do not want him to leave his bunk area." It was a hard order to give Franz's subordinate, but Böhm would not permit Franz's presence to dishonor the obsequies of the man he killed.

Soon, the bos'n had the petty officers and ratings in formal deck formation. Böhm, Baumann, and Brünner took their positions near the tower. The second lifeboat came tossing alongside the first and, after the body was shrouded and weighted, the men in both boats made an attempt to stand.

With no audible splash, the dead seaman Harry was committed to the deep, where he lingered briefly just underwater, ghostlike, and then slowly vanished into the corpse-thickened sea.

Böhm recited aloud the opening verse of the Twenty-second Psalm, as it was numbered in his Bavarian Catholic tradition: "The Lord is my shepherd; I shall not want. He maketh me to lie down in green pastures; he leadeth me beside the still waters," and he nodded his approval when Baumann asked if one of the petty officers might play a verse of a Lutheran burial hymn on his harmonica.

That interval of humanity over, and the men dismissed to their duty stations, Böhm watched briefly as the lifeboats rowed toward shore, then turned his eyes one last time in the direction of his 5,000-tonner. A small fish. Almost too small for the pan. But he would take her. What he really wanted was a 10,000-tonner. Freighter or tanker, it made no difference. The U-boat needed a big number victory pennant on the periscope when it tied up at home, if this whole voyage was to be worthwhile.

With the engines stopped, he could clearly hear the boiling and steaming where cold Atlantic water closed over the still-hot, fractured metal of *Hennapoil*, as he could also hear the crackle of the red flames that spread across the oily waves. Tomorrow, the beaches, fish, and wildlife would be visited by charred bodies, sodden lifebuoys, hatches, planks, ropes, coal dust, and the encrustation of black bunker crude.

Baumann handed him the completed Shooting Report on the *Hennapoil* sinking, which he endorsed.

It was time now to confront Franz.

"Start engines!" he called to the helmsman. "Port ahead full. Starboard on charge. Helm hard-a-port. Come to one-four-zero." To Baumann he said, "Circle around Diamond Shoals, then ask the navigator for a heading to Cape Lookout. We'll bottom out short of there at Ocracoke Light, in green water, on the thirty-six meter line."

He then dropped down the ladder and walked forward, where he found Franz seated on his bunk.

"Stand at attention!" Böhm barked.

He studied the ruddy, gray features of his short-statured, blue-eyed, flaxen-haired I WO.

"In my entire wartime at sea," he began, "I have never seen a German officer fire at helpless survivors in the water. How do you account—how do you *account* for this totally unprofessional, morally repugnant, behavior?"

"The Americans are my enemies, Herr Kaleu. They are the enemies of Germany. We are at war with them. Total war. Their flying boat tried to kill us. So I tried to kill some of them, just as our torpedo killed some of them. I fail to see the difference—respectfully, sir."

"There are circumstances when shooting at enemies is just not allowable," Böhm answered sternly. "One of those times is when your enemy is helpless in life jackets or lifeboats. I thought you would have known that without anyone reminding you. There is a higher code of the sea that takes precedence. Another circumstance is when your enemy is unarmed. These men had no gun or weapons to start with."

"In nineteen forty, the Lion said, 'We must be hard in this war,'" Franz objected. "Standing order number one fifty-four. I haven't heard that he's changed his mind, Herr Kaleu."

"Don't quote Dönitz to me!" Böhm reprimanded him.

"The admiral meant we should not pick up survivors, except captains and masters, if we think they can supply useful intelligence. He never said shoot them. Your behavior is unacceptable not only on humanitarian grounds, not only because it violates the bond that exists between all men of the sea, regardless of nationality, but also because it undermines the morale of our own crew, who would have reason to fear, if something happened to our boat, as it almost did about nine hours ago, that they would be dealt with in the same cold-blooded way. I will not have terribleness on this boat."

After a pause, he continued, in a quiet voice, "Your continued service is required for the effective operation of the boat. Furthermore, I cannot humiliate an officer, as much as I should like to, in your case, and maintain good discipline among the crew. I am therefore deferring any punishment until our return to port. Consider yourself henceforth on carefully watched probation. The kind and level of your punishment will be determined in good part by your conduct during the remainder of our cruise. That is all. You may resume your duties. And speak to no one about what we have discussed."

When what he hoped was a chastened Franz exited to the control room, Böhm closed the curtain on his cubbyhole and sat for a moment on his bunk, where he reflected: there may be some in the navy who accept the principle that war knows no laws—*inter arma silent leges*—but they will not act on it in my command.

As for Franz, Böhm remembered his Sophocles:

> *Long since I knew to treat my foe like one*
> *Whom I hereafter as a friend might love*
> *If he deserved it, and to love my friend*
> *As if he still might one day be my foe.*

Franz was not an overt Nazi, in the way that Peter Krug was. It was not ideology, at least not ideology alone, that explained Franz's unconscionable action. Maybe Krug was right: Franz was simply an asshole. And it took one to know one.

"Whadya got there, Bo?" Ray asked as he came upon his patrol plane commander on a bench outside the Operations Office.

"It's a Little Orphan Annie decoder pin," Bo answered, looking up with a squint in the early afternoon sun. "Writing a note to Belle. I have to encode it."

"You have to *encode* it?" Ray protested. "On a Little Orphan Annie pin?"

"Those were her terms for continuing a correspondence. Said it would keep our letters short, which means telegraphic, unromantic. I borrowed the pin from one of the squadron skipper's kids. Have to get my own. Do you drink Ovaltine?"

"On the rocks," Sam said. "Naw. I did as a kid. Seems this gal really wants to hurt you. First, the Dear John letter. Now this. I can introduce you to others."

"Actually, hers wasn't a Dear John letter. She didn't drop me for somebody else. And I don't mind doing this," Bo insisted. "I count myself lucky to still be in the game. I just can't use any gushy words. For awhile, it's going to be strictly business."

As Bo got back to his encoding, Ray looked over the official notices posted on the board outside Operations.

"Son of a *bitch*!" he said. "Did you see this? The destroyer *Jacob Jones* sunk by a sub at five this morning? Only eleven survivors. Jesus!"

"Not in our district, I hope," Bo said, looking up from his labored sentences.

"No, just north of it. Off the Delaware Capes—but look at this! An oil tanker, SS *Hennapoil*, five thousand two hundred eighty tons, sunk at oh-two-hundred this morning off Wimble Shoals, thirty-five, thirty-three by seventy-five-fifteen. Bo, that's *in* our district. In fact—"

Bo leaped up to look at the notice, then hurried inside

Operations to verify the position on the 5ND Area of Operations chart.

When Ray joined him, Bo said, "Shit, I made a terrible decision."

"I think I know what you're going to say," Ray acknowledged.

Bo put his finger east of the Hatteras Light Ship. "If we had turned north northwest to base here as we were supposed to do instead of proceeding on to the Cape and then north over Pamlico and Albemarle Sounds—"

"We would have gone just east of Wimble Shoals," Ray interjected.

"And look at the time," Bo added, dejectedly. "At almost exactly the time that ship was sunk we would have been on top of her."

"We had no bombs, Bo."

"But we had guns, and our mere presence would have kept that sub commander down."

"He might still have gotten off an underwater shot. I wonder if any tanker crewmen were lost?"

They went outside to look again at the notice. "Ten," Ray said. "Twenty others were picked up by Coast Guard motor surfboats from Chicamacomico. You can't blame yourself, Bo. It would have happened, regardless."

"I wonder if it was our sub that did it," Bo said, sitting down hard. "I'm scunnered with myself."

"You're what?" Ray asked.

"I'm scunnered."

CHAPTER 13

IN THE MID-AFTERNOON LIGHT, the southbound British flag 9,000-ton tramp steamer *Battersea* hugged the Carolina coast as far as its capes and shoals would allow, in order to avoid the three-knot Gulf Stream. Having to pass far out to sea around Outer Diamond Shoal, southeast of Cape Hatteras, had been more of an inconvenience than a danger, for she had been able to do so in daylight, when the U-boats reported to infest those latitudes were on their seabeds asleep—reportedly. Even so, she had zigzagged, mounted double watches, and kept her two lifeboats swung out from their davits.

Now, Ocracoke Inlet stood on the starboard beam, and a confident *Battersea* thrust her blunt bows southwest toward capes Lookout and Fear, the Georgia coastal islands, and Florida. There had been a sinking off Lookout early in the dark morning, as the wireless shack learned from a Morse distress call, but the position was in deep water 400 miles seaward. Apparently, the shallow-fathomed coastwise lanes were out of harm's way from this mark forward on the chart.

Lacking in sea-grace like all deep-sea tramps in ballast, *Battersea* stood high in the water, her red underbody embarrassingly revealed. With most of her hull, upper works, and funnel painted in wartime gray, the rest of her closely matched the steel-blue seas her prow divided, and her only other color amidst that dull unloveliness came from the bright red Merchant Navy ensign that flew from her flagstaff.

Menacingly mounted on the poop was a 4.7 gun.

In lumpy, confused water with no wind to take the tops off the waves—a sugar loaf sea, her crew called it—*Battersea* was making a respectable 12 knots, her screw threshing hard under the high stern, and her smoke trailing bar taut from the funnel. Above, the sky was overcast, like a plain linen spread. The temperature was 35 degrees Fahrenheit. Most of the men just off the afternoon watch at eight bells went to their bunks to nap or smoke, to read or yarn, perhaps to sing a lower deck ditty: "She was a Pompey whore, dressed in the rig of the day."

Others came out on deck in their sweaters, with pipes. A few set up a game of Tombola; some engaged in friendly banter—"Sod you, Jack, I'm inboard"; others gazed lazily toward the Carolina shore, anticipating the evening's first electric lights. A concertina forward played George Formby songs. Aft, an Irish tenor's "The Mountains of Mourne" floated over the undulating swell.

The men on the dog watch, officers, engineers, ratings, manned the ship and kept her sailing on her lawful roads, standing watch at the lee corner of the navigation bridge; ringing the bell at the fo'c'sle on the half hour and singing out "All's well, sir!" to invoke the bridge's "All right"; scrubbing decks around the hatchway coamings, the samson posts, and the ventilators; scaling, chipping, painting; polishing brasswork; cooking; and, down below, in the stokehold, forever feeding coal to the furnace that angered the boilers that turned the propeller in its shaft—fifty-four men in all, most from the British northeast, the red coastline with the virile air, but not all, for here, too, was an engineer from the West Country, a Welsh steward-boy, a Scottish donkeyman, a Portuguese Indian deckhand, a Chinese trimmer, a Lascar greaser, and an Irish apprentice.

Deep-sea tramps were more than their iron plates and wooden housings, more even than their officers and crew. Their whole was greater than their parts. Each tramp had her personality, her character, and her moods. On some it was a special history or experience that established the vessel's unique signature. On others it was the traditions of the owners or the companies: Sir R. Ropner & Co., Ltd.; Stanhope Steamship Company, Ltd.; or the Blue Funnel Line, among them. On still others it was the master, more commonly called in wartime, the captain.

Battersea was known in the merchant fleet as a "Pusser ship"—one commanded by a captain who went strictly by the book and demanded exacting compliance with naval etiquette. More, she was known as the "public school ship," since her captain required his officers to study nautical history, Latin, and Greek.

When the third officer took the bridge to begin his watch, Captain Dudley Rodger Schofield acknowledged his on-time appearance with a doggerel:

Depend upon it, sir:
In time of war, but not before,
God and the sailor we adore;
The danger past, and ills requited,
God is forgotten and the sailor slighted.

"How very true, sir," the third officer observed, as the thickly compact, graying captain, with a face like crinkled chart paper, a briar pipe stuck in its middle longitudes, with eyes that had seen both the malice and the kindness of the sea, equipped with an extra-master's certificate and forty years in ships, stepped out to the open weather corner and sniffed the air. On his visored cap he presented the anchor and crown insignia of the Merchant Navy and on his sleeves four salty-gold rings of rank, the uniform he donned in September 1939, when 4,500 masters, like himself, set aside their company uniforms or their trilby hats and brown tweed coats for the Merchant Navy blue.

Of *Battersea* he was, as the insurance policies put it, "under God" her master—the Old Man—briny and hardcase. But he had his kindly moments, too.

"Excuse me, Captain," the third officer reported, "young Duncan is here to see you, as you ordered."

Schofield turned to see a jacketed, nervous lad, apparently underage, clutching his watch cap in both hands.

"Come out here, son," he said.

When the boy made only mincing steps forward,

Schofield urged him in a less commanding register, "Come, come, lad, I'm not Abdul the Damned."

The youth's face before him now, Schofield inquired, "Your name, your birthplace on ship's articles, make me ask, are you perhaps Jack Purvis's son?"

"Yes, sir."

"He had you late in life."

"Yes, sir."

"A fine man, your father. We served together on the *Rockpool* in the last war. A braver officer I never met. OBE, Lloyds Medal, and Mention in Dispatches. I hope he sank some of that in you. How's your mum keeping?"

"She's well, sir. Thank you, sir."

"No doubt the salt runs in your blood. So you lied about your age at the Seamen's Pool and found yourself sent to me as an apprentice."

"I'll be sixteen in August, sir."

"Where are you assigned now?"

"To the steward."

"Well, eventually you'll get to try every other job on board, except mine, the officers' of the deck, and the engineers'.

"You'll trim coal, oil machinery, rig shifting boards, scrape metal, burnish brightwork, maybe even handle the wheel if I think you're up to it. We'll teach you how to set a course by the stars, and to judge the wind's direction and force by the waves and clouds, how to load cargoes so *Battersea* is both full *and* down to her marks with no space to spare, which is no mean trick, and how to make a reef knot and figure eight, and so on. We'll make a Merchant Jack of you, all right.

"You'll learn most there is to know about the running of this ship, from her stem to her stern, from her keel to her posts. And you'll never forget it. The *Battersea* will stick to your ribs like tinned bully beef."

"I really want to shoot the gun, sir."

"Hah! The gun! You want to be a warrior, do you? Open a fighting account? Well, the seamen gunners had to take a week's course on shore and spend another week in practice. That's what you'd have to do if you want to shoot the gun. When we come up from the sea and pay off, you can apply for that and see if the Dems gunners will take you."

"It's just, sir, I don't think going to Florida for slingloads of grapefruit has much to do with the war."

"And after Florida to Savannah for cotton and to Philadelphia for lumber. I hope you think that's all right." He paused. "So you don't understand the grapefruit? Then, lad, you don't know your Kipling."

Schofield turned at the bridge rail to face the bow and spoke in a loud voice:

Oh, where are you going to, all you big steamers
With England's own coal, up and down the salt seas?
We are going to fetch you your bread and your butter,
Your beef, pork, and mutton, eggs, apples and cheese,
For the bread that you eat and the biscuits you nibble,
The sweets that you suck and the joints that you carve,
They are brought to you daily by all us Big Steamers—
And if anyone hinders our coming you'll starve!

He then turned back to young Duncan. "Rudyard Kipling," he said. "Do you know the name?"

"My father used to read him to me."

"Then learn the point that Kipling makes: *primum vivere*."

"Primum—sir?"

"*Primum vivere*: first you have to live. You have to be alive if you want to do battle. And to live you have to have food and vitamins, which in England means, you need ships like *Battersea*."

He went on to explain how, in a long career of tramping, formerly on unscheduled voyage, time, and bareboat charters along unfixed routes, and, since September 1939, on regulated war transport missions, he had brought into the Thames estuary, or into the Liverpool docks from Dingle to Seaforth, or into a dozen other ports: barley and rye from Australia, rice from Burma, tea from China and Ceylon, peanuts from Nigeria, wine and olive oil from Portugal, coffee from Brazil, sugar from Cuba, citrus and smoked fish from Florida, soya beans from Wilmington, canned goods from Philadelphia, and wheat from U.S. Midwestern states that was carried over the Great Lakes in ice-free months for loading in New York. The *Battersea*, he said, could carry as much wheat as the Yanks or Canadians could grow on 30,000 acres. These and other foods, some, like dairy products and meats, brought by refrigerated ships, carried the red corpuscles that became the lifeblood of Britain's people. Sever the vital arteries, as the U-boats were trying to do, and Britain's defeat would only be a matter of time.

"I see the point now, sir," Duncan said.

"Have you had Latin?"

"No, sir."

"I want you to start. And don't let your bunkmates give you a hard time about it. Latin won't make a seaman of you, but it will make a thinker of you, and put you in touch, if you wish, with great minds of antiquity—with Cicero, Seneca, Pliny, Catullus, Virgil, Caesar, Augustine. I'll give you a beginner's book when we finish here. From time to time I'll go over grammar and pronunciation with you. Are you game?"

"I guess so, sir."

"After the war, you may want to go up for an officer's ticket. Or you may want to go to college. I'd recommend either course. I'm thinking of what your father would say."

"Yes, sir."

"No one can take the place of your father, young Duncan, least of all I, who have never fathered a son. But there is certain advice I can give you that, if you heed it, will make you a better man. *Verbum sapienti sufficit.* Yes.

"Now the advice of the day is this: make the ship your home, your center, your way of life. Forsake the land. Exist for the sea. On board, we live by an established and dependable routine. Life is good, regular, and fair. Here you make true friends. Seek out the company of the better men: 'Therefore 'tis meet that noble minds keep ever with their like.' Here a youth can grow unimpeded, without distractions, into a fine person. I've served four decades under the Old Red Duster and I have seen it happen many times.

"Don't listen to the man who yearns for land so he can go drinking and fighting and whoring. That man is not a true merchant sailor. You'll hear more of that kind of talk in the Royal Navy than you will in Ropner's Navy, which is our company. But you'll still hear it sometimes on *Battersea*, when new men, younger men, sign on. Pay no respect to it. I've never known a man improved by shore leave. Depend upon it, the old saying is rock-hard true for sailors: 'Harbors rot both ships and men.'

"Come on now and let me get you that book." He led the way to his cabin, bellowing a music-hall song:

> *And when we say we've always won*
> *And when they ask us how it's done*
> *We proudly point to every one*
> *Of England's sailors of the King. . . .*

Thump-thump-thump. In the small U-boat sound booth, with tongue-and-groove wood walls to exclude extraneous noise, Puster Kurt Schneewind pricked up his ears at the hydrophone effect reaching the grounded U-boat. Twenty-three sensors on each side of the hull near the forward hydroplanes were feeding a distinct audible wavelength both into Schneewind's earphones and into an electric pulse-timing compensator, which enabled him, by turning a control wheel, to take a rough directional fix on the sound source, estimate its range, decide if it was approaching or receding, and plot its position and course from a black indicator needle that swept across a glass-covered compass rose. *Thump-thump-thump.* It was not the sound of breathing whales or porpoises; nor of a destroyer with its characteristic *swish-swish-swish*; nor of a motor diesel ship. It was clearly the propeller cavitation of a reciprocating steamer, probably coal-fired.

"Herr Kaleu," Schneewind said across the passageway to Böhm, who was reading on his bunk, "I have a south-bound steamer seaward of us, HE bearing Red zero-seven-zero, course estimated at two-four-zero, range four miles."

Böhm sat up and threw his legs around to the deck. "What time do you have, Puster?" he asked, checking his watch against the sound man's.

"German or local, Herr Kaleu?"

"Local."

"Fifteen fifty-six."

"Check. Still three hours of daylight," Böhm noted. There had been a number of ships passing nearby or over-head during the day, as he had been advised at the time or had noticed on the sound room log after his sleep or had heard himself when the traffic was close, through the quiet steel hull. Why now it was this particular screw noise that captured his curiosity, he would ruefully wonder later, but some indefinable impulse caused him to bound into the control room and order Brünner:

"Chief, blow negative! Periscope depth!"

When the depth reached 13.5 meters, Böhm was on his saddle in the tower.

"Up sky periscope!" he ordered.

The high-angle, 90-degree lensed asparagus, as U-boat men called a periscope, came hissing up from its well. Böhm's right foot trained the fixed-height eyepiece around 360 degrees, only pausing at 070 degrees for a quick look at the funnel and posts of the steamer, more concerned with this scope to check sea and sky for war-ships or planes. Below, the engineer and his planesmen jockeyed the regulator valves and buttons to maintain the boat constant at 13.5 meters.

"Down scope! Up attack scope!"

The 7.5-meter long monocular, high-magnification attack scope fitted with reticule, or numbered cross hairs, provided Böhm with a good view of the oncoming steamer. "Forward-connected double kingposts higher than her funnel," he observed. "Good size. Hand me the *Gröner*," he said to Baumann, standing by the deflection calculator.

Flipping through the *Gröner* book of merchant ship silhouettes, Böhm came to the best fit. "British steamship of the Ropner line, nine to ten thousand tons, BRT. I like her. Except for one thing—" He strained in the sight, and, after a moment, leaned back to say, "There's a four-incher on her stern. That I don't like. Not with sunset three hours off. We could trail her and, after sunset, catch up and make a normal surface attack, which would use up a lot of fuel. Or, we can make an underwater launch now when we already have perfect position on her. She's coming right to us, like a duck before the blind. *Audacibus fortuna iuvat.* There is a moment which, when taken at the flood—" He made up his mind.

"Both ahead half, make four knots, come right to one-two-five, open bow caps three and four, set depth at two point five meters." Baumann passed the torpedo order to the forward compartment. "Set for multiple launch," Böhm continued. "I'm choosing a shallow depth because she's got such high freeboard in ballast."

As the steamer loomed larger in the graduated lens, Böhm completed his estimate of her speed from ship type and bow wakes. To Baumann, manning the fourteen knobs and dials on the calculator, he called out the target range, bearing, course, speed, and, "Angle on the bow— Green eighteen." The calculator fed the aiming triangle through the torpedo receivers into the gyrocompass steering mechanism in the eels.

When the range closed to 1,000 meters, Böhm said, "I'll wait for a ninety-degree track." At eight hundred meters, when the steamer filled the lens, he had it.

"Tube three—*launch!*"

"Tube four—" he waited eight seconds, "*launch!*"

"Forty-five seconds, Herr Kaleu," Baumann reported on the first eel.

The boat seemed to shoot forward slightly with each launch. Below and forward, Böhm and Baumann could hear seawater rushing into the regulator cells as the chief made up for the lost weight and maintained trim.

Nearing 45 seconds Böhm fixed his eye carefully on the target. This he wanted to see.

RUMMMS!

Underwater, the exploding warhead had a muffled sound, unlike the sharp report one normally heard on top. Eight seconds later:

RUMMS!

Böhm watched both hits with satisfaction. The first sent up a towering smoke and debris column from the forward hold, while the second punched a hole abaft the bridge, causing a wide flame and water cloud pitted with wildly swinging splinters.

"Port six!" he ordered. "Scope down!" He turned to Baumann, "Another one, and this time it's victory pennant class. I missed the engine room, but she's mortally wounded. The forward torpedo crew can bring down their bunks. They'll be happy about that! We'll keep our scope hidden for awhile to avoid the gun and steer around the stern to her port quarter. Both ahead full!"

Through the tower plating, as they made the turn, Böhm, Baumann, and the helmsman could clearly hear the screeching of torn metal and the bursting of bulkheads in the victim's innards.

"Her screw is still turning at the same revolutions, Herr Kaleu," the puster reported from the sound booth.

"That's curious," Böhm said. "I'd better make an observation. Up attack scope!"

Just seconds before, *Battersea* was proceeding cheerfully on her lawful occasions, toward Cape Lookout. Her bows, lifting and dipping, shouldered the long, easy swell with a sober steadfastness, leaving four creaming wakes along the red paint. Her decks were shipshape and Bristol fashion. The fo'c'sle rang the bell, the galley prepared canteen pies and tea, the quadruple expansion engines ate Cardiff coal, the bronze screw beat its stolid tattoo, and white water frothed in the vessel's wake. God was in his heaven, the master was on the bridge.

Then, with Fate loaded heavily against her, *Battersea* shuddered from two savage explosions, one fore, one aft. The wakeless electric torpedoes had shown no sign of their coming, not even a wheal on the water's surface. Forward, the tramp's thin half-inch hull plates gave way like paper to 280 kilos of high explosive charge and surrendered in a terrible swift uprush of plate fragments, deck machinery, hatchboards, Oregon pine deck planking, flame, water, and smoke that happened so quickly, and with such deafening noise, that no one on board remembered watching the blast develop but could only behold its final, towering result with shock and awe.

Seconds later, another torpedo exploded against the cross bunker bulkhead, destroyed the master's cabin, the engineer's accommodation, the galley, the forward lifeboat and davits on the starboard side, and caused the funnel to lurch forward with a grating clangor. On the bridge, Captain Schofield flew six feet in the air against the gyro repeater, breaking three fingers on his left hand. Standing upright, he grabbed the whistle lanyard with his right hand and gave six short blows to signal the Dems gun crew to action stations. He ordered the second officer, standing watch, to pull the handle of the engine room telegraph to "Stop" but there was no acknowledgment from below, and no cessation of the engine's deep reverberating sound.

"There's no response from the engine room, Captain," he reported.

"Very well, get the chief engineer down there right away to cut off steam! Send the damage control crew forward to start pumps! Have the wireless officer send an SSS and our position!"

Schofield ran to the wind-boxes, port and starboard, to look for their U-boat assailant. He saw nothing. Then, with dismay, he looked forward and saw not only that the ship was listing to starboard in response to water pouring through her gash on that side, but that the water's weight was causing the vessel to go down by the bows.

"The crew forward reports that there is little the pumps can do, Captain," the second officer reported. "The first torpedo took out twenty feet square of plating where numbers three and four holds join the side, so they both are flooding. Also, the bulkheads between them and holds one and two have buckled and they're filling through the fracture."

Schofield could hear rivets and seams shrieking as the bows continued to settle. "Where is the engineer's report on our steam?" he demanded.

"Nothing yet, sir."

A pallor of worry crossed the master's face. He did not feel the pain in his hand. "By Harry, if we don't stop our steam," he said loudly, "*Battersea* is going to drive herself underwater like a submarine! Are we making water aft from the second torpedo?"

"Yes, sir."

"So we can't hope for the screw to lift out and stop our way. And unless we do stop, or at least slow down, we can't lower our remaining boats or they'll capsize. See if you can find that engineer! And I don't hear any gunfire!"

There was no artillery action because there was no target for the gunlayer to aim at. The nine member crew stood resolutely at the loaded piece on the poop, their hands on the training wheels and the lanyard, but they saw no sign of their attacker, and the more their ship listed to starboard and settled by the head, the less chance they would have to bring their gun to bear on the port side, if that was where the U-boat appeared, if it appeared at all.

Finally, the chief engineer emerged from *Battersea*'s vitals to make his report. "The second torpedo blast ruptured an auxiliary steam line, Captain. The second engineer and crew were driven out by the steam. They couldn't approach the valves. I'm going to try to get down myself."

While the chief donned an overcoat, gloves, cap, scarf, and goggles, Schofield addressed the second officer: "Pass the word to the officers that *Battersea* is going under—by her own power if we can't cut off steam. Have the gun crew stand down and all hands assemble on deck in life jackets to abandon ship, on my signal, by jumping from the starboard side. Detail the lifeboat crews to release the lashes to the griping spars and, when the whistle sounds, let the three remaining boats go down if they will. Though they'll probably capsize, their buoyancy tanks will float them. The port boats will probably splinter along the side if they go down at all with the list. The crew can swim to them and ride their bottoms or hang onto their grasping ropes until help comes. The wireless did get our position, did it not?"

"Aye, aye, sir," the officer confirmed.

"All right. The water will be cold, so we'll need help soon." Schofield then went after the confidential papers in their sinkable bag which he threw overside from the starboard wing. From that position he could see that the well deck forward was shipping green and white water against which the winches and posts stood out in helpless contrast.

Meanwhile, the chief went down the steep, greasy iron ladder into the engine room, which was half-blinded by a scalding fog. He knew well the fearsome nature of steam, which deprived the room of oxygen and burned the eyes and lungs. No man could stay in it for long. He made his way as quickly as he could, therefore, by feel as much as by sight, along the tilted catwalk and deck. The engines were still turning, but their rumble and vibration were slowing somewhat, he noticed, as steam dissipated through the pipe fracture. At last, his feet deep in water, he found the main steam wheel and turned it off. Gradually, the engines ceased their loud labor and the propeller shaft abandoned its spin.

From his canting perch on the bridge a relieved Schofield used what little steam was left for the whistle to Abandon Ship. The two port lifeboats made it down the side but in much damaged condition. The lone remaining starboard boat hung up in the after fall where it stayed, swinging, vertical and useless, tearing apart in the swells.

One by one the crew jumped overside from the slowing vessel, some pausing not an instant, others lingering at the rail to screw up courage. A few refused to jump, though they had jackets, and the officers had to force them bodily overside. One ran back to his bunk, he yelled, to retrieve a picture of his wife; he was not seen again. Another clung to the gangway when he reached the water, as though he could not bring himself to leave the ship, and soon became lost from view in the creaming sea. Another stood at the rail with no life jacket. Schofield recognized him. It was young Duncan! Schofield grabbed his megaphone and called to him: "Duncan, where is your life jacket?"

The youth looked around, confused.

"Here!" Schofield called, throwing down his own jacket. "Put that on! Get in the water and swim to the port lifeboats! Now!"

Duncan donned the jacket and, looking docilely back at Schofield, jumped awkwardly into the Atlantic swell. He, too, would not be seen again.

Over the sound of the breaking tramp, Schofield heard one of the men in the water singing an old chanty:

I thought I heard th' Old Man say,
Leave her, Johnnie, leave her!
Ye can go ashore an' take yer pay,
An' it's time for us to leave her!

Once satisfied that everyone was off who was going off, Schofield walked aft and mounted the poop, where he could see how well his men were doing. It appeared to him that most if not all would survive, if hypothermia did not outrace assistance.

He then hauled a wooden stool to the starboard rail, threw it overside, and jumped after it, his captain's hat flying off as he fell.

When he bobbed to the surface, his limbs chilled and

saltwater up his nose, he swam until he found the floating stool and held on, his left hand beginning to hurt now for the first time.

Withdrawing from him was the saddest sight of all his years at sea—the grotesquely tilted, wounded frame of *Battersea* on her knees, crawling slowly under water. Soon, only the stern could be seen above the surface, and the great blades of the screw came up, rotating idly in the air.

Schofield could hear the boilers come apart from their seatings with a deep thunder, followed by a loud sizzling.

Then her funnel lay over and she simply went.

Tears welled in Schofield's eyes, the first, he reflected, since the death of his mother twenty years before. He gazed with immense sadness at the spot where *Battersea* slid under. He loved that ship. Born on the Tyne, buried in Carolina. Services held in the Cathedral of the Sea. May the souls of all the ships departed, through the mercy of God, rest in peace. Amen.

With his high magnification scope Gunther Böhm saw it all as he held back from his victim on her port quarter. At the end, he figured that the last man jumping off was her captain, and he ordered the boat surfaced so that he could make sure.

Taking the usual periscope sightings as a precaution— one problem with a submerged attack was that he could not take out the ship's radio shack with his machine guns and prevent a call for warship or warplane assistance—he saw no immediate signs of danger and proceeded to surface with decks awash.

Under diesel power it did not take him long to pass the survivors hanging on to the lifeboat ropes and others tossing in life jackets, and in whom the sight of his low gray form must certainly have raised strong emotions, to reach the position where he thought the last man to jump might be. The forward starboard lookout sighted him first, and Böhm came alongside at dead slow. Franz was the watch officer, but Böhm called Baumann up, too, to interpret.

"What ship are you?" Böhm asked through Baumann.

"*Battersea*, British, nine thousand tons," came the reply from the stool.

"Are you the captain?"

"Dudley Rodger Schofield, Master, Merchant Navy."

"I'm going to throw you a line and invite you aboard."

"I should prefer not, sir, if it's all the same."

"It's not all the same. You are an officer and a captain, and my prisoner. No captain of any flag is going to die in cold water if I can help it."

To Baumann, Böhm said, "Go below to my compartment and bring up a blanket, some of my socks, and a watch cap, so we can get him down the ladder without his catching cold. Break out a bottle of schnapps from the confidential locker and place it on my drop-leaf."

"*Jawohl*, Herr Kaleu."

To Franz, Böhm said, "Number One, take two of the lookouts and throw the captain a line."

But Franz did not budge.

"Did you hear me?" Böhm shouted in his face. "I gave you a direct order."

"I will not assist an enemy of the Third Reich, Herr Kaleu," Franz said stiffly. "I will not shoot him, as you have corrected me, but I will not help him, either. I would rather be shot myself, respectfully, sir."

"And you damn well may be!" Böhm exclaimed in outrage, and grabbed two lookouts himself, whom he led down the outside ladder, where they opened the watertight 2 centimeter ammunition container and withdrew a cork life preserver on a weighted line, which Böhm, in his angry determination to shame Franz, if that was possible, threw too quickly into the water, not taking care to notice that the coil of line around his right ankle would carry him off, too.

When he finished bouncing down the diving tank plates, got the line unwound from his foot, and emerged from beneath the water, he called to the lookouts, who were poised to rescue him, "Stay! Stay!," grabbed the line in the water, and swam to the life preserver. With the cork ring held before him, he kicked his way out to Schofield hanging on the stool.

"Here!" he said in German, hoping the master would understand, "Take this line, sir, and we'll pull ourselves to the boat!"

Schofield, understanding more the gesture than the words, was reaching over the water with his good hand to take the line when two loud shouts came from the U-boat's bridge, the first from a lookout, the second from Franz:

"Flying boat! Consolidated!"

"Alaarmm!"

Without looking at Böhm in the water, Franz waved frantically for the two lookouts on deck to drop the line and climb the ladder back to the bridge, while the other two lookouts leaped down the hatch. The diesel exhausts closed shut, ballast valves opened to take in sea water, and, after the remaining lookouts and Franz were below, and the hatch cover was locked, the boat perceptively moved forward and down.

Böhm had never before observed a diving operation from the outside this close aboard, and it took a moment to break his fascination with it and to turn his attention instead to the horizon, north, where, yes, there was a flying boat of the same type that had caught them on the surface twice before! It was a hundred meters off the deck, descending, perhaps two kilometers distant. Obviously, the lookouts had been paying more attention to him than to their sectors, or they would have sighted the "bee" well before this. But Franz had done the right thing in diving. Fifty men in a U-boat were worth more than one—or two—in the water.

Böhm looked Schofield in the eye. *"Sprechen Sie Deutsch?"*

"No," Schofield answered, *"Nein.* Do you speak English?"

"Nein." Böhm thought for a second. *"Dicisne Latine?"* (do you speak Latin?)

"*Utique*," (yes), Schofield answered, pleasantly surprised.

The two men smiled at each other briefly, acknowledging the rarity of the coincidence. Then Böhm continued, in Latin, "I regret my decision to sink your ship, for reasons that will soon become clear."

"If that's an apology, I accept it," Schofield replied. "For my part, I wish I could have given back as good as I got."

"Are you a Christian man?" Böhm asked.

"More or less."

"Then I advise you to say your prayers, sir. When the bombs (he used *bombae*) fall in the water, their concussion (he used *concussio*) will kill us."

"Will kill us?" Schofield repeated, as, with a cold wave upon his heart, he looked over his shoulder at the aircraft, now almost on top of them, loud and fearsome with its engines, *bombae* hanging from its wing racks.

Böhm reached across the wooden stool and took Schofield's right hand. "*Vale! Auf Wiedersehen!*" he said over the engines' roar.

"*Vale!* Goodbye!" Schofield called back, and closed his eyes, reserving all further communications to the Almighty—as did Böhm, who recited aloud an Act of Contrition.

To Böhm and Schofield, as to Bo and Ray in the pilots' compartment of their PBY-5, it all seemed to happen in slow motion. The four vaned canisters came off the aircraft's bomb racks simultaneously, in salvo, and made a curving 50-foot descent to the water, where the splashes coincided with their spacing on the wing, the port forward bomb entering some twenty yards distant from the position where the U-boat commander and tramp master hung from their flotage.

The seconds were like minutes as the high explosive charges sought their prescribed depth, where detonators released their awful fury.

In milliseconds each charge converted into a gas bubble that expanded outward radially as a pressure wave traveling through the water at the speed of sound. When the waves reached Böhm and Schofield, whose body tissues were of water density, the pulses shredded the interfaces of tissue with air-containing cavities—in the abdominal hollow viscera, the thoracic wall, and the lungs, where the shearing and tearing of tissue led to pulmonary hemorrhage.

Each man's hands then uncurled from his flotage, vital systems shut down, consciousness became a shadow within a shadow, and the sea closed over him.

The attacking aircraft droned in circles overhead.

CHAPTER 14

IN CASSOCK AND BIRETTA, Tony made his way through the sacristy and into the darkened cathedral, blessing himself from the holy water font, and genuflecting toward the tabernacle. Outside, as he had often observed in Florida before, a gentle rain came down from one corner of the sky while the afternoon sun slanted across from another. Spaced high along the western aisle of the old Spanish nave, stained glass panels that depicted scenes from the life of St. Augustine rejoiced in the direct golden light.

As he walked toward the gospel-side confessional, he took a quick glance across the pews toward the epistle side, where a blue-clad sailor, white cap in hand, was just departing the left curtained kneeler at Tom Murphy's box. So Tom was already at work. Lines four or five deep stood along the wall to either side of his two curtains. Other penitents, bent, shadowy forms, knelt at various points in the pews.

On his own side, Tony saw a similar array of civilians and servicemen waiting to be shriven, though he took care not to notice any faces, and he lowered his eyes as he neared his post—the penitential quiet broken only when the front church door opened and closed, and he could hear the sibilant passage of automobile tires on the wet street surface outside.

He opened the small wooden door to the confessional, placed the purple stole around his neck, closed the door, sat down, and slid open the grill panels on either side. Open for business, he mouthed to himself. Sins to the left of him, sins to the right of him, into the valley of absolution rode the parishioners. Don't be irreverent.

Actually, 4:30 was a good time for Saturday confessions.

He could get in a few things beforehand. This afternoon it was the first three acts of *The Masked Ball* from the Metropolitan on the Blue network. Another advantage was that in football season he could hear Ted Husing do an entire game before the start of confessions—"Hello everyone everywhere, this is Ted Husing high above Mychie Stadium at West Point, where the Black Knights of the Hudson meet the Fighting Illini of Illinois, as the banners of a hundred odd colleges crack in the autumn breeze."

That was some story in the *Record* yesterday: Coach Leahy of Notre Dame giving up on Rockne's backfield shift and going with the orthodox "T." Spring practice beginning next Monday at South Bend—

Footsteps and a rustle of curtain to his right. He closed the sliding panel on the grill to his left and waited until he heard knees meet kneeler. Then—"*Misereatur tui omnipotens Deus, et dimissis peccatis tuis, perducat te ad vitam aeternam. Amen.*"

The penitent, a woman who sounded middle-aged, began: "Bless me, Father, for I have sinned. It has been two weeks since my last confession. I was uncharitable in my speech two times. I had three bad thoughts, I neglected my evening prayers two times, and I denied my husband conjugal rights one time. That is all, Father."

Sometimes they save the big one for last, Tony reflected. Good God! Except for her priest- and nun-induced guilt, the woman was a saint.

"Our Lord is very pleased with you," he told her. "For your penance say one Our Father and one Hail Mary. And spend a few minutes before the Blessed Sacrament thanking Our Savior for his merciful love. Now pray a good Act of Contrition."

Tony then recited the absolution: "*Indulgentiam, absolutionem, et remissionem peccatorum tuorum tribuat tibi omnipotens et misericors Dominus. . . .*"

He ended, as he always did, in English: "Go in peace." He could have added, "And sin no more," as Jesus did, but that would suggest that this good woman was a sinner, which she was not, really, or it would set up expectations that simply were not realistic in the case of serious sinners.

Of which he might have one on the left side, as he guessed when he pulled aside that panel. The whiff of alcohol through the grill was his first clue. The late teens or early twenties male voice was his second. No doubt a soldier from Blanding or a sailor from Jax. You didn't get breath like that this early in the day from locals.

"Bless me, Father. I confess to Almighty God and to you, Father, that I have sinned. It has been two months since my last confession. During that time I have had two fights. I took revenge on a real bastard—excuse me, Father, I didn't mean to say that—I fornicated with three women, I can't remember exactly how many times, I got drunk a lot and took God's name in vain many times, I abused myself at least once a day, I had maybe a hundred bad thoughts, I ate meat on Friday five times and I missed Mass four Sundays. That's all, Father, except that I have a moral problem—is French kissing a sin?"

Talk about straining at a gnat. Whew! Tony had news for him, "That's not your only moral problem, son." He then reviewed the young man's list, pointing out how each of his sins was an offense against God and himself. "Would you hold yourself up as a model person for others to emulate and to follow?"

"No, Father."

"Don't you think, as a Catholic, you have a calling to draw people toward God rather then to repel them, or simply to use them for your pleasure, for your own selfish ends?"

"Yes, Father."

"Now as to your question, the Church teaches that any contact between the sexes outside of marriage that arouses venereal pleasure, that is, excites the passions, is seriously sinful. So if French kissing excites your passions or that of a partner who is not your wife, it's a mortal sin. You, though, have gone far beyond that, by your own account. French kissing is not beside the point, but it is close to it, given your confession.

"I want you to reflect on your life and on how much happier you would be if you followed God's will. You'll do that, won't you?"

"Yes, Father."

"For your penance—do you have a rosary?"

"Back at camp."

"Then recite one decade on your fingers before the Blessed Sacrament."

"Which mysteries?"

"Uh—sorrowful. Now make a good Act of Contrition. . . . *Deinde ego te absolvo a peccatis tuis, in nomine Patris, et Filii, et Spiritus Sancti. Amen.* Go in peace."

Which mysteries!

Closing the panel, Tony reflected on the spiritual direction he had just given, and whether it made any sense. A saint like Jean Vianney, the Cure d' Ars, need only open his mouth and life-changing wisdom poured out. But, unfortunately, he was no Jean Vianney. Was he right to correct that young man's self-interest on the one hand, and then appeal to his real self-interest on the other? Only God knew. On French kissing he gave the textbook answer from Noldin's *Summa Theologiae Moralis.* Of course, one could ask, what did Noldin know? An Innsbruck Jesuit. Easy for him to say.

Cite the authorities Tony could do. But nothing in the seminary curriculum prepared him to provide pastoral guidance—to say the right things in the sacramental forum that might help someone transform his life. At ordination a bishop rubbed chrism on your hands and sent you out to wing it. *Dabitur vobis.* "O what a life and it is thine, O Priest of Jesus Christ." Lacordaire. It was what he had had printed on his ordination cards. What a life, indeed!

A younger male voice cleared behind the grill to his right. A high schooler. Predictable confession: mean to his brothers and sisters, disobeyed his parents, entertained bad thoughts, and, saving the worst for last, was impure with himself so many times.

Tony slid back the panel. *"Misereatur tui omnipotens Deus. . . ."*

"Bless me, Father, for I have sinned. It has been two weeks since my last confession. During that time I have had a terrible experience, and I need to ask you a question. Father."

"Of course. Go ahead."

"Is it true, Father, that what you say in confession is a secret? I mean always remains a secret?"

"Yes, son, it's called the seal of confession. The priest who hears your sins can never reveal them, or anything else you say, to anyone else—ever—not even to the Pope. Secrecy about what takes place in the confessional is the gravest obligation of a priest. I would be excommunicated if I revealed anything you told me. Does that make you feel more comfortable?"

"Yes, Father. I just have this terrible thing and I just feel it's a sin, the worst kind of sin there is, and I can't sleep worrying about it. It's driving me crazy."

"Just tell me what it is."

Tony recognized the voice, something he tried not to do in the confessional. It was Paul Ohlenburg. Definitely Paul Ohlenburg.

"Well—I was involved in—I had something to do with getting a man killed, Father."

"I see. Go on."

"It's complicated, Father."

"I have plenty of time. The other penitents can wait or go to the other confessional. Go on."

Totally unpredictable. Totally. Tony breathed hard into his cupped hands.

The youth described in riveting detail the espionage work of his father—here at St. Augustine Beach!; the arrival from a German submarine of the agent named Homer and the chance encounter of Homer with the night watchman of Marine Studios; the killing of the watchman—so *that's* what happened to him; the burial; the drive up the beach to this boy's house; Homer's explanation of why he had to kill.

"I helped to bury him, Father. I shoveled sand over him with my hands. He was just fishing. That's all he was doing. My father says no, but I feel it was a murder. I feel that I'm—I can't think of the word."

"An accomplice?"

"Yes, Father. I wake up at night and I see that body and the fish on top of him. I see his eyes opening up and staring at me. I throw up a lot."

"What does your father say to you?" Tony asked.

"He says that every German is a soldier in the war and every soldier must kill for the Fatherland, because we're at war, and no one is a non—is a non—"

"Noncombatant?"

"Yes."

"All right. And you've not said anything to the police?"

"No, Father."

"And why not?"

"Because of my father. Because he didn't do anything, Homer did it, and I did it with him. If I said anything to the police, the FBI or somebody would trace Homer right to my father. They'd hang my father. I love my father."

The boy broke into a single loud sob, followed by sniffling and silence.

"That's all right," Tony said. "Take your time."

"I'm okay," the boy said, finally.

"Do you agree with what your father is doing?"

"I don't know, Father. I don't understand. He makes it sound so right. I'm confused. Right now, I'm all mixed up."

Tony stalled for time. What in God's name should he say?

"No wonder you are," he said, finally. "If I were in your shoes I'd be confused, too. You love your father and you love your father's country, which you say is also your country of birth. On the other hand, you love your adopted new country. You respect the orders of your father, yet, on the other hand—the reason you're here today—you believe and honor God's commandment against the unjust taking of life. Furthermore, you're unclear if this is a case of justifiable killing, as in war, or of murder. Does that seem to sum it up?"

"Yes, Father—"

"You are very right to be upset about the death of an innocent man. But I'm sure that God knows exactly what pressures you were under, and that you never *intended* for anything like that to happen.

"Sin is in the *intention*, son, not in the actual deed. You see, if I set out in my car to murder someone but had a flat tire on the way and couldn't get there, I'd still be guilty of murder in the eyes of God, despite the fact that I never carried out the physical act itself. Similarly, if some evil occurs that I did not intend and over which I had no free control, I am not guilty in God's eyes. That's what we mean by intention. Sin is in the intention. But you never intended anything of what happened. Your participation in the burial was forced on you and was not in itself a sinful act, except to the extent of covering up a crime. And I don't want you to feel guilty about that, either, particularly since we may be able to do something about it. Are you beginning to feel a little relieved now that you've got this much off your chest?"

"Yes, Father. Thank you, Father."

It was a leap well beyond what needed to be asked or said in this confession, and he struggled interiorly with the licitness of doing it, but, knowing that he would later regret any surrender to craven scruples, he allowed his voice to speak the words, "You don't have to answer this if you don't want to, but is Homer, as he calls himself, living with you at the beach?"

"No, Father. He moved to town, to the Alhambra."

"So you're done with him for now."

"Yes, Father."

"Do you know what his mission is?"

"No, Father."

"And he's registered at the Alhambra under the name of Homer."

"I don't know, Father. He may be using his real name of Krug—Peter Krug."

Tony fastened the name in his memory: *Peter Krug*. Leaning close to the grill, he said in a voice that sounded to him several notes higher, "Now, as I said before, I think there is something we can do about the body on the beach, something that will make you feel a great deal better. Let me ask you this, son: do you remember *exactly* where the man was buried?"

"Yes, Father."

"All right. Will you come back to this same confessional on Monday afternoon? What time does school let out?"

"Three."

"All right. Will you be here at three-thirty on Monday?"

"Yes, Father."

"Good. I'll have something worked out that will help you. In the meantime, I want to assure you again, everything you have told me is under the seal of confession. Is there anything you wish to confess besides what you've already told me?"

"No, Father."

"All right. I'll give you general absolution for all the sins of your past life. Now make a good Act of Contrition."

All through the formula of absolution, which Tony gave by mindless rote, the thinking part of his cerebrum kept shouting, *Jesus, Mary, and Joseph!*

At supper Tony fiddled with his food while Tom and Larry discussed the winter season upturn in collections. The bishop was still on his way back from Orlando, so table conversation was less arch than usual. In a casual voice Tony threw out the question that had his capillaries racing.

"What do you guys know about acting on knowledge learned in the confessional?"

Tom looked over at Tony, chewing thoughtfully. "You talking about what the seal allows—the *sigillum confessionis?*"

"Yeah."

"The first rule is you can't do it. Then you start looking at exceptions. At St. Mary's, Roland Park, where I went, the moral prof told us that in difficult cases you can ask another confessor's advice on how he would handle a particular sin or its circumstances, without, of course, revealing the identity of the penitent. You can do that, I know."

"Yes," agreed Tony. "They said the same at Dunwoodie."

"You have to be very careful, is what I remember," Larry broke in. "At Roland Park the prof told our class a story to show how a penitent's sin could be revealed accidentally. It was about this woman parishioner who told the pastor, 'Oh, Father, I had the honor of being the first person to confess to your newly ordained assistant.' And then, later, the assistant told the pastor, 'How do you like that? My very first confession and it's a case of adultery.'"

Tony and Tom laughed politely. They had both heard the story.

"What I mean is," Tony continued, "without *saying* anything to anybody, can you act on what you've heard?"

"Example?" Tom asked.

"Well, suppose someone had committed a sin of some kind at Touchton's Drug Store—I can't think of what it might be, shoplifting, let us say—and the reason he'd gone to the store in the first place, he says in confession, was that the store had a sale on toothpaste. Could I then act on that knowledge and pick up a couple of tubes of Pepsodent at the sales price?"

"I don't see why not," Tom said. "The sale was public knowledge, of which you were previously and simply unaware. I can't see how anything public like that could be *sub sigillo*—under the seal.

"If, on the other hand, the penitent revealed something secret, such as that the clerk who handled toothpaste was having an adulterous relationship with him or her or with someone else, you couldn't act on that information, by, say, counseling the clerk to break off that relationship. No, you couldn't do that."

"Of course not," Tony agreed. "In order to act on something secret—"

"You couldn't go over and counsel the toothpaste clerk

because, first of all, it's none of your business, and, second, because she or he would probably figure out how you knew about the relationship, and that would not only be detrimental to the penitent, it would compromise the integrity of the sacrament. I think I remember my major sem notes pretty clearly on that. But, if there are exceptions to that rule you'd best consult a moral theologian—if you can find one south of Baltimore."

Tom laughed.

"Not a canonist?" Tony asked.

"Oh God, no!"

"Thanks, Tom."

He let the matter drop and joined half-mindedly in the conversation that ensued on the advisability of starting a second collection after communion in order to take advantage of the well-to-do Catholic winter visitors in the city.

"We're not going to have them again, I bet," Tom said. "With the war gearing up and transportation restrictions tightening, they won't be down here next year. We'd better lay in some acorns for the hard times."

Excusing himself before dessert and coffee, Tony checked with Tom, "You and Larry are covering confessions at seven-thirty, right?"

"Yeah," Tom said. "It's my week to go double-duty. By the way, the Old Man said he'd take the six-thirty in the morning."

"Okay," Tony acknowledged. "I'll be up early. I'll help him with communions."

Tony mounted the stairs to his room and exchanged his cassock for the street garb of rabat, collar, Brooks Brothers black suit and hat that he wore outside the cathedral perimeter. It was not chilly enough for a topcoat.

He walked out on Cathedral Place and made his way briskly west past the Sip and Bite to the Ponce, tipping his hat to passersby, then around to the Ponce entrance, and across King Street to the white-faced Alhambra Hotel. He thought he would pay a courtesy visit to the owner, Mrs. Olga Mussallem, if she was there—compliment her on the faithful service her sons Wally and Eddie were rendering the Church as altar boys. All right, all right, he knew that was not the real reason. Yes, he knew he was skating on the thin edge. But Krug's registration as Krug or Homer was public knowledge—not as widespread as a toothpaste sale, but still public to all who knew he was a guest at the Alhambra, and that could be many or few, but still public. There was a registry, after all.

Uncomfortable as it was, even scary, Tony thought he had a moral obligation to throw himself into the middle of this situation as far as the sacrament of penance allowed. Human lives were at risk. Maybe even the course of the war? Was that too much to say? God, what a *load!* As long as he didn't *say* anything to anyone. Wasn't that the key? As long as he kept his lips sealed, couldn't he keep his eyes and ears *open?* Yes, that was it. Surely *that* was within the rules. Still, he'd better check. Later tonight. Or tomorrow.

As he approached the hotel, with its veranda of white wicker rockers fronting the entire facade, including the Florida Motor Lines office on the northeast corner, the appearance of the white-painted structure, in the glow of street lamps, took on a somber, ghostly cast, and his ear seemed to catch a faint foreboding message, one that caused his chest and sides to tingle. For a moment, he sensed that he was about to cross into a sinister zone from which, once entered, he could not step back. Still, with whatever bold force it was that impelled him, he opened the door to the lobby and stepped over its threshold.

Never having been in the Alhambra before, he was surprised by the luxuriant expanse of Oriental rugs that ran from the front entrance to a large stairway at the far end of the lobby. Numerous pillars interrupted the tall space, and, like the veranda, white wicker was everywhere— chairs, couches, and tables. A fireplace and what looked like a parlor, or card room, stood to his right. As he walked straight ahead his eyes caught sight of the front desk at the left, just before the stairs, and his ears recoiled from a volley of loud music and high voices passing through a closed doorway also to his left.

A slight, balding man behind the front desk greeted him as he approached, "Good evening, Father. Can I help you?"

"Good evening. I'm Father D'Angelo from the cathedral. I was wondering if Mrs. Mussallem was in. Just wanted to say hello."

"No, Father, she isn't. She's here in the daytime hours only." He put out his hand. "Miles Zeigler, Father. Everybody calls me Zig or Ziggy."

"Very glad to meet you," Tony said over the din from the nearby door—just as two soldiers burst through that door swinging fists drunkenly at each other and abusing the air with obscenities that Tony rarely heard.

Quick as a squash racket, Zig leaped over the desk and placed his small frame between the two men, delivering as he did so well-placed chops to particularly sensitive parts of the male anatomy. As the soldiers bent over in pain, Zig lifted up their faces by their collars and said sternly, "Now you two gentlemen apologize to the Padre here for using such foul language in his presence. Go on!"

One, a swarthy fellow, wet down the front of his khaki shirt, squinted hard at Tony. "Thas's Zorro," he blubbered. "Thas's one tough guy. Zorro I like. Get Zorro a drink."

His fistfighting friend, perhaps less inebriated, grabbed him by the arm and hauled him back through the door, which when opened, revealed, through a smoky gauze, uniformed soldiers and sailors, mostly soldiers, five deep at a long bar, and a brightly colored, much too loud jukebox that was booming Jimmy Lunceford's "Whatcha Know Joe." The vapor of alcohol passed into the lobby and hung like ether in an operating room.

"Sorry about that, Father," Zig said, walking back around to his position behind the desk.

"Not at all," Tony said. "I admired the way you handled those two men, both about twice your size, I'd say. Though I missed the Marquis of Queensberry rules."

"The Marquis never had to work the lobby on Saturday nights, Father. Never had a bar full of plastered soldiers. Never had the cockfighters. Oh, oh, look who's comin' now—the gauleiter."

Tony turned to see an army officer, flanked by two MPs, marching down the Oriental rugs.

"Major Max Edelstein," Zig confided. "Commands something called the St. Augustine Recreational Area. Thinks he commands the Western front."

When the major came abreast of the desk, he nodded toward Tony, "Evening, Reverend," then barked, "Zeigler, you had two lieutenants fighting in your lobby this afternoon. The army is not going to have that. Enlisted men fighting is bad enough, and the Alhambra bar and package store causes plenty of that. But officers fighting will not be tolerated. Tell any disorderly officer you see to use the O Club on the Bay. We will not have disgraceful displays by officers in this hotel. I will hold you and Mrs. Mussallem personally responsible. One more such outrage and I will close this bar and this entire hotel. You understand?"

"Quite so," Zig said, adding, "I hope you're as tough when you face the Germans, Major—if you ever do, which I doubt they'll let you, since you're so indispensable around here. Now say goodnight to the Father."

Edelstein bit his lip, nodded stiffly again in the direction of Tony, said "Father," and marched out, his MPs smartly alongside with their nightsticks.

"It's gonna be a long night, Father," Zig said with a grin.

"You said something about cockfighters?" Tony asked.

"Oh yeah, we have our share. A tournament's on just north of the city."

"I thought cockfighting was illegal," Tony said, surprised.

"Nah. Doesn't harm anyone. Brings a lot of money into the city and county. I mean a lot of money. Sheriff relies on me to keep 'em happy."

Tony took that in as best he could. The disturbed look

on his face caused Zig to speak in a different vein, "Life's a lot different outside the rectory, Father. But let me emphasize, we don't allow any whores here. None at all. Mrs. Mussallem is emphatic about that. She runs a good Christian hotel. Any of our bellhops tells us about being approached by a female guest on a three-two deal, and we call the police and they're gone. I mean, gone."

"I'm glad to hear that," Tony said. "And I'm not surprised, knowing Mrs. Mussallem's fine reputation and knowing her two altar-boy sons."

"You got it right, Father. She is one fine lady. We got a real nice lady guest in the hotel right now, too, judging from her clothes. Was going to wait in the lobby for her escort. Going to the dinner dance at the Ponce. I told her it would be best to wait in the parlor by the door. Said I'd direct her escort there. Wanted to keep her away from this Saturday night noise and liquor, you know, Father? And outta the way of any fights. We have lots of decent folk who come to the hotel and I try to take care of them nice as I can."

"I'm sure you do," Tony said, deciding to take his leave, but disappointed that he had not learned anything about Krug. "Enjoyed talking with you—uh, Zig. Please tell Mrs. Mussallem that I just dropped by to pay my respects. I'll come by again sometime in the daytime."

"That I will, Father. You take care of yourself. Stay outta the bars!" Zig laughed. "Some guys may not *like* Zorro!"

Tony turned with a chuckle and walked toward the front door, to the barroom beat of Tommy Dorsey's "Oh! Look at Me Now!"

CHAPTER 15

AS TONY NEARED the front door on his way out of the Alhambra, he paused for a quick peek into the parlor. At the moment, it was nothing more than an act of idle curiosity, though later he would readily acknowledge that it was as fateful an idle action as he had ever taken in his life.

Seated on a sofa inside the parlor, facing the door, was an attractive woman, late twenties–early thirties, brown hair, formally dressed, whose eyes at once caught his during the instant his head appeared.

"Oh, Father!" she called, extending her right hand, and catching Tony in the motion of withdrawal.

"Yes, ma'am," he said, having now to step bodily into the room.

Sally Parkins stood and said, "I hope I'm not botherin' you, it's just that I haven't seen a priest before in this whole state. I was beginnin' to think they didn't have 'em down here. They're all over New York. Do you know Father McGowan in New York? He would be a lot older 'n you."

"No, I'm afraid I don't," Tony answered. "I'm from New York, as a matter of fact, but they're hundreds of priests in the city I've never met and don't know."

"Father McGowan was the one that baptized me when I was born. His name is on my certificate, which is in a frame back home in New York. But I haven't been to church much, certainly not recently. And I never went to parochial school. I guess you'd call me fallen away."

"Well, you can do something about that," Tony encouraged her. "Did you ever go to catechism classes?"

"Never did. Never heard the word 'til just now. What is it?"

"Instructions in the Catholic faith."

"Oh, them. I asked my mother once—she wasn't all that religious—if I could go to Sunday school or Saturday school or whatever it was, don't know what nomination, near our place on West Forty-seventh between Sixth and Seventh. But she said, shove in your clutch!"

"Shove . . . ?"

"To tell the truth, Father, I gotta be honest with a priest. The real reason I wanted to go was to be with this dude I had a crush on we called Handsome Harold, who actually grew up to be a pretty good trumpet player, and not bad with the horses, either."

"Uh, Miss—?"

"Sally Parkins is my name, Father, honored to meet ya." She extended her hand.

"I'm Father D'Angelo," Tony said, accepting her hand. "Could we sit down for a moment? I can explain what you could do to get your religious life back on track again, one New Yorker to another, okay?"

"Okay," she agreed, and popped down on the sofa.

"You need to begin," Tony explained, "by learning the teachings of the Catholic faith into which you were baptized and by going to church regularly every Sunday and on holy days. Now how do you learn the teachings? By taking a course of instructions, the same course that is offered to converts. Once you finish the course, and have convinced the priest who is your teacher that you truly believe in God and accept all the doctrines of the Church, and that, furthermore, you are prepared to observe the rules and obligations of a Christian life, you can be prepared for confession and Holy Communion and be a full member of the Church."

"Oh," she said, screwing up her face, "I don't know if I wanna go all the way. Are the rules hard?"

"Not really," he said, "once they become a part of your life. Faithful attendance at Mass on Sundays and holy days of obligation, no meat on Fridays, fasting during Lent, and, of course, observance of the commandments. Then you would be expected to live a life of prayer and conse-crated service. It's a way of life, many, many centuries old, that would give your days both meaning and peace. Our Blessed Lord Jesus Christ would give you the strength to live that life through His holy sacraments."

"Can I take those instructions at any time," she asked, stalling, "or just at certain times in the year?"

"At any time," Tony assured her. "In the early church, catechumens, as converts-to-be were called, received their preparation during the period just before Easter. But, today, the Church gives instruction year-round."

"Well—I'm willin' to talk with ya about it. I just don't know about the rules, especially the commandments. Also, I may be traveling soon. Suppose I started and then had to hit the road?"

"You can continue the instructions elsewhere. Could you come by the rectory, say, tomorrow afternoon at one o'clock to talk with me about it some more? Do you know where the cathedral is?"

"I can ask my gentleman friend where it is."

"And let me recommend that you go to Mass tomorrow morning. I'm saying the eight o'clock, but you could also go to the six-thirty, ten, or eleven-thirty. And sit up front so you can see all that the priest does." Tony smiled, "All right?" raised his prominent eyebrows to signal that every-thing necessary to say for now had been said, and stood up. "Well! Until tomorrow afternoon, then. It's been a pleasure meeting you, Miss Parkins."

She stood and extended her hand. "And you, too, I'm sure, Father—oh!" She looked toward the parlor door. "Here's my gentlemen friend now."

Tony, too, turned toward the door and saw a man about his own height, long face, wide mouth, blue eyes, light hair, dressed in navy blue suit, white shirt, and red-blue-gold rep tie, holding a pearl-gray snap-brim.

"Peter!" Sally said excitedly, "this is a Father I just met."

"Good evening," the man said smoothly. "Peter Krug."

He reached for Tony's hand, from which blood drained all the way to his clerical black shoes.

Tony stuttered his name in return. Consciously, but awkwardly, he smiled and took a step. "Well!" he found himself able to say, "I was just leaving. I hope you have both—you both have an enjoyable evening." And, turning to Sally, "I'll look forward—to seeing, to seeing you tomorrow at one." He nodded to Krug. "Good night."

"Good night," Krug said, evenly.

"Good night, Father," Sally said cheerily.

Tony managed to make his feet work, left, right, left, right, toward the hotel doorway, where, once through, he expelled two lungfuls of frightened air.

Jesus, Mary, and Joseph.

Outside, Tony gathered his lapels against the chill that filled his chest. Head down, distracted, hardly seeing where he was going, he started across Granada Street but was hardly off the sidewalk when he collided with the front tire and handlebars of a braking bicycle.

"Oh!" cried the woman rider, as Tony caught both her and her vehicle in the act of collapsing onto the pavement.

"I'm sorry, I'm terribly sorry!" Tony exclaimed as he struggled to steady upright the victim of his recklessness. "I wasn't watching where I was going. I'm terribly sorry."

"Oh, it's you," the woman rider said, straddling her bike with her feet now safely on the pavement, rearranging her hair, and patting down her sweater. "Father D'Angelo?"

"Miss—Hart?" This was really embarrassing. "Are you hurt?"

"No," she said, catching her breath. "Actually, I had been hoping to bump into you—though not in this way."

Tony smiled with relief. He was elated—more than he dared admit—to be in her company again, particularly at this moment when he needed help in regaining his composure.

"I wanted to say again," she continued, "that I'm sorry to have spoken so strongly the other day. I just hope I didn't offend you."

"On the contrary," Tony sought to assure her. "I found your candor very refreshing. Are you out exercising this evening?"

"No, I get enough of that in the daytime. I'm headed for the Iceberg. Why don't you join me? I'll buy you a cone."

Tony thought about it for a moment. *Numquam solus cum sola*. Appearances, appearances. Would it look like a "date"? He decided, no—not if they walked in the middle of the street, she with her bike.

"Okay," he agreed. "That sounds like a nice idea, except for you paying. If I remember, you like satin coffee."

"You have a good memory."

"I just hope my judgment is as good as my memory," he confessed in a low voice as he walked alongside her on the empty street.

"What a strange thing to say. You're having a problem?" she asked.

"Yes. A professional problem. Larger than any I've ever had. I was wondering as I was crossing the street just now, whether I'm thinking about the problem for myself or if I'm simply thinking about it the way I've been directed to think? And if I *am* thinking for myself, is my thinking as good as, or perhaps better than, the thinking of some acknowledged authority? Does that make any sense?"

His expression of uncertainty was quite an admission, Tony reflected. Certainly for a Catholic priest. He would never have spoken in such a way to a parishioner. That he had doubts about anything, much less about Church authority, would have been cause for scandal in the ears of the typical parishioner. He felt at ease, though, talking in this vein to Miss Hart. Curious. He did not know why.

"I think I understand," Belle responded. "I'm very much my own person with my own views, as you've discovered. But I know I shock people sometimes. And I ask myself, do I really have reason to be confident that I know better than others? Including the so-called experts? I think everybody with a free, open, inquiring mind asks herself that kind of question from time to time."

They passed Craig's, then, at number forty-six, Saul Snyder's wholesale grocery, which Belle pointed out.

"In the seminary," Tony explained, "we learned everything by rote, much of it in Latin, all of it *ex auctoritate*— what the authorities said, people like Aquinas, Noldin, Tanquerey, Gredt. There was almost no encouragement given to think things through for ourselves. In fact, one could almost say that, except within certain defined limits, independent thought was actively discouraged."

"Where was this?" Belle asked.

"St. Joseph's Seminary at Dunwoodie, Yonkers, New York. Educationally, all we did there for four years was memorize manuals on dogma, moral theology, canon law, and ritual. We didn't even study the development of doctrine in the Ecumenical Councils. Everything was premasticated, and all we were expected to do was spit back what had been spat at us. Question and answer, question and answer. Many of the questions had not been asked by real people for centuries. Those that had, such as moral questions, were neatly treated in formulas, such as the principle of double-effect."

"Double-effect?" Belle asked.

"Yeah, that's the rule for dealing with situations where an evil is reluctantly and involuntarily caused as the side result of a good action or by the avoidance of another evil. You see," he added, smiling, "my memory serves me still."

"Can you give me an example?" Belle asked.

"Well, when a bomber pilot, let us say, aiming his bombs at a German aircraft plant, knows that nearby civilian residents will be killed by the explosion—"

"He can morally go ahead?"

"Yes, so long as four conditions I won't go into are met."

"Do you think that your typical bomber pilot would run through four conditions in his mind?"

"No, I don't. Anyway—theoretically—the double-effect doctrine reconciles the legitimate conduct of warfare with the moral prohibition against attacking innocent noncombatants. The proportionately greater good effect—

destruction of the enemy plant—compensates for and jus-
tifies the unintended evil effect, the civilian losses."

"Sounds like a very precious distinction to me."

Tony winced. "Well," he said, "we could discuss the
Protestant churches being awash in moral relativism, but
let's not."

"No, let's not," agreed Belle with a mischievous smile.
"Let's talk about what's wrong with your system."

"Ouch! How did I ever get into this conversation?"

"You started it, didn't you? Well, listen, good Father
D'Angelo, I have to admire you for talking so freely about
your uncertainties and vulnerabilities. I don't hear that
often in men. Any men. It's reassuring—and I promise to
guard the confidence."

"Thank you. Somehow I knew you would. Uh, here's
the Iceberg—"

Belle left her bike at the curb and the two entered an
immaculate drug store, populated largely by Negroes of
various ages from the Lincolnville district. Tony savored
the typical and undefinable soda fountain scent. He paid
for two cones, satin coffee for Belle, French vanilla for
himself.

"Thank you," Belle said. "The next one's on me."

As they started back, Tony returned to his theme
between licks. "What I wanted to say is that at Dunwoodie
we had almost no exposure to what was happening elsewhere in the academic world. New discoveries and theo-
ries in psychology and sociology, for example, which would
have been great background for understanding people's
relationships and for giving guidance to parishioners in
trouble. The latest findings in the physical sciences, history, law, anthropology—we heard none of that.
Contemporary Protestant theologies—we learned nothing
about them, either. Our mission was to memorize scholas-
tic syllogisms and erect defensive bulwarks around
anointed truths, or what we were told were truths. I'm
talking about a strictly imposed isolation from modern
currents of thought. And then, after ordination, we were

expected to go forth and preach to that outside world of independent learning. Preach?

"Like the rest of the guys, I wouldn't have had the wit to know what I was missing if I had not made an accidental discovery in the library one day. We had a library, all right, in the main building, but there was little in the wrought-iron bookcases except approved texts on theology, scripture, apologetics, lives of the saints, and things like that. And the library was only open two hours on Sunday and Wednesday mornings. And it had no lights. In my second year, I was appointed a library assistant and, one day while cleaning up—and I know this wasn't right— I jimmied open an office door that had always been kept locked, and it turned out to be the seminary archive. I spent a whole afternoon reading documents about the history of the seminary. And you know what I found?

"I found that back near the turn of the century the seminary rector, a Sulpician, whose name was Father James F. Driscoll, transformed the curriculum to make it completely open to contemporary research and thought. He invited leading scholars of the day, such as Charles Augustus Briggs from Union Theological Seminary, to give lectures at Dunwoodie. He encouraged the seminarians in their spare time to go into the city to pursue courses at New York University. And his Sulpician superior, Edward Dyer, worked out an arrangement with Columbia University so that the seminarians were accepted as graduate students and were permitted to attend lectures there, at no tuition cost. And at the same time, the priests on the Dunwoodie faculty published a journal called the *New York Review*, which was the most open and advanced Catholic theological journal in the country—by far. On a repeat visit to that room I read a number of the issues."

"What happened?" Belle asked.

"What happened was that Pope Pius, the tenth I think it was, issued an encyclical around nineteen-oh-seven condemning what he called 'modernism,' that is, any and all accommodations with modern thought, and the bishops in the United States got scared off any attempts, like Dunwoodie's, to build bridges to the intellectual world outside Catholicism. I mean they got really scared. Archbishop Farley of New York killed the *New York Review*. Then he fired Driscoll as rector and replaced him with the New York police force chaplain. All connections with Protestants, NYU, and Columbia were cut off. Classroom instruction was limited to Thomistic scholasticism, most of it in Latin. And everyone, faculty and students alike, was put on a West Point footing. The repression was on, and it lasted right down to my day—in fact, to this day, some thirty-five years later.

"It's no exaggeration to say that what I discovered in that archive saved my mind. It determined me to make up for what I was missing. Every vacation after that, especially the next summers, including my subdeacon summer schedule, I attended lectures that were open to the public at Fordham, Columbia, and the New School. And I devoured books at the Forty-second Street public library. I can't tell you how many wonderful hours I spent in that reading room."

"Did you tell the other seminarians what you found?" Belle asked.

"Vaguely, in terms of what they were not learning. I couldn't be specific about what the seminary had been like back in the Driscoll years because that would have gotten to the rector, who would have demanded to know how I learned that, and the revelation of my break-in might well have prevented my ordination. It was ironic when, later, in the rector's office, I took the oath against modernism, as we were all required to do as a condition of ordination.

"As for the other guys you asked about, the majority seemed not to be very interested in what I told them. They were by and large content with St. Thomas and scholasticism. Most of them didn't want to study any more than they had to. It's a shame. They were simply not challenged—intellectually, that is, unless you consider mere memorization as growth. During the academic 'reign of terror' that was in place during my time at Dunwoodie, only the good memorizers survived."

"Reign of terror?" Belle asked.

"Oh, that was a purge of sorts. The archbishop and the rector decided that there were too many seminarians, too many guys wanting to become priests. So they weeded out as many as they thought they didn't need."

"I see."

"Here you had the cream of New York Catholic manhood. All around regular guys. Athletic. Very bright, actually. They could have been anything, done anything. But they were never encouraged to grow. As I've expressed it to myself many times, instead of a mandarin's education, they received a cadet's indoctrination. The post-Driscoll seminary limited most of them to rote careers of Mass and the sacraments, CYO, Holy Name, Children of Mary, Johnnie Walker, golf, and the horses."

By this time they had reached King Street and stood outside the Motor Lines office. "Sure you're not being too hard on them?" Belle asked.

"Perhaps so," Tony conceded. "They're all good men. Intellectually servile, but yes, good priests. Have you ever heard of Monsignor Sheen?" Belle shook her head. "No? Well, he said one thing once that I half agree with. It was: the finest three qualities of a priest are kindness, kindness, and kindness. If that's true, then my Dunwoodie friends are doing okay. *Ad multos annos*. Well—sorry to bore you with all that. I'm pretty voluble this evening, aren't I? I'd better say goodnight and get back to the rectory."

Belle mounted her bike. "This time," she said, "it was I who learned something from you. Thank you. Good night."

Tony tipped his hat and watched her pedal west on King. Funny that he had unveiled that much of himself to her. Such an open, free-spirited woman. He wondered where she lived.

He turned to cross Granada again, looking carefully this time to left and to right.

He had not thought that much for a long while about his four years in major sem. Total, mindless regimentation. Rise at five-thirty, morning prayers at six, Mass at six-thirty, first class at nine, lecture, lecture, lecture, chapel at noon, lecture, handball at three, memorization, memorization, memorization, rosary, spiritual nosegays, lights out at ten. No talking above the ground floor, no smoking except in the ballfield area, no "particular friendships," et cetera, et cetera.

Finally, ordination, and acceptance into the "world's greatest fraternity," as the New York clergy like to say. *Haec est vera fraternitas. Ecce quam bonum et quam jucundum habitare fratres in unum.*

That last part was okay. But the mindless years at Dunwoodie were best forgotten. Especially now when he had something far more urgent to worry about.

When Tony reached the rectory, Mattie Mae heard him open and close the front door from her chair in the kitchen. She approached him in the hallway with a bucket of ice.

"Father, bishop say take this ice to his rooms when you gets back."

"Oh, sure, Mattie Mae, thanks for telling me." The bishop liked to have a nightcap about this hour. Tony took the ice and bounded up the stairs. Garvey responded in Italian to his knock.

As Tony entered, Garvey laid his wire-rimmed spectacles on the lamp table that stood by his chair.

"We have a first-class fool in the Miami paper," Garvey said, tossing the *Herald* to the floor. Tony began mixing up a couple of Black Labels and soda on a side table beneath a large framed print of Rogier van der Weyden's *St. George and the Dragon*.

"An authentic tin-plated fool," Garvey went on, "of the sort who should be institutionalized for the duration."

Tony handed him a glass. "Some smokey fluid of Knockando, Eccellenza."

"Says that Floridians themselves need not fear the Germans," Garvey quoted. "The enemy is too far away to present any real danger to us on land here, he says. Any real danger. Doesn't the fool know the global intent of these Nazi thugs? Doesn't he know that U-boats are blowing up ships just off our shores—right now?"

The bishop raised his glass, stared at it for a moment wordlessly, then took an ecumenical sip from the Protestant Morayshire.

"Do you think we'll get involved here in St. Augustine?" Tony asked with a hidden purpose.

"We *are* involved," Garvey answered. "Everyone is involved. This is no eighteenth-century campaign where royal houses dispatch professional soldiery to do battle in distant meadows. This is total war. There are no noncombatants. We are all in the trenches. There is no place to hide. I've told the sisters to prepare our schoolchildren for bombing raids. When the evil force approaches—and you never know in what overt or cryptic form he will appear—each man, woman, and child must do his duty."

A deeper draft from his glass lent passion to Garvey's tongue. "Everyday I pray fervently the prayer for peace: *Deus, qui conteris bella.* . . . But the peace I want is the peace of Pius Twelfth, the peace of justice, not of subjugation, of law and independence, not of tyranny, of national life, not of national death—the peace of the Four Freedoms, if you will.

"I would hate to say that war is a natural state of man. But war happens with such frequency, you simply must take it into account, prepare for it, and, when necessary, wage it. That's what the Church has done since the time of Constantine. That's why we have a 'Just War' doctrine. Even warrior saints are not unknown to the Canon. Joan of Arc is an example. Saint Barbara is the patron of field artillery. For the good of nations and for the good of religion itself, there are times when good simply must contend physically with evil—St. Michael against Lucifer, St. George against the Dragon."

"Are there any priests who have fought in wars?" Tony asked. "Not as chaplains, I mean, but as fighting men?"

"You mean like Friar Tuck?" Garvey laughed. "Yes, there are many examples. Canon Law prohibits it, but, yes, just look at Latin America. Do you know the name Miguel Hidalgo? No? Parish priest of Dolores, father of Mexican independence. A very cultured man, a writer and translator. He led an army against the Spaniards under the banner of Our Lady of Guadalupe, sometime in the early nineteenth century. Another priest, José María Morelos, took up his banner. Both men were eventually captured and executed."

"Not very reassuring," Tony noted, chuckling.

"*Forsitan*," Garvey half-conceded, and then abruptly stuck his right index finger in the air. "Bannon," he said. "Father John B. Bannon. He fought for the Confederacy. Helped man an artillery piece on one occasion, as I recall. There are other examples. Julius the Second, the warrior pope.

"Here in Florida, as you can read in the records, when the English from Carolina attacked the Spanish missions near present-day Tallahassee in seventeen-oh-four, slaughtering the Christian Indians in one of the most bloody and gratuitous massacres of the colonial period, a Franciscan friar named Angel de Miranda rallied his charges at Mission La Concepción de Ayubale and led them in a spirited armed defense of the compound."

"What happened?" Tony asked.

"They gave a very good account of themselves, killing and wounding a large number of the attacking force. But they ran out of musket balls and arrows and had to surrender. The English let Miranda live, but they butchered the Indians, burning some alive, impaling others on stakes. The crime cries to heaven. It cries out just to be mentioned in the history books."

"Those are examples from a long time ago, Eccellenza," Tony objected. "They don't seem to have much relevance to modern warfare."

"Oh, there are more recent examples. When the German panzer corps pushed south into France after Dunkirk, the French Army deployed many of its forces in fortified enclaves, villages and woods, that they called hedgehogs, after the spiny European mammals that roll themselves into balls for protection. Those hedgehogs were ordered to continue fighting even if bypassed by the advancing panzers. In Rome I met a French parish priest and his brother who had been in one of the hedgehog villages. The brother told me that the priest organized, armed, and led his villagers in resisting the surrounding Germans. 'He preached the gospel of peace by day,' the brother said, 'and laid ambushes by night.' There are times, you see, when you must do what you must do."

"Canon Law notwithstanding," Tony said.

Garvey let the comment pass.

There was a far more urgent question in Tony's mind. He thought for a moment on how to phrase it.

"Eccellenza," he began, as casually as he could, "just as speculation, suppose, in the course of hearing a confession, I learned of the presence and murderous activity of a German agent here in Florida. What could I do about it?"

Garvey leaned forward. "You can never violate the seal," he warned.

"Of course not, Eccellenza. But without betraying the seal, could I try to stop such a person?"

"Make use of confessional knowledge, is what you're asking."

"Yes."

"Under certain well-defined circumstances I know you can make use of confessional knowledge. If I had my Kurtscheid—he wrote a fine book on the subject in twenty-seven or twenty-eight—but I lost it when a U-boat sank my luggage in October a year ago. What you need to do in a case like that is consult a moral theologian or a canonist."

"If, because of the knowledge I held, I was the only one who could prevent that agent from doing harm to our country or to individual Americans, would I be justified in so acting?"

Garvey paused to savor his malted barley and to take into his mouth a chip of ice. Then, rolling the ice in his cheek, and looking abstractly to the ceiling, he recited from the Seventeenth Psalm: "But who is God except the Lord? . . . Who trained my hands for war and my arms to bend a bow of brass? . . . And you girded me with strength for war."

He lowered his eyes and repeated the last line in Latin: *Et praecinxisti me virtute ad bellum.*

Tony recognized the Latin easily enough, from Matins every Monday in the divine office. But, for whatever reason, the Old Man was not giving him a directive answer. That was all right. He respected him for that. He would consult another authority in the morning.

And then he would make up his own mind.

With Garvey's nodding approval, he rose, went to the ice bucket, and fixed himself a second.

Perhaps two jiggers this time instead of one would gird him in that resolve. As he stirred, he fixed his eyes again on St. George and the Dragon.

Later that Saturday night, the "Ancient City" and environs presented numerous tableaus of varying hues and intensities:

The multicolored Wurlitzer jukebox in the Mat Shop on Cathedral Place changed 78s from "Amapola" to "My Sister and I," while high school boys drank chocolate freezes and talked of enlistment.

At the Matanzas Theater next door, high school girls tried to watch Walter Pidgeon and Maureen O'Hara in *How Green Was My Valley* while horny dates probed their knees and sweater-clad breasts.

In a white clapboard house on Myrtle Avenue, a father, mother, and two daughters chewed vigorously on wads of Red Man tobacco in order to produce a poultice for grandmother's creeping eruption hookworm.

In the plaza, a GI sat and wept disconsolately as he read and reread his "Dear John" letter, from which three buddies, bent on partying, could not distract him.

At Glick's Famous Bar on Cathedral, local civilian men-about-town Erwin "Drys" Drysdale, Freddie Francis, and Hoot Gibson stood obediently at attention, as ordered by Texas trainees from Camp Blanding, to revere the jukebox lyrics of "Deep in the Heart of Texas."

In a room at the north end of Washington Street in Lincolnville, a bolita operator, having passed around a bag containing a hundred little wooden numbered balls for inspection by his crowd of players, finally tossed it to be caught by a pinched ball, the number of which paid four dollars on a five-cent bet.

At Flagler Hospital, big-faced, blustery Dr. George Walter Potter dripped ether from a can over the gauze-covered face of a sailor whose chest knife wound threatened his future ability to breathe.

In a two-room suite at the Buckingham, thirty-five-year-old Baltimore widow Janet Palmer, Goucher '28, brushed her ample figure and worried what the just-announced wartime rationing of rubber thread would do to her resupply of foundation garments.

Close by the waterworks in West Augustine, Big Margaret's whorehouse (listed in the phone book as "Seamstress") introduced a dozen young servicemen, in various states of intoxication, to the mysteries of womanhood.

At the same time, Dr. Vernon Lockwood, chief surgeon of the East Coast Hospital on King and Malaga, went down the standing line of servicemen who had already experienced Big Margaret's ministrations and made prophylactic injections in their urethras.

In his privately owned potbellied boat, *Moon Regulator*, named after the biggest man in the mythical Negro country of Diddy-Wah-Diddy, a place of no work and no worry, a Minorcan with two helpers from the city worked the waters offshore for shrimp that he could sell, shelled, cleaned, and headless, for four cents a pound.

At Marine Studios the porpoises, their circadian rhythms completely out of whack, and unfamiliar with the advance of human clocks one hour to eastern war time, circled the black oceanarium water wondering how come their feedings were no longer at the regular times.

Whitney Street merchant L. O. Davis, leaving the West Augustine white home with little hope that his missionary work on behalf of Atcheson Baptist Chapel would have much success with this particular family, scribbled in his notebook: "Wife, drunk, thought me a revenue officer—children under the influence of liquor—husband in the swamp making shine—family Roman Catholics."

At Surfside on Vilano Beach, Major Max Edelstein drew two soldiers off the dance floor and admonished them sternly that any more public pushing and shoving over that redhead meant time in the guardhouse, and he was not kidding.

In Denmark's Row on Evergreen Avenue in West Augustine, a group of Negro men forgot their poverty and squalor in fifths of payday Calvert's, while one of their number nursed an inflammation on his arm with dinosaur grease, as he believed black tarry Ichthyol to be.

On Locust Street, while his wife, Claudia, prompted from the script of Clare Boothe's "Margin for Error," Langston Moffet rehearsed his Little Theater lines as the German consul Karl Baumer: "What am I to do with fifty thousand? Start a hundred more camps! Get a broadcasting station! Buy up American journalists! Next Berlin will order me to corrupt Dorothy Thompson, with an autographed picture of Hitler."

At the Castle Warden Hotel, owner Norton Baskin and his wife Marjorie Kinnan Rawlings poured three bourbon nightcaps before showing their houseguest, Nobel laureate Sigrid Undset, to her room.

On Marine Street, Tommy Williams and Bubba Davis weighed the advantages of the dollars gained by theft of linen left on a front porch against the advantages of an airplane ride, and decided to fly.

In her upstairs apartment on Riberia Street, Belle Hart, with a glass of cold milk in hand, read a front-page article in the new March 1 number of the *Civil Aeronautics Journal* urging private pilots to join the Civil Air Patrol.

In his oceanfront room on St. Augustine Beach, Paul Ohlenburg finished his Latin homework while listening to "Saturday Night Serenade" on CBS.

At the rectory, Tony lay in bed listening to the campanile outside his window strike ten o'clock while staring, wide-eyed and unseeing, at the twelve-foot ceiling, dimly lit by a street lamp outside.

And at the Venido Room of the Ponce, under Iberian heraldry in red, blue, and gold leaf, and flanked by tall stained glass windows by Louis Comfort Tiffany, Miss Sally Parkins, in long sleeved black velvet top highlighted by metallic embroidery, with bouffant blue pastel satin skirt, which was one of her better Miami acquisitions, glided gracefully in the arms of Peter Krug to the strains of "I Guess I'll Have to Dream the Rest." She loved the way he led her. It was wonderful to be dancing again. And with such a man! She did not resist or show displeasure when Krug brushed her cheek with his lips. Hardly so. She giggled and kissed him back, on the lips. Minutes later, when they sat out a fast number by the Rainbow Room Sextet, she willingly accepted his warm hand in hers. And she let him know, further, that advances were more than welcome when she laid her right leg softly against his left.

"They're playing another slow number," Krug observed. "Shall we?"

Sally stood gladly, eager to place herself in Krug's embrace. This time, as the 4/4 beat of "The Things I Love" filled their heads, she took the initiative of pressing her body tightly against his; at one point, during the eight-bar bridge, humming in his ear. And for the remainder of their dance floor evening, her closeness, her misty eyes, her half-open mouth disclosed a desire to remove any remaining space or barrier that existed between them.

Not missing any of those signals, Krug knew that their highway partnership was ready to be sealed.

In the semidarkness of Sally's room at the Alhambra, where they stood facing each other before a shade-drawn window, only the closet bulb giving light, Krug slowly removed her slip and bra, smiling thinly at her giggles and purrs. As his palms moved gently across her rounded surfaces he recalled Reinhard Heydrich's words, "Where you can be soft, be soft."

And when, minutes later, in bed, he separated the white columns of her thighs, he remembered Heydrich again, "But where you must be hard . . ."

CHAPTER 16

TONY TURNED WITH the gold-plated ciborium in his left hand to face the congregation. Holding one of the small communion hosts between his right thumb and index finger above the ciborium, he enjoined the cathedral parishioners, whose bodies, at eight o'clock Mass, more than half-filled the nave and two transepts, to behold, under the appearance of unleavened bread, the Lamb of God who takes away the sins of the world.

Then, with altar boy Eddie Mussallem in tow, he descended the altar steps to distribute communion to the parishioners who approached and knelt at the marble altar rail. While Eddie held the paten under communicants' chins, Tony made a small sign of the cross with each host and monotoned: *Corpus Domini nostri Jesu Christi custodiat animam tuam in vitam aeternam. Amen.*

Halfway down the gospel side he looked up to observe that Larry, with the other altar boy, was distributing along the epistle side. Before his eyes returned to the ciborium, however, they jammed stuck at the sight of Sally Parkins in a close-fitting hat kneeling in the second pew near the center aisle. In the brief moment that their eyes met, Sally winked and waved at him.

Unfortunate, he thought. For the remainder of Mass he was plainly distracted—off his stroke. It was not because of Sally's innocent gaffe. It was because her presence starkly reminded him of Krug, whom he had made a conscious effort to exclude from his early morning thoughts and prayers—at least through Mass. *Age quod agis.* But now he found he could no longer do that. He stumbled through the rest of the liturgy. He nearly forgot the ablution, and he had to read the *Placeat*, which he had always easily recited from memory. When he turned to give the blessing, he deliberately looked over the heads of the congregation toward the choir loft.

Tightening his concentration during the prayers after mass, he prayed aloud with particular fervor and purpose the prayer to St. Michael the Archangel, with its militant supplication: "Defend us in battle, be our protection against the malice and snares of the devil. . . . Thrust into hell Satan and the other evil spirits who roam through the world seeking the ruin of souls." But as he unvested in the sacristy afterwards, he realized that Krug continued to encompass his mind.

At breakfast he tried to put the man aside at least long enough to read the Sunday paper. But, again, he was not successful. There was nothing to do but call Eddie Hagerty, his fellow *ordinandus* from Dunwoodie.

"Operator, I'd like to place a long-distance call, person-to-person, to Father Edward Hagerty in Washington, D.C. He's at Catholic University. And the phone is a pay phone in Caldwell Hall. The number is Hobart nine-three-two-four.

"One moment, please."

Plug clicks, line tones, two rings. The Washington operator. More rings. Then—a man's voice:

"Caldwell Hall."

"This is the long-distance operator. I have a person-to-person call for Father Edward Hagerty in Caldwell Hall."

"Hold on a minute," the Caldwell Hall voice said.

Less than a minute later: "This is Father Hagerty."

"Go ahead, sir," the operator said.

"Hey, Fast Eddie! This is Tony D'Angelo in Florida."

"Tony! What a surprise. Great to hear your voice. How is it down there? Great, I bet."

"Yeah, it's pretty nice."

"Bunch of the Dunwoodie dudes are down there now tearing up the golf links."

"Yeah, I'm not surprised. They'd be much farther south than St. Augustine where I'm at."

"And giving Hialeah and Tropical a run for their money, I bet! Hey, what gives?"

"I've got a moral theology question, Eddie, and since you're the only STD in the field I know—"

"Still working on the dissertation, buddy."

"That's close enough. Listen, what I need is anything up-to-date you've got on the use of confessional knowledge."

"Under the seal stuff?"

"Yeah."

"Okay. Well, we went through that. I've got my notes. I can check the sources. How soon do you need it?"

"Would you believe, *quam primum?*"

"That bad, huh?"

"Yeah."

"Okay, let me get on it. Call you back in an hour. Got to help out in a parish at eleven-thirty. Let me have your number."

Tony gave him the number and insisted that he call collect.

At ten-thirty, Mattie Mae called Tony to the phone. After closing the office door and acknowledging Eddie, he made notes of the key concepts and words:

"Okay, here's what I've got," Eddie said. "There's not a lot written on it, actually. The main sources on the seal itself are the Fourth Lateran Council in twelve fifteen and a decree of the Holy Office in sixteen eighty-two. Before Gratian in the eleventh century, oddly enough, there doesn't seem to have been much concern about maintaining confessional content as privileged information. Anyway, you didn't want to know about revealing privileged material, but the use of it, right?"

"Right."

"Okay, the basic rule is this: confessional knowledge may never be used *cum gravamine poenitentis.*"

"*Cum gravamine.*"

"That means when there is any resulting harm to the penitent—anything detrimental, disadvantageous, or displeasing to the penitent—and that includes situations where there is no revelation of confessional material as such.

"Having said that, theologians have noted certain cases where confessional knowledge can be used. For example, the confessor can seek another priest's advice on the handling of a certain type of sin, provided the identity of the penitent is not revealed. We all know about that. Another example: the confessor can use his knowledge for actions that are agreeable to the penitent or at least indifferent to him, again without revealing his identity. All the theologians are agreed on that. A third example: if the penitent discloses something that is public information, such as that the governor has just been assassinated, an event of which the confessor was not previously aware, the confessor may certainly discuss the assassination afterward in the external forum, so long as no sin confessed by the penitent is associated with the assassination and there is no likelihood that the confessor's use of that knowledge would cause the penitent to believe his confidence had been betrayed. You get the drift. Public information is exempted. Only a handful of writers I know about disagree with that—Saint Alphonsus Liguori, for one, who was a strict constructionist."

"So," Tony asked, *"doctores scinduntur?* The authorities are divided?"

"Yeah, just use your common sense. Now there's another possibility. The penitent may give the confessor permission to use confessional knowledge to warn another person or persons of impending harm, and, personally, I would carry it further to say, to prevent that harm. We have an obligation under the precept of charity to shield others from injury. But this is a permission, all the writers agree, that should rarely be asked or used. The circumstances really must be extraordinary. And no *gravamen*, no detriment, must attach to the penitent.

"Very interesting. Very helpful."

"And Tony, if your case is anything like that, I would ask in the sacramental forum if the penitent would agree to give you that same permission in the external forum. Just to be sure. You know what I mean?"

"Yes, I do, Eddie. Thank you, very, very much."

"Anything else?"

"No, I think that's it. Why don't you come down for a visit?"

"Boy, I'd love to. The radiator in my room keeps going out. Maybe someday. I'll let you know."

"Okay, and thanks again."

"And, Tony, be careful. Remember, the penalty laid down by the Lateran Council for violating the seal is confinement in a monastery for life. You don't want that—unless you like cheese."

"Got it! Thanks again. Bye."

"Bye."

Promptly at one o'clock, Sally Parkins rang the rectory doorbell. Tony met her and welcomed her into the office, leaving the door slightly open as he always did when the visitor was a woman.

"So you say you're leaving town quite unexpectedly?" he asked in a surprised tone, acknowledging her first words to him after she was seated opposite his desk.

"Yeah—yes, Father. My gentleman friend, Mr. Krug, and I decided to drive south together. He's an artist, you know, or maybe I didn't say. He's lookin' for good places to paint pictures and invited me to go along. Ain't that, I mean isn't that neat? For some reason, this morning Peter thought we should leave at once. One of those spur of the moment things, as they say."

She smiled. "So, we're all packed, and as soon as I get back from talkin' with you, we're off."

"I see," Tony said, seeing a great deal more than Sally but unable to tell her so.

They looked at each other for a moment. "Well!" she said. "I'm all ears. You mentioned something about instructions."

"Of course!" Tony said, smiling broadly and reaching into a right desk drawer to pull out a paperbound book. "This is the book we normally use for instructions. You can take it with you on your trip." He handed it across the desk.

While Sally paged idly through the text, expressing her disappointment that it contained no pictures, Tony's mind raced through a series of propositions, questions, and judgments: Krug leaving . . . Where to? Why is he taking this woman? She seems to be well below his mind and breeding. But that's based on very brief first impressions. Should he, could he warn her away from him? Not possible. She would tell him. Krug would then know I'm onto him. How would a local priest learn such a thing? The Ohlenburgs . . . Krug would find out if Paul was Catholic, went to confession . . . *gravamen poenitentis* . . . Paul and his father dead, maybe me, too.

It took only seconds for the inspiration to form. Reaching into another drawer, Tony brought forth a packet somewhat larger than the instruction book, and spread its contents on the desk.

"The book I gave you, you can use as background reading," he told her. "But what I want you to study are these extension course instructions, something put together originally by the Knights of Columbus, a laymen's organization. These are instructions you can study on your own schedule while you travel."

"That's really keen," she said, approvingly.

"Yes," Tony went on, emboldened by her positive reaction. "Now you have to be serious about the lessons. If you look at the individual lessons—there are twenty in all—you'll see that each one is paired with a question and answer sheet that you mail back to me. The questions are drawn from the material in each study lesson: 'Why did God make me? What is my purpose in life?' Each time you finish a lesson—I recommend you do one every day—write out your answers on the question form and send the form back to me by mail. I'm writing my address here on a card. Keep this card in a place where you won't lose it—oh, well, don't worry about it: if you lose it just address the envelope, 'Father D'Angelo, Cathedral, Saint Augustine,' and it'll reach me. Maybe I should give you some three cent stamps—"

"Oh, no! I have lots of stamps and smackeroos for more. This is such a neat way to learn something. I like it already. Now do I need to see a priest anywhere while I study?"

"No, not unless you want to. If you decide to return to Saint Augustine, then by all means come in to see me. When you have completed the instructions we can make arrangements for your admission to the sacraments here. But if you decide to settle down elsewhere, just let me know and I'll certify to the pastor in that city that you've completed the instructions and he can go through the final steps with you there."

"And all this time I didn't know how easy it was to get straight with the Church. Thank you, Father D'Angelo. You are one nice guy."

Tony wondered how Sally had become entangled with a man like Krug. Which one inveigled the other? He debated with himself whether to say anything about the impropriety of an unmarried couple traveling together. Would they be sleeping together in violation of the sixth commandment? It was not just knowledge of the catechism that made one fit to enter the Church. It was also demonstration of a conscientiously moral, if not a blameless, life, during the conversion period. But she would read that for herself in the lessons. And probably he ought not to presume any activity on her part that the Church regarded as sinful, for, even if it was a good guess, it would be plain presumption—and perhaps very insulting to her if he voiced it. He could lose her as a potential convert. Yes, let her read the material on the sixth commandment for herself. That was what he decided. But he reproached himself for not acknowledging more candidly the real reason why he dared not risk fumbling the ball on this play.

She stood up with her purse and packet. "Thank you again, Father," she smiled. "You'll hear from me in the mail real soon. And that's a fact."

As he walked her to the door, Tony remarked as casually as he could, "You know, religious conversion is a very personal, a very solitary thing. It ought not to be made subject to a lot of outside influences or distractions. Let the lessons speak for themselves. If you have any questions, you can address them to me. I don't think it's advisable to discuss what you're doing with anyone, lest you hear wrong information and become confused."

"Including Mr. Krug?" she asked.

"I would say so."

Though the scent of danger was strong in his nostrils, there seemed no way for him to warn her. With Krug such an apparent good friend to her, she would regard it outrageous to suggest that he meant her any harm. Obviously, he was using her. But how could he prove that? And how would he phrase such a warning, if he gave one? And it would end in *gravamen poenitentis*, as he had already concluded. So he'd have to forget it.

"Miss Parkins," he ventured, "it's none of my business and I don't mean to be intrusive, but simply to show my concern for your well-being, are you completely certain it will be safe for you to travel with a gentleman you have only just met?"

"You mean Peter? Oh, he's a *dear*. I know a gentleman when I meet one. Don't worry about me. I'm very experienced."

There was nothing more he could say. It was best to let his present plan work itself out. A warning could be given later if it seemed necessary, possible, and credible. In the meantime, he would keep his eyes and ears open. Especially his eyes.

"Goodbye, then, and God bless you," he said. "And please be very careful on your trip."

"I will. Toodle-oo."

Tony waited by the open door until Sally had crossed St. George. Then he stepped out to the black rectory Chevrolet at the curb and pulled the Esso road map of Florida from the glove compartment.

Up in his room, he pinned the map onto the inside of the closet door. He found a red pencil in his desk and tied about a foot and a half of string to it. Then he pinned the knotted end of the string through the top of the map and into the door.

Finally, he sat down with his breviary to recite the hours Prime, Terce, Sext, and None.

But he wondered if, instead, he should be reciting *The Prince*?

Krug's black Pontiac bumped over the coastal highway State 140 south from St. Augustine, past the Ohlenburgs' beach cabin, across the toll bridge at Matanzas Inlet, and along the sand dunes that held the body of the meddlesome bass fisherman. He gave the last site only a glance. His mind was fixed on separating himself from St. Augustine as rapidly as possible, and getting down to business.

The wait for his watercolor paper had been an inconvenience, but he had used the time well. He had three sheets of completed paintings. He had established himself as an artist. And he had picked up a considerable amount of intelligence from soldiers and sailors in the Alhambra bar, some of it corroborated, innocently, by Zig. He knew now that the principal army air fields were Drew and MacDill in Tampa and Eglin at the far end of the Panhandle. But, first, he had to make contact with Lorenz.

No one could track him now. No one could connect him by face or name to his car or license plate, which he had left parked on Cordova Street, some distance from the hotel, and had not used until now. The American hotel system was much looser than the European. One could register under an alias and false address with impunity. No identity card had to be produced, no *formular* or *fiche* had to be filled out for the local police. Payment was made in cash. He would keep all his forged licenses and other cards in the name of Krug, of course, and use them as required, but his hotel registrations henceforth would simply be in other names. He would have to come up with some names. And he would have to explain that somehow to Sally. But Heydrich had been emphatic: "Never leave a trail."

He looked over at Sally and feigned a caring smile. She responded with a hand on his arm. So they were off together, her luggage in the trunk, his, including the foldable easel, stool, color box, three paper pads, and the case for carrying completed paintings on the back seat and floor. Their arrangement was to their mutual advantage. For him it was camouflage and respectability. For her it was companionship and escort service. The sex was also good. And it would probably get better.

"Isn't this swell, Peter?" Sally said, pointing to the shoreline as they approached Flagler Beach.

He readily agreed that it was, looking at the beachfront scenery for the first time now that he had resolved the intentions in his mind. Somewhat relaxed, he even began to envisage how these pleasant sea and shore scapes might be translated onto paper.

To their left were mile after mile of compacted sand beach lapped by curling gray-blue surf and white froth. The ocean scenes were framed, below, by undulating sand dunes topped by palmettoes and sea oats, and, above, by slow flights of brown pelicans in single file. A yellow March sun soaked up the humid air.

To the right of the roadbed, which gave way occasionally to a noisy shell surface, was a north-south intracoastal waterway, seen now and then through screens of moss-bearded scrub oak, magnolia, and cabbage palm. From time to time a white cabin cruiser appeared on the glittering waterway, while, just atop the marshes on the bank, a flotilla of white ibises flying red-orange bills as colors competed for attention.

"Well, you really swept me off my feet, didn't you?" Sally joshed him.

"Oh, I thought it was the other way around," he smiled back. "You were the one who invited me to the dance, remember?"

"This must be what they call a whirlwind romance," she mused.

"I guess so," he laughed. "Hang on to your hat!"

"Speaking of hanging on," she said, running her hand along his right forearm, "how come you wear your money belt when you're making love?"

"Oh, it's just a habit. I hope it doesn't rub too hard against you."

"Why don't you at least turn it around?" That way, Sally knew, she could get her hands into it.

"No, I'm a creature of habit. You have to take me the way I am. Sorry about that."

"Well—it seems strange to me. And why do you wear a knife on your right wrist?"

"To protect the money belt."

"Oh."

"And if *I* may ask a question," he said, "did you say anything to that priest about where we were going?"

"How could I when I don't know myself?"

"Okay."

"Remember, Peter, you promised we ain't goin' anywhere near Miami."

"That's right. We won't be within a hundred and twenty-five miles of Miami."

They engaged in desultory conversation for a while more. Then Sally dozed for a quarter hour, and, on awakening, started reading one of her several copies of *Modern Screen*.

About an hour after leaving St. Augustine, the Pontiac began entering the populated areas, successively, of Ormond Beach, Daytona Beach, Port Orange, and New Smyrna, where the going was a little slower. Krug determined to reach the Canaveral peninsula by dinner time—or, as they said in the South, suppertime.

Eastward, the afternoon sky was a porcelain blue above towering, white-capped, liquid mountains. Westward, it hid behind distant dusky gray masses and smaller clouds that were cotton balls with dirty bottoms. In his mind Krug mixed ultramarine and light red with some viridian and raw sienna.

Finally, the Pontiac pulled into a semicircle of "Tourists

Only" cabins at the dune ridge resort of Cocoa Beach. An illuminated sign above the office cabin promised: SLEEP.

While Sally unloaded what she needed for the night, Krug registered under the name, Mr. and Mrs. Winslow Homer. After inspecting their tiny cabin, the two of them drove a short distance down the road where the clerk said they could get a decent seafood dinner, which they found to be the case, and they lingered long in conversation. That finished, they returned to their cabin. After undressing, and with as much tenderness and patience as he could practice, though distressed by the clanging springs, Krug prepared Sally for what the sign outside predicted.

Once she had entered into that state, he wrote a note, in case she awakened, to say that he would be back a little later, placed a pencil, ten folded leaves of stationery, a penlight, lock pick, and watchcap in his pocket, turned the key in the Pontiac, and headed south to Banana River.

Sally, who had watched his arrangements and departure through slit eyes, got out of bed, turned on the lights, and explored the contents of his luggage.

Bombers and fighters were Krug's first priority, but twice to his knowledge flying boats had given Germany a problem, first when a U.S.-built PBY Catalina sighted and tracked the *Bismarck*, leading to the battleship's destruction, and second, when another Catalina surprised U-*Böhm* and U-*Heyse* in the act of exchanging fuel. He surmised that there must have been other instances, perhaps along the British convoy lanes, when this particular type aircraft posed a danger to the Ubootwaffe.

He had pretty good data on the PBY already, and knew that a PBY-5A amphibian model was now entering service. Such data as he had lacked, such as placement of the Catalina's fuel tanks, he had picked up in conversations with aircrewmen from NAS Jax in the Alhambra bar. From them also he had learned that a new and larger flying boat type, the PBM Martin Mariner, was now operational, and that former PBY pilots were transitioning in them at various sites, one of them NAS Banana River.

Since he had no data at all on PBMs, he steered the Pontiac toward that station, identified at the end of a wooden bridge and narrow paved road by a white-beam rotating beacon. Approaching the final mile with headlights out, he stopped on a sand shoulder and made the rest of the way by foot, leaving his wallet and watch in the car.

After a half hour's walk through difficult off-road palmetto and switch grass, he reached a chainlink fence, where, with a good view of the base buildings, runways, ramps, and the parking apron he counted three PBMs and assorted other, smaller craft. A fourth PBM swung at a mooring in the water about 200 meters off the ramps. Though there had to be guards about, he saw none. On the water side, the fencing extended into a marsh, where it ended. Krug decided to enter the marsh, keeping on his shoes and clothes, and placing his notebook, pencil, and penlight under his watchcap.

Once around the fence and past the marsh, he lowered his body into the cool water and began swimming slowly toward the moored PBM. Nothing on shore around the ramps or on the apron indicated that security patrols were active. Nonetheless, he swam with deliberate slowness so as not to make a sound or a wake.

Finally, he reached the starboard wing tip float of the flying boat and paused to take an extended look around. Still no sign of movement on shore or in the water. He swam noiselessly forward to the floating hull and worked his way around the nose, where the hull appeared wider at the bottom than it was at the top. As he rounded the port side he noticed the gull configuration of the wings, probably designed to keep the two radial engines above the water spray. It was a long swim down the hull. This *was* a bigger boat than the Catalina. Looking over the empennage, he was struck to see that the tailplane had the same dihedral as the gull wing and that the two vertical stabilizers canted toward each other.

At the waist he found a hatch door unlatched and slightly ajar. He grabbed the bottom of the frame and lifted himself up and through. Once inside, he found that he could stand up easily. This was spacious! He removed his dripping clothes and shoes and used his watch cap to wipe dry the soles of his feet. Then, with his penlight held low, he walked forward toward the flight deck, past the waist gunners' stations and the dorsal gun turret, the living quarters area with its bunks, and the galley and mess compartment, which he noticed was equipped with a stove and refrigerator. Aft of the galley, stairs led to a raised flight deck where an engineer's station occupied the aft end. Forward of that stood stations for navigator and radio operator. Then came the pilots' control station with instrument panels, conventional elevator and aileron control columns, rudder pedals, flaps, trim tabs, and power plant controls.

Making another pass of the interior, Krug counted five single .50 caliber machine guns: in nose and dorsal turrets, in the waist on swivel mounts, and at a prone position in the tunnel, or tail. He also noted the locations of armor plate, for protection of the flight deck, gunners, operating mechanisms, and fuel trunks. There was no bombsight in the bow compartment.

Then, in the pilot's data case, he found the *Pilot's Handbook of Flight Operating Instructions for U.S. Navy Model PBM-1*. Prominently displayed on the title page was the notice:

UNDER THE ESPIONAGE ACT (U.S.C. 50:31:32) THIS PUBLICATION SHALL NOT BE CARRIED IN AIRCRAFT ON COMBAT MISSIONS OR WHEN THERE IS A REASONABLE CHANCE OF ITS FALLING INTO THE HANDS OF THE ENEMY.

Krug smiled. No problem.

Reaching into his cap for pencil and paper, he copied out the critical performance data from the flight operating charts, tables, curves, and diagrams, including the engine calibration curve, which showed rpm and manifold pressure settings for most economical cruise fuel consumption at various pressure altitudes. Since the specification and measurement numbers were nonmetric, he copied them as they read, though his notes were in German.

Total fuel capacity, he noticed, was 2,700 gallons. Damn, this was a flying gas tank! And here was something interesting: "For maximum range and endurance, conduct flight at the minimum practicable altitude."

The bombs in this type patrol bomber were carried not on wing racks but in bomb bays constructed into the engine nacelles—maximum bomb load 6,000 pounds. Especially helpful in the handbook was an artist's representation of the cones of protective fire provided by the .50 caliber guns. The drawings suggested to Krug that the PBM was vulnerable to a forward quarter attack by fighters and a forward belly attack by U-boat anti-aircraft. Abwehr post Hamburg should be pleased to learn that.

Finished writing, he made his way aft to the waist hatch, where he stowed the penlight, pencil, and paper back in his cap and redonned his wet clothes and shoes. As he went overside, he wiped dry the spot where he had undressed with two rags he had found in the galley. Slipping into the water, the rags stuffed in his shirt, he made slow breaststrokes toward the shore. The return swim was uneventful until he was nearly at the fence—

"HALT!"

Krug looked up to the river bank just inside the fence and, with a shocking chill, blinked into a flashlight beam directed at his face. The figure holding the light was obviously a navy shore patrolman, though all Krug could make out was white cap, white belt, and white leggings. Then, as the figure stepped forward, the flashlight caught the forward barrel of a gun.

"Halt right there!" the young male voice commanded again. "Come up out of the water!"

Krug did so, saying, lamely, "I was just hunting for clams and oysters, sir." Above all else, he must prevent this guard from summoning others. He undid the button on his right shirt cuff.

"Stand right there!" the guard ordered when Krug was out of the water and climbing the shallow bank. For a moment it appeared to Krug that the guard did not know quite what to do next; then he saw him reach for his whistle lanyard.

At the same instant, Krug lunged at him, grabbing the gun barrel and stock and using them to turn the sailor fully around, where, in quick order, Krug flung the gun away, struck the small of the sailor's back with his clenched right hand, and threw his left forearm bone across the sailor's throat.

What he intended to do next was place the outside of his right arm on the sailor's right shoulder, grab his own right biceps with his left hand, place his right hand on the back of the head, and press the head forward. But this sailor was no Wehrmacht airdrome sentry: he stamped on both of Krug's feet and, with his right hand, grabbed Krug hard by the testicles. The pain forced Krug to loosen his hold and step back. As he did so, and the sailor started to turn, Krug drew the dirk from his right wrist sheath and with his left hand plunged it deep into the sailor's right kidney, where the pain resulting was so severe the victim's scream was beyond the audible range.

On the ground, Krug compressed the neck a sufficient time to guarantee death. Then he pulled the body, still with its cap, down into the river and dragged it around the fence end and about 50 meters beyond, where he pushed it under high marsh grass in a spot where, he was confident, it would not be discovered before morning. At the last minute before exiting the marsh, he remembered the gun and flashlight. Returning to the site of his encounter to retrieve them, he carried them into the black water and dropped them.

• • •

No traffic appeared in the rearview mirror on Krug's return to the cabin. Once there, he gingerly removed his carrying case from the backseat—his balls still blazed with pain—and used a towel stolen from the Alhambra to dry off the car's front seat. Inside the cabin door, which he opened and closed as quietly as he could, he tiptoed the case into the bathroom, where he closed the door and turned on the light. From the case he withdrew one of his St. Augustine exercise paintings. Then, mixing a Pyramidon tablet in an eyecup of water, he copied his data onto the backside of the watercolor. When completed, after an hour's work, he tore the stationery leaves into tiny pieces and flushed them down the toilet.

As he climbed into the double bed, Sally made a slight movement. Krug whispered, "Shhh, go back to sleep."

But he need not have bothered. Sally had smelled, seen, and heard it all—the smell of wet clothing and shoes, the hour-long light around the bathroom door frame, the furtive replacement of the carrying case in the car, and the hanging of clothing outdoors to dry.

As she closed her eyes at last, she wondered: *What the goddam shit is going on?*

CHAPTER 17

AS TUESDAY WAS St. Augustine's biggest tourism day of the week, so Monday was the cathedral rectory's biggest personal-problems day of the week. Usually, Tony looked forward to Mondays. He liked grappling with the problems parishioners brought him. Most were interesting, some were wonderfully challenging. The sessions provided him with a chance to employ the insights of psychology that he had picked up at Columbia and the New School. And follow-up sessions enabled him to acquire a measure of satisfaction that this or that practical piece of advice had actually worked and brought about a positive good in somebody's life. Doctors saw their patients cured, lawyers their cases won, engineers their bridges built. But, with rare exceptions, spiritual advice dispensed in the confessional had no such verifiable result. Only in the office, handling the personal difficulties that parishioners brought him, face-to-face in repeated meetings, did a priest have the opportunity to experience a verifiable sickness cured, a case won, a bridge built. More priests would seize on office problems as a gratifying ministry, Tony thought, if they were educated for it—had the psychological and other social science tools that Tony had acquired. But, lacking that, and insecure about advising people or eliciting from them their own solutions, many clergy were content simply to smile their way through office sessions—kindness, kindness, kindness, in Fulton Sheen's formulation—and kiss off the hours as pretty much a waste. "Oh, I had to listen to that old biddy for sixty minutes," was a common rectory refrain. No wonder, Tony thought, so many older men, as pastors, took their principal career satisfaction from brick-and-mortar construction of the parish "plant"—church, school, and convent.

But for Tony Monday mornings normally were a rewarding time, at 8:15, 9:00, 9:45, and 10:30, allowing fifteen minutes between appointments so that parishioners would not bang into each other, the last appointment having to be cut ten minutes short so that he could make his Latin class at St. Joseph Academy two blocks away— "Goood morr-nn-ning Faa-therrr"—and conjugate the subjunctive pluperfect of *audire* to bored boys and dreamy-eyed girls:

audivissem	*audivissemus*
audivisses	*audivissetis*
audivisset	*audivissent*

Then, lunch at the rectory, where Bishop Garvey was full of that morning's news of Japan's stranglehold on Java, followed by Prime, Terce, Sext, None, and back-and-forth pacing in his room, which lasted until three, when, with a leaden heart and a divided hope that his young penitent would either return or not return, he descended to the empty cathedral and the gospel-side confessional. The anticipation of this moment had clouded his entire day, made his few questions about personal problems that morning less than penetrating, his lunch indigestible, Garvey's lecturing insufferable, the breviary a brainless burden, and his whole sense of priesthood a daunting mystery. Was he really capable of doing that night what he planned to do?

The question festered until 3:35, when, to his responding heartbeat, a body entered the right curtain and knelt before the grill.

"Father?" its voice asked.

"Yes, I'm here," Tony answered. "Thank you for coming back, son. Are you doing all right? Are you feeling better?"

"Yes, Father, a little."

"Have there been any changes, or is everything the same?"

"I don't know anything new, Father."

"All right. Now you remember the last time I said that I would work something out to take care of the body on the beach, and you told me that you remembered the place where Mr. Capona was buried."

"Yes, Father."

"Can you mark it exactly?"

"I think so. It was a quarter mile north of the Studios. I remember it was at the only part of those dunes where there were no sea oats and there was an old driftwood board about three or four yards away, to the right. I thought of using it to help dig the hole."

"All right, now here's what I'd like for you to do. You see, Mr. Capona, being a Catholic and a member of this parish, deserves a Christian burial, and Mrs. Capona deserves to see her husband laid properly to rest. After dark tonight, I want you to place a stake or stick or something with a white rag or handkerchief tied to it into the sand where the body is buried. Will you do that?"

"Yes, Father."

"Then I'll go out later and dig up the body and leave it plainly visible on the beach. Then I'll call the sheriff's office anonymously and tell them there's a body on the beach. They'll identify him and we'll have a funeral Mass. You won't be implicated in any way and neither will I. And you'll feel a lot better about this once Mr. Capona is properly buried. Will you do that?"

"Yes, Father, I will."

"And I will ask you to keep my role in this as secret as I will keep your confession. Will you do that?"

"Yes, Father."

"All right. Now there's one other thing I'll ask of you and then we're through with this whole tragic experience. And, by the way, after today, I want you to forget as best you can everything that has happened. Particularly, I want you to throw aside any guilt feelings you may have. Our Lord forgives you for any small blame you think you suffered from this experience. Forgiveness means that God has forgotten. So you should, too. Just go on with your life. I know you have tensions because of your father's work for the Germans, but do your best to recapture the life you had before this episode. Will you do that?"

"Yes, Father."

"Now here's the other thing I'd ask you to do. I've prayed a lot and studied a lot about this matter, and I've found that, without revealing anything—I mean *anything*—about your confession, I can do something perhaps to prevent other people from being hurt by this man Homer, or Krug, *if* you would give me permission to do so. Would you give me that permission?"

"Yes, Father."

"Would you also give me that permission outside the confessional? In other words, if I go out and kneel in a pew, would you kneel in a pew behind me and say, 'Father, I give you permission to try to prevent others from being hurt by Homer?'"

"Would my confession still be secret?"

"Absolutely. Yes, absolutely."

"Okay. What am I supposed to say again, Father?"

"'Father, I give you permission to try to prevent others from being hurt by Homer.'"

"Okay."

Tony closed the grill and, making sufficient noise to let the youth know he was leaving the confessional, stepped out and took a place, kneeling, in a pew. The youth followed and knelt behind him.

"Father?" he said.

"Yes, son, you have something to tell me?"

"Yes. I give you permission to try to keep other people from being hurt."

"By—?"

"By Homer."

"Thank you, son. Now go in peace. If I can help you further in any way, please come to see me. My name is Father D'Angelo."

"Yes, I know."

• • •

After an early morning's start, Krug and Sally made good time down the coast, Krug choosing the faster US 1, which paralleled State 140 slightly inland from the coast, separated from it by salt lagoons and low-lying islands. Except for stop lights in the few towns en route and occasional cattle that crossed the paved roadbed from open ranges, their Pontiac encountered no obstructions or delays. Sally studied the sparsely settled landscape, today, as yesterday, so strikingly different from her native New York: winter greenery to left and right, pine, scrub palmetto, and prickly pear with yellow blossoms; where the waterway appeared to the left, an occasional, motionless blue heron looking at its reflection on the liquid surface; on the right, oxen standing in ditches chewing water hyacinths; here, a cracker cowman in broad-brimmed pumpkin hat on a Spanish marsh pony driving cattle with an eighteen-foot-long rawhide whip; and there, a farm worker's tin-roofed, single-pen, wood-frame hovel with oil-cloth curtains and a gaunt yellow cur yapping on the broad porch.

Sally wondered if she should say anything to Peter about his weird behavior last night. How many people go swimming, if that was what he was doing, with all their clothes on? Did he fall into a pool? Did the cash in his money belt get wet? Probably. The dude never takes off his belt. And what do you do in a bathroom for a full hour, when there is no sound of running water? Read? Is Peter an insomniac? Better not to say anything right now, she decided. Just try to get a better look at his cards.

Skirting the Indian River, the Pontiac encountered numerous heavy trucks laden with aromatic cargoes of oranges and grapefruit, while, to the right, row after row of dark green groves with oranges hanging like glowing lanterns marched in even ranks toward the horizon; the scene broken at intervals by packing houses or by roadside fruit stands that sold red-meshed bagfuls, citrus candies and jellies, crystallized peels, and "All you can drink for a dime."

At Fort Pierce, Krug found his way into the center of town, where he located a movie theater. The marquee read: DOUBLE FEATURE—SONG OF THE ISLANDS and KEEP 'EM FLYING. Nearby were a coffee shop and a newsstand. He parked the car and the two of them went into the newsstand. Krug bought the local paper and a day-old *Miami Herald*. He invited Sally to pick up all the magazines she wanted. Then the two of them went into the coffee shop for breakfast.

"Now today," he told her over pancakes, "I've got to do some work on my own, scouting sites for painting. It's the kind of thing I have to do by myself. It's long and it's boring. When I actually start painting, I'll make sure you're with me."

"That's what I want to see," she agreed. "But just what do I do *today*?"

"You have your magazines. You can stay here until the movie theater down the block opens and you can watch the double feature. Here's a ten dollar bill."

"A ten-spot," she said disgustedly. "I've got more money than that in my change purse."

"This trip is my treat. I'm sure that's all you'll need today. Now be a good sweetheart and just relax and enjoy yourself. I'll find you at the theater or back here at the coffee shop later today. Tonight we'll go out to the best restaurant in town, I promise you."

"In this burg? What's that, the diner?"

"Don't be naughty. And we'll order some champagne, too."

"Bubble, bubble," she muttered through pouting lips.

State 140 south hugged the west bank of Indian River, past weathered fish houses, rickety piers, boat sheds, and signs: LIVE BAIT, DANCE AND DINE, REPENT. Eden was so small it did not show on the roadmap, but Krug had been told by Abwehr it was south of Fort Pierce between Walton and Jensen. He drove the narrow road slowly, troubled that he saw no place signs. On rising ground to the right there were single houses and occasional clusters of houses, but no signs. When he came upon a man with a cane fishing pole walking toward him on the left, he stopped the car to ask, "Can you tell me, sir, if Walton is up ahead?"

"Oh, you've passed Walton," the man said, pointing. "It's back there."

"Well, I'm really looking for Eden," Krug explained.

The man turned to point forward, "Well, it's ahead up there."

"How will I know when I'm there?"

"You'll see some mailboxes and a dirt road, maybe a mile. Take that."

"All right, many thanks."

When, after a mile, a clump of mailboxes came into view, Krug turned right up a heavily wooded incline. All he could see was an occasional frame house. There was no town as such. To his right, an elderly man in overalls led a mule across a small, bushy field. Krug stopped the car, got out, and walked briskly after him.

"*Autsch!*" he cried, when he felt a sharp pain in his right leg. He looked down to see that his assailant was a knifelike serrated blade of a low, dark green plant.

The old man ahead stopped and turned when he heard the shout. Krug caught up with him and explained that he had been pricked by a leaf.

"Them be pineapple leaves," the old man said.

"Oh, yeah, I heard this is supposed to be a pineapple town."

"Was," the old man corrected him.

"I'm looking for a man named Emil Lorenz. Do you know where he lives?"

"Fellow with the boats?"

"I suppose so."

The man pointed. "See that yeller house, second down?"

"Yes. Thank you. Much obliged."

Krug walked back to his car, which he drove off the dirt

road and parked on the shoulder. Then he walked carefully along a path between irregular patches of pineapple plants until he came to the yellow house, small with white trim, where he knocked on the door.

A slight but well-proportioned man, about fifty, with blue eyes and wispy gray hairs that sprang in various directions from the top of his head, answered the door, flinging it wide open, not at all furtive or suspicious. He wore a frayed white short-sleeved shirt, navy trousers, and tennis shoes.

"Yes? May I help you?" he asked, in a thin, reedy voice.

"My name is Peter Krug."

"Emil Lorenz. Come in."

When Krug had stepped inside and found himself in a kitchen, he apologized, "Oh, I'm sorry, I seem to have come to the back door."

"No matter at all," Lorenz said, "I really don't have a formal front door." He led Krug through a small, neatly kept living room to a screened-in porch facing the river, where he motioned his visitor to a bamboo chair with a faded green and white floral pattern cushion.

"Do you care for coffee?" Lorenz asked, before sitting.

"No, thank you."

Lorenz looked at him carefully. "You say your name is Krug. What can I do for you? Are you selling something?"

"I'm not selling anything, Mr. Lorenz," Krug answered, smiling, "but if you'd like to question me further, I'm sure you'll find my answers reassuring."

"You know, I always like to take people at face value, Mr. Krug. Perhaps you can tell me your business and we can get to it."

Damn. He was not giving away a thing. Krug realized that for Lorenz to ask a penetrating question, one to which Krug alone, or Krug with very few others, was likely to know the answer raised the possibility that Lorenz would betray himself instead of his visitor if "Krug" turned out not to be who he said he was. So Lorenz was standing pat.

Looking at his own cards, Krug was chilled by the

thought that maybe this was not Lorenz at all: perhaps Lorenz had been picked up by the FBI and this man was a trap, luring him into showing his hand.

Krug decided to play a card, anyway, lest their bluffing go on forever. "I'm going to tell you something, Mr. Lorenz. I once knew a man named Böhm."

Now that was a name no FBI man would know, unless the Bureau had elicited it through torture, for which he understood the Americans had no stomach.

"Is that a fact?" Lorenz said, still playing the game. "Is Böhm supposed to mean something to me?"

"Günther Böhm," Krug added. "He recently came to Florida by boat and made a visit to Marine Studios."

"Yes?" Lorenz asked. "I wonder if you're thinking of the man I know who once met up with a fellow named Heyse?"

There! That did it. No U.S. agent could possibly have known the linkage of those two names, now so many afternoons away, it seemed. Krug relaxed.

"And I'll give you a number," Krug corroborated, "one twenty-eight."

Lorenz stood up and went to the kitchen. "Sure you don't want any coffee?" he called.

"No. Thank you."

When Lorenz returned with a cup to his chair, he asked, "Have you had any luck?"

"So-so," Krug replied.

"I'm glad that you came here straightaway, because, to tell you the truth, I may be picked up before our scheduled rendezvous, and I've been worried what you'd do without my help. I certainly couldn't leave notes around."

"Picked up? By the FBI?"

"Yes. Not because they know of my activities, but for general purposes. I think all us registered German aliens living on the coastline will be removed and detained. A number have been already, as you may have read. The U-boats have the authorities very nervous. And they think that German nationals are providing the U-boats shipping information, which is silly, of course. There's so much shipping all lit up, if not by their own lights, then by American shore lights, the U-boats don't need any information from me. They can fire at will."

Krug nodded.

Lorenz stood up. "I think you better come with me to the river." He opened a screen door and Krug followed him into a small lawn, then down a white sand path toward heavy growth of water oak, mango, and cabbage palm.

Looking back, Krug observed, "You certainly have a brightly painted house."

"Yellow keeps the mud daubers from building nests under the eaves," he said. "Just be glad you're here in March instead of April. When the rains come, that southeast breeze we're catching brings saltwater mosquitoes from the beach across the river. They get so thick you can reach out and grab them by the handful."

"How do you deal with them?"

"Well, I put out smudge pots. I even hang one on the lawn mower when I cut my lawn. I wear oil of citronella. And I peel some pines—doesn't cut the mosquito population all that much, but it gives me satisfaction."

"Peel pines?" Krug wondered.

"Peel some pineapples and set them on posts. The mosquitoes crowd those pines and suck the juice until they're so bloated they can't fly anymore. When they fall to the ground, the ants carry them off. It gives me satisfaction."

"I walked through quite a number of pineapples on the way up to your backdoor," Krug said.

"Yes, but the industry here's long dead. This sugar sand ridge was ideal for the pines. Lots of people came in, including many Germans, cleared six acres or so, planted pine slips—they were first brought here from Key Largo in the eighteen eighties—and after eighteen months they had a crop.

"People made money. They built plantations. There was a lively social scene here—dances, beach parties, boating, tennis. Lots of fishermen from here, Jensen, and St. Lucie village joined in. And then, one year, it all died."

"How come?"

"A number of reasons. Flagler's FEC railroad started importing Cuban pines, which were not only cheaper, but ripened earlier. The draining of the Everglades and the timber cutting locally changed the rainfall levels, or at least that's what people thought. And a nematode infestation that the locals called 'red wilt' or 'root knot' decayed the fruit in the ground. Some people turned to citrus or to fishing. But most people just left, just walked out, leaving their houses and all their furnishings, with the doors unlocked. That's how I got my own house and furnishings. An uncle said, 'This place is yours.' Some of the plantation houses were later taken down to avoid property tax."

Lorenz led Krug across State 140 and out a 40-yard pier toward a two-story driftwood-gray boathouse with a pitched tin roof. "I used some of the plantation weather board to fix up my boathouse. I've got so many loose boards in this old pier, I really should do something about it, too."

"Don't you get lonely here?" Krug asked. "I don't mean to pry."

"Don't mind. I had a wife. From Frankfurt. She knew what I did and she was very helpful. We got along real well, like a rattler and a gopher in the same hole. But she died."

"I'm sorry."

Lorenz ignored the commiseration as he turned a key in the boathouse door. "I probably don't need a lock here," he said, "but I'm not a fool." He flicked a light switch. "There's a power line I placed from the house underground to here. People know I have boats and they probably think I work on them a lot, those who care, and it'd be hard to find many who do. You couldn't find a more secluded spot, a less obvious place, for my kind of work."

Krug followed Lorenz inside and saw two medium-size, new-looking boats, one open, the other with a canvas top, in the boathouse water, the first named *Crunch* and the other *Des*.

"The open boat is a Gar Wood twenty-eight footer," Lorenz said, "top speed in the forties. The canvas top job, *Des*, is a Chris-Craft Express Cruiser, twenty-five feet, speed in the thirties, and it's rigged for off-shore fishing. If anything happens to me, take *Des*. It's the better sea-keeper. It doesn't need a key. If it doesn't turn over, then take *Crunch*. Its ignition is set to go, too. Either one will get you out the St. Lucie Inlet, which is seven nautical miles south, into the open sea. Your U-boat is going to be three miles due east of the inlet. You won't need to scuttle the boat. The U-boat gun will blow it up."

"Okay."

"Do you know anything about boating?"

"A little. Enough, I think."

"Whatever you do, don't go when the tide's going out. Look here," he opened the door and pointed to the bare river shore, "see all that smelly seaweed? That's low tide. I can handle the bar at the inlet when the tide's going out and the sea's coming in, but you can't. Don't think you can. Boats will broach unless you know how to get between the sets of waves. Currents can run seven knots in that cut."

"I understand."

"Read the tide tables. I've got 'em posted right over the tackle box. Advance the times one hour to eastern war time. Leave here an hour before high tide."

Lorenz pulled a rope on the ceiling that opened a door that lowered a ladder. "The FBI probably won't care about my boats," he said, walking up. "They'll want to know what else I own."

When Krug reached the top floor, he saw a chaotic storage scene: boxes, rugs, lamps, jalousie window frames, clothing, papers, the typical attic detritus of an American household.

"That pine floor's a false bottom," Lorenz said, lifting up a whole section on hinges. The junk on top of the section fell off. "I just brush it all back when I'm through."

Underneath the false bottom, and an oil cloth cover, lying flat, were a transmitter and a receiver. He explained that they were a 40-watt dual channel telephone/telegraph transmitter with frequency range from 1,600 to 15,000 kilocycles and a superheterodyne communications receiver with a frequency range of 550 to 30,000 kilocycles. "They pull upright on their own hinges to a forty-five degree angle, like so. That enables the tubes to cool. Alongside, you see I've got lots of extra tubes, condensers, resistors, and so forth. And here," he pulled up a folding table, "is my Morse key, my bug. And I've got a little folding canvas camp chair to sit on. Here are the U-boat frequencies and the one-time pad ciphers for each date."

"Where's the antenna?" Krug asked.

"Standing between studs in the east wall framing. I'll show you how it works. I have a radial copper ground wire underwater." He let the equipment and floor sections back down on their hinges, pushed the junk back on top, and, from a coffee can, sprinkled dust over the whole area. Then he went to the north wall and pressed the index fingers of both hands simultaneously on two spots of the upright wood slats. Immediately, two portions of the wall spread open from floor to ceiling. Lorenz completed the opening manually, turning each of the two sections back against the wall and revealing shelves filled with cameras, enlargers, film, paper, and chemicals as well as a drop-leaf table, holding a typewriter, which Lorenz flipped down.

"This is a false wall, as you can see. Special hinges let the two sections come fully out, then turn back. It's where I do my cards and documents. A double-button electric switch throws the latch. For natural light," he pulled a chain in the wall and one section of the roof slid down and across, exposing a large Plexiglas opening, "I have this window. And you asked about the antenna," he pointed to a hand wheel in the false wall, "here I can crank it up from its present hidden position to full height. I only do so at night, since that's the only time I transmit and receive, by one-time pad."

"You certainly did impressive work on my licenses and ID cards," Krug complimented him.

"I have people in Washington and New York who keep me up to date through General Delivery in Fort Pierce. When any new cards come out, I get examples right away."

"Oh, that reminds me," Krug interjected. "The three Army Air Corps IDs. I was looking at them the other day and they have a misspelling, right at the top." He removed one of the cards from his wallet and showed it to Lorenz: INDENTIFICATION CARD NOT A PASS.

Lorenz smiled, and reached for a pack of card stock. "See these? They're the most recent, and the army hasn't caught the error yet."

"Well, I'll be damned."

"I hope they fight as well as they spell." He closed the doors. "By the way, here is where you press the slats to open the wall, in case you need to, which I doubt you will."

"Okay."

"I think I've shown you about everything," Lorenz said, as they walked back downstairs. After raising the ladder, and before leaving the boathouse, he added, "Except for one thing. See this black coffee cup next to the tackle box? If you see it turned upside down, it means I've been picked up here in the boathouse. There's another cup just like it on the window sill in the kitchen. If it's upside down, it means I was apprehended in the house."

With that, Lorenz closed and locked the door, then gave the key to Krug. "I have another," he said.

On their way back to the house, Krug told Lorenz about the naming of Eden on the U-boat chart of the North Atlantic and its coastlines. "No Jacksonville or Miami," he said, "but Eden's there big as life."

"I'm glad we're remembered somewhere," Lorenz replied. "We're off the railroad map and the gas maps."

At the house, Krug said his goodbyes, ending with a click of the heels, a stiff arm salute, and a "Heil Hitler!"

Seeming not to notice, Lorenz opened the back door and smiled thinly. "Heil Hitler," he said.

• • •

After Tony parked his car that night on the sand off State 140, he opened the trunk and removed the spade he had found in the rectory tool room and the Coleman lantern he had borrowed from Mattie Mae's husband, who floundered with it on weekends. Removing his suit coat with nervous hands, he withdrew a large kerchief and a bottle of alcohol from the trunk, doused the kerchief with alcohol, and placed it in his left pants pocket. Then, in flannel shirt and tan trousers, he traipsed over the sand, palmetto, and cordgrass to the dunes, where he stumbled awkwardly down the deep, soft sand to the hard-packed beach, where, following Mattie Mae's demonstration, he got a glow going on the mantle of the lantern. With its yellow light he paced slowly north, half-spooked by the drumroll of the nighttime surf, looking in general for a spot where there was a break in the sea oats, and, specifically, for a stick and a white rag.

No more than five minutes into his search he saw it clearly in the full moon—a white handkerchief fluttering on a stick. He walked up to the site, noticed the absence of oats, sighted the driftwood board nearby, and set the lantern firmly into the sand where the dune began its rise. Then, after looking up and down the moonlit beach to satisfy himself that he was alone, and with a nauseous gulp that betrayed his fear of actually finding the thing for which he dug, he vigorously began shoveling sand to his left side.

It would have been much easier just to tell the sheriff that his deputies would find a body underneath the white marker, and let *them* dig for it. But Tony did not trust the sheriff's department to search for a marker. They might take his message as a crank call and dismiss it. But if he reported that there was a body *on the beach*, he knew that the sheriff would act.

Now the point of his spade hit something with slightly greater consistency than sand. He gently worked the blade around the object and half-lifted it, letting the spade handle fall. He reached for the lantern and held it over the object. It was a large, sand-coated fish.

Digging deeper, he hit another object, which came up lengthwise: the end of a cane pole, as the lantern revealed. He unearthed the pole with some difficulty, pulling its full length free from the entombment, and casting it aside. The German lad had mentioned the fish and the pole. This was the place, all right. As he reached to set the lantern aside so that he might resume digging, the plain form of a man's fingers appeared in the hole left by the pole, and a foul odor, though not as strong as he expected it to be, entered his nostrils. He reached for his alcohol-soaked kerchief and wrapped it around his face.

Tony shuddered. He knew that it would come to this: he would have to touch a dead body, something he had never done before, except to administer conditional extreme unction to a corpse in the hospital or funeral home. He found that he could not reach down and grasp the hand. His emotions would not let him. There was something about a hand.

Instead, he continued digging, slowly now, taking care to expose the whole body so that he could remove it all at once. Here, the left arm and shoulder came into view; there, the two legs came free; now the trunk and head emerged from the sepulchral sand. A cold shiver came over his ribs when he saw that the two dead eyes were open and staring at him! Otherwise, to his relief, the facial features were so caked with sand they were indistinguishable. Where he could see the flesh clearly he was surprised how dark it was. He continued with the exhumation until he was satisfied that he could get a good grip on the torso, then he leaned down to get what purchase he could below the shoulders.

The body moved with his tug, though it was difficult in the soft sand to maintain footing, and he found that he had to haul the rigid dead weight out in jerks. After struggling in this fashion, he finally got the body out of its hole, down the dune, and onto harder sand, where he dragged it a short distance farther in the direction of the foam line, so that its presence could not be missed.

With a great groan of release, he stood erect and looked to the black sky and moon, and prayed aloud against the surf:

De profundis clamavi ad te, Domine:
Domine, exaudi vocem meam:
Fiant aures tuae intendentes in, vocem deprecationis meae.
Si iniquitates observaveris, Domine:
Domine, quis sustinebit?

He left the body to retrieve the lantern and spade, and looked for a last time at the hole. The sheriff would see that it was here the body had been hidden. When he returned to the ungainly bent, stiff corpse, he set the lantern on the beach and knelt beside it. From his pants' right pocket he pulled a copy of the *Rituale Romanum*, and through his kerchief read aloud the prayers, psalms, and Gospel passages from the *Ordo commendationis animae*.

That completed, he stood to go. He had thought originally of anointing the body conditionally, and had brought his gold-plated oil stock for that purpose; but death had occurred so long before, anointing seemed pointless. Besides, he reflected, traces of oil on the body might tell the coroner that a priest had touched the body.

He made a final sign of the cross over the remains of Joseph Capona—"May his soul and the souls of all the faithful departed, through the mercy of God, rest in peace. Amen"—and, with lantern and spade, walked over the dunes to his car, where he removed the kerchief from his face, took off his shoes, stepped into the car, and drove it a few feet off the sand onto the paved road. Then in his stocking feet, he took the spade and turned the sand where the car had stood, so that no identifiable tire tracks remained, although it was not likely that tracks would remain long on that kind of surface. With a rag from the trunk he wiped the spade, lantern, and shoes free of sand and placed them in the trunk. Finally, he started up the engine, ran the car through its forward gears, and steered south to Flagler Beach, making again a detour via State 28 and U.S. 1 to avoid the bridge tender at Matanzas Inlet.

During the drive, he sensed a general decompression of his physical systems, as though a giant clamp that had forced his innards to a knot was unscrewed. He had done the right thing. It was damnably the hardest thing he had ever done in his life. But he had done it. Wherever and however he had gathered the courage for it, he had no idea. Not since he was a kid on New York's streets had he engaged in an activity so physical or practical—at least not since handball at Dunwoodie. His recent life had run to the spiritual and the intellectual.

But now he experienced a certain exhilaration at discovering that he could undertake a physical task, a horrible, sickening one at that, and carry it off without hesitating, without blubbering, and without puking. Did that mean he was a man? Was there more to him than he had thought?

It was three-thirty when he parked the car at the rectory, and, making sure no one was on the streets or in the plaza, he removed the spade and lantern and took them inside. His shoes he had thrown into a marsh on the return drive. The spade he placed back in the tool room. The lantern he would hold onto and use to go floundering with a parishioner several nights hence—though, not liking to fish or gig, the prospect did not entice him—so that there would be no perceived association of either himself or it with the exhumation.

Inside the rectory office, he looked up the number of the sheriff and dialed.

"Sheriff's office, Deputy Andreu," a male voice answered.

"I have an important message for the sheriff," Tony said, half-disguising his voice through the kerchief that was still rank with alcohol. "There is a dead body in plain sight on the beach about a quarter of a mile north of Marine Studios. Do you have that? On the beach just north of the Studios."

"Who is this? How do you know—?"

"Very important. Please act on it right away. Thank you."

Click.

Up in his room, he took off his clothes and placed them, with the kerchief, in an old suitcase. He would dump it somewhere later today. Then he took a bath and got into his pajamas. Probably, he would not be able to sleep. He set the Westclox alarm for seven, just in case he did, so as to make morning Mass. Then he knelt on the prie-dieu in his room and placed himself in the presence of God; though the voice he heard was not God's, but Garvey's:

But who is God except the Lord? . . .
Who trained my hands for war and my arms
*   to bend a bow of brass . . .*
And you girded me with strength for war . . .
Et praecinxisti me virtute ad bellum.

CHAPTER 18

THE DRIVE ACROSS the peninsula to Tampa seemed longer than Krug had anticipated. Probably the hard steering on narrow, rough, asphalt state highways 30 and 79 west from Vero Beach contributed to the feeling. Certainly, too, the flat, open, sparsely settled countryside made one think the road would never end. West of Yeehaw and as far as Lake Wales the scenery was eye-glazing grassy prairies interrupted only here and there by herds of cattle and thin stands of pine.

Reaching Lake Wales, with its lakes, citrus groves, palms, and subtropical flowers, Krug was glad to stop and give Sally, who was visibly more torpid than he, a chance to recharge her batteries, if that was possible. This was not the Florida she was accustomed to, as she had made plain several times, including last night when the dining establishment Krug had picked out proved to be well below her usual standards, and she declared her intention never to eat any crap like barbecue again for the rest of her natural life. And the place had no champagne—probably didn't know what it was, she groused. Krug promised her better in Tampa.

"I'm going to the ladies' room," she said now as they pulled into a service station. "See if there's something here worth seeing. If I don't see a building soon, I'll fucking die."

While Sally was thus engaged and a pump jockey filled his gas tank, Krug learned that Mountain Lake Sanctuary, with a so-called Singing Tower, two miles distant, was the principal local attraction.

"And I'll need a good camera store," Krug told the station manager.

"That'll be Buddy's Camera and Film near the entrance to the sanctuary," the man said, handing Krug his change. "You can't miss it."

"Thanks."

Sally seemed in better spirits when she reentered the car, especially after he told her they were going to see a building—a carillon tower—and that he was going to buy a camera so she could take pictures, and that he might even paint a watercolor.

"Okay, anything that's not boring," she agreed. "Let's go!"

After driving up a low mountain slope, Krug stopped at the camera shop mentioned at the station and found it relatively well-stocked with cameras. He really would have preferred one of the 35-millimeter models with their precision focus, adjustable shutter speeds, and good F-stops—there were even some Leicas and Zeiss Ikons on the shelf, by God—and he lusted after an attachable telephoto lens; but he knew that his tourist-couple cover would only be served by a lesser quality box type, so, reluctantly, he chose a Kodak Target Six-16 Brownie and ten rolls of film.

Inside the sanctuary, loaded camera in hand, Sally made for the tower as fast as she could, while Krug, carrying his art equipment, lingered among the trees, shrubs and multihued azaleas to find a site for his easel. He would need more finished watercolors when he got to Drew and MacDill Fields. These flowery scenes should provide him with two or three acceptable paintings. He hated to hurry because the natural beauty deserved to be enjoyed for its own sake and the artist in him cried for a slower brush. But, following a different imperative, he worked as rapidly as he could, pausing only at twelve noon when he leaned back on his canvas seat to listen intently as the carillon in the tower began a plangent recital.

After another hour's painting, when he leaned back again to study his third and final effort, he felt a hand on his shoulder.

"I've been standing back here *watching* you!" Sally laughed. "I saw the whole picture just *pop* up. It's real pretty. I never saw anything like that done before."

"Thank you," Krug acknowledged. "Did you make some pictures of your own?"

"Shot the whole damn roll. And then I got mad 'cause I wanted a picture o' me in front of that bell tower. Did you hear those bells?"

"Yes. Give me the camera and I'll go into the woods there and change rolls. I'll take a few pictures of you here and then a bunch more when we get to Tampa."

While he worked in the shade, Sally called to him: "That's one of the highest buildings I've seen in this whole state. You know what it looks like to me, but smaller? It looks like the GE Building, you know, at Lexington and Fifty-first?"

"Lexington?" he asked, walking out from the shade.

"Yeah, it's near a fancy all-night bar where my friend Harold takes me whenever he comes in big on a ten-to-one shot at Pimlico, or wherever, which is about once a month. He always says, 'That is one eight-cylinder valve-in-head horse.' That's what he says. I never know what it means."

"Come on," Krug urged her, "show me the bell tower and strike a few poses in front of it. Then we better get something to eat, and start driving again."

After an hour and a half drive, during which their eyes blinked repeatedly at distant water mirages on the highway that mirrored the clouds and sky, Krug and Sally finally entered Tampa, where Krug secured second-floor twin-bed accommodations, under the name Mr. and Mrs. Harold Pimlico, at the Gasparilla Hotel.

As they followed the bellhop with their luggage up the stairs—Krug carried his art equipment—Sally whispered to him, "Why did that desk clerk call you Mr. Pimlico?"

"Because that's how we're registered," Krug answered.

"As *Pimlico?*" Sally asked incredulously. "The track?"

"Sweetheart, wait until we're in the room." After they were, and the bellhop was tipped and gone, he said in his most reassuring voice, "We're not married, but we're traveling as though we were. Someone, now or later, who might want to embarrass us could use our joint registration, under either your name or mine, for mischief-making."

"I don't know who in the hell *that* would be," Sally puzzled, honestly. She had slept in so many beds with so many men the last thing she ever worried about was registration. Getting shot maybe, or syphilis, but never registration.

"Well, you have your fun with Mr. Pimlico and just leave me out of it."

"Fine," Krug agreed. "I thought it *was* kind of funny. Now why don't you relax here in the room for awhile? I'm going to go out with the car and scout some painting locations. At the same time, I'll look for some good places to take some more photos of you. Okay?"

"Okay."

After Krug left, Sally sat down heavily in the room's upholstered chair by the window. Well, there he goes again, she thought—money belt, knife, and all. This dude was something else, like a four in craps, a tough point to make. Would someone please tell her how to get inside that belt? He was holding several Gs in his hand at the Alhambra crap table. How much total must be in the belt? She guessed high. Somehow she had to get her mitts on it. But how? And how much more time did she have to invest in this guy?

Oh, well. She reached for her Catholic instructions packet and started reading lesson two. She had dropped the question-and-answer form for lesson one in a mailbox down the street from the coffee shop in Fort Pierce. Maybe she could get another lesson done this afternoon. She read the words slowly, thinking hard about what they meant, and wondering if she really believed them.

When Krug returned two hours later, he found Sally dozing in the chair. "C'mon, sleepyhead," he roused her, "I've found a good place to take some photos of you."

Sally was groggy but managed to get up on her feet. "I'm not in a picture-taking mood," she complained, stomping off to the bathroom.

"You'll feel better after a few minutes," he encouraged her. "One thing about war time, we have lots more sunlight. Change into something nice. We'll go eat afterwards."

"No barbecue."

"No barbecue. I've found a real nice Spanish place called Las Novedades. They have a full bar—and champagne."

"I'll believe it when I drink it."

When Sally was ready, Krug walked her downstairs and two blocks away to his car. To Sally's inquiry why he did not park in one of the numerous places closer to the hotel he answered that he preferred to park some distance away in order to exercise his legs, a lame explanation that she seemed to accept, though she protested, "Your legs fine, but next time drive to the door and pick *me* up. Please!"

They drove west through the city into the suburbs and then along the fence of a military airfield that Sally saw identified at an entrance gate as Drew Field. Olive drab–colored airplanes were noisily taking off and landing overhead. Abruptly, Krug turned off the roadway and through a gate opposite the airfield marked: National Youth Administration of WPA.

"National Youth—" Sally read aloud. "What the hell is this?"

"It's a government camp where they teach young men skills like plumbing, carpentry, radio repair, and so forth. There're some big open fields alongside the camp buildings—a good place for taking pictures."

Sally did not particularly see why, but she went along with it and got out of the car where Krug stopped. "You see?" Krug said, "there's good light here and some nice natural groupings of bushes and trees."

Sally looked up as loud engine noise descended from a low-flying aircraft.

"Don't mind the airplanes," Krug urged her. "Concentrate on looking pretty." He led her by the hand and positioned her near a line of wild bushes. "Just hold it right there now while I adjust the framing."

Krug went down on one knee so that the camera pointed upward. He stalled for time, directing Sally to assume this position or that, until an aircraft coming over the fence on takeoff filled his viewfinder and he pushed the Brownie's shutter button.

"There! That's one," he said. "This time place your hands on your hips and turn slightly sidewise. Keep your eyes on me. That's right—"

When another aircraft came over the fence, its tricycle landing gear retracting, Krug clicked again. Two photos of the Bell P-39 Airacobra with Sally in the foreground he decided ought to be enough.

Sally used her hands-on-hips stance to declare, "I want some pictures of me straight-ahead, regular, not up my nose."

"Sure," Krug complied, taking six pictures of her at eye-level, after which he looked around to see if someone was observing them. It appeared not. Tomorrow he would rent a boat and take some photos of Sally out in Tampa Bay where, he had discovered during his brief drive around, MacDill Field's Boeing B-17 Flying Fortresses made over-water takeoffs and approaches.

"That's all for now, Sally. Let's go back downtown and get something to eat."

Which they did, and enjoyed greatly, Sally getting smashed and giggly on New York State bubbly, which he encouraged because it made her less acutely disapproving when, at the hotel, he put her to bed and said he had to go out and would be back later.

"You're going out *again?*" she slurred, as he pulled a sheet blanket up to her chin. "You're *always* going out somewhere." She pulled the pillow from under her head—she never used one—and flung it over on Peter's bed, knowing he liked to spread out two.

"I'll be back soon. Now get some sleep." In fact, as he noticed, she passed from stupor to unconsciousness even before he left the room and walked downstairs.

In his car again, he drove out Tampa Bay Boulevard to the north side of Drew Field. By driving back and forth along it and West Columbus Drive, which bordered the field on the south, and particularly by questioning naive soldiers outside the fence, in eateries and bars, he acquired a fairly good picture of the base.

Use of the site as a military field began just a couple of years before when it was a sod-covered cow pasture with a single asphalt runway, and, except for a second runway, not much had changed since. There were a few buildings that belonged to the property's former owner, a man named Drew, that were used now for barracks, a mess hall, and a temporary hangar; a headquarters building that was once a disreputable roadhouse called the Green Gables; and, for the rest, shelter was tents, including a worn-out circus tent, the gift of Barnum and Bailey, that was used for classes and blew over in the slightest breeze. Kitchens were old No. 2 Ranges with tent flies strung over them. Most of the men lived in pyramidal tents pitched in mud. The surroundings were mostly swampy marshlands, although there were some orange groves and woods. Some of the water on the field was knee-deep. All of it was contaminated. The men relieved themselves in straddle trench latrines. There was rampant food poisoning, general sickness, and syphilis. Conditions had worsened in December when seventeen hundred enlisted men from Camp Wheeler, Georgia, descended on a field that was not adequate for the one thousand who were already there. Both enlisted and officer morale were groundwater low.

More to Krug's interest, Drew was headquarters for the Army Air Corps's Third Interceptor Command. Its mission was to train pilots transitioning in the single-seat P-39. Also on the field was an Air Warning Unit Training Center, which taught plotting range and azimuth with aircraft warning receivers. If he had the time, which he did not think he had, he would take a look at that system later.

By ten-thirty he had surveilled the field closely enough to know the entrance gate routine, the MP patrol schedule, and the locations of the principal points of interest, including the parking apron for the P-39s. What he needed now was a uniform—preferably a sergeant's. The officers would all know one another on a field this small. A sergeant's stripes would make a safer cover.

At Chappie's Tavern on West Columbus he had seen a handful of uniformed noncommissioned officers going in and out. He parked in back and ordered a bottle of Schlitz at the bar. There were ten or so corporals and sergeants at tables drinking the same or Ballantine. Krug waited until he saw a sergeant about his own height and weight get up and go to the men's room. He followed him at a careless gait, and, once inside the single bowl space, closed the door latch.

"You don't buy beer, you rent it," the sergeant said to whomever it was behind him.

With the soldier's hands preoccupied with his penis, Krug's arm grab around his throat was easy, and this time he pressed his own penis hard against the soldier's buttocks to deny him a grasp on his testicles; though, as it turned out, this particular fellow made no real effort at resistance and went lamely to his knees, where, maintaining pressure, Krug said, "I'm glad you made sergeant."

Leaving some life in his victim, quickly as he could, he changed clothes and shoes. The uniform was a good fit. But the shoes were too big and he didn't have a cap. Maybe he did not need a cap. He wrapped his own clothes and shoes into a ball and placed it under his arm. Then, cracking the door to make sure no eyes were pointed in his direction, he walked calmly out in the direction of the back door. For one unnerving instant he froze, when a soldier's voice behind him yelled, "Hey, Charley, where you going?"

Krug resumed his step, waved his hand, and, without turning, answered, "Be right back."

It was too risky to go through the main gate. One of the MPs might have known Charley, and Krug's newly acquired sergeant's ID and pass would not have worked. Besides, he wanted to have access afterward to his own clothes and shoes. So, in a remote west corner of the field, he threw his civvies over the fence into some orange groves and clambered over the fence after them. At

Hamburg he had trained on many different kinds of fences, and this one was elementary. He stowed his civvies behind a tree.

Reminding himself to salute if he encountered an officer, he walked casually around the perimeter, headed for the parking apron. As he passed the opening of an empty tent, he spotted a cap on one of its six cots and went inside to grab it. Now he was inspection perfect.

Coming up on the apron, he counted thirty Airacobras in three neat rows. There were no lights, except for the waning moon, and, as far as he could see, no sentries. The P-39 had a distinct look about it, something more than its tricycle gear, though it was the first example of that type gear he had seen. It was the engine air intake and exhausts that were jarring. They were *aft* of the pilot. Damn. The pilot sat forward of an in-line engine and on top of the propeller shaft! And with the engine on the center of gravity, a tricycle undercarriage made perfect sense.

When he reached the apron, he chose an aircraft in the center row, stepped up on the wing and tried the cockpit's automobile-type door. It opened. He climbed inside, sat, and studied the panel. Nothing unusual. After groping about, he found the pilot's handbook. He leaned down and opened it up on the floor where his penlight would not show outside, and copied the numbers. This was a P-39D with an Allison liquid-cooled V-1710-35 engine rated at the number, 150 horsepower. Maximum speed 368 at 13,800 feet; cruise 213; service ceiling 32,100. But no turbo supercharger! And a gross weight of 8,200 pounds. He doubted that this plane could make anything like 32,000 feet.

The technical data also revealed why the engine was mounted in the rear. The manufacturer placed a 37-mm T-9 cannon in the nose where it could fire through the hollow driveshaft. He noted the additional armament: two .50 caliber and four .30 caliber machine guns. Well, that was a lot of firepower, but Krug bet that, heavy as it was, and with no supercharger, if it ever flew in anger the P-39 could not fight effectively above 12,000–15,000 max. The new Bf109Gs coming out of the Messerschmitt factory, with superchargers, takeoff weight less than 6,000 pounds, fast rate of climb, fuel injection, and a top speed of 400 or so, figured in mph at 22,000, would fly pirouettes around these planes.

When he finished with the numbers, he looked around, saw no one, stepped out, and examined the gun mountings in the nose. It was after midnight when he finished, and time, he thought, when he should be heading toward the station hospital.

Krug's experience in the Luftwaffe was that flight surgeons knew more about what was going on than anyone else, with the possible exception of chaplains. Everybody talked to doctors: officer and enlisted, high and low rank, flying personnel and ground pounders. He bet the same was true here.

"Captain Boyer's on duty, sergeant, but he's in the latrine," an orderly answered Krug when he presented himself at the hospital entrance. "Are you sick?"

"Not really," Krug said. "I'll find him in the latrine."

"Round the corner on the right."

"Thanks."

The latrine was a wooden building, not an open ditch such as he had seen in the tent area. Inside, he walked toward the sound of piss hitting corrugated tin.

"Captain Boyer?" he called.

"Yeah?" a voice answered.

"Sergeant Davis. I wanted to—*autsch!*" Krug reached for his forehead and recoiled in pain.

"He got you, too, huh?" Captain Boyer said, approaching, buttoning his fly, and chuckling.

Krug squinted and saw two shoes that he had run into with his head. Looking up, he saw that the shoes were attached to a young officer, in olive drab blouse, pink trousers, and cap, with silver wings insignia, hanging by his neck from a rafter. A kicked-away ladder lay on the floor.

"Yeah, he's dead," Boyer said. "See the lividity of the hands?" He pushed up a pants leg. "See the distention and discoloration of the lower extremities? He's been dead for several hours. The first one this month, officer or enlisted."

"A pilot," Krug observed.

"Yeah. On his last flight. The enlisted men hang themselves in the woods, the officers in the latrines."

"I wonder what that means," Krug ventured.

"Probably nothing more than what's available for hanging," Boyer said. "So what's your problem, Sergeant?"

"I couldn't sleep, sir. I was wondering if you could give me something."

"Sure, come on in the clinic. I'll tell the orderlies to cut this guy down."

"Do many pilots do this, sir?" Krug asked as they walked.

"Nah. This is only the second. It's mostly the enlisted men, city boys who've never had to rough it, are homesick and lonely. This place overwhelms them. You heard what Walter Winchell said, 'If your son's in the Pacific, write him; if he's at Drew Field, pray for him.'"

"What's the problem with the pilots?"

"Oh, it could be stress, or a Dear John letter, or fear of the Peashooter—"

"Peashooter?"

"The Airacobra."

"Oh, yeah, of course."

"They're crashin' all over the place, as you know, mostly engine failures on takeoff."

Boyer paused at the hospital entrance to tell a couple of orderlies about the suicide. "Lay him on a gurney in the operating room and take his clothes off." To a nurse standing nearby he said, "Would you stick on the three EEG leads, just for the record? I'll look at him when you call."

"Yes, sir," the orderlies and nurse responded and went outside.

As Boyer led Krug into his clinic, "Sergeant Davis" ventured, "I wonder if MacDill is any better than this place, sir?"

"You mean, does it have less squalor?"

"Yes, sir." It was not what he meant, but it was a good opener.

"MacDill is built-up, dry, and relatively clean. Lots of mosquitoes and a good number of diamondback rattlers on the perimeter, but not much disease. MacDill's problems are off-base. One-third of all the patients in the station hospital are venereal."

"I wonder if security is any better there than it is here?"

"Nah, I don't think so. They got infantry with machine guns and all kinds of MPs, but I've walked in there twice unchallenged to use the PX. I don't think they have the simplest idea of gate security. Why do you ask?"

"Oh, just curious, sir, if things are done better elsewhere."

"The one thing I take comfort from, Sergeant, is knowing that what we have to fight is another Air Corps."

They were interrupted by the nurse, "We've got the suicide laid out, Captain."

"Okay," Boyer acknowledged. "Let's have a look."

"Mind if I stand in?" Krug asked.

"Not at all," Boyer agreed, and led "Sergeant Davis" into the small station OR. The dead officer's uniform had been removed and placed on a chair. His unclothed body seemed to be about the same size as that of Sergeant Davis. Could Krug be that lucky twice in the same day?

While Boyer read the straight line on the EEG, shone a flashlight into the dead man's eyes, passed a stethoscope over his chest, and began filling out forms, Krug wrapped the man's uniform into a ball and placed it on the hall floor outside the OR door.

Then he said to Boyer, "I think I've seen enough, Captain. I'll head back to the tent."

"What about your sleeping pills?" Boyer asked, not looking up from his notes.

"I don't think I'll need them now, sir."

"Okay, Sergeant. Sweet dreams."

Picking up the uniform and holding it tightly under his

left arm, he made a quick exit past the orderly at the front door. "See you later, soldier," Krug said as he left.

"Okay, Sergeant," the orderly returned, leaning back to stretch and yawn.

Outside, on his way back to the fence, Krug unrolled the uniform ball and shook the creases out. The pants stank, but he could fix that.

So the P-39 had no supercharger. That meant that the U.S. Air Corps had no effective bomber escort. The Japanese had already briefed Abwehr on the Curtiss P-40 in its various modifications, the only other combat-ready interceptor in the Air Corps inventory, which the Japanese encountered in Burma, where P-40s had been flown by the American Volunteer Group since April 1941. The P-40 climbed like a rock. If you could get it to sufficient altitude so it could dive on another fighter, it could outdive him and outshoot him. The thing was a flying machine gun. But it was hard to get it to altitude, and it was not too nimble when it got there, the Japanese said. One pass was about all it could make against the new Zero. So the German 109s and 190s had nothing to fear from that plane, either.

It was time now to look at bombers. That was where performance figures were lacking altogether. At the fence he recovered his civvies and exchanged clothes. And, when he reached his car, he placed both a lieutenant's and a sergeant's uniform in the trunk.

Back at the hotel room, Sally seemed fast asleep when Krug let himself in. He had left most of the officer's uniform in the car, but brought the pink trousers in to wash up their seat. When he finished that, and hung the trousers in the closet, he took his picture case, eye cup, and pyramidon tablets into the bathroom, where he removed one of his Lake Wales paintings from the case, placed the case on the toilet seat cover, and laid the painting face down on the case. Next, he brewed a solution of pill and water in the eye cup and, with a toothpick, began writing.

Forty-five minutes later, he shredded his notes and disposed of them in the bowl. Now, for a few winks, he slipped into the other twin bed. It did not take him long to fall into a fitful sleep. Sally, who had not been asleep when he returned, watched him twisting and turning and listened to his loud breathing. This was a repeat of Cocoa Beach, a late return and a long spell in the bathroom, except that this time there was several minutes of running water at the start.

What did he *do* in there? Count money? Was he robbing and burglarizing at night, and now counting his take? The guy is an artist. Is this the way artists behave? Do they spend a lot of time in the bathroom? Maybe he wasn't out robbing. Maybe he has a broad here. Maybe he had a broad in Cocoa Beach. Maybe they liked swimming together with their clothes on—

She drifted off, and the two of them awoke about eight. Sally took a bath first, and then Peter. She noticed that he kept his money belt with him. They said very little to each other while dressing, Sally wondering if there was any point in continuing this relationship. Then, abruptly, she decided to ventilate it all. "The next time you go out at night, Peter, I intend to go along with you, and find out what in the hell is going on. It is *weird* that you stay out so late alone at night and then come back and spend a fucking hour in the bathroom. What do you *do* in there?"

Krug, who prided himself on never being surprised, was surprised. So she hadn't been asleep, after all. He wondered if she had been awake in Cocoa Beach.

"I'm sorry, sweetheart. I had some private business to take care of. And when I got back, I did a little reading to help get myself sleepy. I hope it wasn't the bathroom light that woke you."

Sally stepped into her shoes. "I think I have a hangover," she said.

"I'll find you some Alka-Seltzer when I go out this morning to scout painting locations. Don't forget this afternoon we're going boating. That should be fun."

Then the two of them went down to the hotel coffee shop for breakfast: freshly squeezed orange juice, eggs over light, grits, toast with butter and jelly, and coffee.

They did not talk much. And they both left the grits untouched.

After breakfast, Krug gathered up his watercolor equipment, all but the carrying case, and left their room, saying, "I'll be back a little after one. We'll have lunch and then go boating. 'Bye."

Sally sat down with her instructions packet and returned to lesson two. A hour and a half later, she had the question-and-answer form ready for mailing.

She got up and checked the dampness of her rose blouse that she had washed before taking a bath that morning and left hanging to dry on a hanger by the window. There was warm air moving through the window, so she was not surprised to find the cotton fabric ready for ironing. She walked downstairs and asked the desk clerk for the loan of an iron. She also asked for a board, but none was available. No matter, the blouse was small enough, she could iron it easily on top of the round writing table. Back in the room, she cast about for something to place underneath.

The *Tampa Tribune* would not do, the print might come off. The pillow cases were soiled by Peter's Vaseline hair tonic. The towels were too wet. Her eyes lit on Peter's flat case standing against the wall. Of course. Peter wouldn't mind. She lay the case on the bed, undid the ribbon knot that held it closed, and pulled out the last three paintings in the series, which she held up to admire. They were all browns and greens with lots of flowers and a bit of blue sky overhead, the scenes Peter painted at Lake Wales. Really nice. Peter might be strange but he knew how to color.

Then she lay the cardboard case on the tabletop, and the three watercolors, one on top of the other, paint-down, on the case. She ran her hand, appreciatively, over the dry clean white reverse side of the top paper. Perfect.

When the iron was warm, she retrieved the blouse and spread it, buttons-up, on the paper. She ran the iron back and forth on the front and two sleeves. She stood the iron on end while she turned the blouse over to iron the reverse sides, and, looking down as she did so, saw brown spots appearing on the paper!

Oh, shit! She had ruined Peter's painting! The paint was coming through! She placed her hands over her face in distress.

Then her eyes slowly widened as the brown spots grew to what looked like words, except that she did not know any of them. She stared, uncomprehending, at the result:

TROTZ SCHWACHER STEIGLEISTUNG IST DIE P-39 GUT
BEWAFFNET—IM RUMPFBUG EINE 37MM KANONE
PLUS 2 X 50 KALIBER MASCHINENGEWEHRE IM RUMPF-
BUG UND 4 X 30 IN DEN FLÜGELN
KANN EINE EINZIGE 500-PFUND BOMBE ODER EINEN
75-GALLONEN ABWURFTANK MITFÜHREN
GESCHLOSSENES COCKPIT UND LECKSICHERE KEROS-
INTANKS
LÄNGE 30'2"/HÖHE 11'10"/FLÜGELSPANNWEITE 34'0"
MOTORLEISTUNG 1150 PS KEIN KOMPRESSOR FLUG-
BEREICH 800
PILOTEN HIER IN TAMPA MÖGEN FLUGZEUG NICHT
DIE LAGE DES MOTORS MACHT ES ANFÄLLIG FÜR EINE
GROßE REIHE VON ANGRIFFSARTEN
SCHLAGE VOR WIR GREIFEN DEN MOTOR VON OBEN
UNTEN UND DEN SEITEN AN

Secret ink?

Sally sat down hard and studied the few words that resembled English:

BOMBE . . . 75-GALLONEN . . . COCKPIT . . . KEROSINTANKS . . . PILOTEN HIER IN TAMPA—pilots here in Tampa?— MOTORS.

Was this about airplanes? BOMBE. Military airplanes? Peter?

She stood up and ran the iron over the remainder of that sheet, bringing out at its top:

BELL P-39D AIRACOBRA DREW FIELD 04.3.42
HÖCHSTGESCHWINDIGKEIT 368 MPH BEI 13.800 FUß
KRITISCHE HÖHE WAHRSCHEINLICH NICHT MEHR ALS
12.000

Drew Field! That's near where they were yesterday! What are these numbers? A date? April 3, 1942. Something to happen on April third? That was all she could guess at, except the words at the top, which might be the name of an airplane.

But what was the language?

Leaving the paper on the table she walked downstairs and called to the desk clerk from the bottom stairs, "Sir, is there a public library near here?"

"No ma'am. The closest is the main library at Franklin and Seventh, and that's about eight blocks."

"What's the phone number for information here?"

"Seven-oh-two, ma'am."

"Thank you."

Retrieving the watercolor paper from her room, she placed a nickel in the hallway Ameche, dialed information, and asked the operator for the number of the main library.

"That number is four-seven-nigh-yun-four," the operator told her.

With the returned nickel she dialed that number.

"Main library," a woman answered.

"Yeah, I'd like to speak to someone who knows languages."

"What language in particular are you interested in?"

"I don't know. That's the problem. I've found some writing and I don't know what language it's in."

"Perhaps Mister Templeton can help you. Hold for a moment, please."

"Arthur Templeton. Can I help you?"

"Yes. I'm at the Gasparilla Hotel and too far away to get

down there. I've found some writing on a piece of paper and I can't read most of it. I was wondering, if I spell some of it out can you tell me what language it is, and what it means?"

"I'll certainly be glad to try, ma'am. Let me get a pad and pencil. . . . All right, go ahead."

"Well, one of the sentences, if it's a sentence, goes—I'll have to spell it out—T-R-O-T-Z, and a space, S-C-H-W. . ." It took two and a half minutes to complete the sentence, after which there was a long pause at the other end.

Finally, Mr. Templeton said, "The language is German. A rough translation would be, 'Despite poor climb performance the P-thirty-nine is well-armed—in the nose a thirty-seven-millimeter cannon plus two times fifty caliber machine guns in nose and four times thirty in wings.' You say you found this somewhere?"

"Yeah. Here's another sentence: D-I-E, and a space, L-A-G-E . . . ," which, when she finished, Templeton translated as, "Engine position makes it vulnerable to a wide range of attacks."

"And here's another," she spelled out, "K-A-N-N . . . ," which he also translated for her.

"You know," she said, "that P-thirty-nine business comes up again, at the very top. I can read it: 'Bell P-thirty-nine-D Airacobra.'"

"Yes, that's an Army Air Corps plane," Templeton confirmed. "They have them at Drew Field locally."

"Well, Drew Field is mentioned here, too, and some numbers follow it that look like a date: 'Zero four, period, three, period, forty-two."

"Yes, that's today's date in European form, the day placed before the month. Ma'am, I must say, I'm very troubled by this document that you've found. The authorities must be tol—"

Click.

She returned to the room and sat down to think. The thoughts came clearly for the first time in days. Peter was not from Chicago. He was a German. A fucking spy! Jesus Christ, and here she's been traveling and sleeping with the bastard. Now she knew what he did at night. He got information on American planes and then wrote it down in secret ink on the back of his paintings in the bathroom. The night he came home all wet must have been because he went after a ship or a seaplane. Yesterday, at that camp, he was not interested in her. He was only pretending to photograph her when he was really photographing those loud airplanes. His artist's work is just a scheme. The pictures give him something to write on. And registering under assumed names—now she knew why.

She reached into the case and pulled out the rest of Peter's finished paintings. One by one, she ran the iron over their back sides. Nothing appeared until she came to what appeared to be a St. Augustine street scene. On its reverse side fifteen brown lines of words and numbers emerged under the iron's heat. The first line read: MARTIN PBM-1 MARINER BANANA RIVER 02.3.42.

Another airplane, she guessed. That was the night they stayed at Cocoa Beach. The night he came home wet. Carrying both watercolor sheets, she walked to the window and looked out on the office buildings, the automobiles and pedestrians below, and the starched-blue sky overhead.

And it was then that she realized, in a flash, what it was that she held in her hands: *aces back-to-back*.

She carried both paintings with writing on them down the hall to the maid's linen closet, where she inserted them between folds of the bottom sheet on the shelves. Then she returned to the room and added a note to the question-and-answer form she was mailing to Father D'Angelo:

Dear Father,
As you can see I am in Tampa. You were right about Peter Krug. He is no gentleman after all. You know what he is? He is a German spy. Can you believe it? And I have the proof. Right now I have to look out for myself. I'll let you know more later.

Your friend,
Sally

She took her envelope downstairs and asked the clerk if he took mail at the desk. He said, no, that there was a postal box on the wall to his right. Sally added, "I'm Mrs.—uh—Pimlico in twenty-two. I'll be checking out today before noon. Mr. Pimlico, I think, will be staying. I'd like to go ahead and have my bags brought down. Would you send a bellhop up in about forty-five minutes? I'll ask you to call me a cab when I'm ready to go."

"Yes, ma'am, of course. I hoped you enjoyed your stay."

"Yeah, very nice." As she turned toward the postal box, she jumped to hear, "Sally!"

"I needed my case, after all," Krug said, as he approached the hotel desk. Sally seemed to him somewhat grim. "Is everything all right?" he asked.

Looking down at the letter in her hand, and turning it slightly with his, he read, crosswise, "Father Anthony D'Angelo, Cathedral, St. Augustine . . . "

"Yes," she responded, thin-lipped and nervous. "I have to mail a letter."

"I'll drop it for you," he said.

"*I'll* drop it," she said sternly, and walked over and did so.

"You seem on edge, sweetheart," he whispered, taking her arm and moving her toward the stairs. "Why are you writing to that priest?"

"I'm taking Catholic instructions and sending in my answer forms."

"Have you been mailing them elsewhere on this trip?"

"Mailed the first one from Fort Pierce."

"I see."

When they reached the foot of the stairway, the desk clerk called after them, "I'll have the bellhop to your room in forty-five minutes, Mrs. Pimlico."

Sally nodded.

"Bellhop?" Krug asked.

"I'm leaving, Peter," she said.

"Leaving?" he asked loudly. "Why?"

"Come in the room and I'll tell you."

When Krug entered the room he saw at once that his carrying case lay open on Sally's bed, with several of his paintings spread over the blanket and sheets. Looking around quickly, he saw the iron standing upright on the table.

"So what have we here?" he asked, rhetorically.

"You want to tell me, or should I tell you?" Sally said, her arms crossed over her rose blouse.

He flipped through the paintings and examined the inside of the case. "Two of my paintings are missing," he said evenly. "I'd like to know where they are." He unloosened the cuff button of his right sleeve.

"They're at the police station," she answered, just as calmly. "I had somebody translate the writing on the back sides. You think you're so damn smart. Well, I can tell you a P-thirty-nine airplane can carry a five-hundred-pound bomb or—or a seventy-five-gallon drip—a drop—a drop tank! Whaddya think about *that?*"

Damn her eyes, Krug thought, she *did* have a translation done.

"Who did the translation?" he asked.

"Someone I called on the phone. And then I called the police and they sent an officer and I gave the paintings to him, with a note about who you were but all rolled up and wrapped in the *Tampa Tribune* and tied shut with one of my belts, and I told him this was important evidence and to hold it until two o'clock this afternoon when either I would go by to reclaim it or they could open it up and get to work. And all you have to do, you Nazi bastard, is go with me to the station and I'll reclaim the package and give it back to you."

"For a price, no doubt."

"Whaddya take me for, a mark? I wasn't born Sunday. Three Gs."

"Three Gs," he repeated.

Then in an instant, he had her hair in his right hand and the point of his blade pricking just outside her right carotid artery.

"This is the biggest crock of *shit* I've ever heard," he

said, menacingly, his mouth inches from her wide eyes. "I've had to kill two people in the last nine days and one more will not bother me in the least. Now you tell me where you *really* have hid those paintings or you will never see shit again."

"All right," she gasped.

When Krug released her hair, she reached for her throat with both hands.

"Now!" Krug ordered, coldly.

"They're in the linen closet," she said, shaking, and moved sideways toward the door.

"Then *get* them. And I will be within a knife thrust of you every step of the way."

She led him down the hallway to the closet, where she retrieved the paintings and handed them to him. He directed her to return to the room.

For the next ten minutes, while Sally stood, trembling, her face forced against the wall, Krug grilled her about Father D'Angelo, about her discovery of the writing, and particularly about the conversation she had had with the librarian.

"And I suppose you told him you were staying at the Gasparilla."

"I may have—" she began, which a touch of the knife in the side of her neck changed to, "Yes, yes, I did."

It was clear now that Krug had to get out of this hotel, and fast.

"It really is such a pity," he said, placing his left arm around her narrow neck. Sally could have proved a very useful person. But there would be no boat ride today.

Professionally, he would miss her.

CHAPTER 19

ON THURSDAY, MARCH 5, Joseph Capona was finally laid to rest. Because of the publicity attending his death, and at Tony's urging, the cathedral thought it appropriate to offer him and his family a Solemn High Requiem Mass. Tom Murphy was officiant, Tony deacon, and Larry subdeacon. Betty Zim played the organ. The Gregorian Chant Choir, under the direction of Sister Damian, S.S.J., sang the liturgical plainsong.

At the conclusion of Mass, the three clerics gathered around the casket in the center aisle, Tom vested in black cope, for the absolution. A cross-bearer in cassock and surplice stood at the head of the deceased between two acolytes, similarly vested, holding lighted candles. At the foot of the bier, Tom began the final prayers: *"Non intres in judicium cum servo tuo, Domine, quia nullus apud te justificabitur homo, nisi per te omnium peccatorum ei tribuatur remissio. . . ."*

From where he stood, Tony could see the tear-streaked face of Joe Capona's widow, Maria. He wondered what must be passing through her mind. Of course, there was much that she would probably never know. She would never know the identity of Joe's killer, or the circumstances of his death, unless young Paul Ohlenburg elected one day to tell her. And if he did not, Maria would never have the satisfaction of knowing that Joe's killer was punished, if he ever was—or of knowing that Joe died in battle, that his death was as much war-related as if he had been shot by a German submarine, which, in a way, he had been.

Tony and Larry stepped aside to permit Tom to circle around the casket, first with the aspergill, sprinkling holy water to signify the preservation of body and soul from the dominion of Satan, then with the censer, throwing clouds of incense to express the honor due a former temple of the Holy Spirit.

When Tom came to the *In paradisum*, Tony wished that it were prayed in English instead of Latin so that Maria could understand and be comforted by it: "May the angels lead you into paradise: may the martyrs come to welcome you and take you to the holy city, the new and eternal Jerusalem. May the choir of angels welcome you. Where Lazarus is poor no longer, may you have eternal rest."

Back in the sacristy, the three clerics made ready to ride out to San Lorenzo Cemetery in the car supplied by Craig's Funeral Home. *Ubi funus ibi tumus.* They said very little to each other, observing the special silence that prevailed when death was violent or untimely. In the background, Betty Zim replayed softly the *Dies irae* as mourners filed out the cathedral.

Even on the way to and from the graveside ceremony the three priests spoke hardly at all, as though some dark, forbidding force had touched and defiled their parish, Tony saying only, "Holding Mrs. Capona's hand in mine gave more comfort to me, I think, than to her."

The others could only guess at what he meant.

When they returned to the sacristy, where they unvested, and to the rectory, the mail had arrived. Tony took his small stack to the dining room and joined Tom for coffee. He smiled to see an envelope from Sally Parkins. He smiled again when he saw that she had filled in the answers correctly. He had had his doubts. Was she all right? He supposed so. All she had written in addition to the answers was, "Fort Pierce is a bore. Sincerely, Sally." Well, maybe by comparison with Manhattan. And what was Krug up to, that murderous Nazi thug? There was no indication.

Tony closed his eyes and recited a brief prayer for Sally's continued safety. When he got upstairs he would have to circle Fort Pierce on the map—and add the postmark date: March 2.

While Tom read the sports pages of the *Florida Times-Union* from Jacksonville, Tony looked idly through the Florida State News of the Day on page five where there were a dozen or so stories datelined, variously, Tallahassee: "Florida Farm Prices Go Up During Month"; Camp Blanding: "Sand Figure Fools Sentry at Blanding"; Tampa: "FBI Searches 59 Homes on West Coast—Enemy Aliens Are Rounded Up in Three More Cities." Tony read through the last story, wondering if St. Augustine Beach was one of those sites; it was not. Tampa again: "Woman Found Dead in Hotel Room," which Tony chose to skim through:

"A young woman guest at the Hotel Gasparilla was found dead on Wednesday afternoon by a policeman . . . identified by documents in her purse as Miss Sally Parkins . . . " *Sally Parkins?* ". . . of New York City . . . Her age given as 31 . . . Police are holding a hotel bellhop for questioning . . . " *Sally Parkins!* "The body is in the custody of the coroner while a search is made for next of kin and local police complete their investigation."

Tony stood bolt upright, scraping his chair across the hardwood floor, and startling Tom, both by the loudness of his voice and by his ashen expression.

"Oh my God!" he exclaimed.

Tom was agape, "Tony, what's wrong?"

Tony gulped and said, in a raspy whisper, "A woman I was giving instructions to by mail—dead—in a Tampa hotel room. . . ."

Tom reached over, found the story, and began reading.

"Just today," Tony continued, "her first answer form arrived in the mail," but he physically clutched his throat to stop from saying what was increasingly obvious and damning: *And it's my fault*.

Silently, he prayed: Eternal rest grant unto her, O Lord . . . And be merciful to me, a sinner. *Mea culpa, mea culpa, mea maxima culpa*.

He should have *warned* her! My God, why didn't he? He should *never* have let her go with Krug. He had a chance to save her and he did nothing! The whole point of getting permission to use confessional knowledge was to prevent others from being hurt. But he allowed himself to become so enthralled by his own clever tracking operation that he placed *its* success before Sally's life.

Use of confessional knowledge, indeed! What conceit, what arrogance, what foolhardiness on his part! And now *another life* was gone, a life on the rebound, maybe. Like Capona's, a life cut short by violence, but not random violence. A purposeful hand had cut her down. And it was not the bellhop's. The problem was, could he ever say so?

Looking at Tom through his mist of self-flagellation, he said, "I'm sorry, Tom, if I seem shaken, but then I am. I feel a responsibility to see that she receives a Catholic burial. Surely, she expressed a *votem ecclesiae*. She had a baptism of desire."

"You're the judge, Tony."

"Tom, I want to ask a very big favor of you. I'd like to go to Tampa. I'll take the bus or borrow a car. I'd like to make arrangements personally for her funeral. Could you possibly cover me while I'm gone? It means you'd have to double-up on confessions if I'm not back by Saturday. And what about my Masses?"

"Oh, that's no problem," Tom assured him. "The bishop's gone to Miami, so he can't help as I know he would, but I'll get an assist from Elkton or Lorreto. Glad to do it. You better get going. If you need to stay longer than you think, just let me know."

"You're a saint, Tom. I'll call you as soon as I know what the situation is."

"Sure. Don't put yourself under any pressure."

"Okay, many thanks."

Tony went to the office phone to call Motor Lines at the Alhambra. A bus was leaving in five minutes; Tampa via Orlando. He could never make that one. Next bus at 3:30. He mounted the stairs to his room, exchanged his cassock for street garb, and packed a small overnight bag, making sure he had his Gem razor, shaving brush, soap, toothbrush, and paste. He took his breviary and, for extra reading, he looked over his bookcase—*The Confessions of St. Augustine* seemed appropriate. He needed that about now. "Too late have I loved Thee, O Beauty of ancient days, yet ever new," he remembered. "Thou wert with me, but I was not with Thee."

The more he thought about it, the more he became convinced that what he needed was not mere transportation, but freedom of movement. He needed a car.

And he needed to talk.

To Belle.

New St. Augustine airport assistant manager Sonny Noell offered to pull Belle's prop through on the blue-with-white-trim 65 horsepower side-by-side Taylorcraft.

"Seatbelt?" he called out.

"Seatbelt!" she confirmed.

"Brakes?"

"Brakes!" she answered, pushing hard against the heel brakes and drawing the control wheel into her tummy. Sonny pulled the prop toward him, checking the brakes.

"Throttle off?" he called.

"Throttle off!"

"Switch off?"

"Switch off!"

"Crack throttle!"

"Throttle cracked!"

Sonny pulled the prop through four times to check compression on the cylinders.

"Contact!" he called.

"Contact!" Belle acknowledged, as she threw the magneto switches from Off to Both.

Sonny gave a heave to the single bladed prop and the Continental engine barked into life, the prop disappearing into a blurred arc. Belle adjusted the throttle setting, gave a thumbs-up to Sonny, released the brakes, and began taxiing out to the downwind end of the runway.

It was great to be in the cockpit again. Restrictions on

private flying had been lifted for pilots planning to fly Civil Air Patrol antisubmarine missions, and a number of local pilots and student pilots were hand-propping each other's or airport-owned rental aircraft. Two Taylorcraft and three Aeroncas displayed the CAP insignia on their sides: a blue circle enclosing a white triangle enclosing a red three-bladed prop. Frank Upchurch and Roy Barnes had been the first to apply the device and, during the nearly month-long no-fly period, pilots painted it on four other craft in expectation that St. Augustine would be named an official CAP base, like Daytona Beach to the south, which was scheduled to be activated on the eleventh. Together with the men who held private tickets, Frank, Roy, Si Davis, Jr., J. W. Richbourg, Carver Harris, Irving Glickstein among them, and one woman student, Jane Quinn, who had not yet soloed, Belle had signed up and received a CAP card and number.

The *damnable* thing was that CAP headquarters had ruled that no woman could fly official CAP antisubmarine patrols! They could fly CAP lost plane searches over land, forest fire patrols, and courier missions. But they could not even ride as observers on official ASW flights. The prejudice of the "stronger sex" aviation community was disgusting. It was ignorant. It was short-sighted. And it was blind. Would they have ruled out the late Amelia Earhart? Are they ruling out Jacqueline Cochran? And Nancy Harkness Love? Could any of the male CAP officials who made this ruling hold a candle to those three? Or to a lot of other women pilots in the Ninety-Niners? Not that Belle thought that she was in the same lofty company. It was the principle of the thing, damn it.

Anyway, a number of the men were planning to fly unofficial, voluntary offshore patrols starting tomorrow, from Ponte Vedra to Marineland, and Belle was going to do the same. The St. Augustine group as yet had no uniforms, no government money, no bombs, and no official status. But they had avgas, eyes, and one-watt radios. And for Belle it was a blessing that official status had not yet come, for it meant that she could fly ASW, too, and do it alone, if she wished. At nights she was spending time studying nautical charts with a few of the men who had flown over-water flights to the Bahamas and Caribbean. And today, with an inflated inner tube as life preserver in the front seat, she was going to test the water ten miles out.

At the runway's end she ran up the rpms to check the mags, left and right, held her heel on the left brake and made a 360-degree turn to look for traffic in the pattern, and then, pointed down the runway, she walked her throttle to the wall.

The nimble aluminum frame and fabric Taylorcraft fairly leaped off the concrete into the warm March air. Belle looked down happily at the country club golf course, the marshes and river, the cathedral and Exchange Bank building, Anastasia Island, and, finally, the gunmetal blue Atlantic. She leveled off at 2,500 feet, higher, she was told, than CAP patrols were flying out of Atlantic City, New Jersey, and Rehoboth, Delaware—500 to 1,000 feet—the first two CAP bases to begin regular patrolling. But she elected to stay high and dry these first times out. There were scattered clouds at 3,500. The temperature was agreeable. Visibility was razor clear. There was no turbulence. It was a good day for flying. Ahead, in the distance, she could make out the small forms and wakes of two northbound merchant ships.

When Belle returned to St. Augustine two hours later, and taxied up to the tie-down area, she was both surprised and pleased to see Father D'Angelo standing by the airport manager's office. She shut down her engine and bounded out to greet him.

"Hello, Father! Did you decide to take that ride?"

"No, Miss Hart, I can't do it right now, thank you. I just wanted to talk with you a few minutes, if you have the time."

"Of course. But, please—call me Belle."

"All right, thank you—Belle. I phoned Davenport Park and they told me I'd probably find you here."

"Yes, I quit my job there so I could fly more regularly. I have some aviation career ambitions. Also, I'm going to be flying antisubmarine patrols. In fact, the flight I just made was my first trial-run at it. Look—could you stand by just a minute while I tie down this bird and fill in my log book?"

"Sure, of course."

He watched her do that, admiring her practical skills, and then followed her suggestion that they walk and talk along the perimeter of the field.

"I hope you don't think it forward of me to ask you a few questions," he began. "My outside-the-seminary training has made me something of an empiricist. I gather as much good thought and advice as I can from various sources, and then, having weighed it, make my own decisions—or at least I think I do. You strike me as being the same kind of person, and—"

"Thank you. I'm flattered."

"And I wonder how you would handle a situation where you learned accidentally in an absolutely confidential setting about the activities of a person who intended great harm to our country and to any innocent individuals who got in his way. And—this is important—there was apparently no one else but you who could stop him."

Belle walked a good ten yards before replying. "Well, Father, I assume that this is a hypothetical case. And you couldn't go to the police?"

"No. I don't see how."

"And it has something to do with the war?"

"Yes."

"Let me answer, then, by saying that if it were a *real* case, and *I* was the one who could do something about it, and without betraying the confidence you speak about, I'd be on my horse—or in a plane—this instant to stop him."

"You really would?" Tony asked.

"Yes. In fact, that's what I'm doing right now, when you think about it—searching out U-boat commanders in order to prevent them from doing harm to our country and to innocent people—merchant seamen."

"Of *course*. That's what you're doing right now. Well, if it *were* a real case"—he chuckled—"I'd be at a disadvantage since I don't have access to either a horse or a plane. In fact, I don't even have access to a car. I wouldn't be able to commandeer the rectory car. And they don't have rental agencies down here like we have in New York. How would you handle a situation like that?"

"Hypothetically, I would ask someone like me, who has access to her late father's car, which her mother rarely uses, if I could borrow her regular car for as long as it was necessary—"

"But I would never ask *you* for *your* car," Tony protested.

"I know, I know," Belle continued. "We're only talking hypothetically. But it would be a perfectly fine, workable arrangement. In my scenario the car would look something like that black Ford parked over there, by the airport office, it would have just been serviced, the tires would be good, and the insurance current."

"But that's not—"

"And, furthermore, it would be found parked on the street outside your rectory in an hour's time, with the keys in the ignition, and my home telephone number on the dashboard in case you ran into any problems."

"But I didn't come here to—"

"Remember, Father D'Angelo, we're only talking hypothetically."

"Of course."

She smiled. "The word we use is 'Roger.'"

Earlier that day, Peter Krug sat in the office of an Atlantic Richfield station across the Tampa Bay toll bridge in St. Petersburg scanning old and current copies of the Tampa and St. Pete papers while waiting for his Pontiac to be gassed and greased. The afternoon before, following the unfortunate business with Sally, he had registered in a new hotel in St. Pete, under the old standby, Winslow Homer. Later that same afternoon, he had painted two beach scenes at Indian Rock. And, after five o'clock, when officers came from work at MacDill and Drew to stroll the beach, he had cased the uniform blouses left in their cars until he found a major's gold oak leaf insignias and a full colonel's silver eagles in order to upgrade the second lieutenant's bars that came with his uniform. Since the police were bound to have a general description out on him, he would wear the uniform full-time now as protective coloration.

The AP report on the Wehrmacht's Eastern operations in the *Tampa Tribune* of March 1 was not encouraging, if it could be believed: "Desperate Nazi attempts to save the 90,000 men of the trapped 16th Army at Staraya on the northeastern front." And a headline in the March 3 paper made him worry anew about Lorenz across the state in Eden: "FBI Round Up 124 Axis Aliens in Tampa Raids." He read quickly through the story: Germans, Italians, and Japanese in the Tampa area classed as "potentially dangerous" were taken into custody during 247 searches of homes, business establishments, and gathering places. Seized in the mass raid, the largest ever conducted in Tampa, were two Swiss rifles, 700 rounds of ammunition concealed beneath a trap door, dynamite caps and fuses, coastal maps and charts, cameras, shortwave receivers, binoculars, stacks of foreign language propaganda, and a bust of Mussolini.

Yeah, Krug mused, I'd watch out for that bust of Mussolini.

When he reached the March 5 *Tribune*, which he particularly wanted to see, he read with acute interest the story on Sally Parkins. Body found by a policeman . . . autopsy being conducted . . . police holding an unnamed bellhop as a material witness. Witness? A not very accurate description of Mr. Pimlico followed. Police assumed that he had a car but had not been able to obtain an identification or license plate. So, Krug was relieved to conclude, there was nothing to worry about in that story. He had not violated Heydrich's principle: he had not left a trail.

And, in another local story, an Air Corps sergeant, who

had been assaulted and unclothed in the men's room of a local tavern, was reported in "improved" condition at the Drew Field hospital. That was okay: since December, humanity began with the rank of sergeant.

"Your car's ready, sir," a smartly uniformed service attendant told Krug, who paid the $2.50 bill and drove back across the water to Tampa's Vera Street, which took him directly south from Drew to MacDill Field, a bomber base that occupied a two-and-a-half by two-mile peninsula jutting out into Tampa Bay. Parking his car a block away from the main gate, he marched up to the MP guards who gave his uniform, gold oak leafs, wings, and Major Peter Krug "indentification" card only the barest notice. The entry was absurdly easy. While he was passing through, in fact, a civilian bus arrived with both uniformed and nonuniformed passengers; an MP stepped inside, looked around casually, stepped back out, and waved the bus through. The Führer, Mussolini, and Tojo could have ridden it into the base undetected.

Once inside, he walked briskly with eyes set straight ahead, as though he knew exactly where he was going, and returned the salutes of junior officers and enlisted men in the U.S. Army style that he had practiced before his hotel mirror. This first penetration was for land reconnaissance purposes only. He identified the principal buildings that stood on the ball-bearing-like sand, including the headquarters of what was marked the "29th Bombardment Group," another building marked "B-17 Operational Training Unit (OTU)," and three hangars; studied the positions and movements of the MPs and soldier-guards; noticed that while officers moved individually and freely, enlisted men moved from point to point in marching groups; identified the runways—eight approaches, six over water—and the hardstands; and for awhile stood on the flight line watching the olive drab, four-engined B-17 bombers taxi out and take off on training flights.

These must be the new B-17Es, he decided. They were considerably changed from the B-17C type the British had used last year, with less than impressive results. The British dubbed the plane Fortress I. More accurately, Herr Joseph Goebbels called it a "Flying Coffin." This new mark had a lengthened rear fuselage, a huge dorsal fin—for greater stability at high altitudes?—an enlarged empennage, and, most significant to Krug, increased armament: twin .50 caliber barrels in the tail, twin fifties in a ventral ball turret, twin fifties in a dorsal turret aft of the pilot's compartment, single fifties on each side of the waist, and a flexible gun, probably .30 caliber from the looks of it, in the nose. This model of the Fortress could put out six fierce zones of fire, certainly far more than Germany's heaviest bomber, the Heinkel HE-177, which was not yet operational. But Krug guessed that the B-17s would have to fly in large, tight formations, if they wanted to mass their fire effectively. He also guessed that there were spots where the guns were blind, where a Fortress could be approached without fear by a Bf 109 or a FW 190. He would have to fly in one to find out.

While he watched yet another Fortress roll out the taxiway in a roar of radial engine noise, he saw a sergeant line chief break away from his regular duties and attend to an olive drab C-47 transport that landed and taxied up to the chocks. Krug backed off somewhat, but not out of listening range, when a full colonel alighted from the aircraft and said to the line chief, "Colonel Howard from Southeast Training Command. Top off my tanks and tell the next Fort crew I'm going to ride with 'em."

"Yes, sir!" the line chief acknowledged.

"Advise the engineering officer, and get me a chute and some high altitude gear."

"Yes, sir!"

"That fits."

"Yes, sir!"

Krug was impressed. No Luftwaffe *Oberst* could have done it better. Obviously, a colonel could throw his weight around here, too, and unquestioned.

He reached into his left pocket and took out his bird

colonel's insignias. It would be a rapid promotion, but, he thought, damn well deserved.

The next morning, while Tony talked with the Tampa chief of police in his office, Detective Jim Boney leafed slowly through the March issue of *Sunshine and Health*, only occasionally looking up to make sure that Frankie Dolan was still in the chair alongside his worn, wooden desk. This current issue of the nudist monthly had a black-and-white photo feature on biking, which gave Boney more leg action than he had seen in several past issues, and a bit of a bounce to the upper structures besides.

Seeing Dolan peeking over at the pages, Boney rebuked him, "Take your dirty eyes back off my magazine, you pervert. You must be sick, you know it? You'll be lucky if the chief doesn't tear your eyes out with his bare hands."

At which point the chief entered the detectives' room, with Tony in tow. Boney hastily stored his magazine in the top drawer and stood to meet the priest.

"Detective Boney, Father D'Angelo, from St. Augustine city. He's come here to talk about the Sally Parkins woman and to try to make some funeral arrangements. I told him how we'd found her next of kin, her mother, and told her about the daughter's death, and got her permission for an autopsy. The father here called her just now and suggested the daughter might have wanted to be buried as a Catholic, since she was plannin' on convertin', but—you tell the detective yourself, Father."

"The mother said, okay, but she wanted to have the burial in New York," Tony said. "Apparently, Miss Parkins had enough money in her purse to pay for the shipment of her body. I'll say a Requiem Mass for her locally at Sacred Heart."

"I explained to the father that there was no sign of trauma on the woman's body," the chief continued, "except for two small marks on the right side of her neck. Detective Boney, why don't you tell the father what happened and how we know she was murdered. Let's sit down."

Boney sat, reached for his typed report, and summarized its contents in a clinical drawl. Sally Parkins, registered as Mrs. Harold Pimlico, said she was going to check out of the hotel and asked for a bellhop and a cab. That was Wednesday morning the fourth, the desk clerk said, around eleven o'clock. Then the husband came in and the two of them went up to their room, number twenty-two. After forty-five minutes the bellhop, named Frankie Dolan—that was this guy sitting here by the desk— knocked on the door. The man, Mister Pimlico, or whatever, gave Frankie some baggage and told him to take it down to the sidewalk. Said Mrs. Pimlico would not be needing a cab, after all, and Frankie did as he was asked. It turned out, though, that Frankie had done more than he was asked.

Boney turned a judgmental face toward the bellhop, who was some thirty years of age, ruddy-faced, with unkempt dark hair and brown eyes, dressed in a dark blue long-sleeved shirt and khaki pants.

"This pervert here . . . ," Boney went on. "But let me finish the bare facts. Once outside, Mr. Pimlico carried his baggage up the street. So neither the desk clerk nor Frankie here got a look at his car, assuming he had one, much less his license number. Frankie was going to follow him up the street out of curiosity—morbid curiosity, it turns out—but just at that moment one of our police cars pulled up at the hotel entrance and the officer asked Frankie to step inside, since he needed to talk with both him and the desk clerk. With the officer was Mr. Arthur Templeton, one of the city librarians, who had called here very concerned that a woman registered at the Gasparilla had found a paper all in German about one of our Air Corps planes at Drew Field.

"Well, the desk clerk said that Mrs. Pimlico had asked about the location of the main library about eleven o'clock that morning, and also that she had asked for the telephone number for reaching information. We confirmed with the information operator that a woman called for the library number about the same time. And Mr. Templeton remembered that the woman caller had said she was at the Gasparilla.

"So the policeman went up to the room and found Mrs. Pimlico's—Miss Parkins's body. We gave Mr. Templeton's notes to the FBI and we put out a physical description on the man Pimlico, whoever he might be. Our reasoning at this point? Harold Pimlico is not the guy's real name. He's a German agent interested in war planes. The FBI is having all the gate guards at Drew and MacDill keep a special lookout for anyone, in or out of uniform, answering his description. The problem is, the description we have is so general, it could be five hundred different guys. I don't think it's going to help at all. MacDill would have to arrest half the people going through the gate."

The chief broke in, "Since we knew from the desk clerk that Frankie Dolan was the last to talk with either of the Pimlicos, Detective Boney did some real hard talking with Frankie, and I have to give him credit."

Boney shifted in his chair to a more commanding position. "The more I talked with this guy, the more I knew he was holding back something. You know what it was? This guy didn't wait forty-five minutes to go up for the bags. He went up after about twenty. And why? Because he's drilled these tiny little holes in the doors of several of the rooms, including number twenty-two, and through those holes he watches women undressing and couples having sex. And, hoping, I guess, to see this particular man and woman in a romantic moment, if you get my drift, Father, he sees—what did you see, Frankie?"

Without looking up, the bellhop said, "Well, I seed the man grab the woman round her throat from behind and choke her 'til she fell down and didn't move no more. I got scared and went downstairs until I figured it was forty-five minutes and time to go back up and knock. The man gave me a bag and a flat case and followed me down to the sidewalk, gave me a tip, and walked off. I didn't say nothin' 'cause I didn't want the hotel to know what I'd been doin'. That's all I know."

The chief explained, "A death like that, with the man disappearing, is suspicious to start with, even with no visible wounds on the body, and I would have asked for an autopsy, anyway. Frankie's eyewitness account describes the death as homicidal, and the autopsy confirmed it. So that's the story."

"What will you do with Frankie?" Tony asked.

"Probably nothing," the chief answered. "We held him more as a material witness than as a suspect or accomplice. We could charge him as a Peeping Tom, but I think he's earned immunity. He's lost his job at the hotel, which may be punishment enough for now."

The chief turned to Frankie. "If we catch the murderer I'm gonna need you for the trial. So don't you leave town. You understand me? Now get outta here!"

As Frankie left the detectives' room, with commendable speed, Tony decided that it was time for him, too, to leave.

There was not much that he had done, and even less that he *could* do, except, of course, provide the chief with Pimlico's real name, verify his physical description, state that he represented himself as an artist, describe his mission as German espionage of some kind, and reveal that he had earlier killed a man on St. Augustine Beach, where he had landed from a submarine. But the last two particulars were definitely under the seal. What of the first three? Was it possible to say something about the first three?

Could he at least tell the chief that he knew Sally was traveling with a man named Krug, give his physical description, and add that Krug told Sally he was an artist? After all, he had learned all three himself or from Sally in the *ex*ternal forum, at the Alhambra and in his office at the rectory. To say that much was not likely to compromise the seal or impose a *gravamen poenitentis*. Or was it? The rule was to be extra careful, particularly in speech. But had he been *too* careful in speaking to Sally? Was he being too careful now in speaking to the chief?

He had already failed once in his use of confessional knowledge. Should he risk failing a second time?—in his use of *non*confessional knowledge?

He decided that the virtue of prudence still dictated caution and silence. Peter Krug was a name he had learned under the seal in the confessional. The fact that he had also learned it, subsequently, in the external forum did not relieve him of the obligation to observe the secrecy of the original disclosure. Krug's identity was not public information, like the assassination of a governor. And the additional facts that he had picked up, Krug's physical appearance and artwork, he would not ever have learned had he not initiated certain actions in the wake of a secret disclosure.

He said his goodbyes to the chief and Detective Boney and looked at his watch. Ten A.M. already. Where was Krug now? he wondered as he walked to his car. With Sally's death he no longer had any way of knowing. The police chief and the FBI had a description out—maybe they could find him. But Tony thought not. The description was too vague. Even with a name, a more accurate description, and a profession in hand, the authorities probably would not be able to locate him. Krug would be a step ahead of them, and even more deeply underground than before. Only a Jack Russell terrier, like Tom Murphy's, could run this varmint to ground.

But who would that be?

If not himself?

CHAPTER 20

BY TEN O'CLOCK Colonel Krug was already back inside MacDill. This time he had driven all the way down Vera Street and through the main gate, where the guards this time examined his face and credentials a great deal more closely than they had yesterday. Probably they had his description. But he passed inspection, nonetheless. No doubt being a bird colonel helped, as did the drugstore-bought pipe clenched between his teeth, and the fact that his description, if it was the one in the newspaper, was so nonspecific. They should have had the desk clerk or the bellhop on the gate, he thought. MacDill was no smarter than Le Touquet-Paris-Plage. From the gate he drove casually into the field as far as the rear of hangar number three. From that point he marched as officiously as he could around the hangar to the flight line and B-17 hard-stands, where pilots and crewmen, either wearing or carrying cold weather gear, were assembling around their individual craft. Among one group he sighted the same master sergeant line chief he had seen on Saturday.

"Sergeant!" he called to him. "Colonel Krug from Southeast Training Command. Line me up with one of these crews. I'll need high altitude equipment and parachute. Make sure there's a mask for an extra man. I'll want a pencil and a clipboard. And I'd like to talk with the engineering officer."

"Yes, sir!" the line chief acknowledged, and sent a corporal scurrying to fill Krug's order.

"You can ride with Lieutenant Parry, sir," the line chief said, "tail number one-nine-zero-two-four."

Krug looked down the line of matte olive bombers until he found the number, then started walking toward it with the line chief.

"You'll be using the jump seat, sir?" the line chief asked.

"Yes. Why did you recommend Lieutenant Parry?"

"Well, sir, I figured you wanted to see how well we're doing, and Parry's crew is our best. But if you want to observe an ordinary crew—"

"No, Sergeant, you read me right."

Coming up fast behind them was the engineering officer. When Krug reached 19024, he turned around to talk with him.

"Captain Ehrlich, Colonel," the officer introduced himself, short of breath. "Engineering."

"Colonel Krug. Have you worked up an average time frame for Twenty-Ninth Group to re-arm, re-bomb, service, and perform normal maintenance checks exclusive of battle damage?"

"Yes, sir. Five hours."

"How would you compare your numbers with a B-twenty-four group?"

"We've had a B-twenty-four group on the field, sir, and I'd rate the Forts better on every count."

"For example?"

"Time to do the turn-around things you named, sir, on a Liberator group, is seven hours. Also, you get twenty hours less usable time before engine change. The Liberator accident rate is double that of the Fort—lots of takeoff crashes, outboard engines going out. And I certainly wouldn't want to ride one in combat, sir."

"And why not?"

"Well, for one thing, sir, that high aspect Davis wing can't take a hit. Attack any part of that box spar and the whole thing'll collapse. The Germans will love that plane. For another, it can't reach enough altitude to evade triple-A."

"When you make a report, Captain, you do not use abbreviations."

"Yes, sir, sorry, sir. Anti-aircraft artillery."

At that moment, a corporal came running up with

Krug's gear and clipboard. Krug stepped aside to write down what he had just heard.

The line chief and engineering officer exchanged looks that said, Boy, this one is a real hard-ass.

When he finished, Krug said to the engineering officer, "I like to get the frank opinions of the officers on the field. Thank you. The Liberator must have *some* redeeming value, though."

"Yes, sir. Ten miles per hour advantage in climb speed, five in route speed. Slightly larger bombload. Greater fuel capacity, so longer range. And you can install additional fuel tanks in its larger bomb bay for even longer range. That's about it, sir, as I see it."

"All right, Captain. I want to talk with you again when I get down."

"Yes, *sir!*" the officer responded. "I'll watch for your tail number."

The line chief approached with an officer who was carrying altitude gear over his left arm. "This is Lieutenant Parry, Colonel."

The lieutenant saluted, "Welcome aboard, sir."

"Thank you, Lieutenant. What's your exercise today?"

"Solo cross-country at twenty-five thousand, sir. A five-legged track—Orlando, Jax, Tallahassee, over the Gulf for gun-testing, Cross City, and home. I've completed our ground check."

"All right, Lieutenant, ready to board when you are."

Most of the ten-man crew entered the Fort through a door near the empennage. The officers swung themselves feet-first up and through a left nose hatch—a six-foot heave. Krug wondered, could he do it? He *had* to do it.

Following the lead of the others, he tossed his heavy protective clothing, boots, flying helmet, and parachute through the hatch. Then, grabbing the hatch frame, he swung up with all his might and main—just barely making it legs-first into a narrow, cramped space. In the pilot's compartment he donned and zippered the fleece-lined pants, boots, jacket, and helmet; and snapped on the parachute harness. Parry and his copilot dropped the jump seat for him. A crewman stowed his chute.

Out the side windows, he could see the ground crew pushing the huge props through three revolutions. While the pilots and engineer went down the cockpit check list, he reached for the pilot's handbook and began copying curves and numbers for: formation climb speed, rate of climb, climb power setting, route speed, return speed, fuel consumption, max operational altitude, service ceiling, max normal formation radius with 6,000-pound load and 1,730 gallons of fuel.

Then he followed the pilots and engineer as they went through the prestart check list.

". . . Fuel transfer valves and switches?"

"Off."

"Fuel shut-off switches?"

"Open."

"Cowl flaps?"

"Open and locked left, open and locked right."

"Intercoolers?"

"Set."

"Turbo controls?"

"Off."

"Generators?"

"Off."

"Gyros?"

"Set, left and right. . . ."

After the lengthy list was completed, Parry called, "Clear!" on the left outboard, or number-one, engine, activated the fuel boost pump, turned the ignition switch to On, engaged the starter, switched to Mesh, and primed through six blades. Abruptly, the Wright R-1820-65 radial fired off a burp of smoke and noise, and the blades spun tentatively. Krug watched the oil pressure come up to normal limits inside thirty seconds. Parry adjusted the throttle to 1,000 rpm. And so on, through engines two, three, and four. The start-up was all a very familiar procedure that Krug had managed many times himself, with two engines instead of four. He had to admit, though, that four 1,200 horsepower–rated engines roaring all together on one plane was an impressive new experience.

Equally familiar were the taxi out and the run-ups. Before takeoff the bombardier and navigator officers came aft to take standing positions, with the engineer, behind the pilots; no doubt to have to have more survivable stations in the event of an engine failure crash. At the downwind end of the active runway Parry advanced the throttles, gripping them together, palm-up, on central horizontal levers. At 60 mph on the airspeed indicator, he pulled back slightly on the control column: it seemed that the preferred angle of incidence was to let this bird fly itself off tail-low. Lift-off came at 100 mph, and, after giving his copilot thumbs-up for the gear, Parry continued a shallow climb until reaching 150 mph indicated, when he reduced manifold pressure to 38 inches and propeller rpms to 2,300.

After passing through 3,000 feet Krug activated his throat mike in the manner he copied from the pilots, "Lieutenant Parry, level off at ten thousand. I'm going to do a walk-around."

"Yes, sir."

"Engineer, I want you to accompany me."

"Yes, sir."

During the climb, Krug studied the bomb load and armament data that were included in the same packet with the handbook. Estimated average bomb load was 6,000 pounds. That was not much compared to the British heavies, such as the Short Stirling's 14,000. But it was more than what the Heinkel HE 177A was scheduled to carry. Next, he studied the machine gun data, especially the .50 caliber. The Browning .50 was supposed to be a superior weapon, with an effective range of 600 yards.

At 10,000 feet Parry eased the column forward, building up cruising speed, then trimmed and cranked in 32 and 2,200. Krug disconnected his headset, stood up, and gestured for the engineer to lead the way.

"We'll look at the tail guns first!" he yelled.

"Yes, sir!" the engineer responded, and led Krug aft across a catwalk in the bomb bay to the radio operator's compartment, past the two waist gunners squatting by their lateral gun apertures, and the Sperry ball-turret gunner, who apparently did not want to curl up inside his belly station any sooner than he had to, and as far as the entrance to the tail gunner's station, where the engineer called the gunner out so Krug could enter.

"I'm going to check the movement!" he told the engineer, and crawled into the small space. The gunner occupied a position above his twin .50s and manipulated them by hand through bell cranks. When Krug tested the movement, he found that the guns traversed 30 degrees to either side of the vertical and horizontal planes. He thought that 109s and 190s might be able to get around the cone of fire those guns put out. The gunner's body, though not his head, was protected from a stern attack by armor plate; there was no armor forward.

Returning to the waist, and knowing that he was too big to get inside the belly ball turret, he elicited what information about it he could from the engineer and gunner. As for the handheld waist guns, he asked the engineer, "What's been your experience so far with these?"

"A bit hard to handle, sir, in this slipstream. If we ever hit anything it will probably be just luck. At least the breeches don't freeze up at altitude, as they did with the RAF on the old Seventeen-C. One of our assignments, today, sir, is to test 'em after two hours at twenty-five thousand."

"You think your flanks are not as well protected as they ought to be?" Krug asked.

"Well, it's not for me to say, sir. The Fort's supposed to be self-defending all around. That's what they keep telling us. We're not supposed to need interceptor escorts. I guess the proof will come in combat."

"All right, let's go forward," Krug ordered the engineer. In the radio compartment, what he had not seen on the ground Friday, was provision for mounting another handheld .50 that the operator-gunner could deploy overhead through a removable plexiglass cover. Behind the pilot's compartment, he tested the Sperry A-1 upper turret, and, while it had 360 degrees movement in azimuth, the twin .50s could not be depressed more than 5 degrees below the horizontal plane. He began to get ideas.

Thanking the engineer, he continued forward alone.

Beyond the pilot's compartment and the navigator's station, where he returned the navigator's nod, was the bombardier's compartment. No Norden bombsight was aboard. A pity. But here, as he had suspected on Friday, was a flexible .30 caliber gun—hardly an adequate weapon against head-on attacks—and his ideas began to build.

"What's been your experience with this gun, Lieutenant?" he asked the bombardier.

"Not very happy, sir. It takes too long to change from one ball socket to another. It's difficult to aim from the front upper socket. And the plexiglass cracks from the recoil. And I don't think thirty cal is enough up front."

"I agree," Krug said.

"Especially," the bombardier went on, "since the navigator and I haven't received the same aerial gunnery training that the boys in back got."

"I understand. Okay, thank you, Lieutenant."

Krug returned to his jump seat and ordered Parry, "All right, Lieutenant. Inspection completed. Resume your climb to two-five."

"Yes, sir." And turning the intercom to all stations, Parry ordered: "Pilot to crew: oxygen, repeat, oxygen." A minute later, the copilot called, "Oxygen check." Each officer and crewman reported in by the usual sequence: nose, top turret, radio, ball, waist, tail, and jumpseat.

Krug leaned back with the aircraft as Parry applied power and went to 300 feet per minute.

He had rarely been to 25,000 before.

Back on the ground, Krug dropped through the nose hatch into the company of Captain Ehrlich. He had been enormously relieved to see, on landing, that his reception party was not submarine gun-toting MPs and infantry. God! he had gotten away with it again. Here, as in Germany, he guessed, colonels were simply beyond suspicion. It had been the most opportune promotion in his aviation career. Now, though, he had to revert to artist. He had a lot of painting to do in order to have room for his pages of data.

"Did you have a good flight, sir?" the engineering officer inquired, solicitously.

"Yes, very good," Krug replied. "Very stable at twenty-five." In fact, the aircraft was amazingly stable at 25,000, and Parry had denied any mushiness in the controls. It was, indeed, a steady platform for high altitude precision bombing. No question about it. "Good crew. The guns tested well. No freeze-ups."

As Krug divested himself of the altitude gear, Ehrlich looked up to the two-story high tail. "Big assed bird, isn't she, sir?"

"Yes," Krug agreed, but a better name, he thought, reflecting on her bristling firepower, was *Viermotoriges Kampfflugzeug*—four-engined fighter. She was certainly that. Except where she was incredibly vulnerable to an attack closing from forward. A fatal flaw. The .30 nose gun was inadequate, and the top turret .50s could not depress worth a damn. There was no armor in the nose, no bullet-proof glass. With luck, a 109 or 190 could destroy nose and cockpit, then rake along the length of the fuselage to take out either the ball or tail gunner. Advice to the fighter arm: take her measure head-on with tracers at 700 meters, give a short burst at 500 meters, do a half roll and out. Come back around front and take out the engines, if needed.

"Guess we'll be sending these men overseas pretty soon, sir," Ehrlich ventured, as they walked back toward the hangar.

"I'm not at liberty to say, Captain," Krug answered.

"Of course, sir. It's just that I heard the Forts were

leaving and were going to be replaced by B-twenty-six mediums."

"Could be."

"I dread it, if it happens, sir. With that high wing loading, the Marauder is hell to fly. A great airplane, but a bitch to fly."

"A hot ship," Krug guessed.

"Too much of an airplane for greenhorn pilots. Too much for the experience level we see around this place."

"Too much?"

"Well, sir, when we moved B-seventeens from here to Karachi the last two months, the pilots had only fifteen to twenty hours of four-engine time before setting out across the Atlantic. But the Fort is a very pilot-forgiving airplane, as you know, sir. Like a Piper Cub. The Marauder, on the other hand, is intolerant of pilot error. If we have the same experience level with the B-twenty-six group, I'm afraid we'll be southern headquarters for pilot error. We'll see 'em pranging in all over Tampa Bay."

"I hope you're wrong, Captain."

"If we're gonna have the mediums, sir, I'd much rather have the B-twenty-five Mitchell—"

"I can't answer those questions, for you, Captain," Krug insisted again. "I want to see your map room."

"Yes, sir. It's in operations. I'll show you, sir."

After saying a private Mass for the Dead at the Jesuit Sacred Heart Church on Florida Avenue and receiving the pastor's telephoned introduction to the Catholic chaplain at MacDill, Tony drove Belle's car to a parking spot near the airfield's main gate, where he was met by middle-height, pudgy-cheeked, dark-haired First Lieutenant Timothy Feehan, from the archdiocese of Boston.

"The name's Tim."

"Tony. Good to meet you."

"I got to know some of your men from New York in chaplains' school," Feehan said as drove them into the base in an olive drab Ford sedan. "You're Dunwoodie, right?"

"Yes. A loan to Florida for a couple of years."

"I'm Brighton myself. And, I guess, Air Corps for the duration."

"I envy you."

"Well, it's a fast-track to the responsibilities and freedoms of a pastor. You don't have to spend your entire life as a curate, like in Boston. Of course, the price you pay is you have to serve two masters—three, if the field CO's a Catholic, which fortunately isn't the case here right now."

Feehan made a hard fast turn against a wood-frame building adjoining the field chapel. "Here's my office," he said.

The two priests, one in khaki, one in black, walked past two enlisted men at desks into a small, utilitarian office where Feehan threw his cap on a file cabinet and showed Tony a chair.

"So you say you've got something confidential and urgent?" Feehan asked, offering Tony a cigarette.

"No thanks. Yes, I do," Tony began. "Confidential, because it's under the seal, although I have the penitent's permission, given in the external forum, to act on confessional knowledge. Urgent, because the knowledge relates to national security and to the lives of innocent people. I believe that I have a duty in charity as well as in justice to do something about the situation, if I can—all the while, of course, protecting the integrity of the seal.

"Which brings me to the question, why am I here? Tim, the key person in all this has just been here in Tampa, probably is still in Tampa, and, if so, possibly is on your airfield. He cannot be identified by name. You won't have it on any muster, or whatever it is you say. But *I* know what he looks like. So I'd like your help, if you can give it, in looking around the field to see if, by chance, I can spot him. It's a long shot, but I feel that I should take it."

Feehan placed his cigarette in an ashtray and sat upright. "Holy shit, Tony! You take my breath away. What happens next if you *do* spot him?"

"I'm not sure. But *primum videre.*"

"Yeah, first you gotta find him. Okay, of course, I want to help. Hell, yes, I want to help! *Citius melius*."

Feehan went to the door and called for one of the enlisted men, "Wozniak?"

A young corporal presented himself.

"Corporal Wozniak, this is Father D'Angelo, a priest of this diocese. He needs to take a good slow look around the field. Never mind why. It may take awhile. Use the sedan, okay?"

"Yes, Lieutenant."

Tony put out his hand. "Good to meet you, Corporal."

"Likewise, Father."

While Wozniak headed for the car, Tony asked, "If I don't happen to find what I'm searching for here, are there any other Air Corps fields in Florida or Georgia where I might also look?"

"There's Drew here in Tampa—"

"I know about Drew."

"And then—I guess you gotta go to Eglin."

"Where's that?"

"Way the hell out in the Panhandle. I'll walk out to the car with you and show you on the map."

When they came to the car, Feehan reached into the glove compartment and took out and unfolded a Sinclair road map.

"See, here, this big shaded area called Choctawhatchee National Forest? It's all been taken over by Eglin Field. It's called the Air Corps Proving Ground. A big testing facility. The main field is near Valparaiso—here. And they're clearing and grading a bunch of auxiliary fields out in the swamps and woods. They say you need boots to make your way around Eglin. They've got a Catholic chaplain up there, a Lieutenant Waldo, but I don't know him."

"That's all right, you've been a great help, Tim. Thanks for your understanding and for the car and driver. I owe you a bottle of Black Label."

"Just solve the problem, Tony. And when you do—as me sainted mudder in Irelan' says, fuck 'im!"

• • •

In the Ops map room Peter Krug found exactly what he wanted: a sectional air map of Eglin Field and a field advisory dated 15 February 1941. Eglin Field, it turned out, was a two-runway main field near Valparaiso, but since October 1940 the name Eglin also applied to an Air Corps reservation surrounding Valparaiso of some 400,000 acres, mostly forested. Eglin's mission was tactical testing of aircraft, armament, and accessory equipment. There were extensive bombing and gunnery ranges, including some overwater in the Gulf. Also, since last January, engineers had begun construction of seven auxiliary fields in outlying areas of the forest. Satellite Field No. 1, two-and-a-quarter miles east of north-south highway 218, below Mossy Head, was now complete, with two paved runways for special projects training, one air-to-ground range, and one bore sighting range. Krug made a rough trace of the graphics and copied down the pertinent numbers. Then, clipboard in hand, he walked aggressively to the rear of hangar three, returning salutes all the way, and entered his car.

As he made the turn onto the gate road, at 10 mph posted speed, and approached the frame building that housed the PX and commissary, he sighted in the distance two men, one in black, the other in khaki, stepping out of an Air Corps vehicle and walking in his direction toward the PX entrance. The man in black had a white square at his throat indicating that he was a priest. Krug would have thought no more about it, *except* that, when he drew closer, he saw that it was—it was that priest from St. Augustine! *D'Angelo!* What was he doing *here?*

Now, suddenly, the priest stopped walking and stared through Krug's windshield like two headlights on bright. Krug recognized the contact at once. *Herrgott noch mal!* He *had* left a trail, after all. But how? Sally Parkins, of course. She must have been in the papers up there, too. He hadn't figured on that. And the priest *knew his name.*

Krug watched him step out to the edge of the road, apparently for a better look. At the same instant, Krug swerved sharply, accelerated, and aimed at D'Angelo's black legs. Just as the priest was about to be crushed, the man in khaki reached out and pulled him back between two parked cars. *Verdammt!*

"So what happened next?" Chaplain Feehan asked a hard-breathing Wozniak.

"Well, sir, that officer's car tore out of there at high speed and right through the gate without stopping."

"Did you get a license number?"

"Father D'Angelo, when he picked himself up, made out a 'two-eight,' the last two digits, he said."

"So what did Father D'Angelo do?"

"He had me drive him right away to his car outside the gate, and then I watched him disappear into the traffic. I think he was going after the guy."

"Well, I'm sure he's grateful to you for saving his ass, Wozniak. As I am, too. That officer must have just lost control of his vehicle. He probably has no idea of how close he came to hurting someone bad."

"Yes, sir. I guess so, sir."

"I wouldn't worry anymore about it. Hey, it's Friday! You deserve a weekend pass."

"Thank *you*, sir."

"Get some prophylaxis afterward, okay, Wozniak?"

"Yes, sir."

Tony looked around Tampa the rest of that day and all of the next, and though he sighted many uniformed men who had Krug's stature and hair color, none turned out to be his quarry and assailant. On Sunday morning he helped with a late Mass at Father John Mullins's provisional Christ the King parish church, and then, taking off his jacket, rabat, and collar, he struck out in Belle's car for Eglin Field in the distant Panhandle.

Passing north of Tampa into Pasco County, he realized that he was truly on his own now, feeling his way, with few geographical reference points in the thinly settled back country, with only a few Catholic rectories, should he need an inn or a port in a storm, once he passed Pasco County. There was a church at Gainesville, a second at Perry, and a third at Tallahassee. Beyond those—what? And this particular stretch of cracker Florida was not known to be friendly to Catholics, much less to priests. Wasn't it at Gainesville that the mayor and chief of police abducted the popular Father Conoley and castrated him on the road to Palatka—in 1923 or so? He decided to steer clear of Gainesville.

In fact, he decided now to skip all the rectories. He had enough cash to stay at tourist cabins. And that would free him up from intrusive questions. He also considered the fact that he had no Mass kit or portable altar stone, and no delegated indult to use them if he had them. So the obligation of daily Mass would have to be dispensed with. No matter. *Ecclesia supplet*. He was making his own rules now.

The narrow, rough state roads took him through alternate stretches of dense pine and hardwood hammock. Where the land was cleared, he could see dilapidated farm houses and roving cattle followed by white herons; but very few humans: an occasional white farmer walking his furrows; a Negro guiding a high-wheeled cart drawn by oxen; or a convict road gang, shepherded by armed guards, chanting with each heave of their shovels:

> LOU-U-ISE—UGH!—SWEETEST GAL I KNOW—UGH!
> SHE MADE ME WALK FROM CHI-CA-GO—UGH!
> TO THE GULF—UGH!—OF MEXICO—UGH!

When he finally reached Tallahassee, he decided to stay overnight at a small tourist court on U.S. 90, which, he was relieved to see on his map, would take him tomorrow directly to Eglin. In his haste to leave St. Augustine, he had forgotten to bring lay clothes. That had not even been on his mind in Tampa, where black clericals had been appropriate, but he wished now that he had taken time out from his search for Krug to pick up some shirts and pants. All he had to wear for a shirt as he drove a short distance down the highway from his room to a roadside restaurant, was his collarless dress shirt with French cuffs. He wondered how that would play in cracker country. He decided that rolling up the sleeves would solve most of his problem.

In fact, there was no problem at all. The restaurant people were about as friendly as he guessed they could be to a Yankee. Catfish, corn bread, turnip greens, and black-eyed peas were not his usual fare, but he was surprised how much he enjoyed them. He even got a kick out of the jukebox lyrics: something about bein' back down South—where you don't wear shoes—and the chicken's fryin'—and a honey chile's waitin' in a little ole shack—and so on. It was wonderfully expressive, but, to a Manhattanite, beyond his cultural limits.

CHAPTER 21

THE NEXT MORNING, gassed up, oil checked, and windshield cleaned, Tony pressed westward on Highway 90. The long drive to the boundaries of Eglin was uneventful except for his stop, between Bonifay and DeFuniak Springs, at Strickland's Country Store: "Salt Pork, Corn Meal, Horse Collars, Clothing for Men and Women." Tony parked in front of the large low building with a tin roof and a wrap-around porch that was filled with potted plants and flowers. Inside the doorway, where three men in bib overalls discussed dogs around a black wood stove, he paused to look around and to acknowledge the storekeeper's "Howdy."

Seeing shirts and trousers hanging in the left rear of the store, he walked in that direction, past wooden barrels of dill pickles and pole beans in bulk, 100-pound cotton bags of scratch feed and cracked corn, 1- and 5-pound paper bags of rice and sugar. Throughout, there was a scent compounded of peppermint, shoes, soap, coffee, and oil cloth. When he reached the clothing section, he decided it had exactly what he needed: corduroy trousers, cotton shirts, and a wool sweater. He tried on the trousers in a curtained cubicle. And here were hunters' boots that Tim Feehan had suggested. He tried on a couple of pairs until he found a right fit.

Carrying his purchases to the storekeeper's counter, he said a word to him about the pleasure he took from the store's redolent atmosphere. The storekeeper replied in a no-nonsense way, "I think you need a collar to go with that shirt you're wearin', mister. I got 'em in both cotton and celluloid."

"No thanks," Tony said, putting his purchases on the counter with its glass front candy case. "These will be fine."

The storekeeper toted up the cost and observed, "You're the second Yankee what's been in heah in the last two days, an' normally I don't get two in three months."

"Really?" Tony asked idly, and then, suddenly interested, asked again, "Do you remember what the other one looked like?"

"Sort o' long and muscle thick with a mouth that went from heah t' heah"—he demonstrated with his fingers—"and talked kinda funny, like you—no offense."

The storekeeper wrapped Tony's shirts, trousers, and sweater in newspapers and reached toward the ceiling for string, which he broke at the right length with a quick move of the wrist.

"Did you get a look at his car?" Tony asked.

"One of those big black cars you see in the city."

"Do you remember what he bought from you?"

"Hunters' boots, sump'n like yourn but my better brand, waterproof, a cob pipe, and field glasses—the last I had."

"Did he say where he was headed?"

"You Yankees are awful curious. Didn't say."

"Thanks. I liked your store a lot." Tony paid his bill and accepted the change.

"You're country welcome. If I were you, mister, I'd keep a close look for cattle and deer on the highway at night, especially cattle. They'll kill you dead." The storekeeper turned to his black stove trio. "Ain't that right, boys?"

"It shore is," one of them confirmed, while the others nodded.

Tony threw his package in the back seat of Belle's car and resumed his drive west through now extensive fields of cotton, tobacco, corn, and general farm crops. It was landscape that Krug had seen himself only two days before.

Unlike the smell of the country store, Krug's scent, though welcome, fouled the nostrils.

• • •

By mid-afternoon Tony reached Mossy Head, where, as his map showed, state Route 218 descended south from U.S. 90 through the Choctawhatchee/Eglin forest to Niceville and Valparaiso. He made the turn and plunged into the narrow paved defile between tall stands of pines and hardwoods, where, about ten miles down the road, he was startled by a formation of loud, low-flying airplanes overhead. When he reached Niceville after twenty minutes of driving, he decided to continue on to Valparaiso, on an arm of Choctawhatchee Bay, where he found one remaining vacant room at a tourist court called Bay View. In the early evening, after bathing and finishing his breviary as far as Compline, he dressed up in his clericals and drove down to the shore of the Gulf of Mexico. He felt refreshed, but hungry. From Fort Walton he drove to Destin along the Gulf Coast Scenic Highway U.S. 98, which lived up to its billing, and, when darkness came, decided to try the seafood at a place called Bacon's by the Sea. The menu featured "giant snapper."

"Is that *red* snapper?" he asked the waitress, when she came.

"Yes, Reverend, it sure is. Are you from around here?"

"No—"

"Well, this area here's the red snapper capital of the world."

Tony smiled. "Then I've certainly come to the right place. With iced tea, please."

He looked around. There were only a few tables empty. This must be a popular place, though not inexpensive, as he saw by the menu. He estimated that about half the tables were occupied by Army Air Corps officers with their wives or dates. They looked relaxed and happy. A number held hands across the table. In the background a jukebox played, "I'll Get By."

He could not help feeling a momentary pang of loss when he contemplated how he might have chosen a married instead of a celibate life. As a bachelor, living in a totally male, except for Mattie Mae, environment, he was isolated emotionally from many positive human experiences, such as these men and women were enjoying with one another. Most of what he knew of such man-woman relationships were on the downside—from his brother, the confessional, and the rectory office. The sweet and loving side he could only guess at from visits to parishioners' homes, and appreciate indirectly through the lyrics of songs like "I'll Get By," "Dolores," "I Hear a Rhapsody," "You and I."

"Excuse me, Father?"

Tony looked up to see a young officer on his left. "Yes? Good evening."

"I happened to see you over here, Father. Can I buy you a beer?"

"That's very kind of you, sir, but no, thanks."

"Is your church around here, Father?"

"No, actually it's in St. Augustine, on the Atlantic Coast."

"Do you happen to know Father Showalter in Omaha?"

Tony smiled. Lay people always assumed that you knew every priest in the country. "No, I'm afraid I don't." He was about to utter a break-away phrase that would let the officer get back to his lady, when he said something very different in order to *hold him in place*, and shield himself from the view of a male civilian who just entered the room—"Is that your home?"—and resembled—*Mother of God!*—more than resembled, *was* Peter Krug!

This time in civilian clothing.

Tracked by his scent!

"Yes, Father, it is."

His heart pounding, Tony managed to maintain a distracted conversation with the officer.

"Do you live here now?" he asked, "Uh, is it Lieutenant?"

"Yes, Father. I'm sorry but I can't talk about what I do—military regulations and all."

Krug was being led to a table in the center of the room.

"Of course. It was stupid of me to ask—"

"Oh, not at all, Father, but you know the military."

"Actually, I don't, Lieutenant. Let me just say, *whatever* you do, I pray that God will keep you safe while doing it."

"Thank you, Father. Will you bless my rosary?"

"Of course." As he did so, he saw that Krug was seated with his back to him—thank God!—absorbed, it appeared, with the officers and their ladies.

Saying goodbye to the officer, Tony struggled to make sense of the moment: the murderer and the man he tried to maim or murder—seated peaceably in the same dining room! But thank God for Tim Feehan's lead. This was exactly where Krug would go next—to spy on more military aircraft, no doubt, perhaps the ones that had passed overhead that afternoon.

Tony felt his chest fill with a new emotion he could not at first identify. He did his best to eat the snapper when it came, and he dabbled in the tapioca pudding, while examining the back of Krug's head and his broad, evil shoulders. As he drained his second glass of iced tea, he decided what his emotion was.

It was anger.

And the taste in his mouth was not tea. It was spit and vinegar.

Having changed into his OD blouse, pinks, wings, and bird colonel's insignias at the Bay View tourist court, Peter Krug and his Pontiac presented themselves at the Eglin Field main gate at 10:15 that night. The guards here, he had found on penetration earlier in the day, and the day before, were as serious as those he found at MacDill on his second visit there. Here, each time, they carefully compared his face to the photo on his "indentification" card and asked his destination.

"BOQ," he answered this time, blandly.

On his earlier reconnaissances of the base he found that on-field guards, MPs, and infantry, were more intimidating, in their numbers as well as in their alertness, than were the casual patrols in Tampa. Their weakness, if they had one, lay in their regularity. Tonight, he would scout and time the patrols assigned to base ops and the Main Field, where twenty-four B-25B Mitchell bombers were parked in two lines on the tarmac. And if the occasion presented itself . . .

There was something very curious about these B-25 Mitchells, which he had seen in the air numerous times since his arrival. He recognized them at once from the Luftwaffe silhouettes: twin engines, twin rudders, slab sides, gull wings. But these mediums were flying back and forth in formations no higher than 450 meters—which was, what? 1,500 feet?—and, as he had observed from various positions outside the base earlier today, were sometimes buzzing just above the hedges. Was this Le Touquet-Paris-Plage all over again? Also, as he could easily see on their low-flying hulls, the Mitchells here had been modified in two significant ways: they had no retractable Bendix electric gun turrets on their undersides, and, instead, sported twin guns in their Plexiglas tail cones, which, according to Luftwaffe data, were supposed to be simply prone observation posts.

After parking at the BOQ and making his way on foot to the flight line, Krug stood in the dark corner of a maintenance building and timed the guard patrols. There were few lights. The last quarter moon was hidden by clouds. After an hour's count, he concluded that one of four walking guards would pass each aircraft every five minutes. That was sufficient interval for him to get in, and, with good timing, to get out. He knew that there were ladder trap doors that pulled down from both the rear and forward bellies. He would go for the rear, and selected the third aircraft from his left in the first line, tail number 02261.

After a guard passed at 11:42, Krug waited ninety seconds and then made his move in a running crouch. When he reached the tail cone, he looked up to check the twin guns for caliber. Curious. Even in the darkness he could see that the barrels had no air-cooling apertures. He jumped to feel one of the barrels.

What the—?

He jumped again at the other barrel.

Wood! These "guns" were nothing but black-painted broomsticks! And the travel slots on the Plexiglas were also black paint!

He had to get inside quickly, and found to his relief that the rear meter-square door came down easily. Once inside the fuselage, he retrieved the door to its up position, and looked about with his penlight, careful not to let its narrow beam show through the tail glaze or the two small windows, left and right.

The broomsticks, of course, had no firing mechanisms. He could only conclude that they were meant to discourage an attack from astern, though hardly to resist one! In the interior space that would have been occupied by the retracted ventral gun turret, he saw that a fuel tank had been installed, probably capable of holding 40 to 50 U.S. gallons. Why? Overhead, the dorsal power turret, with twin .50s, remained in place.

Farther forward, he came upon a large, rolled-up, rubber coated, collapsible fuel cell, with a hose line that led into the crawl way above the bomb bay. He guessed that, when filled, it was deployed in the crawl space, effectively blocking crew passage fore and aft. How much more fuel did that cell provide? Above 150 gallons? Again, why the extended range?

Krug tested his broad shoulders in the crawl space and found that he could get through. It would have been embarrassing beyond description—not to mention fatal— to get stuck and be discovered in the morning by the crew. Once into the pilots' compartment, he looked around for the usual equipment, controls, and gauges. Something was missing from aluminum brackets. Radios, to judge from the disconnected wiring. Removed, he assumed to reduce weight, but why the radio silence?

He poked around for the B-25B pilot's handbook and, when he found it, saw that it was the book for B-25A. Was there that little difference? He began checking performance specifications. As he did so, a piece of paper fell out from between the leaves. He reached for it and read, in a feminine hand: "Thanks for the ride, boys! But too noisy! Ellen."

Had someone else—a woman?—penetrated this aircraft? There was no end of questions raised by this bird.

He stepped back and down into the navigator's and bombardier's compartment. No Norden bombsight in the nose. Instead, he found a curious, seemingly handmade, two-piece aluminum device consisting of an angle bar sight, like the "post and V" sight of an air rifle, screwed to move up and down alongside a plate marked in degrees of declination. So what was *this* all about? A return to the primitive? But why?

He checked out the .30 caliber gun in the nose and then looked at his time. A guard should be coming down the line about now. He looked out the nose glaze and saw one, a little off his time, coming up three aircraft away. Krug worked his way back through the crawl to a point in the rear where he could watch the guard through a window. After the soldier passed, Krug waited ninety seconds and then let down the trap door.

Within another minute he was back in the shadows of the maintenance building, lucky, relieved, and aware—but no wiser.

What *was* going on here?

Perhaps he had to give more time to the plane in the air. He noticed this morning that six planes took off and flew north-northeast, more or less in the direction of Mossy Head. About noon, the same planes returned to base, and in the early afternoon another half-dozen planes flew the same course and returned by five. In the early afternoon he had called the telephone operator in Mossy Head and asked her if she had heard a flight of bombers come over her town at low altitude any time that day, and the answer was, no. So the Mitchells were stopping somewhere short. And he bet it was at Satellite Field 1.

He decided to drive out that way tomorrow morning and see what he could see.

• • •

The original forest highways through Eglin remained open to loggers, hunters, and the general public, except when bombing practice was scheduled, and army sentries held the traffic at checkpoints. It was on one of those forest highways, the same State 218 he had taken from Mossy Head to Niceville, that Tony found himself this morning, in trail, at considerate distance, of Peter Krug's Pontiac.

He had set up the trail immediately upon paying his check and exiting Bacon's by the Sea the night before. He tracked Krug to the Bay View, whose quarters they shared, ironically, and then, following again in his vehicle, watched Krug, in Air Corps officer's uniform, drive to the Eglin main gate. Unable to enter the reservation, Tony waited in his car a short distance outside the gate until, about midnight, central war time, he saw Krug emerge and return to his quarters.

Last night, Tony had slept very little. For one thing, his nervous system would not slow down. For another, he did not want to miss the sound of Krug's car when it started up again, though he need not have worried since Krug did not leave his room until 7:30. Putting on his new brown corduroy trousers, green plaid flannel shirt, sweater, and boots, Tony watched through the curtain as Krug's car moved out the driveway and turned north. When he thought it was safe, Tony got into his own car and followed, though not closely, and when Krug stopped at a diner in Niceville, apparently for breakfast, Tony kept going, past the diner, and waited several residential blocks ahead on a side street.

After Krug emerged and resumed his course north, Tony kept well back. The road was familiar. He looked at his road map. The next town was Mossy Head. Sometimes, on rolling terrain, where gnarled scrub oak fell away to swampy bottoms, he lost sight of Krug's car; but most of the time he kept it in sight as a black speck. There was a moderate amount of military and commercial traffic.

After about ten miles of driving, Krug's car pulled off the paved surface to a stop on the right shoulder, and Tony saw him get out and look east over the top of his vehicle to the sky. Without slowing, Tony bent down and looked, too, seeing, just over the trees, several olive drab airplanes wheeling against the luminous blue. There was nothing to do but drive on past, blowing into his handkerchief as he came abreast. In the rearview mirror, he saw Krug remove equipment of some kind from his trunk and start to walk into the high grass and scrub.

Tony stopped his car over the next rise, where it would not be seen by Krug, and also walked east into the forest floor. It was not like any walk he had taken before. There were no forests in Manhattan, and none to speak of in Yonkers. But he made his way steadily forward, keeping the morning orb of the sun and the sound of airplane engines in front of him.

Krug was familiar enough with the carry of aircraft engine noise to know when he was drawing close to its source. After a mile and a half walk, he figured that he was about an eighth of a mile distant. The Mitchells he had seen in flight were apparently doing takeoffs and landings at this auxiliary airstrip. What puzzled him was the fact that much of the engine combustion lacked the variation in sound frequency, the Doppler effect, generated by airplanes in motion: it seemed that these aircraft were spending an abnormally long time running up their rpms in braked positions on the ground.

Near the wood line, movement in the scrub! Ahead and to the left! Krug ducked behind a pine. Men's voices! Within a minute's time he saw them—two men, soldiers, helmeted, with rifles slung over their right shoulders, walking, talking, laughing, on a track that crossed his from left to right.

Why guards in the woods? he wondered. Security at Eglin Main Field was tight, but this was incredible! What was there about an airstrip in a woodsy wilderness that required guards to prevent intruders? He decided before proceeding farther to wait in place to see if there was another one- or two-man patrol that followed at a certain time interval.

There was—two men again, after exactly twelve minutes, and a little farther ahead, closer to the wood line. And there was another, at fifteen minutes, somewhat deeper; and yet another, at thirteen minutes, and shallower. Krug decided that he could rely on twelve minutes, less two minutes on each side, for forays to the wood line, out and back—eight minutes' clear observation between patrols.

He set up his easel, stool, and paints so that he would have an innocent position to retreat to, if needed. Then, two minutes after the next patrol, he set out on a run for the wood line. When he reached it, he took a look at his watch to check expended time, then, from behind a pine, fastened his eyes across the tall field grass at the airstrip.

One Mitchell was just lifting off, wheels retracting, from his left to right. Two others were in the pattern overhead. A fourth was taxiing into takeoff position. Two others were on the ramp. There were no buildings, there was no tower, only a firetruck and a wind sock. The airstrip had flags placed on both sides along its shoulders, beginning, he estimated, from the position where the aircraft readying for takeoff was holding, about 30 meters ahead of that aircraft, and ranging forward at 60, 90, 120, and 150 meters, or—let's see—500 feet. They had to be some kind of indicators for landing practice, Krug concluded, since normal take-off numbers for a Mitchell were 1,500 feet at 90 mph.

The B-25B in takeoff position now spooled up its rpms, but higher, Krug thought, than what was needed for a mag check. The aircraft struggled against its brakes. Flaps were cranked full down. Trim was probably back, too. Okay, short field takeoff practice, that's all it was. That explained the sustained, high power run-ups. Part of standard training. But the flags had nothing to do with it. Krug could not remember seeing short field numbers in the specifications, but there was no way a Mitchell, at 27,000 pounds—plus gross weight, could get off in the distance marked by the farthest flags.

The Mitchell trembled behind its howling engines and frenzied props. Forward, the nose went up and down on its hydraulic gear. Aft, a small dirt storm formed in the ground effect. Then, suddenly, the plane came off its brakes and lunged forward in a takeoff roll. Abruptly, *before the last flag*, it yanked up in a near-stall—couldn't be going more than fifty!—brought its wheels up and its nose down, built up speed, and remained airborne! *Verdammt!* If he had not seen it, he would never have believed it.

He checked his watch. He had encroached on the two-minute safety margin. He quickly retreated to his easel. The patrol came at thirteen minutes.

Twelve times more, Krug moved forward to observe the practices. They were baffling. Some of the Mitchells were getting wheels up at the next to last marker, but clearly the aim was to hit the last flag. Why? What was there about this amazingly abbreviated takeoff that was so important? On landing, the aircraft were not shooting for any particular flag, it was obvious: they were all over the place. But the takeoffs were precise. He had had to practice short field bomber takeoffs himself in Germany, but never at anything approximating this distance, since there was always ample runway space at bomber bases. Here, though, the bombers were drilling on the procedure again and again, and getting off in the space of a postage stamp. Why? He had never known an aircraft type that raised as many questions as these Mitchells.

Perhaps he could find some answers from the air. Crestview to the northwest had the nearest private airfield, according to the desk clerk at Bay View. He decided to rent a plane.

CHAPTER 22

THE DISTANCE TONY had to walk was not as far as he feared, perhaps a mile and a half, which was no test even in his out-of-shape condition. What he really had cause to fear was stumbling face-to-face on Krug or on the military sentries that he sighted just in time to avoid detection. It was clear that he could no longer proceed eastward because of the sentries, and he imagined that Krug was similarly stalled, so he turned south, hoping to catch a long-distance view of the agent and discover what he was up to. After ten minutes, and about 100 yards away, he sighted Krug at his artist's easel, which held a white square of paper on which there were a few strokes of brown and green. Krug had a corn cob pipe in his mouth, but there was no smoke.

Tony knew that Krug was not here to paint. He was here because of the airplanes. Sure enough, every fourteen or fifteen minutes Krug dashed in the direction of the tree line, toward the sound of the aircraft engines. He must have timed the sentry patrols, Tony figured. After several instances of this, Tony decided to go east himself a short distance, while maintaining a safe separation from Krug, and try to find out what it was that held the German's attention. He hung back farther in the trees than Krug, but he could see, barely, Air Corps planes of some kind taking off and landing one after another. It had no meaning for him, but it must have for Krug. Two times doing this was enough for Tony. He was afraid of the guards. He returned to a scrub oak patch where he could continue watching Krug painting, leaving, returning, painting, leaving—

Until 11:45 when, apparently, the planes all left—he could hear only engines receding in the distance—and

Krug could be seen disassembling his easel. Tony took off west at his best speed toward his car, which he missed by about 300 yards to the north. Funny how you can get disoriented in the woods, he thought. Krug's car was out of sight over the low hill. What should he do? He decided to drive his car slowly north and, if he was not passed by Krug, to turn around and try to catch him headed south.

He was passed by Krug going north. As before, he followed him at a safe distance, and continued on when Krug turned west on U.S. 90. At Crestview, fifteen miles later, Krug stopped at a gas station for less than a minute, apparently to get directions. Tony passed, and in his rearview mirror he watched Krug start up again and take a right turn. Tony steered into a residential driveway, backed out, and drove east to the turn, which he himself took. After four miles, he came to a flying field with a hangar that had CRESTVIEW written across its metal roof. Three small planes were tied down on the edge of a grass field. As he passed, he saw Krug's car parked on the far side of the hangar.

From the shoulder a quarter mile off, Tony kept his eye on Krug's vehicle and, after about fifteen minutes, saw Krug reenter it and drive back toward Crestview. Tony followed and saw Krug driving south on State 54, which Tony knew from his map was another north-south route through the Eglin forest. He continued to follow him, mile after mile, until it seemed to Tony that his adversary was headed all the way home to Valparaiso.

Tony stopped and made a U-turn. He returned to the airfield that Krug had visited and found a man in overalls working on a bright red plane in the hangar.

"Excuse me," he dissembled, "have you seen a man here named Krug?"

"Yessir," the man answered, "A fella by that name was just here 'bout half hour ago. Wanted ta rent a plane."

"Oh, were you able to take care of him all right?" Tony asked.

"Well, yes and no. I told 'im our only rental plane, a J-three Cub, was bein' flown up in Alabama today by a couple of hunters, but it'd be back tomorrow afternoon. So he gave me a deposit to hold it. Showed me his licenses and medical."

"Good. I'm glad it worked out." Tony reached in his pocket for a ten dollar bill. "I shouldn't have worried about his getting a plane." He handed the bill to the mechanic. "I'd appeciate it if you wouldn't say I was asking about him."

The mechanic winked. "You got it."

As Tony walked to his car, the man came around the hangar door to say, "I have ta give 'im a check-ride, ya know."

"That's all right," Tony said, and drove off.

Arriving back at the Bay View in Valparaiso, Peter Krug considered his deadline, the dawn hours of March 13, three days hence, when he would have to be off Eden and St. Lucie Inlet to rendezvous with U-*Böhm*. The deadline was approaching almost too quickly; when he thought of it, his imagination pictured the kind of approach he was recommending for German fighters against the B-17E Flying Fortress: head-on, at a combined speed of 500 mph—"and don't break off the attack too soon!" It was not an approach for the faint-hearted.

In order to have a time cushion he really should be leaving by car today. But he thought he should delay until tomorrow afternoon in order to have an air view of the Mitchells' takeoff field—absolutely essential—"don't break off too soon!"—even if it meant that he would have to take a train rather than risk a time-consuming auto repair job on the road.

If only he could obtain a rental aircraft today, but a call to other nearby airports, such as Fort Walton and Pensacola, had failed to turn up one any earlier than the Cub at Crestview: fixed base operators in other locations told him that, with the lifting of the ban on private flying on Sunday, the reservation list for rental planes was jammed.

• • •

After getting change at a Crestview gas station, Tony used the station pay phone to call the long-distance operator. He wished to speak person-to-person to Miss Belle Hart in St. Augustine. He gave her home number. A woman answered, probably the mother, said Belle was at the airport and gave the operator that number. The airport manager went out to find Belle.

"Belle Hart speaking."

Tony deposited thirty cents.

"Belle, this is Father D'Angelo."

"Oh, yes! how are you *doing?*"

"Fine, thanks. I wanted to tell you that I'm ready to take that airplane ride."

"Wonderful."

"And you said that you liked to go from point A to point B."

"Yes?"

"And does that still apply if point B is a good distance from point A?"

"Well, try me."

Belle started out toward the Panhandle within a hour of Father D'Angelo's call, toting a change of clothes and toiletries in a cloth bag, and in the only plane that was available for cross-country rental that day, a 1940 Lock Haven yellow J-3 Piper Cub. Making a good 70 mph groundspeed along the track of U.S. 90, she spent the night en route at Tallahassee with a FSCW classmate and her husband. From their home she called Father D'Angelo at the Bay View in Valparaiso to say that she would land at Fort Walton on the Gulf, an airport with which she was familiar, before noon the next day.

Resuming her flight in the morning with a full tank of gas, she got on Highway 90 at 2,000 feet and pressed westward, calling up in her mind scenes from the "Ruth Darrow Flying Stories" she had read as a girl. What exactly was the adventure Father D'Angelo had in mind?

• • •

Tony met Belle's Cub when she landed at Fort Walton at eleven-thirty and drove her to a nearby restaurant for a bite of lunch. On the way, he expressed his very deep gratitude that she had come so quickly and so far.

"I ordered my tank to be topped off when I landed," she said when they were seated. "How far do we have to go? With twelve gallons the Cub doesn't have much range."

"To the north edge of the forest below Mossy Head," Tony said. "I'm sure we'll have to remain outside the Eglin reservation, which for all practical purposes is the forest, and that means we'll have to fly east about twenty-five miles, then north to U.S. ninety, and then west just a short distance to Mossy Head."

Belle examined her CAA sectional map, as Tony continued, "From just below Mossy Head we should be able to see that flying field I was telling you about on the phone. Did you bring your binoculars?"

"Yes. Just exactly what are we looking for again?"

"We're going to be looking at a small Army Air Corps landing field built on a clearing in the forest just off highway two-eighteen. I need for you to tell me exactly what you see, and how you would interpret it."

"And can you tell me why?"

"No, Belle, I can't. I'm terribly sorry. There's that matter of privileged information I told you about that I can't disclose. Again, I simply have to ask you to trust me."

"Oh I do that," she assured him. "You have my car, after all. And I wouldn't have flown all the way out here for any other man I know—except one. But can you be just a little more specific about what I should be looking for?"

"No, I can't, because I don't know enough about airplanes and airfields to say. I just want to know what *you* see. And I think, as soon as we finish lunch, we should get going."

Remembering that Krug was expecting his plane by mid-afternoon, Tony wanted to make his fly-by before Krug got in the air. On returning to the Fort Walton airport, Belle instructed Tony how to step into the small passenger space and to strap himself in the back seat of the small, fabric-covered tandem aircraft.

"And here're some rubber tube earphones to put on. They're connected by a hollow tube to my voice piece," she explained. "Through it I can talk to you over the engine noise. It's a device used by instructor pilots in tandem planes like this one. Unfortunately, you can't talk back. If you need to tell me anything, undo your seat belt, lean forward, and yell in my ear. Okay?"

"Okay." He had never yelled in a woman's ear before.

At one o'clock, after Belle had done an outside go-around, gotten a prop pull, and flipped mags, the yellow Cub lifted off and headed east along the shore. Tony was thrilled to see the Gulf of Mexico stretching seemingly to infinity on his right. It was only the second flight he had made in an airplane, and his first in a private craft. When Belle made the turn north along the eastern edge of the forest, making a gradual cruise climb out at 55 mph—she said that she would level off at 5,000 feet—Tony was relieved to find that he could see a great distance into the forest. And when she turned west at the top of the forest, and came abreast of Mossy Head on the right, Tony could make out the narrow north-south cut of State 218 through the woods to his left. With the highway as a marker, and with the help of the binoculars, he soon was able to sight the airstrip on the highway's east side—not only that, but a flight of twin-engine airplanes circling the field and landing.

He leaned forward, handed the glasses to Belle, and shouted: "Directly to your left, an airstrip, and olive-colored airplanes landing!"

Belle took the glasses, eased the throttle back to 45 mph slow flying under the maxi-wing, and peered through the lenses. After half a minute, she asked, "Is that what you wanted me to see?"

"Yes and no! I want you to see the planes when they're taking off—which they do again and again!"

"Then I'll fly on past and come back on the same track," she decided.

Twenty minutes later, she was back, headed east, due north of the strip. Now, she could see one of the Air Corps planes readying for takeoff.

"It's either a B-twenty-five or a B-twenty-six," she said. "A twin-engine medium bomber—can't tell which from this distance. There he goes—off the ground awfully fast, I'd say, and before reaching a double white line painted across the runway."

"What does it mean?" Tony yelled.

"I don't know," Belle answered. "It looks like short field takeoff practice. I'll watch the next one."

She did. And the next one. And the next one. "They're lifting off before that double white line," she said. "And it's a very short distance, almost the takeoff distance of a Cub. I'm exaggerating, but that's how short it is. Almost the distance of an aircraft carrier flight deck."

She paused. "No . . . no. It can't be that. But it's not impossible. There's a white line painted down the center of the strip and it ends at the double white stripe, about, what? an eighth of the way down the strip. It could be practice for short jungle strip takeoffs, or . . . those lines may really be meant to mark off a carrier deck. Could the navy fly *bombers* off a carrier? Perhaps, effectively, they're doing it right here."

"So you really think that's something important going on?" Tony yelled.

"I can't be sure," Belle answered through the tube. "But if it's medium bombers training to take off from carriers, it's *damn* important—excuse my language."

Tony looked out the window to his left and—*O my God!*—no longer saw the ground on that side, for his whole frame of view was filled by another yellow Piper Cub!—only tens of feet away, its pilot, in the rear seat, with glasses, studying their faces!

Peter Krug decided to drive out early, after lunch, to Crestview, just in case the hunters in that rental Cub got back early from Alabama. He was not disappointed.

"Shot their limit already," said the mechanic, who seemed also to be line man, check-out pilot, and general factotum. "She's topped off. You ready for a check ride?"

With the mechanic in the front seat, and his case of finished paintings, which he now never let out of his sight, alongside him in the back, and after a quick familiarization with the aircraft's controls and very few instruments, Krug began his takeoff roll down the grass strip. He had not had a stick in his hand since January. The tail came up quickly and the main gear jumped off the grass seconds afterward. The little craft handled nicely, he decided, as he went around the pattern—downwind, base, and final—to a gentle three-point landing. It was no Fieseler Fi156 Storch, to be true. The Storch could carry two passengers in addition to the pilot, cruise at 93, and max out at 109. But the Cub was all he needed for an observation platform, and he wasn't complaining.

When the mechanic stepped out with a thumbs-up, Krug took off, kept the nose down the length of the runway to build up speed, then pulled up in a steep climb to test the aircraft further. It had a lot of pep for 65 horsepower. He made a left turn out of pattern and headed east to the point where State 218 entered the Eglin forest. At 4,500 feet, he placed the binoculars strap around his neck, held the stick between his knees, and sought the auxiliary airstrip through his lenses. And there it was!—with the last of a flight of six Mitchells landing on its paved surface and one of their number poised near the far end of the runway for takeoff. It was not the aircraft, though, that froze his attention. It was the runway!

White painted lines across the runway! Probably corresponding to the last of the flags, which he could not see from this altitude. And another white line down the center of the runway that ended at the double white line.

These bombers were flying off a *simulated carrier deck!*

Of course! That's it!

He slowed the aircraft, watching the first bomber takeoff. Damn, if it didn't get off in the space defined by that double white line. He watched the second bomber do the same. They were getting off in 150 meters without the advantage of a carrier's head wind. This was like Thunderbolt at Le Touquet. Except that this was a live Made in *America* bombshell.

The Air Corps pilots were going to fly these Mitchells off a carrier to—where? Not Germany or the occupied countries, since the Americans already had Aircraft Carrier England. And not to England, since they didn't need a carrier to get them to England—they'd fly themselves there, hopping from island to island, if that's where they were headed. No, it had to be a target in the huge-distanced Pacific. A target that could only be reached with the help of a carrier. And what target did the Americans most want to hit right now?

Tokyo.

Remember Pearl Harbor.

He had to get word out to Hamburg right away. Only a U-boat's transmitters could reach Germany, which, in turn, could reach the Imperial Japanese Navy. He would call Lorenz at Eden as soon as he landed.

All his questions about the Mitchells had been answered. Tokyo is why the Mitchell pilots had installed fake guns, to discourage Japanese Zero attacks from astern; why they added an extra fuel tank and cell; why, no doubt to avoid detection during approach to target, they were practicing formation flight at 450 meters; why probably they installed the handmade bombsight—the Norden being useless at the low altitudes where they would fly.

He began a right turn and slow descent to Crestview—when, through the full-width Plexiglas window overhead, his eye caught sight of another yellow Piper Cub ahead and above him by some 150 meters! *What the*—?

He added power and, after reaching altitude, easily overtook the other craft, which was on slow cruise. Coming from behind, he knew he was out-of-sight, just as he had been outside the other pilot's view when he was below and aft. Advancing the throttle on the left wall of the cabin, he pulled close alongside the other plane's port side with the binoculars in his right hand.

There were two people on board the other Cub, a blondish young woman in front, who turned to look at him, startled, and a man—*Verdammt!*—a man in back, who, though he was not in clericals, resembled that frigging Father D'Angelo. Krug adjusted the focus. It *was* D'Angelo! How had he followed him *here?* What was he doing in the *air?* And now D'Angelo apparently recognized *him*. He watched the priest lean forward to shout something at the woman, who suddenly accelerated forward and then made an evasive diving turn left, reversing course, below him.

Krug followed, hoping that the time on his Continental engine was lower than the time on the other plane's engine—which he had cause to doubt when he found it hard to keep up with the other craft as it banked below him, the woman checking him out through her overhead window.

Though out-circled, Krug held the advantage of altitude. With his rudder hard left, stick forward and left, he dived on the other craft, his thrashing propeller aimed at its tail.

As Belle pulled out of her dive, she put the top of her head outside the port window and looked back to see the other plane following her. "What's going *on* with that guy?" she asked through the voice tube. "You called him dangerous? I would *say* so."

Tony, his stomach still moving in a different direction from the rest of him, loosened his belt and leaned forward as best he could. "Yes—I know something about him!" he yelled. "He would like to see me dead! If he's got a gun, he'll use it."

Belle whipped her ailerons into a sudden right bank, then level again, so that she could see her pursuer through the right window. The other Cub was diving on them! Was it going to chew them up with its prop?

Belle dived too, with throttle wide open to build up speed. "Be sure your belt is on tight!" she warned Tony. Abruptly, she pulled the stick back into her tummy and the plane shot up in a loop. On its vertical climb, Belle saw the other Cub whip by to the left, only inches away.

"Shit, that was close!" she exclaimed.

"Whadaya think I'm doing?" Tony gasped to himself as he hung on to the little there was to hold onto, and, as the Cub fell inverted out of the top of the loop, grimaced as dirt from unnumbered shoes fell off the floor into his face.

During the upside-down descent, through the overhead window, Belle watched the other Cub ahead of them banking left, intent, it seemed, on making another run. At the bottom of the loop, rather than continue straight ahead at their adversary, she made as tight a turn to the right as she could, hoping to break outside his turn and gain some separation. But the turn slowed them, and, near its completion, she looked back to see the other Cub coming on fast. She checked the altimeter: 3,500 feet. A quick turn to the left to estimate the distance between them, then—she pulled the throttle all the way back, laid the stick in her tummy again, and when the steeply climbing plane slowed and trembled into a stall, she pushed hard on the right rudder.

The maneuver caught their pursuer out of position. If he was intending to bite them to pieces with his prop, he would have to do that when the planes were both going at near-equal speeds. Otherwise, he would go down, too, in a mid-air—which he seemed to realize, since he broke off the attack and made a slow roll off to the left.

Belle's Cub went into a right spin, spiraling down toward earth, seemingly out-of-control, and thoroughly frightening Tony, who made an audible Act of Contrition. After a 700-foot drop, Belle applied left rudder until the plane righted itself and pushed the stick forward to gain flying speed, then fed in a touch of power. As the Cub pulled out into level flight, Tony looked up and around for their foe. Damn, if Krug wasn't *spiraling down right after them!*—like a Satanic fallen angel, sliding and turning on an invisible rail.

Belle wondered if the safest thing might be to land at an airport where the two of them could find help.

"Did you say you went to an airfield in Crestview?" she asked.

"Yes," he yelled.

"Try to find it," she urged him, taking the binocular strap off her neck and handing the glasses back to Tony, while she concentrated her own attention on the other Cub, which to her distress, she could not find! Where *was* it?

With all of their maneuvering, Tony estimated that they were to the west of Mossy Head. The forest was to left and south, and the bisecting highway 218 was behind them. Ahead was the other forest highway 54 that led to Crestview. He saw the town in his glasses.

"Straight ahead!" he yelled, just as their plane shuddered violently and whipped sharply to the right! They were *hit!* Then *hit again!*

Belle dove to escape, then leveled off. The rudder pedals flexed freely back and forth. The cables were shot. The moveable rudder panel on the vertical stabilizer probably was gone. She would have to steer with the ailerons and elevators alone. Could she land with them alone?

"If he gets the rest of the tail," she shouted into the tube, "we're goners! Come on, come on, Continental!" she coaxed the engine.

Her mind laced with hope against hope, Belle flew on toward Crestview, knowing that their only chance was to outrun their attacker in a straightaway race. For mile after mile, she jockeyed the plane forward on its ailerons, banking and yawing, but flying steadily forward in a shallow full-throttle descent. She dared not turn to look back, for a turn would bleed off miles per hour. So far, she had the speed advantage, why she didn't know. A fresher engine?

Now, with Tony gesturing forcefully to the right ahead, she saw a building with CRESTVIEW written across its roof in white letters, and a grass field alongside, north of the town. She pushed her nose down a tad farther and headed for the grass: 500 feet . . . 400. . . . She could see the wind sock. They could make a straight-in approach. Thank God! 300 . . . 200. . . .

She spoke for the first time in what seemed an awfully long time to both of them.

"Are you okay?"

"Yes!" he yelled back. "And you? Are we going to make it?"

"Yes. Tighten your belt. We may bounce."

100 . . . 50 . . . 25 . . .

Belle kept up a relatively high airspeed on final in order to maintain directional control with the ailerons. Just before touchdown the plane yawed suddenly right. But immediately afterward the left gear touched down and bounced, throwing them into the air again, where Belle held the aileron hard over right and the plane righted itself enough for both tires to hit together, though on a different heading. Two more bounces and they were down, rolling to a crawl.

As soon as she could, Belle braked the Cub into a left turn back to the airport hangar and taxied over the rough grass at her best speed. At the same time, she saw with relief that the other Cub had not followed them to the ground. She searched the sky for it, and finally saw the yellow wings at a low altitude to the south. It could still land.

She first realized that her heart was pounding and that her hands were shaking when she pulled in front of the hangar and cut the mags. An adrenalin flow had kept her steady when she had to be, but now the realization of what they had just been through was showing in her heartbeat and nerves.

Tony saw the mechanic he had met yesterday standing in front of the hangar wiping his hand on a rag and watching them climb out of the stricken Cub. Could he help them?

Tony, too, was feeling the aftereffects of the stressful

experience. Getting out, he leaned against the fuselage and tested his legs. Then he walked with Belle to the rear of the aircraft to study the tail. The entire moveable fabric-on-aluminum rudder was gone. A part of the non-moveable vertical stabilizer had also been chewed away. Cables dangled on each side.

"Well, I ain't seen nothin' like that b'fore," said the overalled mechanic, who came alongside. "Get yur tail caught by a buzzard?" he asked Tony, who leaned his head toward Belle.

"She's the pilot," he answered.

Belle spoke part of the truth, not knowing how far Tony wanted to carry this, and not having a chance to check signals with him beforehand.

"We had a small mid-air," she said. "With another yellow Cub."

"Musta been with my plane I rented, huh?" the mechanic ventured. "Wonder why he don't come in. He's a friend o'yourn, ain't he?" he asked, remembering Tony's visit the day before and the ten dollar bill.

"I'll make a report to the CAA," Belle said. "And I'll want you to repair the tail, if you have the parts."

"Oh, I got anotha rudda. Ain't no problem. But it'll take a coupla days. The otha part o' the tail I gotta dope an' all."

"I understand," Belle said. "I'll come back, by bus or something. I'm from St. Augustine."

While Belle and the mechanic talked repairs, Tony walked over to Krug's car, opened the driver's side door, and saw that the keys were in the ignition.

When he returned to the plane, the mechanic was saying, "Well, it musta been my plane's prop that done this. Couldn't ha' been no other part of the plane 'cause he's still flyin'. Don't he know what he did? Wonder why he don't come down."

Tony wondered, too. But he did not want Belle and himself to be around when Krug did land. He took a ten dollar bill from his wallet and handed it to the mechanic.

"Here's another ten-spot for services to be rendered.

I'm going to call you from the road to find out where that other pilot goes after he lands. Okay?"

"Sure 'nough, okay."

Belle retrieved her cloth bag from the Cub.

Then Tony took her by the arm and led her to Krug's car, saying over his shoulder to the mechanic, "Tell my friend that I've borrowed his car."

"But how's he gonna get aroun'?" the mechanic asked.

"He'll find a way. What's your telephone number here?"

"Eighty-seven."

"Eighty-seven. Okay."

As Tony and Belle drove off in the Pontiac, he said to her, "I've got your car at Fort Walton airport. We'll exchange this one for yours, pick up my things at Valparaiso, and get you home."

"Thank you," she answered. "But whose car is this?"

"The man who tried to chop us up."

"And we're stealing his car?"

"Borrowing it. After what he did to us this afternoon, I think he deserves a little inconvenience, don't you?"

"I think I'm seeing a new side to you, Father."

"Yes, I suppose so. Perhaps it's about time."

"Why don't we press charges? Why don't *you* press charges, since you say he wants to kill *you*?"

"He'll disappear. I have a feeling things are moving too rapidly. I may be the only one who can nail him. The police would slow *me* down, not him."

"But I'd at least like to know who the man is and why he tried to kill you—and me with you. Don't you think I have a right to know at least that?"

"Yes, Belle, you have a right. No, Belle, I can't tell you. It's a terrible position to put you in and I'm extremely sorry. My God, today I put you in jeopardy of your very life! I can't be more sorry than I am for that, and for the fact that I can't even give you the name of the man who was trying to kill us. I'm trying awfully hard to keep a solemn secret. Maybe too hard. Maybe I'm being too scrupulous. Anyway, my main desire right now is to get you away from this danger and safely home. And, also, I'll take care of the costs to repair your plane."

"Well, it's all very mysterious to me, and I'll pursue it another time. Right now, it's not danger I'm concerned about. I'm scheduled for an antisubmarine patrol tomorrow afternoon, and I'd like to be back in time for that."

"We'll drive. On the way, I'll have to make a call to the Crestview airport to find out, if I can, where our attacker is going next."

"You really are on to something, aren't you?"

"The most that I can say is, yes."

When Krug finally landed at Crestview, it was after the most uncertain, indecisive moments of his life.

Flying back and forth, aimlessly, he simply did not know what to do next. Should he land at Crestview, pay the mechanic for damage to the prop, and drive off to Eden? No; the priest would probably have the police there. Should he land at another airport, like Fort Walton, and abandon the plane? Perhaps; but he would have no ground transportation. Should he keep this plane and fly on to Fort Pierce with the nicked prop, which vibrated but otherwise seemed okay, leaving his car at Crestview and his suitcase at Valparaiso? No; the prop might not last, and the Cub was so short-legged he would have to land at airports all along the route for refueling, and the police could warn fixed base operators within a 300-mile radius to be on the lookout and not to refuel him.

He really had gotten himself in a box this time.

Finally, and uncharacteristically, he decided that honesty was the best policy. He would land, explain that he had a mid-air accident that was his fault, and offer to pay for repairs to both planes.

Which is what he did. But, just as he feared, there was a uniformed sheriff's deputy waiting alongside the mechanic when he taxied up to the hangar. And the other Cub with the torn-up rudder! But no sign of D'Angelo and the woman.

"I'm afraid I had an accident with your plane," he said to the mechanic after getting out.

"Well, I 'spicion so," the mechanic acknowledged, fingering the dented brass leading edges and the splintered wood blades of the Sensenich prop. "You're darn lucky this laminated prop didn't fly apart on ya. It's junk now. And look what you did to the other plane," he said, pointing to Belle's Cub in front of the hangar.

"Can you replace the prop and rent me the plane through tomorrow? I'll be glad to pay you whatever it costs. And I'll pay for the other plane's repair, too"—he looked over at Belle's Cub—"which I see got beat up kind of bad. The pilot did a fine piece of flying to get it down. Is he around," he dissembled, "so I can apologize?"

"It was a she and a man passenger. No, they're gone. And I don't have a new prop. Have ta order one."

"Can you rent me one of these other planes tied down here?"

"They're privately owned. No way I could. You said you'd pay. Have ya got cash? I reckon one hundred for the new tail and two hundred for the prop."

Krug peeled off $300 and handed it to him.

"And I hav'ta report the accident to the CAA," the mechanic answered.

The sheriff's deputy spoke up for the first time. "You got some identification, mister?"

Krug gave him his two private pilot's licenses, peace time and wartime, as well as his Selective Service card.

The deputy looked them over, nodded, and handed them back. "I got a call from a hog farmer that said he saw two yeller planes hit each other and a piece fall off one of 'em. Well, no one was hurt, and you paid up, so I'm gonna git me some barbecue. Runnin' late on eatin' t'day, Virgil," he added, winking at the mechanic.

"Do you have a phone?" Krug asked the mechanic, who pointed to the back right corner of the hangar. "I have to make a long-distance call. I'll get time and charges from the operator."

"That'll be fine."

Krug placed his call to Lorenz person-to-person through the Fort Pierce exchange. But there was no answer. Damn! He had to get Lorenz to send word out about the carrier bombers right away, so Japan could get ready. He would try again from the Bay View in Valparaiso.

When he exited the hangar he looked across to where his car had been parked. "Where's my *car*?"

"Your friend took it what was in the plane with the woman," the mechanic said.

"My *friend*? He's no friend! Where did he take it?"

"Don't know."

Krug summoned back the deputy before he had a chance to drive off and gave him a description of the vehicle and the license number. "Damn!" he added. "And I have to get to Fort Pierce"—which he regretted saying as soon as the words left his lips.

"Ain't there an L and N leavin' tonight fer Jax?" the mechanic asked the deputy.

"Seven sharp," the deputy said, and made a fast turn out of the airfield's dirt road, yelling as he did so, "Still no dang barbecue!"

"If he don't find your car," the mechanic offered, "I'll git you to the Crestview train station in my pickup."

"Can you drive me to Valparaiso to pick up my suitcase?"

"In the pickup? Hell, it can't git that far."

When Tony called Crestview airfield on the road from a pay phone in DeFuniak Springs, there was no answer. When he called an hour and a half later from Marianna, the mechanic picked up.

"I'm the man who gave you the ten-spot," Tony said. "What can you tell me about the fellow who rented your plane?"

"He said you ain't his friend," the mechanic replied.

"Yes, he's right. And I apologize for deceiving you—"

"And that you stole his car."

"Well, I didn't. I'm driving my own car. Did he say what he was going to do?"

"Said he had to git to Fort Pierce. I took 'im down ta Crestview station. Leaves at seven on Louisville and Nashville number one. But the L and N only goes as far as River Junction. He was madder 'n hell about havin' to leave his suitcase. All he had was a flat cardboard thing. An' he forgot an' left his field glasses."

"So they haven't located his car?"

"Nah, the deputy called and said no. Where'd you put it?"

"After the train leaves at seven, call the deputy and tell him to look in the parking spaces at Fort Walton airport. I'm afraid I carried the keys away in my pocket. What was it you were saying about River Junction?"

"The ticket agent said he's got to change there to Seaboard Mail and Express that leaves at midnight eastern time and gets into Jax at six-fifteen. Then he's got ta buy another ticket south. He's got a wad of money. Is he a gangster?"

"You could say that. Okay, six-fifteen A.M. at Jax. I think I owe you another ten-spot."

"I think ya do, too."

"What's your name and address?"

"Virgil Bass, Rural Route Two, Crestview, Florida. God bless America."

"Amen to that."

CHAPTER 23

THE FORD V-8 DRONED on eastward through the night into the early morning hours, the mile markers on U.S. 90 flipping by like page numbers in a book. Tony and Belle exchanged the driving responsibilities every two hours. And as people who are only acquaintances are wont to do on a long trip, they revealed much of their personal selves to each other.

"For most of my classmates," Belle, who was driving, said, "college was just a way station before marriage and children. But not for me."

"What was it for you?" Tony asked.

"It was a chance to grow up, to learn how the world works, to debate ideas, to test myself in sports and aviation."

"Is it too personal for me to ask—did you have gentlemen friends and go out on dates? You're a very attractive person."

"Thank you. Yes, I did. From the men's school at Gainesville. And I have a gentleman friend, as you put it, right now. But our relationship is on inactive status for the time being because he's in the military and I'm trying to get overseas to ferry airplanes for the British—something that Jacqueline Cochran has set up. How about yourself? Do you have any lady friends?"

Tony laughed. "A fair question. The answer's no. It's not allowed."

"Do you have a problem, then, with the two of us, just you and I alone, late at night, side by side? Does your church have some rule about that?"

She smiled, more as a tease than as a provocation, Tony thought.

"*Numquam solus cum sola,*" he answered.

"That's Latin, I guess. And it means—?"

"A priest should not be alone with a woman in a tight space."

"Like this."

"Like this."

"Don't you feel guilty?"

"You certainly know the right terms don't you? Everything in Catholicism is calculated to induce guilt. Do you ever see the sun dial on the face of the cathedral campanile?"

"Yes, it was off two hours, I think, the last time I saw it."

"Well, that's because of the introduction, I don't know when, of eastern standard time, and then, recently, war time. But I mean the Latin inscription on the dial, '*Pereunt et imputantur*': 'The hours pass and we must give an accounting for them.' That's what the Church does: it provokes guilt."

"How are you going to account for these hours tonight?" Belle asked.

"*In extremis extrema tenenda sunt*—our traveling together is something perfectly correct because it's something that must be done. Besides, I'm enjoying your company, I hasten to add."

"Just breaking the rule gives you a little exhilaration, doesn't it?"

"Yes. As a matter of fact, it does." He laughed.

"Well, I think if you can dodge death in the air the way we did yesterday, you can certainly resist my advances on the road."

Tony looked over to see Belle's face creased with that now-familiar mischievous smile, and laughed again. "I don't want to laugh too loud," he conceded, "lest you think that I discount the power of your charms."

"Thank you for that. You know something? Calling you 'Father D'Angelo' is too stiff and formal for what we've just been through. And too distant for a couple of still-young people on a private night passage. I think I'll call you 'Solus,' if you don't mind."

"Okay—'Sola,'" he agreed, surprised at the pleasure that filled him.

Still nursing her wounds, U-*Franz* sighted the lights of Savannah to starboard on her scheduled cruise south to Eden and the St. Lucie Inlet. The air attack ten days before had bent the starboard propeller shaft, forced water through the shaft stuffing boxes and the diesel exhaust valves, set the motors on fire, knocked out the electrical controls of the hydroplanes, and jammed the main oil pressure pump.

Repairs had been made to all the equipment except the propeller shaft, which turned with a fiendish rasp that unnerved everyone in the after torpedo room, and was an injury of such scale it would have to wait return to the Keroman yard at Lorient for straightening or replacement.

Overall, it had proven easier to mend steel than it had to mend the softer substances of mind and emotion. The boat's interior was thick with unassuaged grief and anger. The shock of losing their commander had afflicted every grade and rank, with the seeming exception of Oberleutnant Wolf-Harald Franz, formerly first watch officer, now interim commander.

Only Franz appeared unaffected by the tragedy. Only Franz was calm, sharp, business-as-usual. And only Franz was in charge—obdurately so.

Baumann's attempts on several occasions to reason with him on issues facing the boat were as abruptly rebuffed as were his offers to share responsibility for future operations. Baumann was particularly disturbed that Franz had conducted what he judged to be only half-hearted efforts to locate their commander, Böhm, either dead or alive.

Agreed, the hours-long vigil of the flying boat overhead had made it impossible to surface until well after sunset, when Franz cautiously tested the black air and found it vacant. As best the navigator could tell from dead reckoning, the damaged boat surfaced in the general vicinity of the flying boat's attack, but there was no trace of Böhm, or of the merchant master, or of the U-boat's life preserver.

"Needle in a haystack," Franz had observed on the dripping bridge. "I doubt we'll ever find him—or his body. Almost certainly it would be the latter. No one could have survived the concussion of four bombs."

"Still, we have to keep searching," Baumann had insisted.

"No, we don't *have* to keep searching," Franz had answered, coldly. "What we *have* to do is sink ships, complete our mission, and get home. That's what we *have* to do. I'm not going to waste precious fuel hunting for a cadaver. One more hour at slow cruise and that's all. I'll send a report to Kernével advising the Lion of our loss and assuring him that I have assumed command."

And that was what Franz did. But in the intervening ten nights he had not sunk any ships. Four times he made surfaced approaches, choosing to man the UZO himself, though Baumann was now I WO, but lost his target in haze on the first try, missed (incredibly) with a two-eel fan shot on the second, miscalculated the data on the third, and set the depth too deep on the fourth. That was how Baumann summed it up.

In the boat there was widespread bad feeling among the crew. Word of Franz's decision to give minimum time to hunting for Böhm or his body had been circulated through all the compartments by the lookouts who heard him; men of far lesser rank wondered how much time he would spend looking for *them*, should something happen. Further, a crew's confidence, trust, and general morale rested on the commander's success in sinking ships; and Franz had sunk none. And, in marked contrast to the leadership style of Günther Böhm, Franz had instituted severe punishments for perceived minor infractions of the rule book; the result: seven men committed to hard lying—an unprecedented number in U-boats, Baumann thought—and an energy-sucking malaise among the rest.

Baumann, who knew all the crewmen personally and

enjoyed the respect among them that Franz did not, argued with Franz that his iron discipline was self-defeating. "You're killing the spirit, which means the fighting effectiveness, of the crew," he attempted to persuade him.

"These men were coddled by our classical scholar," Franz answered acidly. "Their performance is classically casual. With me they will have to meet a higher standard of discipline, dress, and hygiene."

"At least their classical scholar, as you call him, sank ships," Baumann riposted.

"That impertinence will be duly noted in your fitness report," Franz rebuked him.

Baumann despaired of getting through. The man was steel-clad. What of the days and weeks ahead? How would the men handle their resentment, their sense of futility, their fear—emotions that had never characterized this boat before?

Were he a petty officer or rating, and were he present in the forward torpedo compartment at mess time, he would have heard those emotions expressed in gallows talk about punishments probably yet to come.

BTSMT. STURM: "If he puts you on report and presses charges back at base, you'll think hard-lying is luxury travel."

MATR. VII WAGONER: "If it's only mild punishment we'd get full rations and only have to do some extra work and close order drill."

STURM: "But that drill is done with gas masks on, and a lot of seamen break down."

MATR. II KRAUSS: "I know a machinist's mate who was sentenced to nine months. He served four of them in a work battalion at Freiburg-Breisgau. The treatment and the food were horrible. He was under hard punishment. When he finished his term, they sent him to an army punishment company in Russia for three months before letting him rejoin his navy unit."

OB. FK. MT. SCHNEEWIND: "Radiomen get the worst punishments. They say a radioman in the navy has one foot in the grave. Making mistakes in deciphering messages is the worst offense, next to missing them altogether. They're numbered, you know. A fellow I worked with on another boat fell asleep and missed some signals. When he returned to base, he was sentenced by his boat commander to twenty-one days in an isolated cell on bread and water. Twenty-one days is the maximum term a commander can give. For anything over that, you have to have a court-martial."

MECH. OB. GEFR. BORCHERT: "God help you if they send you to Torgau."

WAGONER: "What's that?"

STURM: "The navy prison. I've never known a man to come out of Torgau alive. They say that even if you survive it you can never be reinstated into the service—any service."

MASCH. MT. BORCHERT: "AWOL more than three days gets you one to ten years. Desertion is death."

MATR. II ERBEN: "How?"

STURM: "Firing squad or hanging, I don't know. They do it at Kiel. Taking the property of a fallen comrade means death. Homosexual conduct, you can get shot for that."

KRAUSS: "I wish they would shoot some of those girls in the communications service."

STURM: "The *Blitzmädel?*"

KRAUSS: "Yeah, they all have the clap."

SEIDEL: "Not all of them. Some have syphilis."

BORCHERT: "Catching venereal disease now gets you a three week cure and, *then,* prison under hard arrest for two weeks."

ERBEN: "Damn! That's gonna kill my style back in Lorient."

WAGONER: "Where in Lorient?"

KRAUSS: "The Café les Trois Soeurs."

WAGONER: "You mean the Café Sechs Titten."

They all laughed.
It was their first laugh in ten days.
But it was hollow and short-lived.

Daily routine inside the reeking cockleshell continued on automatic. Men performed their assigned duties with regularity if not with spirit. Anomie was pervasive. Franz snapped at the petty officers, who snapped at the ratings. The chief bos'n worked on the petty officers, reminding them of the maxim: officers teach men how to die; NCOs teach men how to live. It was up to the petty officers to keep their men going in face of Franz's tyranny and their own hard-lying.

Most of the ratings suffered, too, from *Blechkoller*—"tin neurosis," induced by prolonged nervous strain in a tin-can environment—where the ears of *Hein Seeman* succumb to the endless staccato of push rods and rocker arms; where his nostrils yield to the foul emanations of boat and bodies; where his eyes redden and glaze under the harsh twenty-four hour light; where his leg muscles hang flabby from disuse; and, most critical, where his mind softens from lack of hope.

As the men grew more edgy, and their nonduty hours were spent striving with what energy was left to get through each hour as it came around—sleeping, day-dreaming, reading dog-eared Zane Grey and other German-language American Western pulp for the second or third time—they began to long for home with growing intensity. When the cook came around with the obligatory daily pail of lemonade, they lusted instead for Beck's, Pilsner, Münchner Löwenbräu, Martell, Hennessy, and even *vin rouge ordinaire* at the Café Sechs Titten—anything to remove their minds from dismal reality.

Belle dropped Tony off at Union Terminal on West Bay Street in Jacksonville. At 4:30 it was still dark and she was an hour away from St. Augustine. When she got home, she assured Tony, she could get in a good sleep before flying her afternoon ASW patrol.

"Oh!" Tony remembered, as he opened the passenger side door, and reached in the back seat for his bag, "I forgot to tell you that when I spoke with the Crestview mechanic on the phone, he said that the man who attacked us paid in cash for the repairs to both planes. But I'll still pay for your trip back out there to pick up your plane."

"Please don't," she said. "I have a nice income from my father's trust fund. I can afford it much better than you." She put out her hand. "Goodbye, Solus. I won't forget our adventure together."

"Goodbye, Sola. Neither will I. Maybe some day I can tell you what a service you rendered. Thank you from a grateful heart, and God bless."

Tony was well ahead of time to meet the Seaboard Mail and Express when it pulled in at 6:15. From a secluded position, he watched Krug alight and walk from the platform into the cavernous Tennessee marble terminal waiting room. The German was dressed in a dark, long-sleeved shirt, tan trousers, and boots. He carried a flat case—for what? His expression was grim and unshaven, probably the same as his pursuer's, Tony reflected.

Krug walked directly to the ticket window and purchased a ticket, which he looked at briefly and placed in his shirt pocket. After checking the time on his watch, he walked across to a coffee shop and sat down to order.

Tony went immediately to the same ticket window and told the agent, "The gentleman who just purchased a ticket from you—I want to go to the same place. We're together."

"Walton?" the man asked.

"I thought we were going to Fort Pierce," Tony said, hesitantly.

"Walton's a flag stop just south of Fort Pierce," the agent said. "Actually, he's gonna get off at Eden but you have to buy a Walton ticket."

"I'll buy a ticket to Walton, then," Tony said, recovering, and placed a $20 bill on the counter.

"FEC local twenty-nine," the agent said, handing him his ticket and change. "Departs eleven o'clock, track three, arrives Walton five-fifty, or, if you go on to Eden, five-fifty-five."

Tony thanked the agent and walked to a corner of the waiting room where he could watch Krug without being seen. It was going to be a long wait, nearly four and a half hours before departure. He wondered if he could stand that long. He wondered if he could stay awake that long. At the terminal newsstand he purchased a copy of the *Florida Times-Union*, less to have something to read than to have something with which to cover his face when he could get on board, sit, and sleep. He also purchased sun glasses and a loud tourist hat.

At Norfolk seadrome, Bo Burke and his crew, in PBY-5 Bureau No. 2359, lumbered into the early morning air, bound for Florida, except that neither Bo, Ray, nor Sam was piloting. They, their crew, and their gear were being flown by a regularly assigned VP-83 patrol plane commander down to NAS Jax, where their orders were to pick up their original Bureau Number Cat, now repaired, and fly it to NAS Banana River. The USN Gulf Sea Frontier headquartered at Key West, which included almost the entire Florida peninsula in its command, had exercised authority granted it by the Navy Department on February 25 to obtain operational assistance from Jax, which was the southernmost base of the Eastern Sea Frontier. GSF needed a long-ranger to patrol a wide arc going seaward from Cape Canaveral and back to St. Lucie Inlet. Since Bo and his crew were the only experienced operational crew that Jax could offer, it was so long, Norfolk, hello, Banana, to join that station's six PBM Mariners and the OS2U Kingfishers, five of which had just two days before been established as Squadron VS1-D7. GSF wanted the Mariners to concentrate on transitional training, and the Kingfishers were too short-legged for extended seaward patrols, so Bo, much to his liking, would have the first choice on bombs.

The move was a hurried one for "Bo's Boys," as they had come to be called at VP-83, but not so hurried that Sam Singer was not able to crank out a new stanza for them to sing on the way down:

And so to Banana, to make a fourth drop,
Our first three were surely a flop,
But armed with some gin,
Not to mention some sin,
We'll bring our bad luck to a stop.

From the navigator's compartment, 3,500 feet high in CAVU, Bo and Ray looked out over the featureless Atlantic—calm, flat, unmoving, gray-flannel, but brilliant orange where the rising sun reflected off it—the domain of U-boats, which were sleeping somewhere beneath and within it.

"I've been thinking, Ray," Bo said as he maintained his gaze seaward, "that maybe we should have bombed in salvo when we bombed in train, and in train when we bombed in salvo."

"How would we ever know for certain?" Ray asked. "The tactical doctrine they gave us at Jax is that a salvo drop is preferable to an intervalometer drop when the target is still partially visible on the surface, and that's sure as hell what we did off Ocracoke."

"Yeah, that's what they said."

"But, then," Ray continued, reaching into his pilot's case, "you look at this 'Section B-3, U.S. Fleet Doctrine for Anti-Submarine Warfare by Aircraft' that they handed us Monday, and it reads: 'The lethal radius of a four-bomb salvo theoretically is not quite double that of a single bomb of the same type plus the underwater dispersion between bombs. That dispersion cannot be predicted with any amount of accuracy.' Yeah, here's the key point: 'One bomb exploding within lethal range is quite sufficient to do lethal damage. Salvo drop on a diving, still visible submarine is therefore not appropriate doctrine.' So how do you like that?"

"Navy speak with forked tongue," Bo said. "Actually, I don't think they know. They're just feeling their way, like us."

"Yeah."

"I think that right now luck probably plays a greater role than doctrine. One of these days—or nights—Bo's going to get lucky and a bomb from our boat is going to pop right inside that lethal range, and Bo's going to win a Kewpie doll."

"I know you're right, Bo," Ray encouraged him, and laughed. "It's gonna happen. All we need is a little bit of Lady Luck."

"I'll tell you what we'll do next time, Ray. We'll compromise. If we can catch a sub diving and come in on its swirl, we'll drop two in train. If the charges bring her to the surface, we'll come back and drop two in salvo."

"Sounds good to me."

The blue and white trim Taylorcraft crabbed left into the wind in order to maintain course parallel to the coast on Belle's first ASW leg north to Jacksonville Beach. Westward, the sky was darkening, a sign, she thought, of typical Florida afternoon cumulus buildup. The temperature was warm, so it was to be expected. The CAA had no special weather advisories for the P.M., so Belle concentrated her attention on the ocean surface fewer than 1,000 feet below. It was calm and featureless; except for two northbound merchant ships, which she easily out-ran, about ten miles off shore.

At Jax Beach she made a slow 180-degree turn to the south and crabbed right on the return to St. Augustine. The sun in the Western 4:00 P.M. sky that she studied over the inflated inner tube that occupied the cabin's right seat was slipping away beneath overcast and about 3,000 broken. Below, she watched the two ships and their wakes come toward her, and wondered if their captains considered that she might be doing them a service, though it seemed to her that they might help themselves somewhat if they zigzagged.

Ahead, off St. Augustine, she noticed that scattered clouds and low-lying scud were pushing off the land and over water. The Western horizon was darkening there, too. She wondered if she should continue her intended patrol south to Flagler Beach. There probably was no need for concern. The air above St. Augustine airport was still relatively clear and enough gas was sloshing around in her tanks to make Flagler or Daytona Beach in case St. Augustine closed in. She kept her attention on the sea, looking for a U-boat's feather wake, and wondering what language she would use if she saw one and called it in on her one-watt radio.

South of St. Augustine, she found the weather a bit more menacing, with imbedded dark masses. Wind intensity picked up, and her little craft began to rock and bump in the gathering turbulence. She reduced airspeed accordingly.

By the time she reached Flagler Beach and began her turn-around, weather to the south had deteriorated to the point where she doubted that she could get in to Daytona Beach if she wanted to. Making her turn, right, into the wind, she was surprised at how strong it had become. It seemed that her Taylorcraft was standing still as it faced the shore, which now, she discovered, as she continued the turn, was lost to view behind unbroken cloud and scud. And to the north, off St. Augustine, she could no longer see the water below!

She was flying above overcast. For the first time, her heart beat palpably and her hands became moist. She had to descend to an altitude where she could regain ground and water reference. Reducing power further, and watching the altimeter, she bounced her way below the 700 feet overcast only to find herself over 500 broken in light rain with about two miles visibility. She had never before experienced such a rapid deterioration of flight conditions. Could she push hard West through this stuff and regain sight of land?

She tried to do just that, hanging on the gauges. But the turbulence she encountered was so severe, the head wind so strong, the rain so intense, and the visibility so limited, she had to turn back out to sea, aided violently in that direction by the overpowering air currents. *Don't panic*, she told herself. Don't become disoriented. Stick to the panel.

Pilot error, she reprimanded herself. She should never have continued into doubtful weather. But she could punish herself later. Right now, she had to keep her head. She reached for the radio earphones and hand-mike: "Taylorcraft NC-two-three-six-nine-one to St. Augustine airport. Over." Only static crackled over her earphones. "Taylorcraft NC-two-three-six-nine-one to anyone. Do you read me? Over." She repeated the call ten times.

No answer. From anyone. Atmospheric conditions may have shot communications all to hell. The radio was only a one-watter. And maybe she was too distant. Speaking into the mike was like trying to reach land with a megaphone. She checked her fuel—one eighth to empty. Damn! Would she have to ditch? Yes, yes, yes! There was no way in to terra firma. The turbulence would tear her to pieces. Only seaward could her little craft continue airborne—and for how long? Grimly, she checked the magnetic compass: 85 degrees. She tried flattening her course to 50 and found that she could stay ahead of the weather. But she was still going out to sea. Only to sea could she find her way visually, and only to sea could she escape the low ceiling, rain, and turbulence. Only to sea and a crash.

It was 4:50 on her watch when, ominously, the four-cylinder engine coughed and lost power. Belle pushed the nose down to maintain airspeed. Altitude: 500. The engine resumed normal combustion for a few minutes as the last quarts of usable fuel fed from a new angle in the exhausted tank. Four more times Belle made her futile radio calls. Then, abruptly dry, the engine quit altogether and, in the strangely peaceful silence that followed, the plane descended gently toward the ocean surface.

Belle knew what she had to do. She cut the switches and cracked open the doors. For warmth she had already decided to keep on her leather jacket, the crinkled black and brown leather flying helmet she wore without the goggles, and her canvas tennis shoes. Now she checked the pockets of her slacks to make sure she had her wallet and the St. Christopher medal that Solus had given her during their drive from Eglin. She wondered if she should throw the inner tube out just before she ditched or try to get it out afterward. The main thing was to stall the aircraft just before touching water. She fastened her safety belt as taut as she could, knowing that, as soon as the wheels hit, the plane would flip over on its back.

Her only hope now was that, when her failure to return was noticed, and the storm abated, her fellow pilots would mount a search for her. There were hours of daylight left. She had only to keep her head. Forget the sharks and barracudas. Just keep her head.

After Franz trained the observation periscope through its full 32-point reach and sent it hissing back down the housing well, he shouted below from his seat in the tower, "Surface! Decks awash! Lookouts to the bridge!"

Thirteen-point-five meters later, Chief Engineer Brünner and his control room hands had the tower clear. Franz disengaged the hatch spindles and stepped out onto the frothy bridge platform, the lookouts right on his heels. With 7 x 50s he quickly checked the horizon and sky around the double-plate steel coaming, then called, "Starboard ahead one-third! Clear tanks! Steady on one-six-zero!" down the pipe; immediately after which the puster sang back from his station: "Herr Leutnant, voice transmission in the clear: 'Taylorcraft NC-two-three-six-nine-one to anyone.' Repeated three times."

"Very well," Franz acknowledged.

As the first diesel exhaust fumes and noise came up the starboard port aft, the bridge watch steadied into their rhythmic routine, lenses sweeping the four quadrants of what was, that afternoon, a choppy sea and a dark messy sky, wind force 6 or 7 westerly. Rain columns obscured the horizon to starboard, though some sunlight and blue could still be seen in the distance to port.

Of a sudden, the port aft lookout broke ranks with his fellows and shouted, "Herr Leutnant! An aircraft going down!"

Franz turned to train his glasses alongside those of the immobile lookout. Against the thin line of pale blue sky northeastward he could see the dark form of a single engine aircraft descending gradually to the water. At his best focus he saw that it had wheels down, so it was fixed gear and not likely to be military. But what would a civilian plane be doing this far out? It appeared to be ditching in distress.

"Both ahead full!" he ordered. "Come left to zero-five-zero!" Ordinarily, a U-boat would dive at the sight of any plane, military or civilian, but this one was crashing and ought to be investigated.

As the U-boat made its turn, the tower leaning to starboard, and the port diesel thundering in, Franz, holding his glasses as steady as he could, watched the aircraft turn slowly toward them, into the wind. It was then that he sighted the still propeller.

"Dead-stick," he said to the lookouts as he went forward to the voice pipe. "Deck force prepare to recover survivor!"

Turning again to the stricken plane, he watched its final moments. It was a smaller plane than he had first thought. Just before the wheels touched down, a large black object came out the starboard door. Then the wheels hit and the engine dug in with a white splash and the fuselage overturned forward, where it floated. The pilot extricated himself and swam back toward the black object, which must be a life preserver.

Böhm would be amazed if he saw this scene—Franz going to the assistance of an American survivor! Franz laughed at the thought of it. But this pilot might have very useful information about coastal defenses and favorable notice would be taken of that at flotilla headquarters. The Lion should be impressed by his resourcefulness; enough, Franz thought, to make up for his attack failures, perhaps enough to win him his own boat and crew.

• • •

When he came alongside the still-floating aircraft, Franz saw that it was no more than a brightly painted *sport* plane. What the hell was a plane like that doing out here in a war zone? There was an insignia of some kind on the fuselage, probably the emblem of a flying club. He would interrogate the pilot and if there was nothing useful to be gained, he would throw him back like a too-small fish— although, to keep the crew docile, he would direct the puster to transmit the survivor's position on the 600-meter wave band.

With the U-boat close aboard, the pilot raised his arms above the inflated rubber tube to catch the extended arms of two deck force crewmen on a rope ladder. Both the pilot and the tube were brought aboard, the pilot surprising all the deck force with his slim build and delicate features.

The chief bos'n stood him up by the shoulders and checked him for side arms. Unzipping the leather jacket, he felt inside for a shoulder holster. Abruptly, he stopped and drew back! Then, stepping forward again, he undid the pilot's chin strap and pulled the helmet off by the crown.

Belle's damp blonde hair fell to her shoulders.

Stunned, the bos'n made an about-face and shouted to Franz watching from the bridge, "Herr Leutnant! It's a *woman!*"

CHAPTER 24

WHEN FEC LOCAL 29 pulled out of the straw-colored station at Fort Pierce, Tony asked the conductor on which side of the tracks the Eden station would appear.

"The left, sir," the black-clad conductor replied.

"Okay. Will you make sure the train stops there for me?"

"Sure. There's another man getting off."

"Yes. And I'd like to ask you to do me a favor. Let me get out on the right side, opposite the station."

"I can't do that, sir. It's against the rules."

"Just this once," Tony suggested, handing him a ten dollar bill. "And I want to get off on a different car from the other fellow's."

"Just this once," the conductor said, placing the bill in his vest pocket.

It was the fourth time Tony had offered ten-spots. Were they bribes or payments for service received? If the former, were they justified by the good result that was intended? Did the end justify the means? He would have to sort it out later.

If Krug had walked through the coach cars looking at passengers, Tony had not seen him. First, because he had slept for four hours with his hat and newspaper over his face. Second, because, on awakening, he had gone to the toilet where he remained for the rest of the multi-stop trip, telling the few people who knocked, in a false voice through the door, that he was sick—to go to another car.

And that was another thing—the lies. Like the lies he told to the airplane mechanic in Crestview. Did the exigencies of wartime excuse them? He thought so. He hoped so.

At 5:35 on his watch, when the train slowed down for

what had to be Fort Pierce, he had emerged from the toilet to strike his deal with the conductor.

Now the train slowed again as it passed Walton. The conductor came by to show Tony the between-cars steps where he could alight. When the Eden flag stop was reached, and the cars banged and groaned to a stop, Tony grabbed his bag and jumped from the lowest step to the ground. To the west of the tracks stood a thick patch of scrub palmetto into which he flung himself and his bag, no doubt startling other passengers at their windows.

The train quickly jerked away on its narrow course, and, when the last car cleared, Tony looked up carefully from his prone position to see Krug in a leather jacket standing with his case in front of the tiny Eden station, turning slowly to observe everything within his circle of vision. Then, apparently satisfied, he began walking east down a dirt road.

Tony remained motionless where he lay. And it was a good thing he did. Five minutes later, Krug reappeared at the tracks and made another searching observation. Was it Tony he was concerned about? Or the FBI? Then, again, he turned and walked eastward.

Tony examined the landscape on either side of the dirt road opposite. It was dense with trees, bushes, and high grass. He left his bag in the scrub and dashed for the trees about thirty yards north of the road. Although the going here would be tough, the growth provided him effective cover. As quietly as he could, then, he moved forward, pausing from time to time to listen for Krug's step, anxious that his quarry might reverse his course once more or wander into the tree line.

Tony slogged along without interruption for fifteen minutes until the interjection "Ouch!" audibly left his lips. He looked down to see a thick spread of sharp-leafed plants into which he had wandered and from which now he gingerly extricated himself.

Suddenly, where the woods thinned ahead, he saw movement crossing from right to left! It was a human figure. Tony stopped behind a tree. After a moment, he identified the figure as Krug. The German was walking slowly, head down. Tony looked along his line of march and in the distance sighted the paint of two houses half-hidden by trees and bushes, one white and one yellow, about 100 yards apart.

When he saw Krug move past the white house toward the yellow one, Tony moved forward to another concealed position with a better view. From there he could see Krug stop and knock on the door of the yellow house. When, after numerous knocks, no one came to the door, Krug walked around to the other side, out of Tony's vision. Then, after a few moments, he reappeared on the side of the house, where, cupping his right hand against the glass, he peered through the window.

Abruptly, Krug walked quickly off in an easterly direction. Tony followed as best he could, keeping to the high cover. After about 200 yards, he broke into the clear and saw ahead of him a crossing roadway, a river, and a boathouse at the end of a long, weatherworn pier.

Krug could be seen walking with his case along the pier. When he reached the boathouse door, and after first looking up and down the river shore, he placed a key in the lock and entered. After the door closed behind him, Tony ran to a better position where he sat down to rest and watch. He looked at the time: 6:45, and twilight.

No more than ten minutes passed when Tony was surprised by a sudden grinding noise from the direction of the boathouse. It lasted some twenty seconds. A minute later, there was a muffled roar, which Tony thought might be a boat engine. His guess was confirmed in a few moments when a covered boat sortied into the water, highlighted by yellow light from the boathouse, with Krug barely visible at the controls. The boat turned to the right, or south, and picked up speed, leaving a considerable wake that lapped the shore. Tony moved out of his concealment as far as he dared and followed the form of the boat until it was no longer visible in the graying air.

Damn! Had he lost Krug now?

Thinking it was safe to do so, he quickly walked the length of the rickety pier and tried the door. It was open! Inside, he took a quick look around the brightly lit interior. There was a second boat in the water below, an open runabout of some kind, with the name *Crunch* in gilt letters on its stern. The east end of the boathouse was completely open, its large door pulled up flat against the ceiling by chains. That was the grinding noise he had heard. Along the three walls were catwalks and shelving that held fishing equipment—rods, reels, tackleboxes, nets—and miscellaneous boat parts. He looked up to see a pull cord and a panel in that part of the ceiling which was not covered by the boat door. He pulled on the cord and a ladder-type stairway came down.

Before making another move, he walked along the right catwalk to the boathouse opening and looked out in the direction of Krug's boat. He saw and heard nothing. So he returned to the stairway and climbed up. Switching on a light, he discovered a typical storeroom or attic containing furniture, other household goods, equipment of various kinds, and papers, which he looked through briefly—nothing of any interest.

As he descended the stairway he wondered, whose house, boats, and boathouse were these, anyway? Another agent, like Ohlenburg at St. Augustine Beach? If so, where was he? How did Krug know to come here? Had he been here before? Where was he now with the boat?

After letting the springed ladder door back up, his eyes opened wide at something leaning against the wall near his shoes: *Krug's case!* He opened it at once and looked inside. Paintings. Watercolors on paper. Eight or nine. Very good professional work. Nothing else inside the case. But Krug would not have deliberately left his body of work behind, would he? Tony thought its presence here meant that Krug would be back.

Enormously relieved, he looked south out the pierside door, and, detecting no sign yet of Krug's boat, walked back along the pier, across the road, and into the trees, where he established a comfortable position from which he could keep watch. His empty stomach growled.

At 8:25 he heard an engine on the river to the south. Five minutes later, he sighted the black form of a northbound boat. When it slowed and turned in toward the illuminated boathouse entrance, he knew that another of his hunches had proved correct. For an hour after the boat door noisily lowered, Tony made no visible or audible contact with the German—until, briefly, Krug opened the pierside door and looked out, at what it was not clear, his form a black silhouette against the boathouse light. Then, he closed the door and Tony did not see him again for most of the remaining nighttime hours. Near one o'clock he found himself nodding off, but he did not worry much about it, since he was sure he would awaken if the boat door reopened or if Krug walked along the creaking boards of the pier.

Belle sat stoically in her dry but foul-smelling seaman's clothing at the wardroom table. Across from her, Interim Commander Franz and I WO Baumann sat examining the contents of her wallet, spread out in neat rows, damp but readable.

Baumann translated each document and card for Franz. "This is a license from the State of Florida to drive an automobile," he explained. "These two are licenses from the Civil Aeronautics Administration to pilot an 'airplane single engine land.' Here's a medical certificate and a—"

"What's this?" Franz asked, picking up a card marked with the same insignia he had seen on the fuselage of the woman's plane.

"Civil Air Patrol," Baumann read.

"Ask her what that is," Franz directed.

When Baumann did so, Belle raised her eyes from the table and answered in a straightforward fashion, "It's an organization of private pilots who fly missions to help in emergency situations like forest fires and lost airplanes, and so on."

When this was translated, Franz exploded, "You're a liar, woman! There are no forest fires out here in the ocean! Do you take me for a fool? And if a plane was lost this far out to sea, your government would not send a tiny sport plane like yours to hunt for it!"

Franz slammed his fist against the table. "You were reporting on U-boats! But you have no uniform or military identification! You are a spy!" He turned to Baumann, "Translate!"

Belle was startled by the commander's guttural outburst, and for the first time felt fear in the hands of her captors. Grateful though she was for her rescue, she thought now that she had been saved only to be punished, perhaps killed, and she was not reassured when she heard Baumann's translation.

While Baumann was speaking, Franz got up and went to his commander's cubicle, where earlier, behind its curtain, he had permitted Belle to change out of her wet clothes. He returned immediately with a piece of paper and, while still standing, read from it. "Standing order number one fifty-four," Franz said in a loud voice. "From Admiral Karl Dönitz, Commander-in-Chief U-Boats. To all commanders: 'Do not rescue any survivors or take them with you. Have no concern for lifeboats. Weather conditions and distance from land make no difference. Be concerned only for the welfare of your U-boat and try to achieve additional successes as soon as possible. *We must be hard in this war*. The enemy started the war to destroy us, and so nothing else matters.'"

Franz thrust the paper in front of Baumann, adding, "The Lion made only two exceptions, captains and masters, if they can provide useful intelligence, and this woman is neither. Tell her I want detailed information on American coastal air patrols off Florida and if she does not supply it I will throw her and her tube back in the sea."

As Franz glared threateningly at Belle, Baumann read every other sentence of Dönitz's order and Franz's demands, interspersing, "Be advised this man is a cold-hearted warrior. . . . He will treat you badly, just as he says. . . . If you do not know the information he demands, make it up."

Belle nodded obediently when Baumann finished. "I don't know the military flight schedules, but I'll tell you what I do know—"

Baumann translated into German as Belle spoke, "And that is: several hundred patrol planes that were originally destined for shipment overseas to the British have been temporarily reassigned to antisubmarine patrols off Florida. These include PBYs and PBMs, oh-S-two-U Kingfishers, and even a squadron of the new B-seventeen-E Flying Fortresses. The intention, I overheard military pilots saying, is to give saturation coverage to every merchant lane in Florida waters, both Atlantic and Gulf, and to make it suicidal for U-boats to operate here."

"When will these forces be in place?" Franz directed Baumann to ask. "And where will they be stationed?"

"The end of this month," Belle answered. "The principal bases will be Jacksonville, Banana River, Key West, Tampa, and Pensacola."

"Can she draw silhouettes of all these planes?" Franz asked.

"Yes," Belle answered.

"Then give her some paper and a pen," Franz ordered Baumann. "And when she's finished, dump her in the forward torpedo room until I decide what to do with her. I will not have a spy—a civilian resistance fighter—a partisan, and you know what we do to partisans in Russia and France, don't you, Baumann?—I will not have someone of that contemptible ilk defiling the officers' or petty officers' quarters."

"Yes, Herr Leutnant."

When Belle received the paper and pen she immediately began sketching a PBY. It was easy to do. She knew all these planes cold, as did most schoolboys, like Paul Ohlenburg. Pictures of the planes were in all the newspapers. If a spy wanted to know what a given warplane looked like, he need only open *Life* magazine. She was not giving anything away. And if the commander believed her story of massive ASW air patrols, she might be doing more at this table to keep the U-boats away from Florida than the entire State CAP could have done in the air.

Maybe this commander was a fool, after all.

But wasn't the other officer a decent sort? More immediately, what would happen to her when she finished her sketches? Would she be thrown back into the sea? Or would she be taken to Germany?

She reached into the left pocket of her seaman's pants and fingered the St. Christopher medal she had sequestered there. Irrational though it seemed to her Protestant soul, she prayed, "C'mon Chris, I need you!"

When Belle finished her sketches, Baumann had the cook bring her some food: a hash of corned beef, boiled potatoes, pickled cucumber strips, and salt herring, served with bridge-watch coffee, which she found intolerably strong. The meal completed, Baumann called the chief bos'n from the control room to take Belle forward, as Franz had directed. Before letting her go, he promised her, "I'll do my best to protect you."

"You have already," Belle replied. "Thank you."

The bos'n then led her through the narrow tube of boilerplate and weld.

While every "Lord" in the forward torpedo room would have been willing to give up his bunk-time so that Belle might have a woman's right to comfort and a decent chance to rest, the chief bos'n made Franz's order perfectly clear to every hand: the prisoner was sentenced to hard-lying, and no one was to ease the state of her confinement; with the two exceptions that Puster Schneewind, the only rating who spoke English, should instruct Belle in the use of the head, and that she should receive the same rations as the crew.

At 0910 German war time, 0210 U.S. eastern war time, Franz made one of his chilling inspection turns through the boat and seemed satisfied that Belle was where she was supposed to be, flat on the cold steel floor plates without so much as a handkerchief under her head. After Franz returned aft, Schneewind came forward from the radio room, where he had been relieved by another Funkmaat, to report that Franz had doused the light in his cubicle for a few hours' bunk time in order to be fresh for the pick-up of Peter Krug at dawn. He said that the other Funkmaat would make a "click" on the loudspeaker system if Franz should awake within the next couple of hours or if the chief bos'n gave signs that he was going forward to their station.

Then he knelt down alongside Belle and invited her, in English, to get up off the plates and to sit comfortably on the edge of a lower bunk. He gave her a hand to pull up on.

"Don't worry about us here, Miss," he assured her. "We respect you as a lady. We want you to feel at home, as far as that's possible."

"Thank you," Belle said, smiling for the first time since her capture. She looked around at the dozen young bearded faces that circled her with their own wide smiles.

"I *will* say though," Belle continued, "no home I ever entered smelled as foul as this place. The stench is *terrible*. How can you stand it?"

When Schneewind translated this, the Lords looked at one another and laughed loudly. Then one of them, Krauss, reached under his mattress and produced two small photographs of women, one middle-aged, the other young. "*Heim*," he said.

"His mother and his girlfriend," Schneewind explained.

"Inge," Krauss said softly, pointing to the girlfriend.

"She's very pretty," Belle observed. "Thank you for letting me see these."

Borschert pressed forward a snapshot. "Anna," he said with a toothy grin.

Wagoner produced "Monika," Seidel, "Ulrike," and Erben "Hilde," and various others their girlfriends, too.

Belle was moved. She stood up and slowly walked the circle shaking each man's oily hand, letting the palms linger briefly together, as a way of allowing each one to touch, however vicariously, his sweetheart at home. It was not anything she ever thought she would be doing.

When she sat back down, Borchert, after several half-starts, and encouraged by his fellows, managed to sing, in English:

Come on and hear
Come on and hear
Alexander's Ragtime Band . . .

The others laughed and applauded him. Then, in the awkward silence that followed, Belle sang the rest of the stanza:

Come on and hear,
Come on and hear,
It's the best band in the land . . .

The men edged forward as a sign they wanted her to sing some more.

Belle never thought of herself as a singer. She had a very ordinary voice. But she had sung a featured song in the Junior Minstrels at college, and she thought she could remember the words. To help her do that, she went over them with Schneewind, who then explained to his crewmates the general sense of the lyrics.

Then, reflecting on the bizarre irony that the last time she sang this song in anyone else's hearing it was in the sheltered confines of FSCW in Tallahassee—a life and a peace ago—she reached for the opening notes of "These Foolish Things Remind Me of You."

While she sang, Krauss, Wagoner, and Seidel stared at their photographs. The rest fixed their eyes on Belle or gazed abstractly into a murky distance. Toward the song's end, Borchert and Erben sobbed and shook.

During the silence that followed the song, Belle knew that she had reached her own emotional breaking point, and she covered her face with her hands while the tears flowed.

How her mother must be hurting at this moment! Would she ever see her again? Would she ever see Bo, who cared so much about her? Or her new friend Solus— had he heard the news of her disappearance? How could he? He had gone south on a train.

Schneewind touched her elbow and said, "Why don't you lie down now on this bunk, Miss? If the commander or the bos'n comes, we'll have to remove you right away to the floor, you understand."

"I understand," Belle said, sorrowfully, and lay her head on the blue and white check pillow, which smelled even worse than the ambient air. But it made no difference when sleep soon practiced its consoling ministry.

Krug forced himself awake and looked at the phosphorescent dial on his watch. Four A.M. He stood up and turned on the boathouse light. The Chris-Craft cushions had made for a fairly comfortable mattress, and he felt refreshed for the U-boat rendezvous. Not only refreshed, but downright excited as he anticipated handing the puster a message about the B-25s for immediate transmission to Abwehr—though, he acknowledged, his enthusiasm did not run to a U-boat breakfast, not after more than two weeks of fresh American fare.

Lorenz's tide tables, advanced to war time, scheduled high tide for 5:17. Dawn, he knew from daily observations, would be about 7:15. He would have to get through the St. Lucie Inlet two hours before dawn in order to avoid the perils described by Lorenz. And, speaking of Lorenz, where, he allowed himself to wonder, as he looked at the still upright coffee mug in the boathouse—where had the FBI spirited Lorenz after his apprehension in the house? Fortunately, the Bureau had left everything in the boathouse intact, and, if Krug could judge from his inspection of the loft above, the most sensitive materials undetected and unexamined.

Whew! He had brought down an old pair of binoculars he found upstairs.

The trial run to the inlet last evening took only sixteen or seventeen minutes to cover the seven nautical mile distance. Once through the inlet at high tide, he would still have to go three nautical miles seaward to reach the position, where U-*Böhm* was supposed to be waiting. Had *better* be waiting.

For a moment he wondered if he should try to raise the U-boat on Lorenz's transmitter and get the word about the B-25s to U-*Böhm* in that way in case something thwarted the rendezvous. In the end, he thought not. Lorenz's transmitter could be a fall-back option in case the rendezvous went sour.

He decided to go ahead and make his start now. He could stand in the river off the inlet and wait there for the tide. After placing his case in "Des," well under the canvas top where it would be safe from spray, he opened the boathouse door with the chain and pulley and looked out at the Indian River water. There was no traffic. The sky was overcast. He walked back along the catwalk and released the bow and stern lines. Then, after placing the binoculars strap around his neck, he shut off the boathouse light and stepped inside "Des," where he switched on the ignition. At once, the inboard engine caught and rumbled. All right so far. Releasing the spring line, he edged the boat out into the river, and after reaching what he thought was midstream, swung south.

Tony was awakened by the noise of the boat door opening. He raised himself up from his woodsy lair and watched as the boathouse light lay a band of yellow on the river. Then, just as suddenly, the light went out. When the boat engine sounded, he walked down to the shore to see where Krug was going now. Just barely, he could catch sight of the boat in the inky black. It went forward slowly and then, building speed, turned south.

Before, when Krug took the boat out in the darkness,

he left the light on, which he used for his return. This time he turned it off. Did that mean he was not coming back? Tony ran to the pier and made his way to the boathouse, which was still unlocked. He closed the big boat door and switched on the light. When he did so, he saw that Krug's case was gone.

Definitely, this time, Krug was not coming back. Tony stepped into the open Gar Wood boat with its sleek wood deck and front-and-back seating compartments. He had never driven a motorboat before, inboard or outboard. He studied its controls. They seemed simple enough if he could get it to go. He stepped back up to the catwalk, cut off the light and opened the boat door. Then he untied the lines and sat down behind the wheel in the left front seat. Remembering what Belle had done in the Piper Cub, he cracked what looked like a throttle and pushed what might be a starter. The engine surprised him with its affirmative and loud response. He guessed that the boat was in neutral, since there was no forward movement. Another lever with a round ball on top seemed to be a gear shift and he pushed that forward. The boat leaped ahead with such force that his neck whipped back as the boat departed the boathouse like a shot from a barrel.

He retarded the throttle, which obviously he had set too high, and when the boat slowed down he turned the wheel so as to take a southerly heading, but one close to the right shore in order to veil his pursuit. Maintaining half-power, which he judged visibly from the distance the throttle lever could traverse, he scanned the river in front of him for any sign of Krug.

After twenty minutes he caught his first dim glimpse of what he assumed was Krug's boat. He could just barely make out the off-white canvas top. It was proceeding slowly along the left shore when first seen, slightly ahead, then, slowly it came to a stop and remained stationary. Had Krug thrown out an anchor? It certainly seemed so. And if Krug had cut his engine, Tony must do so, too, and right away lest he be heard. Which he did.

On boarding *Crunch* Tony had noticed that the rear seat compartment was filled with nautical and fishing gear of one kind or another. He wondered if an anchor might be included. While the boat drifted, he crawled back to see, or rather feel around, since it was still dark under a starless sky. Amid what felt like ropes, a life preserver, fishing hand lines, sinkers, lures, and—ouch!—gang hooks, he discovered an iron four-pronged anchor, which he saw was connected by line to a cleat on the inside of the transom. He lowered it to the shallow river bottom and shortened up the slack in the line. Then he donned the life preserver, crawled forward to the controls, and waited—but not for long.

At 5:15 by his watch, he heard Krug's engine start up. Immediately, Tony reached back and hauled up his anchor, which he threw into the rear seat. Then he switched on his own engine and fell in behind Krug at what he hoped was a safe distance. Was Krug planning on meeting someone? Tony could not see any other boat.

Krug turned to his left, or east, and pressed steadily forward in the direction of the Atlantic. After ten minutes, Tony's craft began to feel the water. The flat river gave way to waves and whitecaps. The bow lifted and slapped down hard against black currents. This was an inlet, he guessed. They were going out into the ocean!

Fifteen choppy and scary minutes later, during which he had had to reduce power to prevent himself from being swamped, he entered calmer water. He was actually out in the ocean itself now, he reasoned, rising and falling on more agreeable swells. Land features receded from view to either side. And ahead of him, perplexingly, Krug's boat could no longer be seen in the predawn air.

What to do now? He had no reference points. Which way was he headed? He stared hard at the boat's compass and seemed to make out "80" next to an "E," which he assumed meant East. Reducing power to a crawl, he maintained that heading as best he could.

Had he lost Krug now, for good? There was just no way

to know, as he mumbled to himself, until "dawn came up like thunder outer Sahara 'crost the sea."

This was absolutely something he had never done before, drive a boat, much less a boat in the ocean. He fully sensed the isolation, the disorientation, and the uncertainty that the experience imposed on him. But those feelings were countervailed by a fierce determination to see this chase through to its appointed end.

CHAPTER 25

"BO'S BOYS" were relieved when the big wing leaned right and P-10, out of Banana River, settled onto her homeward leg to St. Lucie Inlet. They had made no sightings along the 200-mile arc they patrolled that night and everyone was a mite bored.

Their aircraft had come out of NAS A & R in fine repair and flew as sweetly as she ever did. While Ray in the right seat searched ahead with glasses, Bo fine-tuned the throttle quadrant to 2,000 rpm, 30 inches, and checked the gauges all around. Established course 295-degrees true, true airspeed 115 knots, altitude 1,200, oil pressure on the money, still plenty of usable fuel. He looked out the windows to either side and ahead. They were in the base of 5/10 cumulus, visibility 5 to 6 miles, sea mirror-calm, wind 4 knots from 260-degrees true, ten minutes to sunrise.

Bo switched on the interphone mike. "Look alive, everybody. This is the time when subs submerge for the day. We might see a swirl. We might see a periscope wake. Wipe your glasses and your mark-one eyeballs."

Sam Singer spoke back from the navigator's table. "Speaking of that, Skipper, I've got a new stanza for our song."

"Okay, let's hear it."

Sam cleared his throat:

We fly in the dusk and we fly in the dawn,
We search for a submarine's scope,
We're sure we could wreck her
By hitting her pecker
But so far no scope so we mope.

Bo repeated the last line and laughed.

To his left the cloud bases were catching first light.

In U-*Franz* crewmen scrambled to their stations. The forward gun crew took up position around the 10.5-centimeters Bootskanone. Other gunners brought up ammo belts for the 2-centimeters C/30 AA machine guns on the rear bridge flak platform. The deck force assembled on the fore casing to make the pick-up.

As I WO Baumann made ready to mount the ladder to command the forward gun, he overheard Franz commanding the chief bos'n, "I don't want that woman spy interfering with our operation or sabotaging our equipment. Take these handcuffs and shackle her to a stanchion."

"*Jawohl*, Herr Leutnant."

After the bos'n had gone forward, Baumann bristled. "I *object* to that," he said to Franz. "Suppose we're attacked and have to abandon ship—"

Franz cut him off, "She'll be the last one I'll be concerned about."

"It's not honorable," Baumann protested.

Franz brushed past him and up the ladder, saying as he went, "The victors define what is honorable."

Baumann went forward at his best speed and caught the bos'n returning from his mission.

"Good job, Bos'n," he said. "You can give me the key."

"*Jawohl*, Herr Leutnant."

When Baumann reached the gun deck, he looked in the direction of shore, and saw nothing but flat sea, mist, and broken cloud cover. Turning, he saw that the sun was throwing up its first faint suggestions to the east. Under him, the boat rocked gently on the warm Florida swells, while one diesel drove the hull forward at dead slow, parallel to the beach. Above, the bridge watch swept all corners of the horizon while Franz trained his 7 x 50s in the direction of the gauzy shore.

The boat had spent the night on the surface and, with the help of the fathometer, had followed the 40-meter line south to what the navigator was certain, based on dead reckoning—there were no stars—were the latitude degrees and minutes of St. Lucie Inlet. At the navigator's direction, the puster had transmitted a cipher message to Lorient announcing that the boat was going to be on time at its scheduled rendezvous point, which he identified as DB 9739.

At 1430 GWT, the starboard forward bridge lookout broke the silence with a yell and pointed to the southeast. Franz stared intently through his lenses in that direction.

"A small dot, Herr Leutnant," the lookout explained.

Thirty seconds later, Franz lowered his glasses, then raised them again.

"That's interesting," he said. "I see *two* dots."

When the first thin band of orange-gray light appeared on the horizon and the overnight sea mist began to lift, Tony sighted Krug's boat ahead and to the right, about three football fields distant. It was not moving fast but, like his, tossed casually on the swells, as though waiting—waiting for what? Not for daylight itself, or Krug would have set out from Eden later, wouldn't he? So far, the German seemed not to have noticed him.

Then, abruptly, ahead and to his left, about half a mile away, a strange dark form with a narrow upperstructure materialized. As its silhouette became more crisply defined, displaying guns, periscopes, and men on deck, Tony realized it was a submarine! At the same instant, Tony heard Krug's engine speed up.

Krug was meeting a U-boat.

Tony revved his own engine and headed toward Krug's craft. Krug *mustn't* reach the U-boat. He *knows* too much. He knows about the *bombers*. And the *carrier*—if Belle was right. Rashly throwing his throttle to full power, Tony aimed his prow directly at Krug, who now, with binoculars raised, was staring back. Tony was surprised how rapidly he was intercepting him. He certainly had the angle on him as Krug made for the U-boat; and he also seemed to have the faster boat.

No more than thirty yards now separated *Crunch* and *Des*. Tony allowed himself to wonder for one moment only, *what in God's name was he doing?* But the moment quickly passed and adrenalin replaced reason. Ten yards distant, and Krug turned sharply away to his right, leaving Tony in the shallow trough laid down by his prop. But Tony's faster boat would not be eluded. At the last instant, he threw seat cushions against the bulkhead and hurled himself down behind them.

The banging, grinding collision knocked him about badly, particularly when his boat, still at full power, careened off to the left and nearly turned over. Tony reached up to ease the throttle and take a look. His prow was smashed and splintered pretty badly, and he figured that he was taking water. But Krug's boat, he saw, was hurt, too, as the German ran back and forth between the stern and his controls, seemingly unable to get his engine, or his prop, or both, to run.

Tony resumed his seat behind the wheel and circled around toward Krug, whose boat was now barely making way, its engine sputtering and black smoke curling from its stern. Tony aimed his prow at Krug's forward hull, threw his throttle to full, and dove for the cushions before impact. This time the collision was fiercer and, as *Crunch* glanced off, itself gravely wounded, Tony felt hurt over his entire body. Again, though, he managed to reach up and reduce power. Then lifting himself painfully for another look, he saw with satisfaction a five- or six-foot gash in Krug's wooden hull that extended down to the waterline. Krug himself, apparently unhurt, had climbed to the front deck where he was waving both arms frantically toward the U-boat in the distance.

Tony got his legs to move well enough to regain his seat. He saw that Krug's boat was beginning to settle on its left side. He brought *Crunch* alongside and pulled his gear shift into neutral. Then, with no further thought to his bruises, he climbed back to the rear seat compartment, grabbed the anchor and, releasing its line from the cleat, hurled it over the side of *Des*, where it bit in the open rear part of the boat. While Krug was running back down from the front to dislodge the anchor, Tony took up the slack in the anchor line and refastened it to his cleat. Then he put his engine into gear. Under power, the anchor cut deeply into *Des* and held despite Krug's energetic efforts to wrest it free, and Tony found himself pulling the larger boat away from the U-boat, however slowly.

Krug glowered at him across the twenty feet of line that bound them together and spoke for the first time, "Damn you, priest! Damn your meddlesome ass! Why do you follow me? What is your *problem?*"

"The problem is yours, Krug!" Tony shouted, looking back from his wheel. "I'm not going to let you get to that sub!"

"You have no *business*—a goddamn priest!"

"I'm stopping you not as a priest but as an American."

"You're supposed to be a man of *peace!*"

"There is a time for peace and a time for war—"

"I will kill you, priest!"

"A time to heal and a time to kill."

"Do you hear me? I will *kill* you!"

"A time for being born and a time to die."

Krug dove into the sea and began swimming the short distance to Tony's boat. Alarmed, and mad at himself for not having thought of it earlier, Tony leaped into the rear seat and grabbed the long fish knife he had seen there earlier, which he now used to cut the anchor line. Then he jumped back to the throttle and pushed it all the way forward. The crumpled and waterlogged boat edged away, just as Krug laid a hand on it.

Now, as he circled around the stern of Krug's crippled *Des*, which was drifting off, he saw Krug begin swimming back to it. Suppose he got it going again? He could yet make his rendezvous with the submarine, which was still standing by, whose crew must be staring aghast at this encounter, wondering which one of them was their spy and who the other guy was.

In extremis extrema tenenda sunt, Tony decided, with a speed that surprised him afterward when he thought about it. He wheeled about his stricken craft and, ice in his heart and "Lord have mercy!" in his throat, he aimed the jagged prow at Krug's upper body. When he came close enough at slow speed to be heard, he yelled, "Stop swimming! Halt! Or I will run you down!"

Which he prayed that he would not have to do, since it was killing in the first place and killing a defenseless swimmer in the second. He remembered in a flash the ancient maxim, "He who would play the angel becomes the brute."

But while Tony procrastinated, Krug fooled him by swimming directly at him, reducing the distance between them and making it impossible for Tony, in his broken boat, to accelerate enough to do him mortal damage. Tony tried to force the gear into reverse but could not. He threw it back into forward and started to turn away under full throttle when Krug grabbed a splintered board on the prow and hauled his body up on deck.

Tony swung the wheel back and forth in an attempt to throw Krug off balance, but the German held on and sprang aggressively over the windshield at Tony and— unseen to Krug until, in midair, it was far too late to do anything about it—Tony's upraised knife.

Just as the long blade drove home in Krug's chest, the boat was rocked violently by the wave action from two successive nearby explosions, and Krug, knife affixed, was propelled overside into the sea.

Still in the cloud bases, but with improved visibility now that the sun lit up the sea below, P-10 droned closer to the terminus of its search sector. At exactly 0743, Ray, who was still on glasses, shouted, *"Tally ho!"*

Bo immediately grabbed his own glasses and followed Ray's lead. "Damn!" he exclaimed, and reached for the mike. "General quarters! General quarters!" he yelled. "Sparks, transmit to base and all ships!"

To Ray he said, "First pilot identify and observe for action report."

Then he cut autopilot and pushed over into a power glide at 2,400 and 43, building airspeed to 140.

Ray activated the bomb release key.

Singer ran through the compartment to the bow gun turret, where he loaded and charged the .30 caliber. Aft, the tunnel .30 cleared.

Sparks transmitted a contact report to base on 8,210 kcs and, directly afterward, broadcast on 3,000 kcs voice frequency: "All ships, all planes: P-10 attacking sub immediately. Position follows. . . ."

"All right," Bo said, "as we agreed, we're going to release only two DBs on the intervalometer, then make a second run for a salvo of two. Understood and set?"

"Set," Ray confirmed.

With the submarine now in full view, Ray scribbled on his clipboard: "Target German 740-tonner fully surfaced, sighted two points off the port bow at 0743—UB dirty gray, very rusty, two periscopes, two guns, no net cutter, no clearing wires, no deck railing, AA manned—large number men on deck, UB has slight way on, course 160° parallel to shore . . ."

Ray interrupted his notes to say, "*There's* something odd—a couple of small boats just to the east."

"Might be fishing boats," Bo suggested.

"Yeah, but would a UB normally surface in the presence of fishing boats?"

Bo knew that coming out of the cloud bases with the sun at 180-degrees relative he had a very good chance at a "Class-A" attack, the sub exposed on the surface. But two miles off, it was clear that P-10 had been detected: crewmen scrambled up the bridge ladder and down the hatch and the sub began a forward submergence.

"Okay, it's gonna be Class-B plus," he said to Ray. "With so many men to recover from deck and bridge he was slow to get under. Start your stopwatch on the swirl, if she's lucky enough to get one."

"Aye, aye."

Bo banked sharply to 160 degrees so as to come up the track of the sub and lay down a straddle. At one-half mile, with P-10 at 200 feet off the deck, Singer opened up with his gun, one burst over, the next short, and the following fifty rounds glancing off the still descending conning tower at an angle of five to ten degrees to the sub's fore and aft axis.

Bo's bomb run was out of the NAS Jax textbook: 125 knots at 100 feet altitude in level flight, a stick of two Mark 17 DBs wired for intervalometer release at a spacing of 40 feet with hydrostatic fuses set at 25 feet depth. The sub was turning to port as it submerged, but the conning tower was still visible as P-10 came over its port quarter to starboard bow at a relative angle of five degrees to the sub's course. Bo eyeballed the release and hit the firing key on his yoke.

"Two dropped port and starboard!" the plane captain reported, as Simmons in the tunnel sprayed 30 M.G. and Bo made a sharp evasive turn to port. Looking back, he saw two towering plumes of water rise, one forward, one abaft, of the conning tower, lifting the sub's pressure hull back to the surface. As he climbed higher and the explosion columns subsided, he could see that the sub was throwing oil as a silvery-green iridescent oil slick, smudged by thick brown patches and foam, formed around her, and a geyser of dirty white compressed air and water blew from a point abaft of the tower.

"She's wounded, Ray!" Bo shouted exultantly.

Ray could see for himself now. "She looks like she's trying to dive again. She's got a propeller churn track."

"Yeah, her stern's going down but not her bow. Let's complete this turn and come at her again with the salvo."

"Aye, aye."

When they were at 270 degrees on the return Ray observed, excitedly, "They're abandoning ship!"

"Well, they damn sure are," Bo confirmed. "Pourin' outta that tower hatch like rats from a hole. Let's finish her off. Set for salvo?"

P-10 made a shallow bank into the second bomb run, this time at 75 feet. At the optimum instant two vaned canisters of high explosive splashed together in a perfect bracket.

Franz struggled to make sense of what he was watching. There were two different small boats, two different men, and they were colliding into each other. Was one of them Krug? If so, which one? Or were they a couple of crazy American fishermen? And how could U-*Franz* decide? He was about to order up diesel power and make a run in that direction when the port aft lookout cried:

FLUGZEUG!

Franz turned to see with horror that a flying boat was almost on top of them. The lookouts would be made to pay dearly for this! He leaned to the voice pipe and shouted:

ALARMMM!

Then he shouted the same to the gun and deck forces on the fore casing. It would take time—dangerous time— to get that many men below. Indeed, he had to slam the hatch shut with two men still on top. Regrettable, but it had to be done for the good of the boat.

Even so, before the conning tower could be fully submerged, two explosions, five seconds apart, convulsed the U-boat—

Click-CLAANG!

Click-CLAANG!

Mighty forces made the floor plates tremble and the steel ribs moan. Mere mortals sagged from the concussions. And Chief Engineer Brünner knew that this time the breakage might be fatal. In emergency lighting he tallied the reports from various stations: The boat had been blown to the surface. Down by the stern, ten or fifteen degrees. Starboard fuel bunker ruptured. Overhead compressed air line severed, so pressure hull compromised. Saltwater in the battery acid and chlorine gas forming in the bilges. Fuse box aflame giving off yellow smoke. . . .

Brünner turned to Franz, standing by him in the control room. "We're on the surface stern down."

Franz said, "Dive the boat!"

"I don't think it's safe," Brünner replied.

"Dive it anyway, damn you!"

Brünner rang the bell and gave the order. The control room crew hit all the right buttons and turned all the right hand wheels. The electric motors produced way. But no submergence showed on either the periscope elevation indicator or the depth manometer. The reason soon became apparent.

"The forward diving planes are jammed in an up position," Brünner reported. "We can't override by hand. We can't dive."

"Then we'd better abandon the boat," Franz replied, angrily. "Damn it to hell!" He wheeled around to Baumann, also standing by. "Get on the loudspeaker and tell the men to prepare to abandon ship. Remind the puster to take with him all secret materials. You take the confidential papers."

Then back to Brünner, "As we leave, you open the sea cock and set the timer on the scuttling charge."

"What about the woman?"

"Forget the woman. She was dead the day we found her."

"That doesn't seem right," Brünner protested.

"You'll do as you're told," Franz ordered. "Now act!"

When everything was set, and the puster, in his life vest, showed Franz that he had the *Schlüssel M* rotors for random dumping and the saltwater-soluble cipher and position books, Franz gave the final order on the loudspeaker mike, *"Alle Manner aus dem Boot!"*

On a U-boat, unlike a surface vessel, it was the commander who abandoned first, so as to take the first shot, if there was one to be taken. After Franz the rest of the life-vested crew went up the verdigris-covered ladder, as practiced numerous times in training, Brünner the last, after setting the charge.

The last except for Baumann, holding the soluble

confidential papers, who lingered in the petty officers' compartment until Brünner was up and out. Then he placed the papers inside his shirt, donned one life vest, and grabbed a spare. Just as he turned to run toward the forward torpedo room, the boat suddenly plunged more sharply on her stern, and Baumann had to pull himself laboriously up the gangway and through the circular bulkhead hatches by seizing hold of anything that protruded from the hull. Behind him he could hear seas crashing through cracks in the hull.

When finally he gained sight of a none too happy aviatrix hanging from her cuff in the torpedo room he called out to her, "I'm coming! It's all right!"

After reaching Belle, and bracing his feet against a reserve torpedo, Baumann pulled the cuff key from his pocket and unlocked her restraint. Belle fell awkwardly into his arms, where he helped her into the second life vest.

"Oh, thank you, thank you!" she exclaimed.

Baumann found something for her to hold onto in the steeply canted space while he wrestled an aluminum ladder up and against the forward torpedo access hatch. When set, he climbed the ladder, disengaged the spindles, and opened the hatch cover. But almost the moment he started back down to get Belle—

Click-CLAANG! Click-CLAANG!

Baumann was thrown against a torpedo hoist I-beam where his skull shattered in a profusion of blood.

"Oh, God no!" Belle gasped, barely able to breathe in a body jammed rigid by the twin concussions. When at last she could move her limbs, she grimaced at the pain from the contusions caused by their being slammed about. With them, though, she worked her way down to Baumann's side to revive him if that was possible. But, feeling his reddened chest, she detected no sign of breathing.

"Please, God!" she prayed, as she tried his pulse, but there was none.

So there was but one life to save now, and it was her own.

Excruciatingly, she clawed up to the foot of Baumann's ladder and lifted herself high enough to place a foot on its lowest rung. By dint of will alone, she climbed, rung by rung, while the bow of the wounded U-boat rolled in its final throes, and she had to hang on to the ladder rails with a fierce, unyielding grip.

Finally, she was able to look out the hatch. The view was nearly horizontal to the sea, whose swells lapped just below the opening. With one determined, ultimate effort she pushed herself out and into the water where she gently floated off and away.

It was odd, she thought. She had arrived on the U-boat by life preserver; she was departing it the same way.

The sun was bright orange. She blinked her eyes in its light. She looked behind her briefly when the U-boat, in its death ride, slipped beneath the surface with a frothy gulp. Then, she looked around for company. There was lots of it: crewmen everywhere floating in their vests. She paddled to the nearest one. His head hung low as though asleep. She tried to rouse him. When he showed no response, she felt his pulse.

Dead!

She went to another. It was Schneewind, who had befriended her. He, too, seemed unconscious hanging in his flotage. She felt his pulse.

Dead.

She looked around at the rest and hollered, "Is there anyone alive?" But there was no response, only the soft sound of swells merging with each other, U-boat crewmen, faces down, bobbing on them in a macabre dance. And dead fish all around.

Then there was an underwater explosion, no doubt from the U-boat, and though it ruffled the surface and made her legs tingle, it left no lasting effects.

In the distance, some couple of hundred yards away, she sighted what looked like two pieces of wreckage, one white in color, the other brown. She paddled in that direction, looking into the U-boat faces as she passed through the briny mortuary. She saw Franz, the only one for whom she had no pity. Why had everyone died? There were no marks on anyone.

As she drew closer to the wreckage, it began to look like two capsized boats. Where had they come from? What happened to them? Even closer, she saw that a man lay on one of the boat bottoms. He seemed to be alive. He was wearing a life vest different from the U-boat equipment.

"Over here!" the man hollered, seeing her approach. Then, he left his flotage and swam out toward her. "Grab a hold here!" he shouted. "I'll help you!"

When he was within ten feet of her, he stopped still in the water and stared into her eyes.

"Miss—?"

She stared back. "Fa—Fa—Father D'Angelo?"

"Belle?!"

"Solus?!"

He swam to her and placed his right hand on her cheek. "Belle! Is that *you*? What in God's name are you *doing* here? Are you all right?"

"Yes, I am, thank God. Is this a dream? What are *you* doing here, Solus?"

"I can't tell you everything, but I'll tell you what I can. Come, let me help you to the boat bottom."

When they reached the wreckage, which they climbed onto as best they could, Tony called Belle's attention to the navy plane that continued to circle over the site of the sinking.

"You know I hadn't even noticed it before," Belle said.

"Well, we have to keep waving at it so it'll land and pick us up. So let's wave like we've never waved before!"

While they did so, Belle explained how she had gotten trapped by bad weather, and was picked up, and was saved by a German officer when the U-boat was bombed, and how all the U-boat survivors in the water were dead.

In his turn, Tony explained to Belle as much as he could about his own experience, including the fact that the man he had confronted at sea was the same man who had attacked them in the Piper Cub.

"What happened to him?" Belle asked.

"I don't know if he died of the knife wound or drowned, or both. After the two bombs exploded—I didn't even see or hear the plane, either, until after the bombs, I was too preoccupied, too, I guess—my boat, what was left of it, was hit by a small tidal wave from the explosions. The boat capsized and, afterward, when I looked around I didn't see him anymore. All I saw was his picture case floating off on the swells."

"You still can't tell me who he was?"

"No."

"Well, I can tell you who *you* are. I never thought I believed in your Catholic guardian angels, but I do now. I think I've had two of them: the German officer and you."

Tony laughed.

"When I was a kid in parochial school, we used to pray, 'Angel of God, my Guardian dear, to whom His love commits me here—' I never thought I'd end up being one myself. Now keep waving!"

Their arms hurt more than either would let on.

Making their third low pass over the scene, Bo and Ray were struck by the fact that none of the U-boat survivors was swimming, or waving, or making any movement at all.

"I wonder if they're all dead, Ray," Bo said, "and, if so, how come?"

"Beats me, Bo. The rescue vessel you radioed for can probably tell us. But look over there to the right! Those two boats we saw earlier are sinking! And there's some people, two people, I think, hanging on to them. And they *are* waving."

"Yeah, I see 'em," Bo acknowledged. "Fishermen, I guess. We better pick 'em up. Go back and break out the rubber raft. It has a paddle they can use to get to us. Call me when you're ready."

"Aye, aye."

Ray went aft to the tunnel and pulled the Mark II Type Raft from its case. He attached one of the plane's sea anchors on five feet of line to prevent the raft from drifting with the wind. Then he called Bo on the interphone.

"Ready for the drop, Bo."

"Okay, Ray, stand by."

When Bo had the aircraft 50 feet off the deck and some 30 yards from the drop point, he called Ray, "Drop it!"

Ray pushed the raft bundle through the tunnel hatch while holding on to the rip cord of the CO_2 bottle. As the bundle left the plane the raft began to inflate.

Bo began a climbing turn around to set up the sea landing. When ready, he established a final approach laterally between the swells. Just above the nap of the water, with the lightest of touches on the yoke, he put the Catalina into a full stall. The hull swished and settled in.

Back in his seat, Ray directed Bo toward the raft, one of whose occupants was paddling in their direction.

"Okay, Ray, go aft and board them through the starboard blister hatch."

"Aye, aye."

After Ray and the waist gunners had finished assisting the survivors out of the raft and inside the aircraft, which was filling with fumes from the engines, Ray went forward to report, "They're not fishermen, Skipper. You won't believe this. One of 'em is a woman. And the other is a priest."

"You're kidding."

"No, I'm not. The woman said she swam through the Germans and they're all dead."

"I'll be damned. You get us back in the air, Ray, and I'll go aft to talk with her."

"Got it."

The survivors were wrapped in blankets and sitting on lower bunks when Bo reached them. The woman stood up slowly when she saw Bo's face and placed herself in his arms.

Bo's mind lurched.

"Belle?" he asked, incredulously.

"Bo," she replied in a thin voice.

He lifted her head gently from his shoulders and looked at her purple-mottled face and red eyes.

"Are you hurt, Belle?"

"I'm all right," she answered in a near whisper.

"Jesus Christ, Belle, what are you doing *here?*"

"Getting rescued, I hope." She glanced behind her. "This is my guardian angel, Father D'Angelo."

Bo looked at him blankly. "Father," he acknowledged.

"I have lots to tell you, Bo," she said, " but I'm so tired right now."

"Don't talk anymore. Here"—he led her back to the bunk—"lie down and let me strap you in."

Which he did, and then kissed her lightly on her bruised cheek, while Ray fed full throttle to the twin 1,200 horsepower Pratt & Whitneys, and Tony, strapped in another bunk, stared, astonished, at his hands, and remembered, *"Et praecinxisti me virtute ad bellum."*

CHAPTER 26

SUNDAY MORNING, APRIL 19, 1942
When he finished reading the *St. Augustine Record*, Bishop Garvey pushed it across the breakfast table to Tony and observed the young cleric closely as he read the full-page headline and story:

JAPAN ADMITS KEY CITIES ARE BOMBED
U.S. AIRMEN CREDITED WITH ATTACKS ON TOKYO AND OTHER MAIN CENTERS

(AP) Japan announced yesterday (Saturday) that her capital, her two greatest ports and the center of her warplane production had been bombed by planes carrying the bright red, white and blue insignia of the United States Air Force and that most of her home islands had spent hours under raid alarm.

The blow fell on the heart of the empire. Bombs dropped on Tokyo, Yokohama, Nagoya, and Kobe, the high command said. The raid appears to have been the most daring of the war. The full story, with disclosure of the bases from which the attack was launched, may not come for a day or two, or longer . . .

Garvey watched Tony lay the paper down, sit up straight, brace his shoulders, and gaze determinedly into space. There was no question about the change that had come over him since his leave last month.

The bishop decided to make a guess.

"Tony," he said, "when you first came to join us, I nicknamed you 'Cosmas' to go with your lookalike Larry's 'Damian.' It seemed appropriate at the time. But now I think I'll call you 'George.'"

When Tony did not ask right away, why? Garvey knew that he had made a pretty good guess.

He lay his glasses on the table and added: *"Nomen est omen."*

Seven blocks away, a jubilant Belle Hart showed the telegram she had just received to her mother and gentleman friend:

> YOUR APPLICATON APPROVED RAF AIR TRANSPORT AUX-
> ILIARY STOP REPORT AT YOUR EXPENSE 27 APRIL 1000
> HOURS TO HDQTRS ATA RAF FERRY COMMAND DORVAL
> AIR STATION MONTREAL STOP BRING ALL LICENSES
> AND CREDENTIALS INCLUDING LOGBOOK AND MEDI-
> CAL STOP
> MARY NICHOLSON FOR
> JACQUELINE COCHRAN

Taking the telegram back, she kissed it, and then, arms outstretched like the wings of a plane, she twirled around the living room, singing, "Femina perfecta, femina perfecta. . ."

Her mother smiled and left the two of them alone while she returned to the kitchen to snap beans.

After Belle stopped her aeronautical display, she asked Bo if he still had his decoder pin.

"Of course," he said, reaching into his pocket.

"Give it to me."

When he did, she laughingly threw it into the wastebasket. Then she placed herself in Bo's arms and they kissed for a long time—a very long time—long enough, Belle thought, for her mother to become concerned.

But then—she also thought—what the hell!

AUTHOR'S NOTE

The Navy Department document given on pages 47–48 of this work, from the Director, War Plans Division to the Chief of Naval Operations, dated May 22, 1940, may be found in the National Archives and Records Administration, Washington, D.C., Record Group 38, Box 245, "Records of the CNO, Headquarters COMINCH 1942—*Secret.*"

During World War II the United States Merchant Marine suffered a higher rate of personnel killed in action (2.8 percent) than the U.S. Army or U.S. Navy, and was second only to the U.S. Marine Corps (2.9 percent) in that category. Altogether, 5,662 merchant seamen lost their lives or were declared missing as a direct result of enemy action; another 609 became prisoners of war and thousands more were wounded.

The British Merchant Navy lost more heavily: 30,248 dead, one-fifth of their original number, more per man than in any of their nation's fighting services. Tramp steamer crews suffered the highest percentage of casualties. Certainly, as British historian John Keegan has written, these seamen "were quite as certainly front-line warriors as the guardsmen and fighter pilots to whom they ferried the necessities of combat. Neither they nor their American, Dutch, Norwegian or Greek fellow mariners wore uniform and few have any memorial. They stood nevertheless between the Wehrmacht and the domination of the world" (*The Second World War*, London: Penguin, 1989).

More grievous still were German U-boat losses during the war. Of 863 boats that sortied on various operational patrols, 754 failed to return to their bases. Of 39,000 U-boat crewmen who put to sea, 27,491 perished in a hecatomb whose dimensions were without parallel in any other arm of the belligerent nations; 5,000 others were captured.

"First acquired by the Navy in 1937, the PBYs became the most successful flying boat operated by the Allied Forces in World War II and the most produced flying boat of all time. The 'Catalinas' were the Navy's principal patrol bomber." Placard alongside PBY-5, displayed at the National Museum of Naval Aviation, Pensacola, Florida.

The U.S. Army air raid on Japan, utilizing B-25B Mitchell bombers, was launched from the U.S. Navy carrier *Hornet* while 650 miles east of the Japanese home islands on April 18, 1942. Commanding the raid and flying the lead bomber was Lieutenant Colonel James H. "Jimmy" Doolittle. The bombers struck Tokyo and three other cities, catching Japanese defenses completely off guard. Though negligible material damage was inflicted on military targets, the raid had enormous psychological effects, mortifying the Japanese high command, which had guaranteed that the home islands would never be attacked, and greatly lifting American morale after four and a half months of unremitting defeats in the Pacific. More important, the "Doolittle Raid," as it came to be called, prompted the Japanese Naval General Staff to approve the plan of Admiral Yamamoto Isoroku to attack Midway Island on June 4, 1942, which led to the United States' first great victory in World War II.

Of the eighty airmen who left the *Hornet*'s flight deck—all without mishap—seventy-one returned safely to the United States.

Some controversy in recent years has centered on the question of which Auxiliary Field at Eglin Field in March 1942 served as the takeoff practice field for Jimmy Doolittle's B-25s. Some have named Field No. 9, now

Hurlburt Field, others Field No. 3. The archival records establish that it was Field No. 1. See the following two documents in the Historical Archives, Eglin Air Force Base: (1) HAAFPGC/I, Captain Joe Angel, "History of the Army Air Forces Proving Ground Command, Part I, Historical Outline 1933-1944," prepared by the Historical Branch, AAFPGC, Eglin Field, Florida (undated, circa 1945–1946), page 62; (2) "Report on Master Plan for Eglin Field, Florida," U.S. Engineer Office, Mobile, Alabama, June 1944, Appendix 1, page 1. Also: Melvin M. Kessler, Retired Chief Historian, Eglin Air Force Base, to the author, November 18, 1993.

"I landed at Eglin Field on March 3, called all the men together, and told them that they would be training for an exceptionally dangerous mission. . . . I stressed the importance of secrecy repeatedly and said that any violations could mean that the lives of hundreds of people would be at risk. . . . If anyone got particularly nosey about why we were at Eglin or what we were doing, they should give me his name and the FBI would take it from there." (Gen. James H. "Jimmy" Doolittle with Carroll V. Glines, *I Could Never Be So Lucky Again*, New York: Bantam Books, 1991.)

"Ellen," mentioned on page 313, is Ellen Lawson, widow of Ted William Lawson (died January 19, 1992). Captain Lawson, pilot of B-25, tail number 02261, wrote an account of the raid on Japan (edited by Robert Considine) entitled *Thirty Seconds Over Tokyo* (New York: Random House, 1943), which was later made into a motion picture in which the character of Ellen figured prominently. During the training program at Eglin Field, Ted Lawson spirited Ellen aboard his B-25 on one of the crew's flights. After changing in their car into cowboy boots and a borrowed airman's flight suit and hair-concealing cap, Ellen marched in her best macho swagger to the aircraft. Aboard, she flew over the takeoff practice field, which she described to the author of this book, and then over a bombing range in the Gulf, where the crew made dummy bomb drops. Several months pregnant at the time, she experienced dizziness and nausea—a condition relieved, she says, by the navigator's instrument cover. "I was thrilled with the ride, noise and all" (Mrs. Lawson to the author, September 20, 1993). Mrs. Lawson kindly agreed to make the first disclosure of her experience in this novel.

In Spring 1942, FBI agents swept up a German alien and his high school–age son who operated tourist cabins at St. Augustine Beach. The son was a sometime swimming and fishing buddy of the author. Neither father nor son was seen or heard from again by local residents.

The story told in this book first took shape in my mind in 1985 while doing the research that led to the publication five years later of *Operation Drumbeat*. In that year I paid a visit to the interior of the Type IXC U-boat *505*, preserved at the Museum of Science and Industry in Chicago. There, on the navigator's table, was the original 1940 North Atlantic Chart, *Nord-Atlantischer Ozean Wegenkarte*, described in chapter 4. I was struck by the fact that, where the east coast of Florida was depicted, neither Jacksonville, Florida's largest city, nor Miami, Florida's best-known city, was mentioned, while prominence was given to a coastal town, unknown to most Floridians, named Eden. What was it, I wondered, about tiny Eden, with fifty or sixty inhabitants at the time, that caused German nautical cartographers in Berlin to imprint it on a chart of the entire North Atlantic?

I decided that this story was the answer.

For technical and other assistance of various kinds, generously given in every case, I am indebted to the following persons: William R. Adams, Carl Austin, Kenneth A. Bastholm, Edward L. Beach, Everett E. Blakely, Robert A. Bryan, Herbert and Kathryn Bubenik, Keith

Bullivant, Sarah Charles, David Childs, Birgit Petra Clager, David Conrad, Harry H. Crosby, Harry Cruver, Murray Curtin, Kenney Delany, Archie DiFante, Herbert J. Doherty, Page Edwards, William F. Enneking, Raymond Fitzpatrick, Emmett Fritz, Philip Gagan, Dot Gannon, Florence Goldstein, Gene Goodbread, William F. Hamilton, Claude A. Harvey, Elwood "Woody" Keister, Eugene Kennedy, Stetson Kennedy, Melvin M. Kessler, William Kessler, John B. Kidd, Richard A. Knobloch, Ellen Lawson, Bailey Lee, Vernon Lockwood, William R. Maples, Murdo MacLeod, Carl C. McDonough, John McCullen, Charles L. McClure, James D. Mooney, Arthur R. Moore, Eddie Mussallem, Hardgrove Norris, Pete and Olive Peterson, Henry A. Potter, Jane Quinn, Robert R. Rea, Leonidas Roberts, Richard E. Schreder, Constance L. Shehan, Thomas J. Shelley, Charles F. Sidman, Ken Snyder, Lewis A. Sussman, James Swift, Maggie Taylor, Roger Thiel, Sandra Thurlow, Jerry N. Uelsmann, Frank Upchurch, Michael Walker, Alfred Wetmore, Roy Whitcomb, Judith Williams.

Two special thanks are owed: to my editor at HarperCollins, M. S. "Buz" Wyeth, Jr., whose masterly navigation brought me safely into port; and to my spouse, Genevieve Haugen, who was alongside me on the bridge or in the cockpit, car, train, or boat for every single mile of this journey.